All the Flowers

in Shanghai

All the Flowers
in Shanghai

DUNCAN JEPSON

WILLIAM MORROW
An Imprint of HarperCollins*Publishers*

ALL THE FLOWERS IN SHANGHAI. Copyright © 2012 by Duncan Jepson. All rights reserved. Printed in the United States of America. No part of this book may be used or reproduced in any manner whatsoever without written permission except in the case of brief quotations embodied in critical articles and reviews. For information address HarperCollins Publishers, 10 East 53rd Street, New York, NY 10022.

HarperCollins books may be purchased for educational, business, or sales promotional use. For information please write: Special Markets Department, HarperCollins Publishers, 10 East 53rd Street, New York, NY 10022.

FIRST EDITION

Designed by Diahann Sturge

Library of Congress Cataloging-in-Publication Data
Jepson, Duncan.
   All the flowers in Shanghai / Duncan Jepson. — 1st ed.
      p.   cm.
   ISBN 978-0-06-208160-5
   1. Young women—China—Shanghai—Fiction.   2. Arranged marriage—Fiction.   3. Shanghai (China)—Fiction.   4. China—Social life and customs—20th century—Fiction.   I. Title.
PR6110.E66A79 2012
823'.92—dc22
                                                               2011012662

12 13 14 15 16   OV/RRD   10 9 8 7 6 5 4 3 2 1

For all the daughters,
forgotten and unloved

Acknowledgments

To my wife, Charmaine, for your love, patience, and support.

To my good friend (and agent), Marysia Juszczakiewicz, for all your help, hard work, and determination.

To my editor, Wendy Lee, for believing that a man can tell a story on a woman's behalf.

To Lynn Curtis for helping me tell the story.

Thank you.

Chapter 1

I still know your face. I see it clearly as it was at the very
beginning, not how it was left after I had hurt you.

I did not see the brightness of new life in your eyes when
you were born or cradle your warm fleshy body to my breast,
and wish now that I had. I wish I had just looked . . . but I did
not let myself because to me you were stillborn. You were not
a living person to me then, but an object of hatred, created
merely to be beaten and scarred.

When I think back through the tiredness and hunger we
have endured for years now, searching through the pages of
my memory that still serve me faithfully, I know I saw your
lovely face when I was a young girl. It was in 1932, while I was
out walking with Grandfather in those public gardens adjacent
to our house, now forgotten and laid waste to, like the rest of
Shanghai. I am certain now that I have always known and loved
your face; it was only terror and pain that held me back from
you. But all that I suffered then seems nothing compared to the
suffering now being inflicted across this country and I know
that I should never have let anything stop me from loving you.
I wish that all those years ago I'd had the courage just to look
at you, to feel the need and unconditional love in your fragile
little body.

This simple gift for your wedding and the two books I have

written for you are all that will be left of me, perhaps all that is best. Sitting in front of the weak and pale flames of our stove, so far away from home, I have dreamt of you and wish the madness of the country would subside just for one day so I might travel back to see your wedding. But it is impossible to make even a short journey, we have nothing, we cannot even feed ourselves. Every day we silence our stomachs with grass and straw and live off worms and seeds but soon the frozen ground will put even these beyond our reach. They say that no one is hungry in the People's Republic.

I hope that what I have written in these rough pages of cloth will show you how we were so bound to tradition and history that we could not see what was so obvious and that though I have always loved you, I never understood that love is nothing unless it is expressed.

Chapter 2

I t was a long time ago but you may remember those public gardens. The side of our house ran next to the wall surrounding them but Grandfather had made a passageway for us to enter directly. The gardens by the main gate were beautifully designed but our private entrance was toward the center where the landscape was more wild and uncultivated and fewer people ventured. At this point, the gardens were nearly a half a mile across and tall trees populated a large area on the side opposite our house. Between was a wide expanse of grass, and in the spring and summer gorgeous flowers would create a colorful mosaic across the wild pale green. A river ran through the middle and there were small bridges and muddy banks where a few fishermen would sit all day trying to catch ugly catfish. Willows and bushes lining its banks occasionally joined to form a canopy, providing shade for birds. Many years ago, Grandfather had been the head gardener for the old Imperial Gardens near Nanjing, and during our long walks together would tell me the names of each tree and flower in an awkward-sounding language that he said was as old as Chinese.

Once, in the summer of 1932, we stopped at the edge of the treeline and Grandfather pulled down the branches of a tree to show me its leaves.

"Xiao Feng, see this." He held down the branch, which

strained under his grip. "This is the leaf of the Empress tree which is also called *Paulownia tomentosa*. It is a fine tree. Notice that its huge leaf is smooth on the upper surface and rough underneath. This is to protect it and let the water run off more easily when it rains."

He released the branch from his hold and we watched it spring into the air, quivering wildly until it came to rest. The noise it made alarmed two birds who flew up and past us. He put his hands on my shoulders and guided me to the tree trunk.

"Now look up. What do you see?"

I looked but saw nothing. I shrugged.

"Xiao Feng, look hard. What do you see?" He looked at me and smiled then glanced up again into the tree's branches. "Just leaves, heh? This is called the mosaic. The branches overlap and then the leaves so there is no path for the light to reach the ground. So in spring and summer all the light is captured by the tree and it stores as much food as it can from sunrise to sunset. Then in the autumn and winter, when there is little light for it, the leaves fall and the tree sleeps. But though the tree will leave us we can trust it, we can rely on it and believe in it, because it always returns." He paused, looking from me back up into the mosaic of the leaves and branches. Then he said softly to himself, "They are not like people who do not return to you. We must wait to join our loved ones, mustn't we, Xiao Feng?"

"But why do I need to know this, Grandfather?" I asked.

He was looking away from me and my question caused him to look back suddenly as if I had caught him entranced in some potent dream.

"Because . . . I can only tell you what I know." He laughed. "One day there may be nothing left for me to tell you and we will walk in silence then."

I looked up at him and felt like crying.

"Are you going to stop talking to me?"

"No, silly girl, it may be that I cannot tell you anything more about the world," again he laughed to himself, "and it may be that you don't want to listen and will want to leave these gardens and find some of your own."

He looked down at me and smiled, and in the warmth of his smile the tears on my face dried.

"I don't think I will ever leave these gardens and walking with you. I'll always come back."

"That is nice to hear and I wouldn't let you go anyway. What do you think, heh?"

I looked up at him and smiled and he winked back at me. His skin was weather-beaten and his hair was white, but his eyes still moved carefully and thoughtfully, particularly when he studied plants and trees or talked with the gardeners here.

"Now that we have agreed we will live here forever, I should tell my friend. We can also look at the fish he has bred to stock the river."

Sometimes I think I wasted too much of my childhood listening to Grandfather, having the same beautiful and sad conversation repeated, step by step, walking through each year. I should have been learning how to live, how to survive. He should have taught me how to avoid the traps and obstacles in life, not contented himself with pointing out new leaves as they unfurled or the delicate buds of the flowers with names in an ancient language from a distant land. Grandfather should have told me about people—about men in particular—what they need and must have; he should have warned me to be aware of the terrible pride of the human heart.

But I realize now he did not know how to survive himself; like the trees and the plants he loved so much, who were at the mercy of the seasons, he could reach no deeper into himself than his pride would allow. And yet, unlike his beloveds, he would not hibernate in order to bloom and grow stronger in spring, but would emerge a little weaker and little more afraid as each year ended. As I sit here alone writing these words in this little house, free from all the gilt and riches of my marriage, with only a mannequin for company, I think of his kind face and its lines that never ended in anything but the warmth of a smile. I feel guilty for betraying my memories of happier times, spent wearing a path through the flowers and grass, because although those moments are painted in colors now dead to me, these are the memories I cherish most.

It was a time when all the clothes I wore were hand-me-downs from Sister. She had slightly shorter legs than I did, and my shoulders were broader: she would never admit it but my body was more elegantly formed than hers. Your body is the same. Mine had height and poise, but Sister's had a swing and a way of moving. Her walk would turn heads and, when her face was made up and her hair was done, bodies would turn around, too. Several times I saw men turn to follow her, just to get another look.

Her appearance was most important to her. She would ask Ba to buy her lipstick and skin creams, some even imported from the West, to make her look like the beautiful Western ladies, and if he refused then Ma would pretend to buy it for herself and give it to Sister. Occasionally, as she dressed for the evening, I would stand just inside the doorway to her room, shyly watching her apply her lipstick while the maids combed her hair and dressed her.

"Why is it that you come here to watch me?" she would ask me. "No matter how long you watch, you never dress any better than those peasants who come into town selling sugarcane or offering to sharpen our scissors and knives."

She paused to direct one of the maids to brush her hair harder.

"You play in the gardens and you get so dirty. You're the same as those poor people who walk down the streets, banging pots and ringing bicycle bells, trying to attract us to buy their horrible wares." She started to imitate their loud rasping offers of cheap sugarcane snakes or sweet pastries and cakes. "Feng, you must take pride in yourself, you must be better than they are or you will end up like them—dirty and shameful."

"Grandfather likes my clothes. He says that they're the proper clothes for a child," I replied quietly, hoping that my speaking softly wouldn't make her angry with me.

"But you aren't a child, Feng. You are now seventeen and a young woman. Come here."

I remember walking toward her and standing behind the maids while they worked on her hair. I saw her face in the mirror but now I was so close I dared not look directly at her. My nostrils filled with powerful scents, not natural and subtle like those of the flowers in the garden but overwhelming and threatening. Sister swung around on her stool and looked at me; the maids shifted position to continue their work.

"Look how plain these are." She fingered the short collar of my cotton blouse and pinched the material of my trousers. "When I find a husband, there will be a grand wedding and you can't come dressed like this, Feng Feng. What shall we do with you?" She looked at me, pouted a reproof, and rolled her eyes. But instead of looking back at me she looked askance, pausing as if to acknowledge a concealed audience, and then she smiled and turned back to her maids.

She looked over the things laid chaotically across the surface of her dressing table and snatched up a small pot of rouge. Snapping back to face me, she scrutinized my cheeks and mouth. She reached out with her right hand to hold my chin. I flinched but already she had me between her fingers. I quickly stopped struggling as with her long middle finger she dabbed a little of the red from the pot, waited for the rouge to soften, and then gently caressed it onto my lips and cheeks.

"There, you see . . . nearly a woman." She started to laugh. "Feng Feng, you will break many hearts with your elegant face and farmer's clothes!" She went back to directing the maids and selecting her jewelry then, forgetting all about me.

I continued to stand behind her, looking at my reflection. I looked deformed and unreal, my face no longer mine. With a few quick strokes of her finger, she had created a mask that immediately propelled me into adulthood, and had laughed at the grotesque effect. I stared for a few moments longer and then wiped off the rouge with my sleeve. I heard her directing the maids curtly and looked down to examine the red that now stained the white cotton of my blouse. I looked at myself in the mirror. I was once again like a peasant.

"One day maybe you can come out with me. Perhaps those large flat feet of yours can learn to dance?" Sister laughed to herself, then looked up into the mirror and over her shoulder at me. "What would you say, Feng Feng? What would we make you wear? I think you might look funny."

She laughed out loud and wagged her head from side to side playfully, pulling a face by blowing out her cheeks and glaring widely, so that her eyes looked huge and her pupils shone with a dark fire.

But my only trips out were to school and back, though occasionally Grandfather would meet me to walk me home and we would take the alleyways through Shanghai's Old Town. We would look in the shops together at food being prepared, dresses being made, and people selling cheap items. I would linger to watch people make *jiaozi*, fried dumplings, which would explode when I bit into the soft white dough, the beautiful oily sauce staining my lips and dripping down my chin. These shops were all very narrow, some of them just gaps in the masonry.

The Old Town had been constructed over several centuries as increasing numbers of peasants and immigrants settled there from the countryside. The buildings were mostly two-story, of rough, deep brown wood with tile roofs with narrow alleys running between them. People made their lives in these slivers of space—a hole in the floor with a fire beneath or a big oven, a *kang*, to heat the living area in the cold Shanghai winter evenings.

We would pass hundreds of peasants lining the walls and everyone would have to duck when a woman or a man walked along with a pole slung across their shoulders, carrying goods or food for delivery. At that moment we would all stop and crouch against the walls. Suddenly, I would find myself next to a peasant and their family. I would stare at them and their desperate smiles, parting cut and cracked lips to reveal broken teeth; their shabby clothes so worn that the colors and shapes blended into a dark mass of waxy material, with head, hands, and feet projecting outward. I held Grandfather's hand tight then, as it seemed one of them might reach out and grab me, yet I could see that many of them were too weak to stand and barely strong enough to keep hold of their few belongings.

"Why do these people stay here?" I tried to whisper into Grandfather's ear.

"There are many people in China. Fortune has blessed our family but she cannot bless everyone, so those who have been unlucky come here to sell what little things they can and to beg for money and food." He bent forward slightly as we walked, to speak quietly to me. "They are here to remind us to give thanks to the gods of fortune. You should remember that when New Year comes."

"Should we give them some money then?"

"Well, you can buy something from them, but don't tell Ma and your sister because then they will be angry with me for bringing you here . . . and extremely angry that you have spoken to these people. We should be careful. If anyone should see you here they might tell other people, and this is not the sort of place our family should visit." He sounded a little anxious.

I looked at the faces of the poor people around us; rouge would not be enough to fix them; vanity and beauty were luxuries beyond their understanding. These people had worked and suffered so long that they had gone past hope and felt nothing more than empty resignation and exhaustion. I did not realize that the country was full of such people: hungry and, to Sister, seemingly worthless but whose bellies were filling with anger.

As we came out of the Old Town and joined the pavement of the main streets, I was confused and needed to question him further.

"If I should not go to the Old Town, why do you take me?"

"Because I would like you to see the things that are important. Things so many in these changing times don't care about." He looked down at me, his face very serious, then he smiled and gave me a wink and said, "It would have been easier if you had been a boy, of course. What a pretty grandson you would have made!"

When we walked into the house, Sister was standing in the entrance hall and saw the sugarcane snake I was eating.

"Where did you buy that?" she yelled, and snatched it from me.

"I bought it from one of those old vendors who travel the city. Give it back."

"Are you stupid?"

"No."

"Well, I think you must be. Because if someone had seen you buying this they would say our family associates with beggars and street vendors." She scowled at Grandfather. "You should have stopped her."

Grandfather muttered something in reply then said aloud, "I told her so."

Sister looked back at me.

"Xiao Feng, you should know better. Ma will be very angry with you. Are you intent on ruining everything?"

She wasn't expecting an answer from me. It was just a lull before she gave vent to her anger.

"You will never understand, so you simply need to remember that everything you do brings shame on our family. I don't understand why you would even associate with such people anyway."

I watched her shout and bare her teeth behind her perfectly red lips. My mind wandered to the hard, sore lips of the people I had seen earlier, crouching against the walls. Sister's lips were like perfect fruit and her skin like pale silk, but her voice was far more rude than anything those ragged people would ever say. Sister always seemed much older than I have ever been: instinctively aware of how adults live and what adults want. She was right: I did not understand yet. And even now, after all these years, I realize her understanding of life, how to win at it, had always surpassed mine. She was always more conscious of her direction; of where she was and how she would advance to her next objective. My childhood simply seemed to continue as it had started. It was not for me to be concerned with the niceties of afternoon tea parties and noisy evening dances. I spent my time with flowers and grass, running to school and eating noodles on the street. I was not required to know anything more than what I learned from Grandfather and Ba. I had not been chosen to fulfill anyone's hopes and dreams. Instead Grandfather had showed me how to mirror Nature's quiet acceptance; not to scheme and plan and get my own way. I had not understood or felt desire, nor were there any high parental aspirations for me to live up to.

Ma heard Sister's shouting and arrived from the kitchen across the other side of the courtyard.

"What is it? Why are you shouting? People may hear us."

"I'm scolding her for spending time in the Old Town and speaking to the people there."

Ma looked at me.

"How did you get there?"

"I go there often, but this time I took Grandfather. He told me not to enter the alleys but I think it's safe."

"*You* think it's safe? Who are you to decide? I heard your sister call you stupid and I was coming to reprimand her, but you *are* stupid. Those lanes are full of people who carry disease and could steal you away to some village in a distant province. You would never survive. Those aren't the sort of people this family wants to know."

She waited for a few seconds to see if I had anything to say in reply but I at least knew when to be quiet, to say nothing and act dumb.

"Do not go there again! What do you say, Feng?"

"I understand. I won't go there again."

Grandfather shuffled his feet behind me. Ma turned and went back across the courtyard and into the kitchen. I wanted to cry and shout but knew that I must obey. Sister looked past me to Grandfather and then turned to the maid who had been standing watching at the side of the room.

Sister held out the sugarcane stick in front of the maid. "Please take this away. You can finish it if you want—and if you see Feng with another one then you will tell me immediately."

Sister was actually only five years older than me, but I think by the time I had been born Ma had already started molding her into the likeness of a grown woman, one who would care for little other than the things she would be instructed to love and pursue. Sister was generally unkind to me but I could not hate her for that because she always seemed so far above me, living a life of such complexity and sophistication I could only marvel at her. She was like a visitor from another family: unrelated to my shyness, beyond Ma's belief in crude traditions and repetitive tribulations, far removed from Ba's and Grandfather's naïve belief in the teachings of Confucius. I did not love her, either, and she did nothing to make me love her, yet every day I still liked to see her and was glad of the touch of glamour she brought to my life.

She had always excluded me from mixing with her friends, not directly but subtly, as she shrugged aside anyone who was too quiet or too slow to keep pace with her own delicious charm and relentless activity. Encouraged by Ma's ambitions for her, she had been quick to create a life for herself that made no concessions to helping out anyone unable to keep up. I was quiet by nature and, like a lame child, would always be left behind in the race to follow her. I never envied her or sought to be like her, knowing that would be impossible. At the time, I believed that Grandfather's stories and wisdom were all I needed to know.

On certain days, at half past six in the evening, as I sat eating my supper of rice and vegetables with Grandfather, I would see Sister standing with Ba near the front door. We would be sitting in the kitchen on the opposite side of the courtyard, which lay at the center of the house. She would leave her bedroom on the upper floor. Grandfather and I would watch her walk alone beside the balcony rail then appear at the bottom of the steps that ended by the kitchen. We would watch her cross the courtyard then enter the sitting room and, because the maids would leave open all the inner doors to the courtyard unless it was very cold, we could then see Sister again, standing in the entrance hall with Ba. She would wait there patiently to be collected by her current suitor, who would always arrive at a quarter to seven accompanied by his father.

Sister would be dressed in a cheongsam, the red-and-gold flower-embroidered silk furled around her body so gracefully that it appeared like a beautiful scroll, and about her shoulders she would drape an elegant short fur stole that Ba had given her. As Grandfather watched, he would whisper to me, "Xiao Feng, I do not think the gods could have picked more perfect colors for your sister." He would chuckle to himself. "You and I spend so much time together in the gardens, yet the most beautiful creature Nature could ever conceive is right here, heh?"

He would give me a little wink. It was true. Sister's hair was beautifully set and gently waved, like white women's hair, and she would wear the fur stole nestled around her neck, and carry a small bag. She always smelled of Florida Water, the perfume of the time, and whenever she walked past Grandfather and me the scent would hang heavily in the air, always just long enough for it to linger in our imagination.

"Your grandmother would be so proud of you," Grandfather would shout out to Sister as she waited. She would smile in acknowledgment, but not with gratitude.

"Next time you must remind me to give you your grand-mother's old cheongsams. I think they would fit you perfectly."

"I think Grandmother was a little fatter than me and those patterns are no longer fashionable. They're too old for me, Grandfather," she replied quickly, eyes fixed on the door while she spoke to him.

"Just like me, I suppose." It was Grandfather's turn to smile now but Sister did not see.

He mumbled something to himself and looked up briefly at me.

"Your sister is more radiant than Grandmother, isn't she?"

I did not know, as she had died long before I was born.

During those few years I saw a succession of very differ-ent young men appear at the house to court Sister. Many were headstrong and foolish, living off family businesses and the hard work of others. Sometimes the same man would reappear a few times, his parents bringing Ma gifts and perhaps a big box of foreign cigarettes for Ba. Although our family was not rich or well-known, Sister was considered a woman worth marrying— beautiful, well-bred, educated, and thoroughly schooled. Not all her suitors were polite, though—one or two did not show Ba the proper respect. They did not give him face, merely sent a servant into the house to collect Sister, who would then be led to the car where the suitor of the day and his father sat waiting.

People knew that my parents were looking for a good match for her, and it was widely known that they had made the appropriate preparations to achieve this. Ba had saved a large dowry for her, and both he and Ma had ensured that Sister knew every aspect of etiquette, from table manners to Western dancing. She had been raised to put her husband first, but until she found the right man she saw every other woman as a rival, and was ruthless in her desire to surpass them all.

Some suitors came in sheepishly, like poor relations looking to borrow money, bowing and kowtowing so their fat backsides stuck out. The best of them came dressed in Western clothes, dapper suits and finely made fedoras, and the more traditional in beautiful black silk *ma qua*. In the summer, the fat ones would be dripping sweat from the brims of their felt hats, embarrassed and apologizing to Sister for the constant need to mop themselves with an already soaking handkerchief or, worse still, the sleeve of their disheveled suits. The handsome ones would stand like the Western movie stars I used to see on the film posters, striking poses and glancing over regularly to catch a glimpse of themselves in a window or mirror. I loved to watch them when occasionally they had to wait for Sister and Ba.

Ma had her favorites, though I suspect Ba liked none of them. She would rank them according to family background, their job, and family business. A big family business, like shipping, trading, or banking, was what she preferred; professions were acceptable, but Ma was practical and considered capital preferable to intellect.

I liked certain suitors for their smiles and eyes. Some of them had warm brown eyes that greeted me welcomingly, without suspicion or disdain, and smiles that immediately disarmed me. I never went to speak to them, but sometimes I was there when they entered and would stand quietly by. I realized I looked awkward in my ill-fitting clothes but some of them were so handsome that I would forget myself. I would just stand and look at them, and sometimes if they noticed me they would smile, which made me look away in confusion and slowly retreat from the entrance hall back into the courtyard and the kitchen. Their looks were less important to Ma, but she did like height and Chineseness: she wanted wide eyes, black hair, and smooth skin. She did not want anyone too thin or with a dark complexion.

Sometimes Sister would see me hiding as she waited.

"You can come out if you want. You can come and join me and see how the grown-ups live. It is much more complicated than your safe little world with Grandfather, constantly dirtying yourself in the gardens next door!"

One evening she looked at me impatiently and ordered: "Xiao Feng, come here!"

Even though there was no one else in the room, I moved quietly. I stood with my back to the door and we just looked at each other.

"Those trousers are funny . . . you always look like you've just come from the countryside. Perhaps," she teased, "a village is the best place for you."

Sister continued looking at me and I could not move; my feet seemed suddenly to be made of stone. I remained standing there expressionless, caught in her stare. The suitor arrived and she released me. After greeting Sister, he turned and smiled at me. I blushed and slipped back into the house.

Then, for many months, this same man came to collect Sister. He was not as you see him today, but with skin as smooth and shiny as a honey-glazed roast pig. He was always a big man, but he was thinner at that age and had an air of hesitancy that sometimes made him seem vulnerable. This was most notice-able when his father was with him because although the suitor himself was a big man, with large hands, a barrel chest and wide face, he would still manage somehow to shrink behind the slightly smaller frame of his father. His eyes would look away while his father barked out his opinions to Ba. Grandfather said the young man would probably have been a very pleasant and generous person had his father taught him strength of character and a sensitivity toward others as well as pride. I did not like his father; he seemed to me like a mean-spirited man and one who knew that he had power over others. He and his son would arrive preceded by their driver. They would march to our front door, knock hard, and stand waiting impatiently. After the maid let them in, Grandfather and I, from our vantage point in the kitchen, would watch them wait for Sister and Ba if they were not already there.

In those days, the young man could be rude when his courage was bolstered by his father's sour-faced presence, and take an arrogant air, not paying proper respect to Ba or Grandfather by calling them "sir" or offering gifts. But mostly he would stand meekly behind his father like a child, waiting for him to say a few polite words to Ba or Grandfather, and then at his father's signal they would both nod and lead Sister away for the evening.

When the young man came on his own, which happened rarely in the beginning, he would stand quietly twiddling his thumbs or scratching his head while he waited for Sister. If he saw Ba, he would leap forward to shake hands, like a huge dog eager for a walk. When Sister came to join him, they would leave Ba standing alone in the entrance hall, a weak and unconvincing smile forming on his thin pale lips as he watched the young man lead her to his large black chauffeur-driven car.

Sometimes I would be awake when she returned, her heels striking the stone paving of the courtyard, and I would listen until I heard her close her bedroom door. It was never too late, perhaps half past ten, though everyone else had gone to sleep by then. I would hear her singing foreign songs to herself. She would dance in the courtyard, her heels beating out a strange and happy rhythm on the stone. She had learned the words to three songs in English and would sing these again and again so that she could pronounce the words perfectly. Sister could not speak a word of English except for those three songs. In these quiet moments, when she did not know I was listening, I felt closest to her.

Eventually a routine was established and the shy young man would return twice during the week and on Saturdays. Even though everything was prearranged, Ba would still try to be there when he arrived to collect Sister. Grandfather explained it was a father's duty and yet I do not think I ever saw Ba actually do anything. He never refused any man's approaches, and Sister's hand could be taken by anyone who passed the requirements set by Ma.

Once I found the young man standing alone waiting for Sister.

"Xiao Feng," he spoke softly to me. I quickly glanced up at him then returned to studying his shoes. "Don't you think your sister is beautiful? She is probably too beautiful for me. My father is very impressed by her, though."

I kept looking at his shoes, which were very large.

"I have been learning to dance like your sister. Have you seen her dance?"

Ba appeared at that moment. The young man smiled at me then bounded forward to shake his hand.

I had only ever heard Sister dancing late at night in the courtyard and it had sounded lovely and silky, the sharp rhythmic footsteps echoing off the walls and filling the empty rooms downstairs. I loved the ringing sound in my ears; forever afterward it would summon up my most beautiful images of Sister. I had heard that at the tea dances she would attend at Western-style hotels, young couples would dance close together, holding each other and sometimes even changing partners. Grandfather said the music they danced to was loud and aggressive. He also thought it rude and ill-mannered of them to touch each other in public that way. I thought of Sister there with this awkward young man, her dark eyes burning up at him.

After a time the young man started buying Sister jewelry and this made Ma very happy. In fact, she seemed to be happier about it than Sister, who acted unimpressed. These presents were things that Ba could never have afforded. The young man would always present the gifts before he and Sister left for the evening and on those occasions Ma would appear. Afterward she would stand with Ba to watch them go.

"How much do you think their family pays for the jewelry?"

Before Ba could answer, she would reply herself.

"I think they have special discounts at some of the best jewelers. It must be wonderful to live like that!"

Ba remained quiet.

Ba and Grandfather rarely said anything to confront other people, as if they simply could not find a way to force the words out. In their self-imposed silence, their eyes would focus hard on a distant object, gazing past any imminent awkwardness in the desperate hope of finding escape. They shared their thoughts only by passing comments aloud as if speaking to themselves; the words spoken softly, under their breath. They might as well have been the declarations of a beetle sheltering under a petal for all the notice the world took of them. If by chance you happened to hear them, then you could discuss things or argue with them. But neither of them would ever force a direct confrontation in order to make a point. Mostly, they avoided quarreling, preferring always to be "polite." They would tell me this was the Confucian way. Grandfather would say it was better to drink your tears and eat your sorrow than to lose face. I wish they had spoken up, though. I wish they had said something when it was necessary. They opposed very little except when they felt they must save face, but I know now it is sometimes better to lose face than to lose a life.

Ba always paid uncomplainingly for Sister's elegant and extravagant upbringing, no matter what Ma wanted. She had realized even before marrying him that he would never be rich. He was clever, creative, a talented architect, but lacked the ability to play the subtle games necessary to secure promotion and advancement.

Ma's family had immigrated to Shanghai from a small town in the north of China many years ago. Her parents worked with textiles and were good at dyeing cloth but poorly educated. They worked hard and were able to earn a reasonable living and send Ma to school, trying to ensure she gained a greater level of sophistication than they had. Ma also forced herself to learn other things that she thought would advance her position, such as good table manners, dancing, politeness, and some foreign customs. She gleaned these from wherever she could. Her whole life revolved around making better connections and marrying well: helping herself and her family to rise above their low position.

Although Ba did not share her ambitions, he recognized in the youthful girl he first met a strong sense of discipline and a willingness to educate herself, and found he could love her for these qualities. He had been raised by his own father to be happy with simply completing his day's work to the best of his ability. His family had lived on the fringes of Society, enjoying an acquaintance with the rich and powerful but knowing that any further intimacy would always be denied them. But they were content with that prospect, and since they represented a step up for her, so was Ma. Within their own family, though, which she had decided would consist of a single child, Ba passively agreed with her plan to stop at nothing, sacrifice everything, so that their offspring made the right marriage. Another child would serve as the warm blanket for their old age and that would not need education and sophistication.

Being a member of Society required strict conformity to all its petty and remorseless rules and customs. After Sister was born, Ba knew he would have to set aside a lot of money for her dowry, dance lessons, music lessons, elocution, even skin-whitening treatments. But it was never enough. They should have sold the jewelry Sister was given, but Ma insisted it should be kept. It would have repaid at least some of Ba's outlay, but no, everything must be kept as proof that they were not desperate and had no need to sell the gifts they had received. Such was Ma's dream: to marry a daughter into Society, to the wealthiest family in town. Entering into such an association would bring Ma herself good standing and esteem. Or so she believed. Ba never told her that he felt such an ambition was wrong, that she was being selfish. Over the years he had come to understand that, like so many others, he had lived without any dreams to inspire him. Perhaps he'd decided hers were better than none. Although I have missed my father over the years, I recognize that he was a coward in some matters, and I think he knew it, too. Alas, I believe he even became comfortable with it.

I spent the end of that spring and much of that final summer at home sitting in the sunshine in the tangled grass. Only the first day of summer, the day our family was to meet his, it felt like a storm was coming and rained all day, which surprised everyone as the fortune-teller Ma had consulted to decide on the wedding date had told us it would be a lucky day. He had promised water and fire would be balanced and there would be a clear sky until nightfall. Grandfather and I had intended to walk in the gardens but the rain came down and prevented us, so we sat in his small day-room watching the rain drip from the wooden shutters, the portrait of Grandmother looking down at us. Her expression was very soft and wide-eyed. If he studied it for too long Grandfather would withdraw from us and become terribly sad.

"There is too much rain, too much rain, water everywhere," he repeated to himself, as if acknowledging that everything was already lost. "Today will not turn out well." He looked down at me as I sat on the floor by his feet playing with a white paper bird I had folded. I was not sure what he meant, so said nothing.

"Grandmother would have postponed it and asked the fortune-teller to pick another day . . . but then, she would never have allowed your sister to grow up like this."

"But isn't this what Ba and Ma want? Sister, too?" I blurted out. I must have been holding this thought inside me for a long time, because I was almost shouting at Grandfather, feeling angry for some reason I did not understand.

"Xiao Feng, your day may come. And then we will find out what you want, heh?" He was whispering now. "Losing you will be a terrible day for me." He gave me a little wink then put his finger up to his lips as if to tell me no reply was necessary.

Grandfather looked at me and touched my cheek.

"This family, the Sang family, are great people. Yes, I think it is what your parents want. We must hope it is everything she wants as well," he finished softly.

At two o'clock, a pair of huge automobiles parked outside our front gate and the young man and his family appeared in full ceremonial splendor. They came into the house with servants holding up umbrellas to protect them from the rain, but the hems of their clothes, their silk cheongsam, *ma qua*, and trousers were soaked. Water dripped across our wooden floor and carpets, leaving stains that forever afterward marked the course of their regal and overbearing procession.

At that age, most adults seemed identical to me. I had no idea or experience of how ageing tells its story on our skin; people simply looked old. The younger members of the family seemed slightly brighter and more energetic but all twelve of them were large, loud, and grotesque, except for the young man who seemed even shyer by comparison. They moved slowly and heavily; outsized colorful silks concealed their actual size but in turn made them appear bigger. Their faces and hands protruded like swollen pink fruit.

The servants tried to dry them down with towels. After waving them away, the family came into the lounge where the women sat with Ma. The First Wife and the other women were decorated in fine jewelry, jades, and gold bracelets over the sodden silks; beautiful things ruined.

I hid in the kitchen with Grandfather, who had been ordered to stay away. Ba had told him to make sure the kitchen door was shut, so we could not be seen, nor did he want us wandering around upstairs and peering rudely over the balcony. I was happy to be in the kitchen as I knew that the cook would prepare us some dumplings and soup, which we could eat on the little table by the door. It was a plain basic room, walls painted white, with two huge deep cooking pans set on the stone oven, heated by the open fire beneath. All the spices and herbs were stored on shelves lining the walls, and at one end of the room was a large chopping board on which the cook used to chop vegetables and herbs or kill birds and fish. It was the only room in the house that was shared and enjoyed by all, and since it was really the cook's domain, Ma and Sister had little influence there. There was safety in the kitchen.

The servants and I opened the door a little and peeked out to see what was happening in the sitting room. Across the courtyard, we could just see that three of the parents were talking to each other animatedly but Ba was saying nothing. He looked fragile and pale sitting next to this important family in their rich clothes and jewelry. They seemed to suck all the life and energy from him, leaving him able to do little more than nod dumbly at the young man's father.

Enjoying her imminent triumph, Ma smiled at everyone with nothing more than the daydreams of the glory to come in her head. Sister looked beautiful and relieved somehow, as if this moment marked the end of a long night's restless sleep. She stood by her suitor, who was wearing a Western-style suit that was slightly too short for him. He looked ungainly. Yet with Sister beside him, he looked like a man, and you could see why his parents had decided she was the right wife for their oldest and dearest son.

I went back to Grandfather and told him what I had seen, and he smiled at me and to himself. It was one of those smiles that are so close and warm and wide that you can never forget it. Even now, thinking of him smiling like that feels like the warmth of the sun on a bright day when you close your eyes and let the heat just wash over your face.

"So here is their beginning, Xiao Feng."

Chapter 3

Ba and Ma started preparing for the wedding. During the next four months, they spent most of their savings; this ceremony was to be the culmination of their life's work. Nothing would be left for my wedding. I was expected to stay at home and look after my parents in their old age.

They brought each member of our family to the house and had each of them measured for new clothes. I think the tailor visited our house every day for three months. His servants brought beautiful bolts of cloth, mostly silk but also some coarser dark foreign materials with dull simple patterns, which Grandfather told me were even more expensive than the silk. I could not understand why anyone would want to wear a whole suit in such rough cloth.

The bolts were laid out on the table in the dining room and had to be moved every time we had a meal. Often Grandfather and I would eat in the kitchen to save the maids from having to replace everything, which could cause many problems for them, because Sister would often stand in the dining room feeling the textures of the cloth and they would have to work around her. She would stand for hours, staring at the rolls of silk, cotton, and thick foreign cloth, as if lost in fantasies of herself wrapped in dresses or gowns. I would watch her sometimes from the other end of the reception room.

"Xiao Feng, I know you are watching me again. Come in here and let me teach you something," she told me one day.

I was motionless. I did not want to be alone with her in that room, knowing I would be trapped and she could tease me mercilessly.

"Xiao Feng . . ." though she called to me in a soft loving voice, she was ready to taunt me, I knew. " . . . Feng Feng, come in here! I'm not going to bite you."

In soft cotton slippers my footsteps were barely audible. When I reached the dining end of the room, she was surprised to turn around and find me already standing behind her.

"Feng Feng, why must you creep around like a cat?" She held out the corner of a bolt of dark blue silk. "Feel this. It's so smooth, it's like holding a fine mist. These are the things our family can never hope to enjoy. You don't understand, but to be someone, to receive respect, you must have the best of everything. You must have these things and everything like them."

I touched the silk. It was indeed lustrous and fine, but no finer or smoother than the flower petals Grandfather had shown me.

"But how does having these things make people respect you?"

She had started looking at another full bolt of bright yellow silk on the other side of the table, speaking as she unfurled it.

"You are a funny girl. How did we grow up so differently?" Her head remained bent over the silk she was examining but her eyes looked up at me, framed prettily by her fine arched brows. But they were hard, challenging me to make another foolish remark. She continued before I could do so, "It is all about what everyone can see. If you are perfect then everyone will respect you, they will look up to you. They will give you face."

"But is anyone perfect?" I replied hesitantly.

"No, but if you never let other people see that you're not, and you never admit to anything bad about yourself, then because they won't risk showing you that *they* are not perfect, they won't challenge you and they'll leave you alone and give you face. Anything less than perfect, though, means you will be treated accordingly. You will be less than others. For example, your ragged clothes . . . what do they say about you and us?"

"They say nothing."

"No. They say you are poor . . . or wealthy and don't care . . . but they tell everyone that you have low standards," she said decisively.

"Low standards? But who can live only according to the highest standards?" I asked more forthrightly.

"The Sang family can live like that. The emperors lived like that. They are mandated by heaven. Gods."

"It doesn't seem a good way to live to me. Like gods."

She dropped the silk she was holding and walked around the dining table to me. Putting her hands on my shoulders, she forced me to look her square in the face.

"Feng, it is the only way to live. It is what everyone wants."

She frowned at me and shook me slightly.

"You must grow up. Foolish, foolish girl."

She left me, to return to studying the silk. I could not imagine wearing clothes made from this material. What would be the point? I left the rolls in their dazzling piles.

Sister was right: I didn't understand.

Ma and Ba had also bought many other beautiful things for Sister's dowry, all the items that they believed necessary to impress a wealthy family: embroidered silks, piles of foreign cloth, tall vases painted with dragons and flowers, beautiful scrolls and calligraphy, expensive tea sets and preserved fruits, showing them that we were perfect. As well, of course, as all those things that the Sang family said were required by tradition; many of them things Ma and Ba would never possess themselves, such as gold jewelry, jade bracelets, and large tins of foreign foods. The house began to resemble the shining factories Grandfather had shown me in photographs from Europe and America. Deliveries arrived and gifts were dispatched constantly; all the maids were directed to work only on the wedding preparations, to ensure that nothing was misplaced or incorrectly distributed. It would be a terrible loss of face for our family if tradition and custom were not followed, and that included which invitations and gifts went to which people, in the correct order. In keeping with much of my childhood, Grandfather was left to supervise me and our time was spent drifting through the long grass of the gardens, hearing Ma scream at the maids in the house nearby.

Sister became increasingly tired and short-tempered; she had no patience with anyone who made a mistake, as if each fumble could jeopardize her whole future. With the wedding approaching, Sister would ignore me unless she wanted me to help her, and even then treated me more like a servant than her sibling. At the time I thought that because she had found what she wanted, she saw my feelings as irrelevant, no longer of any interest to her. She saw no bond between us; I was just another person who had existed in one place and period of her life. Ma had not taught her to care for me and so she would not miss me when she left. I would not be part of her new life with her new family; my destiny was to remain here, at home, though Grandfather would occasionally try to tell me about marriage. I think he hoped that one day I would find someone.

"Men and women don't really understand each other and I don't think they ever will. It is natural for a man to enjoy many women, some wives and some mistresses. Look at the emperors of ancient times . . . they had hundreds of wives and all very beautiful. But I think love can make us different," he told me while we were out in the garden one day.

He stopped and pushed back his hair from his face. A strong wind had set the long grass dancing. Grandfather put his hands on his hips and stood looking around at the swaying trees and the sun sinking slowly behind them.

"It's just like this . . . look . . . the trees and the sun. The green leaves and brown branches and this huge ball of yellow gleaming behind them. It does not make any sense. One huge object far away and these trees so insignificant in comparison, but from where we stand here they look perfect together. How can we explain it? That together they create this perfect picture."

He looked at me and smiled.

"I wish you could have known your grandmother, because she was the most loving person I have known. I can tell you, I was a better man for being with her. She always put everyone else before herself. My family had warned me that I should not marry her," he shook his head, "no, they did not like her. Even after we married they would say I should have chosen better, because she was always very weak and would become ill easily. They would nag me that she would always suffer from poor health and that our children would be weak as well. Tell me that I should take another wife."

He paused and touched my cheek.

"You probably won't understand." He breathed in sharply as if in pain. "I will never understand why she had to leave us and prove them right. If only she could have given us a few more years together . . ." He smiled his big smile.

"Your grandmother died because of her bad lungs."

I knew that; had heard how he sat with her while she faded a little more each day, forgetting even their young son in the pain of imminent loss.

Grandfather pressed one palm to his chest; his skin was loose and marked with dark freckles, I noticed. His face, too, was dark from the sun and his lips had thinned over the years. He had quite a sharp nose, not big like a foreigner's but a little pointed. Despite his age, though, he still had strong cheekbones and thick hair.

"I looked after her until the day she left me. We had just fourteen years together. Not very long, was it?" He continued to stare at me. "How old are you now? Older than fourteen, I know. Sorry, Feng Feng, I forget. But I'd say fourteen years of happiness is preferable to none at all. I am not sure this is a good match for your sister, but what can we do? Just you and me, heh? It is out of our hands." He laughed wryly.

"Even if she had a second chance, she probably would not choose any differently anyway. She seems to know little of love or even to be interested in it, but every marriage should have a little love, no matter how many wives a man has." He chuckled to himself then and I was lost. "She may be treated as a servant by her new family, seen as being there only to bear them heirs. It is probably all my fault for allowing your father to marry your mother. People don't respect education anymore, now it is only about power and money. After thousands of years suddenly things have changed."

He drew a deep breath, one that would transport him back in time—back to happiness.

"People told me to get another wife but I was not lonely for company, I was lonely for her. Do you understand that? I hope you will . . . one day."

He sucked his teeth and sighed a little, hurling a small stone into the river. We watched the ripples spread out and fade back into the river's current, then walked back to the house.

Three days later during another walk in the public gardens we met a young boy fishing by the river. I could not stop looking at him. He had cropped hair and large eyes whose deep brown pupils held a stillness and peace that fascinated me. Grandfather introduced himself to the boy.

"How is the fishing today?" he asked.

"It is a good day. This is one of the best places to fish on this stretch of river. You see, in this particular place the fish become transfixed by the sight of the weeping willow branches as they sway in the breeze." The boy spoke so confidently, I could not stop myself from staring at him. His eyes followed Grandfather's mouth closely as they spoke together, pupils narrowing in concentration. This was not his dialect but he was determined to express himself. "Sometimes the fish are so mesmerized you can pluck them with your bare hands, straight from the water," he announced.

"Really?" Grandfather laughed. "I have worked helping the gardeners here for many years and no one has ever noticed that before. You do not live here in the city, do you?"

"No, grand-uncle, I live in the countryside."

"Are you a fisherman at home?" Grandfather asked him.

"I'm learning . . . my father is teaching me. But the fish are a lot cleverer at home than in this river. It's easy here."

"What is your name, young man?" Grandfather asked him.

"My name is Bi, grand-uncle," he said respectfully.

With that the boy stepped down from the bank and entered the river. A breeze was blowing across the garden and the branches of the willow tree swayed in time with the ripples in the water. Bi stood very still. After a few minutes a fish swam between his legs. It floated just beneath the surface. Very slowly he slid his hands into the river and cupped them around the fish. He held it momentarily under the water.

Throughout this, I stood dutifully by Grandfather's side. I had not been able to stop myself from staring at Bi while he had talked and kept watching as he stood in the river. Suddenly he looked up and threw me the fish. I caught it but it thrashed wildly against my hands and fell back into the river where it swam away. I gasped in shock and the boy and Grandfather laughed. Then Bi smiled at me directly. I felt my cheeks flush, and looked down and away from his eyes.

"Now you will be hungry tonight!" Bi laughed.

"No, we have a cook . . ." I quickly replied, then stopped.

Grandfather and Bi laughed together again.

Next day Bi was in the same place. Grandfather and he sat by the bank and continued their discussion on fishing, the wind, and the river. Eventually, Grandfather formally introduced me and allowed me to sit on the bank and watch the boy fish. I sat there while Grandfather helped the gardener prune the saplings. In the beginning we were mostly silent. Bi fished and I watched the river and the insects hovering and skirting around the reeds and lilies. It did not feel awkward, because I did not want to talk. I had nothing to say and being quiet with Bi did not make me feel nervous or anxious.

"You don't say much. The girls in my home town can't stop talking." I sensed him looking at me but stayed perfectly still, staring into the water.

He had a sweet smell from his childhood spent in the countryside, like the scent of fresh flowers and fruit in the market. I realize now I should have forced myself to treasure each breath I took that carried the scent of such innocence.

The weeks drifted by as the wedding preparations advanced. I could pass through the busy house, unseen by everyone. Bi and I spent more and more time by the river. Sometimes we would just sit together, looking into the water as it flowed around the rocks on the riverbed. He concentrated so hard on his fishing that often I could gaze at him for several minutes without him noticing. Sometimes I could see his bare chest between the buttons of his shirt. I would snap a quick glance then pretend I had not. I kept looking, though I did not know why. His skin glowed with a light sweat, pale and unblemished. He had none of the scars of older men who have been beaten by the world.

"So where do you live? It must be nearby as all of you city people never travel far without your servants."

I remained silent when he asked this.

"You will have to say something eventually. You wouldn't survive long in *my* village. The only time you can be silent there is when you are sleeping. We are always fishing, farming, cleaning . . ." He paused, trying to convey to me how life was lived there. "The women work harder than the men, but it is the men who do the teaching. That is what my father says. Then, at the end of the day, for a short time after supper, it is peaceful and you can watch the moon and the stars. That is the best time. The time I like most. I hope you can see it one day."

As the weeks passed, he showed me how to build a dam, to make a fishing rod, to take the scales from a fish. Little things, but I remember them still. Most of all I loved to sit in silence with him and follow the movements of his eyes as he looked for changes in the current where fish surfaced. Sometimes, as he concentrated on the water, I would stand behind him and throw small stones into the river. I would watch his head turn and his eyes dart after each splash before he realized it was me. After school each day I would run home, leaving my friends to play without me, and ask Grandfather to take me to the gardens. I am sure he knew why I wanted to go there so urgently, why I could not wait as soon as I arrived home, not wanting my supper or greeting Ba and Ma, but he always took me. He never stopped me or explained to my parents why we were going, just let me be carried away by feelings I could not properly explain even to myself.

Then one day Bi arrived outside my school as I was leaving

to return home. I had left the school yard and turned the first corner on my way back. He was there, standing in front of me, holding two fried *dofu* sticks.

"I thought I would see where you went to school. But now I also know that you can speak, because I saw you there with your classmates. So I thought, if you won't speak to me, then you can at least eat with me." He held out one of the sticks.

We walked on but it was hot and we stopped to sit on a wall and finish our food. He finished quickly and continued talking to me while I took smaller and smaller bites, content just to listen to him.

"I also heard that your sister is getting married. At home a marriage is celebrated by everyone in the town. The groom's family bring many presents, such as sheep, goats, pigs, and ducks. They also give the bride's family fruit, jewelry, money . . . the list is extremely long. I don't think your family will receive many goats and pigs, do you?" He laughed, pressing his nose to make himself look like a pig, and I laughed with him.

"The wedding celebrations there last a week, but after the first night the bride becomes part of her new family. I think it must be strange to become part of a different family."

Suddenly I had to ask something.

"But what does the bride's family give?"

"The bride's family? Oh, suddenly you are speaking to me! I don't want you to stop . . . Well, the bride's family accepts the gifts and gives many of them back. These are very old traditions. It is respectful not to keep them. I don't think the bride's family gives anything except the dowry, but I know that when the bride goes to her new family she will take a chest that contains a quilt and other things for the house. Why do you ask?"

"My family is giving all the gifts."

"Well, maybe your family is very rich."

I hesitated.

"I don't think we are."

"Well, my mother tells me that the traditions change from place to place and can be different with each family. I think people just make them up." Bi laughed again and shook his head.

He paused and looked away from me then suddenly looked back at me.

"Did you like the *dofu* stick?"

"Yes, it was tasty, but wait until you have eaten the dumplings made by our cook."

I wanted to keep talking to him but did not know what to say.

"Would you like to come and eat dumplings at my home?" I asked.

"I remember you said you had a cook. Does she make them very sweet? Because dumplings have to be sweet."

He licked his lips and rolled his eyes playfully.

"Yes, they are delicious, very juicy and sweet," I promised.

"Good. But I must warn you, I can eat many dumplings." He stuck out his chest and rubbed his stomach.

"They are the best."

I did not know why I had said this; I had forgotten all the lessons on good manners I had received. Bi had already accepted my invitation before I realized that Grandfather should be the one asking him, and because I was too young and a girl, Grandfather would not agree. We stood up and continued home. Bi was excited by the busy streets and was constantly looking at people and what they were doing. We walked in silence as he looked around. When we neared my home he turned to me.

"I think I should leave you to walk alone from here. Your family does not know me so I should not be seen with you."

I nodded.

"Remember to come and eat dumplings with us," I reminded him.

It was his turn to nod and then he walked away toward the gardens.

When I told Grandfather what I had said to Bi he was not pleased.

"Feng Feng, it is not right at all that you should invite a boy to our home. It is not your place to ask and brings shame on our family."

I thought he would refuse me then.

Instead he sighed. "However, I introduced you to the boy, and as he has already accepted the invitation it would be completely wrong to take it back."

A few days later Grandfather asked Bi properly, and shortly afterward we all sat down together in the kitchen, eating tasty dumplings prepared by our cook from Beijing. They had plenty of juice and oil inside, which needed to be sucked carefully so that not even a drop was wasted. I liked the way Bi nimbly manipulated the dumpling between his chopsticks and spoon, so as not to lose any of the flavor. He smiled at me as I watched him. He was so gentle and patient, taking his time to unfold each twist of the dough and reveal the meat inside. Sister walked by and remarked that my friend was handsome, giving me a little wink. I had never been so happy. I felt like touching Bi and kissing him on the cheek, but I did not know how and my face burned at the thought.

Grandfather must have seen. Suddenly he asked, "Xiao Bi, what is your favorite dish at home?"

"My favorite food is chicken dumplings, but the best food of all is the Huang He carp. My father and I go to the river and spend all day catching the biggest fish we can. When we get home it is soaked in fresh water for three days to wash the smell of the earth away. Then it is cut into pieces: one fillet is fried and the other is cooked with a sweet-and-sour sauce. With the head and tail we make a tasty soup," Bi told Grandfather proudly.

"It sounds wonderful. Maybe if we visit one day we can try it," Grandfather replied.

"I hope so."

"I am sure Feng hopes so too," Grandfather said, which made me blush again.

I said nothing but continued watching Bi. When we had finished, the three of us walked to the front door and he left us. We watched him walk away down the street.

"I think my own father, your great-grandfather, must have been like this young man: simple but brave, ready to speak his mind," Grandfather commented. "Bi may succeed one day, like Great-grandfather, who came from the countryside and became a captain in the Imperial Army, commanding a troop of men. What do you think?" He looked down at me and smiled. Without waiting for my response he returned to the house, leaving me on my own.

I stood watching Bi walk away from us and dreamt of how he and I would meet again in the future.

Chapter 4

A week later I came home to find Ma and Ba arguing. This rarely happened as Ma would normally give her husband face outside their bedrooms and generally, in turn, he would not openly contradict her priorities. Their marriage was a clumsy dance of conflicting and sympathetic convictions and demands, with each person responding to the other's actions in silence. But this time I could hear them shouting from the street outside the house. The absurd volume of their quarrel was a clear indication that they seldom fought with each other this way. They were standing just inside the courtyard, clearly unaware of all that was going on around them. Ma was very angry, so much so that she was nearly crying. Her hands shook at her sides and wisps of hair had fallen from her bun. I had never seen Ba so aggressive. He kept raking his hands through his hair and glaring at her, breathing hard.

I stood quietly watching them, frightened by their ferocity. Ma turned and saw me.

"Feng, go to your room!"

I stood still.

"Ping, take Feng to her room . . . or to her grandfather," Ma ordered the maid.

I moved slowly as she led me away, trying to hear as much as possible. Once Ping had led me to my room I quickly returned to the balcony to try and eavesdrop further.

"We will have the wedding!" Ma looked at my father, her eyes demanding his immediate agreement. "We cannot miss this opportunity. How could you even suggest that we should stop it? We must make the date earlier so she can still go through the ceremonies . . . The doctors have said as much."

"No. The doctors said she should have a proper examination. They said that *if* we must go ahead, then it would be better to bring it forward, so that her condition is less noticeable. And it would be better for her health that way, too." Ba talked slowly, trying not to shout again. He looked down at the ground, maybe hoping that when he next looked up Ma would suddenly agree with him.

"Exactly! Exactly what I said. We should bring it forward."

"Only if we want to go ahead with it."

"After so many years, how can you consider anything else? You must be joking!" Ma knew he hated confrontation and that he would not answer her immediately.

"The doctors are saying we should only bring it forward if we don't plan to stop it," he patiently replied.

"Well, we *don't* plan to stop it. We will never stop it!" She began to shout at him again. "Only a fool would suggest this. Nothing can be changed when she is married. Once it is done, nothing else will matter. Don't you understand?" She looked at him hard in order to provoke him. Then her mouth formed a derisive smile, her lips curling bitterly, and she cocked her head slightly to one side and looked directly at him. "But then, you always have been a fool. This is the best match we could possibly have hoped for. If we had more money or a better position in Society then we could choose . . . but we don't. Only a fool would think this way." She paused before delivering the final insult. "Are you a fool?"

Ba stepped closer to Ma. It looked as though he might slap her then but he stopped himself.

"I will make all the arrangements so that nothing need affect the wedding plans," she declared and walked off, leaving him staring after her as she disappeared inside the house.

Ba was a naturally lean man who never seemed to grow fat. His friends would joke that this was the reason he'd never be rich. Grandfather, too, had the same slight build, nervous smile, and thick hair. When they were anxious, they would run their left hand through their hair and pat it down at the back. They both had the habit of looking away from things, as if they hoped that when they finally looked back they could begin anew. Their expression glowed when they were happy, and although sometimes there seemed to be little wisdom in their faces, there was always kindness.

I am sorry that I cannot tell you much more, but I do know many people saw weakness in their natural generosity and warmth. Ba had always been exploited, particularly by Ma, but I believe that colleagues at work or the occasional business associate also took advantage of him. He did not try to force his own opinions, believing in politeness, in listening to others, giving them a fair hearing. Ma was not a particularly hard or domineering woman but she had what I now understand to be a narrow-minded indifference to other people's opinions, thinking only of her own advantage. On this occasion Ma chose to ignore his views and simply turned her back, for she knew he would do nothing to resist.

I watched Ba for a few minutes then ran to Grandfather to tell him what I had heard. He said nothing after hearing my story, just sat in the hardwood reclining chair, undid the top button of his shirt, and looked at Grandmother's portrait. He was silent for a long while, though I repeatedly asked him what it all meant. Eventually he pulled himself up out of his chair.

"Xiao Feng, we must keep this to ourselves. Do you promise, little one?" He leaned toward me and whispered, "I think your sister is pregnant. Your mother and the fiancé's family probably want to bring the wedding date forward so no one will notice and we don't all lose face. It is shameful. It is *so* shameful." He sank back down.

My first thought was that we would have a baby in the house and I smiled, asking whether I would be its auntie. Grandfather suddenly became very serious and raised his voice to me.

"Feng, don't be so stupid! This is very serious . . . it'll ruin our family name. This is what can happen when a family tries to rise to a different level. It would be better not to have the baby than to bear such shame. Everyone will know."

He looked so solemn that I was dumbstruck. He got up and left me sitting on the floor in front of his empty chair. The room remained still and silent and I with it, until a servant came in to sweep the floor.

I seemed to be the only one who was looking forward to seeing this baby. Grandfather and I resumed our walks in the gardens. When I met Bi next, I desperately wanted to tell him everything. But he seemed as calm and serene as he had every other day, and all the thoughts bubbling inside me suddenly seemed much too silly, so I kept silent. I smiled and sat quietly beside him, kneading my toes in the grass. Grandfather looked agitated, mumbling that he was going to see if one of the fig trees had blossomed. As soon as he had left, Bi turned to me and shifted a little closer.

"My father told me that girls like flowers." As he said this, he shyly produced three pretty peonies with white petals and beautiful yellow centers.

"I *do* like these! Thank you. They are called *Paeonia lacti-flora*. They are very pretty.".

"What did you say? Is that Chinese?"

"It's something my grandfather taught me. He told me it's an ancient language, as old as Chinese but the people who spoke it have all gone. He said they had huge cities and temples like we do. He told me they were magnificent."

I held the petals to my face and breathed in their freshness. They smelled of daybreak. I laid them in my lap and caressed the petals between my thumb and first finger. They were soft and delicate.

"I never thought I would find someone in the city who liked flowers. You should come and live in the countryside. In summer there are flowers everywhere. Is living in the city good? It looks very busy and noisy to me."

"Except for going to school, I am not allowed to go into it without my grandfather . . . and he only likes to come to these gardens."

"We should go and have a look together."

He tempted me, but I knew we should stay in the gardens. Even my being with him would make my parents very angry if they found out.

Grandfather returned and stood over us, looking at the flowers that Bi had given me.

"Bi, did you give those to Feng Feng? *Paeonia lactiflora* . . . very pretty. Xiao Feng, I hope you named them correctly?" Grandfather gently asked us, though he was obviously still agitated. "Xiao Feng, remember to cut their stems a little before putting them in water when you get home. Then they will not wilt so quickly."

"I will, Grandfather," I replied. "I'll see you at home."

We watched him walk away.

When I went back to the house later I saw Grandfather speaking to Ba. They stood close together, Grandfather straight-backed and Ba looking down, his hands by his sides. They talked slowly and erratically. They talked as father and son, Grandfather speaking and Ba listening respectfully. When Ba tried to interrupt, Grandfather held up his hand, signaling that he must wait. When Grandfather had finished speaking, Ba told him something that obviously stunned him. They stood together in silence for a moment before Grandfather retreated to his room.

I don't know what they said but everyone in the house began to work even more feverishly, as if sheer haste and activity could bring the wedding day upon us more quickly. Each separate task had to be accomplished perfectly: a misplaced stitch or poorly wrapped present might upset the gods and bring a curse upon us, ruining the day. Grandfather lost all interest in the gardens and sat in his chair, pale and anxious. I had not yet seen any of the doctors Ma had mentioned during her argument with Ba, but after Grandfather spoke to him I saw them start to arrive.

The first was a local man who visited every day bringing Sister many traditional medicines made from fresh herbs and dried animal parts, which needed to be brewed into medicinal teas. He was a withered old man who looked like the desiccated creatures and twigs he brought with him. He would shuffle around the outside of the house, checking for objects that would create bad feng shui then remove them before coming inside to visit Sister. There was also a man who practiced Western medicine, who came carrying a neat little bag of bottles and pills. He wore spectacles and was smartly dressed in a gray *ma qua* and Western shoes. The doctors generally saw Sister alone in her room, coming at least once a day. They must have been expensive, as I noticed that Grandfather needed to give Ba extra money to pay for them.

There was now only three weeks to go before the wedding. Sister spent much of the day resting in her room and would only go out in the evenings with Ma. I rarely got a chance to see her, but when I did she looked thinner and paler. Her skin had become gray and translucent, the whites of her eyes cloudy, pupils raw and angry. Her pregnancy was not really noticeable, but when I commented on this to Grandfather and Ba they said I should not speak of it as it would only bring bad luck. I wanted to be sure that the baby would be born healthy, but I was secretly glad Sister was so weak, because it meant she was too distracted to bother with me. If she'd had the strength, I knew she would have told our parents that I liked talking to Bi and was meeting him in the gardens. Fortunately the attention of every other family member, maid, and servant was focused on one thing only.

I continued to spend my time as I pleased. Even Grandfather now seemed too distracted to notice.

In the early evening, once the seamstress was gone for the day, I would sometimes go to the top of the house to see the wedding dress Sister would wear for the important tea ceremonies. The dress was made in a proud startling red—the luckiest shade. After the seamstress had completed her daily work, she would slip the dress over a mannequin, which stood in the corner of the otherwise empty room. The seamstress was now working on the embroidery, which was very fine and complicated. In the half-light of dusk cast through the window at the end of the room the dress looked ghostly. Several times I stood in the doorway, just looking at it, too frightened to enter on my own.

I thought it best to spend as much time as possible away from the house so I would sit in the gardens, reading or lying in the grass, staring at the sun. I used all these opportunities to see Bi, who would be busy fishing or weaving grass crayfish baskets.

"I would like to tell you more about my life. Do you want to hear?" he asked me one day.

I nodded in reply.

"My town is in the heart of China in the countryside . . . it's called Daochu." He looked at me as if I should know it, then smiled. "You've never heard of it?" He laughed. "It is near the old capital city, Xian. I used to go to the ancient ruins with my friends and we'd stand on the tall wall that surrounds the city and pretend to be Imperial soldiers. That was a long time ago. Now I go with my father to tend the fields and fish." He paused and looked at my hands, then slowly up at my face and straight into my eyes. "Seventeen years ago, when I had just been born, there was a terrible drought and both my grandparents died. I like watching you with your grandfather. I think it would have been good to have grandparents.

"I have not told you this before but my mother is the seamstress making your sister's wedding dress. You are very lucky that she is making it. She is a great seamstress and can do the old Imperial stitches . . . even the great forbidden stitch. Her family have known these things for many generations." Suddenly his excitement faded and he paused, looking away from me. He started twisting the grass between his fingers. "But today she will finish her work and tomorrow we will go back home."

My heart started to beat very fast and I could not think. I wish I had said something to him then but in that moment I had no words, just the feeling that I was suddenly part of the garden, left rooted there to watch things pass me by, like a flower gently nodding in the breeze, no longer part of this conversation. As if expecting me to say nothing, Bi continued speaking.

"I liked talking to you, and I liked sitting here with you. You're very pretty. In my town it is traditional for the men to marry young. When my mother makes the wedding dress for my bride, I want you to be wearing it."

I was lost. Had nothing but silence to offer in reply. He stood up and held out his hand to me. I took it and we stood facing each other. I had never been so close to a boy before. I looked at his eyes, the strong lines of his eyebrows, then down to his mouth, his hands, his feet. The hems of his trousers were all muddy and wet.

He touched the corner of my long blouse, below the last button. I realize we were young and childish but he held it as if he were holding me, tethering me to that spot in the grass by the river, and although he did not touch my skin, I felt that he did. Looking down, I could see his hand so close to my body, my skin. I wanted him to touch me instead of the cloth, but that would be wrong and improper. As he talked he kept holding this tiny piece of me and I thought it might be acceptable to take his hand. I almost reached out, wanting our fingers to be entwined in a knot that no parents could ever untie. I did not do any of these things, though. I remained still, just watching his warm eyes looking at me so tenderly.

He reached up and cupped my cheeks with his hands. I let my face fall gently between them. I should have pulled away but I could not. I felt my eyes start to fill and carefully he used his thumbs to catch my tears. I smiled and coughed a little, and he smiled back at me. Then our lips touched.

It was my first kiss. As I recall it now, so that I can tell you, I think of it as tender and loving, but the power of these two emotions were unknown to me then. The kiss was soft, lovely, and left me wanting more. It took only the briefest of moments but it has lasted my whole life.

As he withdrew his lips he also let his hands fall from my cheeks and return to holding the corner of my blouse. He played with the fabric again, perhaps not knowing what to do next. We stood perfectly still and the only sounds were those of the river and the trees.

"Shall we sit down again . . . maybe a fish will leap into our laps for supper?" he suggested.

After a few hours spent sitting together, talking about the river, Bi got up, telling me it was time for him to go. We did not seem to be able to say anything more to each other. He looked at me for a long time, almost drinking me in. Then I watched him follow the course of the river out of the gardens and sat there myself for a few moments more, staring at the water until the light grew gray and I had to return home.

He had left me his fishing rod, which I took with me. I leaned it up against the wall outside my bedroom door. Later that evening, Sister walked past and the hook caught the stitching of her dress and pulled a small thread. She immediately looked down, grabbed the rod and broke it, all the time screaming for me. When I arrived, eating a sticky rice cake, she knocked it from my hand and shouted at me for ruining her dress. She threw the broken rod at me then, which caught me and cut my arm slightly. I looked down at her clothes and could see it was the tiniest of stitches in an old dress.

She noticed me looking at it and grabbed me by the chin and cheeks, forcing me to look at her instead. Her hands were bony and her fingers bit hard into my flesh. I saw that her face looked gaunt and hollow. I had not studied her closely for weeks and realized that the makeup she wore had concealed the change in her. I had only caught glimpses of her, leaving and entering the house, her room, or having conversations with Ma and Ba. From a distance, her carefully groomed facade had always seemed exactly the same.

"Why are you so stupid? You hide in those gardens with that foolish little boy, ignoring the things that will teach you what you really need to know. How do you expect to learn anything useful there? You leave this dirty thing here, to cut me and ruin everything . . . Your safe little life is not going to last forever, you know! Soon you will understand what it means to be an adult. That there is more to this world than just playing. You may even have *my* life, though you don't deserve it."

She screamed so wildly and relentlessly at me that I was too scared to move. The maids had stopped work and I could see them watching from a safe distance.

I began to cry. Her fingers still gripped my face and she forced my head up and back. Even though I was taller, in her Western shoes with heels she could nearly look me in the eye. Tears rolled down my cheeks toward the floor. I could see Grandfather walking past in the background. He stopped briefly when he noticed us then scuttled down the stairs where he must have waited as I did not see him appear in the courtyard below.

"Cry! Cry! And keep crying because *this* is how I would like to remember you. It won't change a thing. You have done nothing! You do not work or practice. You don't deserve anything. So when it happens, enjoy it all—all that I have given you. For you it comes completely free. But remember me and Ma every day. *Every single day.*"

As she stopped screaming this at me, Sister released her grip on my face and pushed me away. She stared at me for a second as I staggered back a step and then she slapped me once, twice, on the cheeks that Bi had just held so gently. It did not matter how hard she hit me. Now I had something of my own and no one could ever change that. She continued to punch and slap me until Grandfather came hurrying back up the stairs and grabbed her hands. I stood still, looking into her bony face and wild eyes. Grandfather led her away. As she was helped back into her room she let out a loud animal howl that echoed around the courtyard and hung in the air like angry spirits, even after she had closed her bedroom door.

I snatched the broken rod from the floor and went back to my room where I lay on the bed and trembled. After several hours Ba came to my door. He stood silently on the other side for a long time before he asked me how I was. I could only lie there, feeling anxious and scared. I did not understand what had happened, I did not understand what Sister had said to me. I had never seen her so angry, but she'd looked frail, too, as if anger was the only thing keeping her upright. I said nothing to Ba and after some minutes I heard him walk away.

I lay on my bed and thought that the only thing I could do was run away with Bi. He would be leaving in the morning. I could escape early and meet him at the station. In his home town I could still go to school, and we could fish together and enjoy the country grass and flowers. I closed my eyes and imagined what his town must be like; perhaps it was one of those beautiful ancient towns on stilts by a river's edge; the tall wooden houses almost falling into the muddy banks and rope bridges crisscrossing to different buildings from each side. In my mind I drifted through these places, walking the unsteady planks of the bridges and watching white cranes pick food from the shallows below.

But I had never even left the safety of my bed before, the bolsters that I had hugged and straddled since I was small. It was not an elaborate bed, though each of the four posts was carved into the likenesses of animals: pigs, rabbits, cows, mice. My bedcover, though a little faded over the years, was still the deep blue shade that always made me think of sleep and childish dreams. When I was upset I would lie on my bed and trace the shape of the carved animals with my finger. This time I let my fingers follow the shape of a mouse's body and whiskers. The touch of the smooth polished wood felt familiar and comforting. Eventually I slept.

Later Grandfather came to my room with a maid and brought me some food as I had missed supper. He sat with me and watched me eat a bowl of congee and a steamed roll. I was still trembling as I put the soup spoon into my mouth. He looked at me so closely, it was as if he was trying to preserve this image of me. I continued eating with him staring at me in silence. Once I had finished, we sat and looked at each other. I huddled on the bed with my arms around my knees while he sat near the door. After a few minutes, he started to smile. It was a weak and uncertain smile, one that made me feel worried rather than reassured.

"You should not blame your sister. She is suffering greatly and is feeling very sick."

I did not care, I just wanted her to leave me alone. I looked at Grandfather expectantly but it seemed he did not have anything else to say to me. I felt what I had always known: that I was second and less important to the family. I must always give way. It was not that Ma and Ba did not love me, more that they preferred to follow tradition and custom rather than to break them. Their devotion to the first child was simply greater than it was to the second, and they could not help that. I could neither win more love from them nor alter their devotion to the eldest. I realize now that this was not something they chose but a thousand-year-old instinct.

As the maid had already gone back to the kitchen, Grandfather took my bowl away himself. As he took it in his hand, he lingered to press his other hand to my cheek. His rough skin—hardened by a lifetime spent planting and pruning—briefly traced the salty lines of my earlier tears. He looked down at me a moment longer then turned and left me to sleep again.

In the morning Sister's fiancé arrived with his father, who summoned Ba very rudely, telling the maid to get him immediately and without delay. When he arrived they all sat down and one of the maids was told to bring some tea. The father did not wait for the maid to return but spoke to Ba abruptly. Whatever was said brought Ba back to his feet immediately so he was standing over his unwelcome guest. He looked at the fat old man, seated in our house like a conquering emperor settling into another's throne, and it unsettled Ba, intimidated him in his own home. As they talked, something was said that shook Ba. He sat back down and then looked at the floor; then he leaned forward as if about to confront them, but at the last moment remained silent. The father continued talking at him and in the end Ba simply nodded and offered his hand. They shook and then, after a few more words, the father led his son away, leaving Ba standing there staring after them. Eventually he turned and saw me, looking back with his eyes full of an emotion I was too young to understand then.

I had noticed that during the last week or so the doctors had all ceased coming to the house. I assumed that meant my sister was better and we'd just have to wait while the baby was born. Hopefully that meant she'd be in a better mood.

I went to knock on her door, but as it was slightly open I went straight in. She was at her mirror applying her makeup, still looking very ill. I asked if she was feeling better. She did not reply. Then I said she must be happy that her wedding was coming soon, and pleased to be becoming a mother. She began screaming at me then and crying so hard it was difficult to make out what she was saying.

"I hate you! You have done nothing and will get everything . . . you will get it *all*. I warn you, though, you will not like it. And every time you feel hurt, remember what I told you last time: think of me and of how much I hate you. *Because you don't deserve it!* Now get out of my room."

As she screamed at me I retreated until I collided with Ba, who had heard Sister shouting and come to her room. The screaming stopped as she started coughing. Little red spots sprayed across the floor at my feet. I looked at Ba, who quickly pushed me out of the door and closed it. I stood outside waiting for him but he did not come out. Grandfather pulled me away and went into the house, calling for a maid to fetch the doctors. I saw Ba come out after several hours, and then the doctors arrived and they went into the room with Ma and Ba. It was already dark and I was tired. I sat waiting in the kitchen with Grandfather. The maid made us strong tea, the kind we had at banquets. Normally I was only allowed to drink two cups but today the maid let me drink as many as I liked.

Eventually I fell asleep. It was Ba who woke me. I was still sitting at the table in the kitchen with Grandfather watching over me. Ba told me to go to Sister's room.

I entered quietly. Sister was lying in bed with Ma sitting holding her hand. The room smelled airless and bad, and was dark except for the light from two candles. I could not make out Sister's face from where I stood by the door. I went closer and could see she was very ill. Her skin was white, and without the usual makeup she looked old and drained. Ma was crying.

Sister grabbed my arm hard and pulled me close to her. She tried to say something that I could not understand. Her nails dug hard into my skin, and I wanted to pull away but Ma told me to stand still. Sister could not make herself understood. Her eyes flickered in all directions, barely looking at me. She continued mumbling. I wanted to leave and run to Grandfather, but Ma insisted I must stay. Sister's words were slurred and drowned by saliva. Finally, without saying anything audible, she fell back, looking exhausted. I realized I already knew what she'd been trying to say. I pulled my arm away and stepped back next to Ma.

Ma whispered to me, "You should have behaved properly. This is your elder sister and you must give her the respect she is due. Please go and pray to our ancestors for her. You should leave now, you are only upsetting her."

She opened the door for me and I left. I went straight to Grandfather, who hugged me tight. He was still in the kitchen, where he had been all evening. I told him that Sister looked terribly ill and asked him what was wrong with her.

Grandfather nodded and simply said, "Yes," but ignored my question.

The maids were already sleeping, so he made some noodles himself, with spring onions, ginger, and two dumplings. We ate in silence, framed by the half-light from outside and the flame of a single candle set on the chopping board, and while Grandfather ate, tears slid gently from his cheeks into his bowl.

The next day I woke to a loud thud. I came out of my bedroom to find some men taking a stretcher into Sister's room. Seeing me, Ma came over and quickly took my hand, leading me to the kitchen.

"Xiao Feng, please sit down and listen to me. You must listen properly. Your Sister has been very ill."

She took a breath and I had time to look at her. Her hair was not neatly arranged as normal and she looked pale and tired. She hunched her back when she would usually stand so straight.

"Your sister died early this morning. Your father and I will organize the mourning arrangements, for people to pay their respects to her and us."

"But I thought she was to have a baby?" I asked.

"Baby? What baby? Feng, this is not the right time to be so foolish. You must grow up! Your Sister was very ill and the doctors could not heal her. There'll be a lot to do so we expect you to help." Ma drew in a sharp breath through her nose. "Nothing has gone right . . . the fortune-teller was wrong. It's a curse on us." It seemed as though she would cry then but she restrained herself.

I did not understand at the time, but I know now that I saw in Ma's distress and bitterness someone who had spent the last months battling against fate, someone who had exhausted all her hope and prayers attempting to prevent destiny from fulfilling its dread work. It was all true: the men were carrying Sister's dead body, Ma was grief-stricken, the doctors were presenting their bills, and now, in keeping with tradition, the maids were no longer allowed to clean the house. Yet none of it felt true. Ma called for the cook.

"Please can you make Feng some Ovaltine? She must keep up her strength for the mourning period and funeral. There is much work to do," she continued without looking at me. "Feng, after you have finished your drink, go to your grandfather. He will look after you and tell you what you must do."

The tightness and shininess of Ma's skin that had allowed her to keep her youthful looks, that had made Sister, too, such a beauty, had suddenly gone. I realized my mother was now an old woman.

Chapter 5

All the wedding preparations came to a halt. Ba and Grandfather stayed close to Ma until the funeral was finished. It took place in our house and lasted five days before she was cremated. Sister's body was laid out in its coffin in the courtyard and every evening people came to pay respects. One evening her fiancé's family arrived and, after a short time spent paying respects, the father took Ma and Ba aside to discuss something. They talked at length and as they did, Ma kept looking up at Sister's photograph at the head of the coffin. My parents nodded many times. When the conversation ended, father and son paid their final respects and left. Ma and Ba resumed their places, seated on the left of the coffin, as other mourners came to see them.

The photograph of Sister, chosen by Ma, had been taken when she was at her most beautiful. It remained on the altar until after Sister's body was cremated. On that day, we followed the coffin to the crematorium and watched it pushed into the flames. My parents burned small paper-houses, imitation money, and paper servants to help Sister in the next life. Ma cried and Ba held her. I stood in silence with any memory of Sister's bitter words lost in the strange and awkward newness of this experience. I felt nothing.

Sister had died of cancer, a badness that had slowly grown

inside her and ate at her. She had never been pregnant, Grand-father had been wrong there, and when he found out the truth he had agreed with Ma and Ba not to tell me. Sister had fore-seen everything that was to happen. I had understood nothing.

At the end of the funeral, the three grown-ups went to their rooms. I sat on the floor in front of the altar in the courtyard, looking at Sister's photograph. It should have been taken with the coffin but had been forgotten. When she had her strength back, Ma would insist on burning it along with the mourning clothes that we had worn for the last few days. It had been taken by a photographer who'd insisted Sister should wear bright red lipstick and a Western hairstyle, both of which she'd liked anyway. Ma had reservations about it, because she felt it looked too Western, but now that did not matter. The photographer had been satisfying his own desires but in that he had captured Sister as she had lived, an image created purely to please her suitors and Society. There was nothing more.

I stared at her thickly painted lips. I should have left the pho-tograph for Ma but I took it with me. I needed still to see those lips and dark eyes that could be so selfish and callous. I wanted to remember the Sister who had never loved me, only scared me, who had lived for herself and the admiration and respect of those she wanted to join. This photograph represented the person she'd wished everyone to remember after they had been introduced to her, but eventually she had left our family not for a wedding ceremony but in a funeral procession. A life spent with Ma, Ba, and Grandfather was all that seemed to be left for me. If Bi returned perhaps I would run away with him, for I understood there would be nothing for me here. I was simply the daughter who had survived. I would be taking care of my parents as they grew older.

Grandfather found me sitting quietly in my room. He came

over and kissed me on the forehead. He saw the photograph then, kissed me again.

"I never liked that photograph."

I looked down at him on the edge of my bed.

"I thought you, Ma, and Ba liked it. She looks older, like a woman." My sentence trailed away as I was unsure of myself.

"She looked too old but it was not for me to say anything."

His words also faded away slowly.

He sat down heavily on the bed and took my right hand in his but his eyes did not look up at me, just stared at the wall opposite us, drifting across to the open door and out into the space above the courtyard. His grip tightened on my hand.

"I should have stopped them from using that photograph. It is not how we should remember her even if that is what she was becoming." He paused and sucked in his breath slowly. "It is difficult, Xiao Feng, sometimes it is very hard to do what you know should be done. I should have raised my voice earlier but I could not. I just cannot do what I know I should."

He became very agitated, letting go of my hand so aggressively that he almost threw it down into my lap.

"Grandfather, I don't think it is that important to Ma and Ba. They liked this photo very much."

He stood up and went over to it.

"Perhaps you are right, everything will be fine."

I could only see his back, his legs outlined by his trousers seemed so thin that they would barely support him. I saw the back of his head move closer to the photograph.

"Yes, I wish I had the courage to tell them. Tell them all."

He turned and looked at me and smiled, yet I knew his smiles and this was watery and hurt, something that he had forced for me. His eyes were wet but he continued smiling hard at me.

"Xiao Feng, I will see you later as I'm going for a walk by myself."

He and I never walked together in the gardens again and he spent most of his time sitting listlessly in his chair, as if waiting for something.

A week later Ba and Ma came to my room with two maids, who were holding Sister's wedding dress.

"Xiao Feng, you must wear this for Sister's fiancé. The maids will help you get dressed," Ma instructed.

I looked at the dress. I had not seen it properly until now. It was beautiful, but it was still Sister's.

"This dress will be too short. All Sister's clothes were too short and wide for me."

It was also very unlucky to wear anything left by a dead person but I did not want to talk about this.

"Your Sister's fiancé will be arriving with his family and they want to see you wear it."

"But why do they want to see me wear the dress? They have never even asked to see me before," I quickly replied.

"Stop asking so many questions! They are thinking of buying the dress from your father in remembrance of your sister and they would like to see it worn."

I did not want to see them. To me they resembled ugly toads, belching their foul stink, bulging eyes squinting at everyone before them. I did not want their toad eyes to look at me even if it was only to see the dress being worn.

"A local tailor has worked very hard to make basic alterations to the dress and alter it to your size, but the seamstress will be coming back soon to work on it properly. You need to be ready in five hours. The maids will bathe you first."

Ma and Ba did not explain any further but left, leaving me to drift to thoughts of Bi and his return. The maids undressed and washed me. I normally only took a few minutes to dress as Ma and Ba had never given me beautiful clothes or the assistance of maids; those things had been reserved for Sister.

The wedding dress, the *kua*, was of red silk with beautiful flowers and symbols embroidered on it in gold thread. The stitching was exact and careful, meticulous work I know well now. It reminded me of Bi and I wished he were here to see me. I had never worn such clothes before; dresses like this must have made Sister feel very special, floating above everyone, almost untouchable. But Bi would have laughed at me for wearing such intricate and elegant clothes. The wedding dress his mother would have made for his bride would have been beautiful, too, but it would have been simple, reflecting the peace of the countryside that Bi loved so much. Still, even I was surprised by the way I looked after the maids had finished.

I did not resemble my sister, being obviously more innocent and childish, but I am sure my face was prettier. My hair had never been arranged properly before and I enjoyed seeing the maids brush it out. It was black and strong and their repeated touching and brushing made me feel older, more like a woman. With all this attention I barely remembered that this was to have been Sister's wedding dress, and what should have happened to her. For these few moments, I was intoxicated by the feeling of everybody revolving around me.

Sister's fiancé arrived with his father and mother and they all sat in silence, with Ma and Ba, sipping tea. As I entered, Sister's fiancé smiled when he saw me and started whispering to his father, who immediately nodded in reply. His father also smiled and as he did, his face spread out into three chins and his tiny eyes disappeared beneath his thick eyebrows. He resembled a happy smiling toad. I served them all tea and sat quietly while they talked. I sat and dreamed of sitting with Bi in the gardens, kissing each other again. I was so lost I could almost taste his mouth.

"Feng, please pour Mr. Sang some more tea." Ma woke me from my dreams.

The dress was restricting, and bending over to pour tea was quite difficult, but I felt regal in it and enjoyed being the center of attention. It was all a new experience for me but I felt I understood now how Sister had become so selfish and vain. To be the focus of such close attention every day would have made it impossible for her to think of anyone but herself. Even for a short time it was overwhelming.

I sat there in silence and gazed out of the window behind the seated adults, losing myself in thoughts of going to tea dances like Sister, dancing and laughing, though I had never received the lessons she had and could not dance. Through the window I could see Grandfather leave the house and start walking up the drive away from us. I hoped he was finally visiting the gardens again; they would bring him a peace that I think he'd needed since Sister had died. I had not visited them myself since Bi left, and would have liked to accompany him. I would have liked to have sat on the grass again and watched the river. The adults continued their discussion, ignoring me, so I returned to watching Grandfather. His steps were tired and slow and he stumbled when only a few weeks ago he'd walked purposefully. At the top of the drive, by the gate, he turned and looked back; his eyes were shadowed and his hair disheveled in the wind. He stared hard for a few seconds, then turned and disappeared into the road.

The conversation stopped and I was asked to leave. It took nearly an hour to remove the clothes and all the makeup and I was so tired, I simply fell asleep. A maid had been ordered to come and wake me for supper and to dress me again. This time I was given a proper silk cheongsam like Sister used to wear to dinner. It was fragile to the touch and weighed almost nothing. It did not fit me perfectly but it still looked very pretty. I liked to see myself and enjoyed the maids brushing my hair again. I had become the center of the house and everything was being done for me. I thought nothing about how this had happened; I just let myself be carried along by the attention paid to me. For this short time I wanted nothing else but for this feeling to last forever.

When I arrived at the table, it was set for three people and I asked why Grandfather was not eating with us and was told that he had gone on a pilgrimage to sweep Grandmother's burial place in the countryside and would not be back for a few weeks. Ba looked sad and tired but Ma was very excited. The maids did not serve the food fast enough for Ma, and she hurried them out of the room as soon as they had finished. Before they had left, Ba started to say something but Ma quickly interrupted. She looked me steadily in the eyes, holding my gaze as if she believed she could hold my spirit as well.

"Feng, in two months, after the mourning period has finished, you will be married to Sister's fiancé."

No. I cannot.

I instinctively looked around for Grandfather and caught a glimpse of myself in the mirror. For a moment I saw Sister's face staring back. Ba said nothing; could not bring himself to look at me, it seemed.

Ma's lips formed a smile but her mouth betrayed something more.

"Your sister died and her fiancé's family want the wedding to go ahead. They asked if our next daughter could take Sister's place. The Sang family have made it clear that there must be a marriage . . . it would be considered a terrible loss of face for them if one did not take place. They also believe it is time their eldest son had a son of his own, and there is no time to find him another bride. They all thought you looked very beautiful in the wedding dress."

I could not move. I feared that if I did I might cry.

"Of course, we agreed and so you will be married to him. It

is a very good match and you are very lucky. Do not disrespect your sister and humiliate us by making difficulties."

Face is everything. The family, the great Sang family, had told their friends, business associates, relatives, and many other very important people that there would be a wedding. They had said that their son would now be marrying a beautiful, talented, and humble woman who knew how to respect a large and highly regarded family like theirs. This mighty family was only just willing to live with the shame of changing the date, and all the gossip and questions about the new bride that would then be conducted in private and not-so-private circles. If a wedding did not take place at all, how could it be explained that their son, the progeny of such illustrious ancestors, had not received what was due to him? To them?

"When your sister died, they expected Ba to do what was right, to do what was honorable, and that was to ensure everything proceeded: they expected him to offer his second daughter in place of his first. It was their right to expect this and we understood completely." Ma had finished speaking and the harshness of her tone brought the conversation to a close.

I did not want to marry this man. I did not want to see him and his father. I did not want them to visit me and take me away. I did not want to dance with this young man as Sister had done. But I could not argue or disobey, and like Sister before me I must assume that they were right. The family had told Ma and Ba what they wanted, and this had been accepted. I must respect their decision and follow it. I had no other choice.

In the following days, Ma very quickly made the necessary arrangements: she ordered dresses, informed relatives, and consulted the fortune-teller as to the favorable dates, colors, and symbols. It had all become our responsibility as we had failed the Sang family once and consequently ourselves lost face. The seamstress had been recalled to ensure that Sister's dress was a perfect fit for me, and she would arrive in a couple of days. I hoped Bi would return as well. I longed for him to take me away.

I'd had many dreams of Bi since he had returned home. Sometimes they were like little poems, brief scenes lasting no longer than the time it takes for an autumn leaf to fall from a tree. They had become more vivid since I had been told I must marry Sister's fiancé, and often in the morning my mood would be colored by the things I had dreamed the night before. In many of them Bi was talking with Grandfather. I could never hear their conversation as they spoke softly, but Grandfather was nodding and smiling. I would approach them and Bi would turn and kiss me then, his lips barely touching mine; even now, as I sit here broken and alone, looking at his picture, I can imagine this kiss and when I do I feel nothing else. He takes my hand and then we are sitting at the little table in the kitchen eating dumplings. It is very cold and our breath hangs in the air. I see the juice from the dumpling he is eating sitting in his spoon and he offers it to me. I swallow and it warms me. He smiles with satisfaction and I feel warmer still.

Then I am at my school desk in an empty classroom looking out of the window. It is a cold day in winter, the grass short and white with frost. The people outside are wrapped in heavy coats and large boots to protect them from the chill north wind. Bi floats by the school window, smiling at me, and suddenly he appears at the desk next to me. We look at the textbook together. He leans on his elbow and stares hard at the writing, then looks up at me and smiles. He can't read and it does not matter. He just stares at me with eyes that are warm and irresistible. I read the text to him; it is the story of Guanyin, the goddess of mercy. I finish the tale and he takes my hand, which feels hot in the cold classroom. We share the sticky rice I have brought for my lunch. His chopsticks break and we use mine. I am eating from one end and he from the other. A teacher enters the room. She reprimands him but I cannot understand what she is saying. She is extremely angry and wants to hit him.

I wake up then. I want him to come and find me. I want his eyes to look at me and hold me there. I want his sweet smell of the countryside to fill me.

Five days later the seamstress arrived again. She immediately started making alterations to the dress, removing and replacing the work of the local tailor. I had been forbidden from returning to the gardens, which was all I wanted to do, so I would sit on a stool near the door to the attic where the seamstress worked. She sat at the other end, close to the window where the light was good. Although I could not see her face I could see her thick black hair and slender neck and back. Most important, I could see her hands as they worked the needle and thread. I wished she would talk to me.

For many hours I sat and watched her, too afraid to ask about Bi. I just wanted her to tell me that he was her son and he had talked of me. I wanted to know that he had been thinking of me and was coming to see me. I could not help but hope that he had come with her and was waiting below in the gardens for me. I could not go and see—Ma and the maids were constantly watching me. Sister's maids now followed me everywhere, making sure I was careful and did nothing that would disrupt the wedding. Ma would not let anything more cause her or my new family any further loss of face.

So I sat quietly and watched the seamstress while a maid watched me. The seamstress's hands swayed left and right as she built up the complex stitching. I loved her hands; they were so peaceful. I could see that they had never been used to destroy or hurt, only create things that she hoped would be important and dear to people.

This dress was the final act in the completion of Sister and Ma's relentless striving, and though Sister would never wear it, and to me it would be a prison, the seamstress must continue to follow their directions and create something beautiful. A beautiful cage in which a man, like those who sat in the market, could keep his little bird. He could bring out the cage and force his prisoner to sing whenever he wanted to be amused, to show off to his friends or simply to make the little bird suffer. It was the one he would hang up on his porch so he could listen to the birdsong whenever he did not want to feel he was alone.

I watched the seamstress building me my cage, and the maid who was watching me scratching her knees that were swollen and raw from cleaning the floors. Suddenly the maid was summoned away. I stayed there a few moments more, then, when I could no longer hear her footsteps, I ran from the room and into the gardens.

I had not been there since Bi had left. As summer had changed to early autumn, the grass had grown wild and the trees had lost their shape and needed pruning. The path that Bi and I had walked, tracing Grandfather's steps as he accompanied the gardener, was gone and I could not recognize the part of the riverbank that used to be ours. The place where we'd sat had disappeared under long grass and flowers, as though the moments we'd spent together there had all happened in another life. A light wind swept through the tall reeds by the riverbank and brushed my cheeks. I had not brought a coat and my arms felt cold as I stood there alone. The sun seemed farther away. Its heat no longer warmed the gardens, and the flowers and trees were preparing themselves for the cold weather and snow. The perfect picture Grandfather had shown me had become dismal and threatening.

Bi was not waiting for me. Grandfather was not waiting for me. Still I kept searching although by now I could hear the maids shouting after me. They had already come into the gardens and were close behind. When they arrived they immediately led me back to the house. I did not struggle, knowing I must do as I was told.

Again I sat watching the seamstress. She glanced up at me and I looked directly into her eyes, and there I saw him.

"Where did you go, young miss?" she asked me.

"Just in the gardens next door. I was looking for someone."

"My son told me you would often go there, and that you are very clever. He said you know the name of every flower and tree in a strange and ancient language, the original names."

Hearing that he'd thought of me, I could not speak. I wanted her to tell me more but could not ask. My lips and tongue were lost to my control. I could only wait, mute. She returned to her sewing while I stared as hard as I could at the back of her neck, as if my gaze might force her to look up and talk to me again. Silence still.

Perhaps my own silence would tease her into filling it.

"He told me you were a very pretty girl and I think he is right," she said finally. "You will look very beautiful in this dress—perhaps more so than your sister. I was sorry to hear that she died, I never spoke to her, but she was a beautiful young woman."

Her accent was from the countryside, with a thickness and melody to it that made me feel warm and comfortable. It was not as clear or refined as that of city Society, but then it was not as sharp or cold, either. I wanted this accent for my own. I wanted to speak this way, too. I wanted to hear about her son, not about Sister and the dress. I kept staring at her but she did not turn to look at me, just continued sewing. Her long black hair was tightly coiled, high on her head, showing her smooth bare shoulders and neck above the line of her blouse. I wanted to lean my cheek against the back of that neck and put my arms around her, just rest and sleep in the warmth of her body. She looked so peaceful.

Instead I sat at the back of the empty room, watching her, a peasant in Sister's eyes. Perhaps she would hold me as she had held Bi when he was a child, allow me to cry on that same shoulder so she could take my tears back to him. I wanted her to wrap her arms around me as she would him when she returned home. I watched for another hour and then I was told by the maid that it was time for supper. Before I left I wanted to say one thing, something for her to tell him, but I had no idea what it should be.

"Auntie, please tell him that I remember him and that the only reason I was so quiet was I liked listening to his stories. He will understand," I said, finally.

She looked up at me and smiled.

The seamstress stayed for three more days but I was not allowed to talk to her again or even be in her company without a maid present. I wanted to know what she would say to her son. If she would say she had seen me. If she would say to him she thought I was pretty and would have been a good match for him. I wanted to know if she had understood how I felt and if she would explain it to him. I wanted to tell someone that I yearned to see Bi and no one else, and for someone to tell me that it would happen, but I saw no one except for Ma, Ba, and the maids. I hoped Grandfather might return early and tell Ma and Ba that it was not the right thing for me, to marry Sister's fiancé. He had made the doctors come for Sister so he could change this for me.

When the seamstress finished she was sent directly from the house and so I had no chance to say good-bye or to pass her another message to give her son. I continued to dream of Bi, and spent my days waiting for sleep so that I could enter the world I shared with him.

Chapter 6

For the first time I could remember the house felt empty and I was alone. The courtyard was still, and I could sit in any of the three front rooms without worrying I would meet anyone. The sitting room was not very comfortable, containing old heavy wooden chairs with marble backs and some dark lacquered chests on which Ma had placed Tang ceramics that Grandfather had given her. She had originally partly covered the chairs with embroidery made by her parents, but had felt this to be out of place once Sister's sophisticated suitors started to come to the house. Grandfather had always filled the house with flower arrangements. Those that remained since he had left had died and there was no one to replace them. Ma and Ba did not seem to notice, even when they started to fill the house with the acrid smell of death. Perhaps that was as it should be.

Occasionally Ma would find me sitting in Ba's office, which adjoined the sitting room. In the winter it was a warm and comfortable place, lined with his drawings and notes and always with plenty of paper and pencils on his desk. He also had a bookshelf packed with journals and thick books. One day she found me curled up reading in the armchair by his desk, one that she would sit in sometimes while they discussed money.

"I'm glad I have found you . . . I wanted to tell you how very lucky you are. Getting married is not something every girl is fortunate enough to do, particularly to a man with such a good family background. Of course, it should have been your sister . . . they all thought she was so beautiful and talented. Please, never let her memory down. Do not disrespect her name and ours."

Ma had sat down in Ba's chair. She always sat with a perfectly straight back and her cheongsam was always tidy and clean. She wore very little makeup but always ensured her eyebrows were plucked properly and her hair neatly pushed up into a bun. She did not move without a clear purpose and hated people who fidgeted or moved carelessly, with exaggerated gesticulations. She always wore a warm smile, which stemmed from a genuine belief that what she said to people was in their best interests. That conviction was reflected in her eyes, which she would focus intently on the other person until she had finished speaking.

I listened but I wanted to run.

"You will be the First Wife of the eldest son of a very highly regarded family. This is your sister's legacy to you and you should be very grateful. Your sister herself told me she was so very happy to give this opportunity to you, if the Sang family asked.

"I wish that your father's family had been so well-respected and influential in the community. We would have been a great family. Think of all the things I could have done."

She paused, perhaps to remind herself of all those things, something she had probably done hundreds of times before, each time hating Ba a little more. I wanted to ask what she would have done differently but I could not.

"But will it be like Grandfather and Grandmother?" I suddenly asked.

"What do you mean?"

"Grandfather wants to be with Grandmother all the time.

Even though she died so many years ago, he has often told me how much he still wants to be with her."

"Women have to be sensible. We cannot all live like your grandfather, hiding in gardens and playing in dirt. This is a very good match for you, you are very lucky. As I have told you many times before, you need to learn quickly not to be so foolish!" Ma snapped.

She looked at me, giving me the opportunity to reply, but I had nothing to say. It was too late for that. She finished and left me alone. I stayed in Ba's office and waited to see if he would come in, but after several hours I realized there was still no one in the house except for Ma and myself. By the time I left the room, it was growing dark as the maids had yet to light the candles and lamps. It was mid-autumn and the days were quickly growing shorter and colder.

Ma and I never spoke about Sister again. I floated around the house like a ghost, waiting for the first day of the wedding ceremony. Ma forced me to practice how to walk in my dresses, change my clothes, how I should behave and perform during the tea ceremonies. The wedding ceremony itself required me to change four times; there was another dress for the tea ceremonies and several more for the banquets. Ma did not explain any of this with any of the excitement and anticipation she had shown while discussing it with Sister, merely ensured that she had instructed me in everything she felt I should know in order to behave correctly. It was a job that must be done. Alas, all this teaching did not stay with me more than a few minutes after I had been instructed. I did not want to think of it.

The whole wedding ceremony would last three days, with several banquets and tea ceremonies in which I and my husband would serve tea to both families. My eighteenth birthday would fall in the week following the wedding. I imagined my new family might welcome me with a celebration then; perhaps Grandfather would be invited to visit.

In between the practicing, the fittings, and the loneliness, I thought about my husband-to-be. He still looked to me like a giant glazed piglet, with his fat shiny face and flat nose with pronounced nostrils. His hair was always worn neatly parted and swept across to his left ear. He was not elegant like Ba but round and heavy-looking. Grandfather had told me he had been to university and was near the top of his class, the first of his family to attend, and he did look very clever behind his glasses. He had spoken to me when he had been waiting for Sister and had seemed friendly and kind enough, his name was Sang Xiong Fa and I would be his wife. I did not want to marry this man or any man.

Since Grandfather had left, my parents and I would have dinner together. I would sit on one side of the table and Ma and Ba on the other. Every night we ate in silence, Ma picking small pieces of food and Ba quietly and slowly chewing. We both waited for Ma to say something, but she never did. There was only one question that would break our silence. I thought of nothing else, because everything, I felt, stemmed from this question. Yet I could not speak a word about it until Ma had spoken to me. I could not speak out of turn, and she seemed content for all of us to keep silent.

The night before the ceremony I realized I must ask. I simply could not stop myself. I could not sit and eat another meal with them, because I could not eat anymore. Everything that came from our kitchen seemed tasteless and without nourishment. Toward the end of the meal, the maids had served the rice and left. We started on our bowls and I spoke. Ba looked up, startled that I had dared to speak. I looked at Ma but all I could see was the narrowing of her pupils. I stared at her hard and asked the question again. She kept on eating but I could see her eyes hardening, holding me again and forcing me to be quiet. I was determined that this time it would be different.

"Why?" I asked.

She continued to look at me without any reaction, then glanced down into her bowl and continued to eat. After another mouthful she reached over and put some food on my plate.

"You should eat to keep your strength. You do not want to be ill for the ceremonies." It was her only response.

My question would remain unacknowledged because it needed no answer: the answer was already part of history itself. Unlike the ancient dead empire whose language described the flowers and trees, China had flourished and survived for five thousand years. It had survived because it must. It had survived by forcing its people to adhere willingly to ancient customs and rules, no matter what self-mutilation and pain that entailed or what self-deception was required.

Ba glanced at me, then quickly focused on something behind me. His gaze returned timidly to me, but only for a moment. He continued to eat.

I finished and left to go to my room, where I sat waiting for tomorrow. Ba came to my door. I could hear him breathing on the other side of it. I felt his hand press against the paneling and after a short while it sounded like he was crying. A long time later he walked away. I did not understand why he could not come in and talk to me. I wanted him to tell me there was nothing to fear, but he could not.

I was woken at around half past four in the morning to wash and dress. It was still dark and the servants were tired. There was a chill in the air and everything was cold to the touch. We worked in silence, my only distraction a few moments spent running the stitching of the gown between my finger and thumb so that I could feel the work of Bi's mother.

After bathing, I stood naked in front of the mirror, waiting for the maids to dress me. My body looked young and weak. I had rarely studied myself so closely. Physical relationships with people were never discussed, and comments about one's own body, apart from height and weight, avoided. Only lower-class people would even mention such things.

I looked at myself more closely. My skin was still slightly brown from the summer sun and, although that would fade, it would never become the milky white so many women, and men, sought. I saw my own height and felt large, even though I knew from comparison with Sister's that my body was slender. My legs had little scars on them where the grass had cut me when I ran through the gardens. My feet were muscular and flat from treading the hard ground. My breasts were small and my nipples seemed too big. I wondered if I would have a baby that would suckle from me one day.

The maids plucked my eyebrows and rubbed my skin with balm. A woman entered to apply the makeup and to coil my hair so that it disappeared into the wedding headdress. Once that was done I saw that I looked like Sister. I did not recognize myself. I put on the dress and stood waiting. The palanquin would arrive in three hours to take me to my fiancé's house. I could not even cry, could not feel or understand what any of this meant.

I waited with Ba in the entrance hall.

The palanquin was beautiful, its paneled sides carved with animals and symbols and lacquered in red and gold. Fragrant cut flowers were hanging from the sides. A muscular man with his head shaved Manchurian-style stood at each corner, ready to slide the poles in place and carry me away. Ba and Ma were ready to say good-bye to me. Ma said how beautiful I was, nearly as beautiful as Sister, and repeated that this was a great day for me. Then she smiled at me, and for that I will always hate her. That stupid smile, passed from one generation to another, thoughtless and involuntary, of poisoned dreams passed on. Ba looked at me then helped me into the palanquin.

"You look beautiful. And look at this," he said, brushing the lacquered side with his fingertips, "what a way to leave your old family and join your new one. It is magnificent."

I could not meet his eyes.

"We will see you at the wedding ceremony."

His voice trailed away as the curtain was drawn across. I could hear the poles slotting across the sides and then I was lifted up with a jerk and we moved away. I sat quietly even though I was regularly bounced from the seat as the bearers stumbled on the uneven roads. Although the morning chill still lingered, the air inside the palanquin soon became hot and moist from my labored breathing. A sliver of light cut through the drawn curtains, catching and dancing on the embroidery. The bright white line highlighted the beautiful fine stitching, picking out the rise and fall of the needle through the cloth. Eventually I peeped out from between the curtains and could see the streets around our house and the tops of the trees in the gardens in the distance.

The fresh air from outside relieved the closeness. I suddenly saw Grandfather walking back toward the house on the other side of the street. He was hurrying, then stopped and gazed straight at the palanquin. He looked tired, the skin sagging from his face and his hair thinner. He strained to stand straight-backed. His gray eyes followed us as the Manchurians bore me onward. As he watched he was mumbling something to himself, and I noticed the tremor in his arms and hands. He did not see me and it was the last I ever saw of him.

We drew away. People filled the space between us. I saw him stand and stare a moment longer, then he looked down and started to make his way back to the house. I shouted out to him but the sound was deadened inside the wooden palanquin and never made it beyond the thick curtain.

I could not stop crying. Tears ran down my face as we continued to bounce along. Occasionally I was thrown to one side and had to readjust my headdress. Unexpectedly, I began to laugh then. I did not know what was about to happen to me, and while I became lost in my thoughts of the fat young man and his family, we arrived at the Sang house. I heard someone shout out for a door to be opened and then I was carried into a courtyard.

Through the curtains I could see the large boxes that contained the presents from Ma and Ba. Some had been opened and had fabric hanging over their sides or straw poking out; others had been emptied. I saw some of the traditional and customary items, more expensive versions of the things Ma had once shown me from her own dowry: gold jewelry, dried fruits, tea sets, bedspreads, lotus seeds, and the sons' and grandsons' bowls. There were also other gifts that my parents had added, such as expensive ceramics and scrolls, unnecessary by tradition but they reinforced our eligibility and gave more face to the Sang family. This was Sister's world, it was alien to me.

The curtains were abruptly pulled back and in the sunlight I saw the high walls of the courtyard and the four ugly Manchurian bearers standing in front of me, their knotted cues resting on their shoulders. Three servants arrived and helped me from my seat. The courtyard was vast and paved with smooth marble slabs, unlike the small yard at home with its gray stone. The servants led me and the Manchurians followed. To scare away evil spirits others let off firecrackers and various musicians started banging cymbals and playing the whining *erhus*. Smoke from the firecrackers clouded the courtyard and trailed uselessly into the sky.

When we entered the house, I realized it was very large, several stories high, and could not help stopping to look around me. A servant pulled me forward but I did not stop staring as we walked. The entrance hall had dark wooden paneling and above it there were three more galleried floors, each framed by dark veneered railings. I could see people leaning over these wooden railings and peering down at our small procession. The ceiling was far above. The walls of the hall were lined with beautiful and ancient scrolls, and at intervals were ornate shelves containing deep blue Qinghua porcelain, Tang green-glaze cups and dishes, Song Dynasty porcelain pillows (one shaped like a little boy and another like a little girl), a rare green Longquan celadon and a green mallet vase from the great Hongwu period, and many delicate ornaments of colored glass. Grandfather had shown me pictures of these things when we discussed flower arranging and how there must be a delicate balance between the flowers and their vessel. I knew these were all rare and expensive possessions; that my parents' painstakingly assembled gifts meant nothing.

I was led to a room at the end of the hall and told to stand at the center of it. A servant waited with me. The room was completely empty except for a maid and me. Like the hall, the floor of this room was of polished wood and on the walls hung huge scrolls showing waterfalls, cranes, and quiet misty mountains, with calligraphy that flowed beautifully but which I could not read properly. The shutters of the room were closed and I felt hot under my layers of heavy cloth. As I stood there I began to sweat.

Suddenly two much older women entered the room. I recognized them from the family visit months ago, on the day it had rained so heavily. They were dressed very traditionally in beautiful long *kua* of brilliant and vivid red with gold inlay, like burning sunsets. Each dress had thick gold trim with large phoenixes embroidered on it. I stared into their faces, which were fat and thickly painted to cover their aging looks. They were grotesque.

Why would Sister choose to live with them? I did not understand why she would want this. The women came close and stared hard at my face. One poked my cheek and another lifted my hand high and reached down into my long sleeve to feel the skin under my arm. She pinched it near my armpit. They muttered to each other with each new poke and pinch. I was too frightened to say anything. One of them lifted my dress at the hem to look at my feet and ankles. I do not think they were happy with my profile, hands, or skin. The ugliest woman, the one with the most makeup and no neck, pushed her face close to mine.

"Do not forget, I am the First Wife of the house. She," pointing to the other woman, who was standing by the door ready to leave, "is the Second Wife."

In the quiet after they had shut the door, I started to cry. The servant, who I had forgotten was there, quickly came up to me with a cloth to stop my makeup from being ruined. I stood waiting and crying for the next two hours and all that time she caught my tears.

Eventually I was summoned and led to some double doors. The young man was standing by them waiting for me.

My bridegroom looked smarter and less pompous in his black silk wedding suit and long red overcoat embroidered with dragons and characters for good luck. The small hat he wore with its red pompom made him look like a round-faced schoolboy.

He smiled at me and said, "I can only just see you behind that veil, but I can still see enough to know you are very beautiful. I think the guests will agree with me."

I wondered if he thought of Sister, but Ma had told me not to mention her during the ceremony because it would be bad luck.

"We must go now. Are you ready? I should tell you not to be nervous, but I am a little nervous myself." He winked at me with a quick smile then signaled to the servants to open the doors.

I only managed a weak smile in reply but he could not have seen this through the veil. Everything was moving so fast now that I did not have time to take it all in. The doors were opened and we entered a large room lined with hundreds of people. At the other end stood two large chairs and there sat his father and the First Wife, in their full silk robes. It could have been the Imperial Court, with everyone assembled to pay their respects.

I looked clumsy walking down the aisle between the guests as my stride was too long, making me out of step with the rest of the procession. The servant had to keep whispering instructions to me. I started to panic, and although I could not hear anyone say anything I think I felt every insult directed at me. Beside my parents-in-law stood numerous other family members, dressed elegantly and expensively. All of them stared hard at me as I approached and I could see them whispering to each other. I learned later that thirty-four members of the family lived in this house, each with their own apartment and agenda, which mostly centered around obtaining more money and influence over the current head of the family, my father-in-law.

Kneeling down on a cushion before my new parents, I was so anxious that I forgot about the hundreds of people looking on. As I glanced up at First Wife from my position at her feet, she looked to me a misshapen thing, like the little creatures Bi and I would mold out of mud while we played by the river. Inside I felt like laughing, but my face was tight and taut with fear. My bridegroom and I were to serve tea to his parents and then to mine. I didn't know whether I should smile as I gave them the tea, or even look into their eyes. I was just relieved I did not spill it. As the cups were passed back to us, the parents gave us a red packet containing money. From its thickness, my parents-in-law gave their son a modest *li shi*. Ba and Ma gave their new son-in-law a *li shi* that seemed huge. I never realized they had saved so much. After thanking them, we got up and all the guests cheered. It was quite shocking to me to look at my new husband. I was now married.

There would be three banquets to celebrate and I was expected to toast all the guests at each meal. My husband drank alcoholic drinks and First Wife suggested I try some, as not to drink on the first night would be rude. There were thirty-five tables of fifteen people each and we toasted each table. As we approached a table everyone would stand and raise their glasses and we would all drink. Ma had tried to teach me the etiquette and manners needed for the wedding ceremony but everything overwhelmed me. There were simply too many gestures of politeness and custom for me to remember and repeat. I had not had enough time to practice and learn. Nothing made any sense. I called the relatives by the wrong names and gave incorrect greetings. I knew it was disrespectful but I was helpless as there was no time to apologize. By table eight, after three glasses of wine, I started to feel ill but First Wife insisted that I must toast all the other tables, too. If necessary, the servants would hold me up. They diluted my wine with water but by the last few tables I could not see anything and could barely stand. Eventually I tripped and fell, and I remember the laughter as they picked me up.

I was taken to my new bedroom. Lying flat on my back, I stared at the ceiling. My vision blurred around the edges, the details fading and then becoming clear again. A sudden sharp pain sliced through my forehead to behind my eyes, the room began to spin, and I passed out.

The servant who had stemmed my tears before the ceremony, a woman called Yan, stayed by my side all night. In the morning she brought me some congee, which helped soothe my stomach. She sat on the edge of my bed, which was very impolite for a servant, but it was the only friendship and warmth I had been offered for the last two months, apart from those moments with Bi's mother, and I was glad of it. She told me that I had missed the rest of the banquet, but my mother had told everyone I was tired out by happiness and the excitement of the occasion.

Yan sat and watched me eat. After a few minutes she broke the silence.

"Young mistress, you must be careful in this house. You must watch what you say to people here. There are many rivalries between the members of the family, many old grudges, but it would take me hours to retell them and anyway I should not be talking that way to you. Remember, after your father-in-law, First Wife should always be given the most respect, the most face. Even your husband must follow this, no matter what. She is his mother."

I did not fully understand what Yan was telling me. I was already afraid of the whole family and did not want to know the other people in the house.

The congee was warm, the smell of boiling rice summoning memories of Grandfather in the kitchen and of afternoons when Bi, Grandfather, and I had sat talking.

"Thank you, Yan," was all I could offer in reply. I did not wish to allow her, a maid, to see my ignorance.

My thoughts wandered and I did not notice her leave the room.

Other servants entered then to dress me for the day of continued celebrations. I was tired and did not know these maids. I felt shy in front of them and was uncomfortable with them touching me. Their attention was suffocating. I felt afraid of all the things I did not understand and that might hurt me. It was time for me to meet my new husband.

As we entered the hall on the second day, there were jokes and twisted little smiles as we passed by the members of the household, walking arm in arm. Xiong Fa patted my elbow gently as we walked, which I found calming, then smiled at me.

"Are you feeling well?" he asked.

"I think so."

"Today we will have another tea ceremony, and then this evening we will have a banquet to receive the more distant family members, acquaintances, and business associates. You will be sitting next to my mother, the First Wife. You must give her face, and should offer to place some food on her plate. Please be attentive. It is best if you serve her at the start of the meal. Do *not* wait for her to serve herself or she will be able to say you were not polite, not giving her proper respect. Please do this correctly. You are young, so let me advise you that following the etiquette and customs, all the small things, will make your life here easier. And, please . . . do not worry."

He looked at me and winked again. I felt a warmth behind his words that surprised me. This was the first time I realized that when his family was not observing him, Xiong Fa did not follow them and could behave differently. That night he was gentle and thoughtful toward me. I was nervous and held my breath to stop shaking; I closed my eyes very briefly, perhaps in their presence he forces himself to become more like them: proud, aggressive, and frightening.

"I will serve First Wife properly." I tried to sound confident looking up at him.

"Good. And please, do not drink anymore." He laughed.

We walked down to the end of the hall together and knelt before my parents-in-law to serve them tea again. People clapped and cheered as we did this and I felt relieved to have completed one of my duties correctly. I saw Yan standing at the back, watching me and smiling, and did not feel so lonely. There was at least someone here for me. After the second tea ceremony, my parents-in-law and Ma and Ba gave us another large *li shi*. After this I had another change of dress and went to rest.

I stood at the window of my apartment, which was a large room with a big four-poster bed and two overstuffed arm-chairs. There was a dressing table near the window and a deep walk-in wardrobe behind it. The room looked out across the courtyard to the door through which I'd entered in the palan-quin. There was a light rain falling and the dark marble of the courtyard glistened like wet leather. Everything there stood in its correct place: the stone lions at each corner, guards posted to either side of the gate, and a huge Qinghua crock with large golden koi swimming in it. The large ceramic pond was the axis of good luck around which this perfect world turned. Every-thing here was completely still and in perfect symmetry, only the remaining unopened boxes disturbed its neatness, but they would soon be gone. The rest of the house was swarming with family and guests but once the celebrations were finished, it, too, would be required to be as ordered as that courtyard.

I stared at a guard to see if he would move, until Yan came in to help me dress for the banquet. The man did not move a muscle. Yan got me ready in silence. Then, as she was passing me my jewelry, she took my hand.

"Remember what I told you this morning."

I nodded. My hand rested in hers momentarily and then she let go.

During the previous night I had not noticed that the banquet hall was so long; it was the largest room I had ever seen. I had never imagined a space like this inside someone's home. The room was decorated Western-style with a huge chandelier at the center of the ceiling and a stage at one end where a group of musicians played music similar to the tunes I had once heard Sister singing. Thinking of her playfully singing to herself late at night was the first happy memory I'd had of her since she had died. It should have been her walking the varnished wooden floor to sit at the head table with her parents-in-law; it should have been her being examined from every side. She would not have suffered from their scrutiny or felt any loneliness among these hundreds of people. She would have enslaved them all, and I would not even have been invited. I would have been safe at home with Grandfather.

My husband beckoned me to sit first and moved my chair for me. I was not sure if I should sit down before him, this could be a test to see if I knew my manners, but he nodded to indicate I should. He took his own place at the table and there was then a toast to Xiong Fa and myself, after which came a huge roar that was very exciting. It was as though everyone agreed with the marriage and had accepted me.

We were sitting with my father-in-law, First Wife, Second Wife, Ba, and Ma, and other relatives of my parents-in-law. I remembered what Xiong Fa had told me, and when the food arrived he nodded to me. It was all beautifully presented. I decided on a piece of fish as it looked the most delicately prepared dish. I took it in my chopsticks and placed it on First Wife's plate. Second Wife looked at it closely.

"Jie, look at the piece the girl selected for you to eat! Look at those bones—she wants to choke you already and does not even know yet how bad you can be." She giggled.

I blushed and felt my cheeks burn.

"That is all right. Now you should take a piece." First Wife gestured to me to take some fish.

I took a piece from near the tail, which I thought would show them that I was not greedy and was leaving the best pieces to them.

"She should have chosen a better piece though she may not know the difference," a frowning Second Wife noted to First Wife.

"Well, we expected it. You saw the size of her feet and those huge muscles on her legs? She is like a fisherman's wife," First Wife commented.

I wished I could have been. My excitement turned to fear again as I began to understand the nature of this family and what had now happened to me. I wished myself anywhere but there, though I had not yet found the words to express this.

For the rest of the meal I continued to eat modest portions of all the dishes. At the end of the banquet, after more toasts, my husband escorted me back to my room accompanied by Yan. The next day would be the last day of the wedding ceremony and then I would be living in my new home as First Wife of the eldest son of the Sang family. It was what Sister had been brought up to achieve, her place.

I sat in my room looking at myself in the mirror while Yan worked around me. I looked hard, past the makeup and artificial glaze I had been given, and saw another face. Your face, I know that now. I looked at it for a long time. I wish the image had stayed with me longer, for every day afterward, but gradually it faded away in the anger and pain to come. I wished it had stayed with me always.

I will tell you now about your great-great-grandfather Sang. About forty years before this, he came from Hebei Province and started a business selling goods from Shanghai port and taking them into the interior provinces and cities. People in the center of China loved to own exotic things from the West as well as India, Malaya, and Java. He built a big business, bought ships and offices, then constructed a palatial home for all the members of his family. Having worked hard and suffered much, he constructed the huge Sang house to keep his family safe from all the difficulties he had endured. Now the same building that had offered them security kept his progeny isolated from the rest of the suffering world.

I did not want the security of this house; it was not built for me. I wanted to leave there and then, change back into my simple clothes, and run outside. I wanted to find Bi and ask him to hold my hand. I wanted to watch him catch fish and tell him the names of all the flowers, as Grandfather had taught me.

Sleeping in my new bed, I realized that my old one at home had been that of a child whereas this was meant for an adult woman. I felt lost lying in it. It was too big for one person, made from rose and walnut wood with little scallop-shaped patterns in the grain. My new family had given me silks, gold, jewelry, and other wonderful things; so many things I had never thought about before. Ma would have appreciated them so much more than I, but they were nothing compared to the achievement of the most important aim in her life, the thing that best defined her as a wife and mother. There was nothing here I wanted, but I knew that by acquiring it all for myself I had been a good daughter to her, the best, and that was all that ever actually mattered. Our family had kept face and, by association, gained position.

Yan broke the silence.

"Tomorrow is the final ceremony. After this you will be part of the Sang family. From tomorrow your husband may decide to spend the night with you in your room."

She could see I did not understand the implication, so she came closer to me and sat down on a stool next to the bed. I was still young but felt humiliated by my ignorance; that a maid knew something I did not. In my embarrassment and confusion I snapped: "It is not correct for a servant to sit so close. You should not do this."

Yan did not appear shocked by my reaction, but stayed where she was. Tears started to roll down my cheeks. Still she remained seated.

"You must leave, it is not right that you speak to me like this. Do not do it again," I said petulantly.

She did not move but another maid knocked at the door and entered.

"Can I do anything for you, mistress?"

"No," I said, more calmly. "Everything is fine. I have just woken up from bad dreams. I was startled, that is all."

Yan waited patiently for me to stop crying before she left me for the night. I lay there alone at last, scared of all the things I did not know and fearful of all the unknown things that could yet happen to me.

Yan woke me early to dress for the final day. We took it slowly and she was gentle with me. Once she had bathed me she started to brush my hair, talking to me in a soft voice as if reading a bedtime story to a child.

"My husband was an Imperial guard. He was not very senior and was stationed in a port in the north. You will not remember but the country was at war with itself then and many people challenged the Emperor. There were warlords, bandits, and foreigners everywhere, all threatening his rule. In the beginning we lived in the barracks but then when my husband was promoted we moved to a small house in the countryside where we had a small farm.

"He was a quiet man and though his life was one of fighting and war, when we were together it was always very peaceful. He never mentioned his job, the things he saw and did. We would just work together, planting, harvesting, and looking after our house. When he came home we rarely left each other's side. I loved him very much. Then, after eleven years of marriage, he was killed by a gang of bandits who were trying to steal a shipment of foreign goods he was guarding.

"With so much horror in his life, I always felt that our life together was threatened, that it would suddenly come to an end one day. I didn't think it would last as long as it did. We weren't lucky like your parents, we never had children to look after us. There wasn't much after he was gone and I couldn't keep the farm on my own, so I stopped and came to Shanghai." She paused here and sighed. "I wanted to work for people who still had a future and a life before them. Now I look after you. Maybe my luck has changed." I looked up at her reflection in the mirror and saw her smiling at me; then she continued brushing my hair.

"Do you think I'll love my husband like you loved yours?" I couldn't stop myself from asking.

"I don't know. He's not a bad man, but he's the son of his parents. You must do what he says, but always keep a place for yourself."

I thought hard for a while and realized what she meant.

"I think I once had such a place."

"You must try to keep it, even if it is only in your imagination and your dreams."

She finished brushing and went to collect my dress. It was the only one hanging in my wardrobe as yet. I sat in my *du dou*, looking at myself in the mirror again. Yan had combed my waist-length hair and put it up. I still had not become used to looking at myself like this; was not accustomed to seeing my semi-naked body, my bare skin, the shape of my neck, my red lips made up in the Qing style and the makeup on my cheeks.

I felt cold and did not recognize myself. I looked like an adult. I looked like a wife.

In the hall again, we knelt down to serve tea to my new family once more. Again, we were given many different and expensive gifts. My father-in-law demanded that ceremonies were performed repeatedly and exactly. Customs must be observed correctly, he believed, because they then brought people luck, and luck brought wealth and long life. He was the guardian of his family's history and future, and my father-in-law would do all that was required to avoid any damage to that legacy. Ma had told me before the wedding that I was only able to marry into such a family because Sister before me had followed every rule, every point of etiquette, correctly and meticulously. Nothing she did could ever have been questioned or left open to interpretation. It had all been perfect.

This time Ma and Ba stood in the background while my new family made the toasts. Ma smiled and talked to everyone, whether they greeted her or not. It was the beginning of her new life in Society by association. From now on, she would rise in her own social circle by telling people into which family her daughter had married. If they heard nothing else, she would make sure they heard the family name. But she would never be welcomed here.

For Ba it marked an ending rather than a beginning. We would see each other only once and after that I would hear little news of him. I was told he spent most of his time with Grandfather, continuing to work as an architect with a building company as the loans he had taken out over the years needed repaying. He had helped Ma achieve her grand aim and with that satisfied, his life was quiet.

Like many people who feel that the world is inherently good, Ba did not worry about the future but believed that matters would resolve themselves for the best. He had originally married Ma believing that she would live with him in the unambitious yet comfortable way that he enjoyed. He did not wish to be continually tested, to have demands made on him. He was too tired. As Grandfather had loved the botanical world so Ba had loved the urban life with its constant distractions of dances and tea parties, banquets and drinks after work. But he did not aspire to be at the center of it all. For him it was enough to enjoy the spectacle from the fringes, which he felt to be his rightful place.

Ma loved to accompany him to the occasional lavish event they were invited to, but Ba had never deceived himself that they belonged there, as she had. She wanted it but he knew no one would give them face; that perhaps people even laughed behind his back because his clothes were not as tailored as theirs and his ideas and ambitions not as grand. He accepted this, and had been wise enough to keep his distance from the great and the good, careful never to step over the boundaries he had set for himself. He was tempted and others tempted him, sometimes genuinely wanting him to join them and at other times to goad and to belittle him. But he had managed to keep a clear and realistic view of his situation and to avoid costly social complications and consequences—until he was overwhelmed by the scale of Ma's ambition for Sister.

Ma saw neither complication nor consequence and so did not create any boundaries of her own, refusing to recognize the way he sought to protect himself from suffering and humiliation. She indulged herself and drew him after her, to a place where he was unprotected from taunting queries and demands. In the dying hours of the evening, Ma laughed and sang in the presence of my new family, confident that her life was now complete, whether anyone else agreed with her or not. Ba stood aside and let it all wash over him. For him it was finished now.

I wondered what would happen later tonight; what Yan had

meant when she spoke of it. I had so little knowledge. Sister would certainly have known what was to happen, she and Ma would have discussed it if Sister had not already known, but Ma and Ba had told me nothing. As I sat at the banquet next to my husband, I reflected that he had been quite friendly to me so far. I did not want to be married to him, but he did not seem to mind the fact that I was his wife. I thought then of Bi and how we'd sat in the gardens together. I thought of him holding the corner of my blouse and how our lips had touched. I thought of my dreams of us together; the feeling I had just remembering our kiss was so powerful it beat inside me and overpowered every other sense, so that for a moment I could forget the last few months. I remembered watching and talking to his mother, the seamstress, while she made this dress. I ran the stitching between my finger and thumb under the table as I thought of all of this. I did not know this man next to me, he did not interest me, but I was now First Wife of the next generation of the Sang family. As Sister had predicted, I had inherited her life and her future.

Most women in those days still entered marriages created by their parents and matchmakers, and in the countryside many couples did not even meet each other before the wedding. In the city, though, Grandfather once told me, a few women were now thinking like foreigners and looking for love. But I did not believe I knew anything about love. How did it feel? What could I expect from it? When did it happen? If Sister had lived I might perhaps have been free to discover these things for myself.

After I had gone to my room on the preceding nights, Xiong Fa had stayed up drinking with his friends. Sister would have stayed with him, but I was too young and I think he knew this. Tonight, though, was to be the last night of celebrations and I would stay with him and his drinking friends. One named

Cheung Liu had a small thin face with slitty eyes and yellow teeth. During the meal he kept knocking into me as he leaned over to pour drinks, and eventually caused me to drop food from my chopsticks. Xiong Fa put his hand on his friend's shoulder and, with a seriousness that seemed suddenly out of place, said to him, "Liu, be careful . . . control yourself. You must be kind to my new wife."

Liu looked shocked for a moment then smiled and replied, "Hey, you had me fooled there. Don't pretend with us, your old friends, to be so protective and upset. We know you! Soon you will be busy looking for your second wife. You are a Sang man and we all know what that means."

His friends laughed with him but I saw that Xiong Fa did not smile back. Instead he looked at me. His eyes were apologetic.

The dinner drew to a close with more toasts and Xiong Fa looked drunk. He and I exited first, followed by all the guests. Outside Ba came over to me and held my hand. He had never touched me like this before, holding my hand so tight in his. The party was ending but there was still some time left before the guests would have to depart. He had used Brylcreem in his hair and it was combed back Western-style. He looked as handsome as I had seen him on all those nights I had watched him arrive home late with Ma when I was a child. He was wearing a Western-style suit with a black bow tie around a white wing collar, appearing smaller in the narrow tailored suit, as though he was about to fade away. He looked at me and continued to hold my hand but did not smile. I hoped he was about to tell me something, to say something significant before leaving, but he merely pursed his lips and stared past me into the distance. His eyes refocused on me then. He clasped my hand even tighter and kissed me on the forehead.

"Xiao Feng." He paused and smiled at me. "Well, you are Xiao Feng no longer. Now you are Mrs. Sang Xiong Fa. Remember, in three days' time you and Xiong Fa should be coming home to us for the traditional dinner with the bride's parents. Do not worry if you cannot, though. I realize with all of this," he looked around, "you might be too busy.

"Besides what would we be able to offer you and your new husband? The food here is glorious, the kitchens famous. I think Cook at home could no longer impress you." He breathed out, trembling slightly. "Aiii, my young daughter, I never thought this would happen."

I wanted to be held by him but didn't have the courage to reach out.

We stood in awkward silence for a moment. After that he released my hand. I wanted to tell him that he was still my Ba and the food did not matter, but no words entered my mouth.

Ma came up to join us. She had been having a wonderful time and now smiled widely at me, saying again how lucky I was to be joining such a fine family, one of the largest in Shanghai. She looked at me, and then around the hall at everyone busy saying good-bye to each other. She turned back to me but said nothing more, just scrutinized me from toe to head. She turned to Ba then. I could see she was tempted to reenter the party, take in the last of the wine, food, and laughter, but she resisted, perhaps out of the little pride she had left. Ba took her by the hand and she followed him to say farewell to Xiong Fa's parents and the other departing guests.

I stood alone for a second before I was suddenly pushed into the family line so that each guest could file past, giving their congratulations and farewells. Most people said nothing to me, a few said I was a beautiful bride, but all of them scrutinized my clothes, posture, and face. I could only manage a half-smile, I was so tired. Face after face bent forward, filling my vision with fatty jowls and my nose with the stench of stale food and wine. Spitting laughter, these sagging faces hung and swayed above me like dripping wax. After an hour we had finished and Yan led me to my room. As we left I looked back to see First Wife and Second Wife looking at me, talking and shaking their heads.

I was relieved when Yan finally closed my bedroom door. It was finished. I was suddenly very tired yet anxious about what would happen next. Everything had led to this moment, the plans carefully formulated many years ago. But for Sister's benefit, not for mine.

Yan struggled to undress me as I was so tired and weak I could barely move. I sat in front of the mirror in my *du dou* and she spent a while brushing my hair. She said she had been told not to remove my makeup but to get me to bed. I asked her why but she said only that I should remember what she'd told me that morning: I should do what my husband told me. She helped me untie the *du dou* and then led me to my bed, laying a sheet over me, which she folded back so that my shoulders were exposed. She fanned out my hair across the pillow and blew out the candles and lamps, leaving just one candle burning near the door.

I lay still, but only because in my curiosity I was lost in thought and had forgotten to move. In the silence, wondering what might happen, I suddenly became nervous. My only comfort was that my husband had been very kind during the last three days, particularly when he'd told his friend Cheung Liu to be careful when he knocked me, and in the morning when he'd asked me how I was. I did not know what to expect from a husband, but mine seemed very thoughtful, like Grandfather would be when guests came to the house. While I waited I could only wonder what I would do tomorrow. The wedding celebration had finished so perhaps I could go back to the gardens, at home. I thought my husband would like the quiet there after the noise of the last three days' celebrations, and I could introduce him to Grandfather if he still wanted to see me.

The door opened and Xiong Fa walked in unsteadily. He was still dressed in his marriage robes. He sat down heavily on the edge of the bed. He said nothing but stared at my face and the curve of my bare shoulders. His eyes traced the line of my hair spread across the pillow. He stroked it and then my cheek. No one had touched me like this before but it was gentle and kind and I did not feel afraid. His hand stayed on my cheek, making small caresses. He smiled at me.

His face came closer. He pressed his lips against mine and I tried to move away, but he grasped me under the chin to hold me still. Again I tried to pull away and then started to struggle. I wanted him to leave me alone. He reached down and pulled the sheet down to my waist, exposing my breasts. I immediately crossed my arms and he smiled at me again. He paused, then took hold of one of my wrists to move my arm back. I must have looked scared, because he let go of me and waited a moment before letting his left hand slide slowly down my side, moving from my waist to my thigh.

I automatically clenched my legs together, though I did not know why. I was panicking and terrified. His hand stroked my stomach. I tensed, wanting to bring my knees to my chest, to curl into a ball, but I did not dare move and merely clenched them together a little tighter. His fingers moved down from my stomach to between my legs, tracing a line through me. I felt them push slightly inside and clenched hard against them. Tears started to well up inside me. Though I wanted to hide them, they trickled down my cheeks. He saw them and stopped. He withdrew his hand and just sat there, letting both hands fall into his lap. I started to cry, lying perfectly still and silent, hoping like an injured animal that he would stop hurting me and leave.

"Perhaps we should try again tomorrow night." He breathed out and the air smelled sharply of wine. "Good night."

He got up, bent over, and kissed me on the forehead. I could only see him for a second. Because I was so rigid with fear, I could not move my head to watch him leave the room. My tears continued. I felt for the sheet and once I had it between my fingers slowly pulled it over me. I lay there in safety for a few seconds then vomited over the bed.

I was woken in the middle of the night by Yan, who looked concerned. I told her I was well enough, but very tired. I saw that the vomit had been cleaned up and my nightclothes laid out. I closed my eyes again and tried to pretend she was not there. The light from the candle kept me awake. I seemed to stay awake for hours, trying to sleep, and though I kept my eyes firmly shut, the faint yellow light danced over my eyelids, making me restive and agitated. When I opened them again, she was still sitting in the chair across the room, watching me. A light breeze broke through the slats in the shutters from the open window and entered the room. It made the flame of the candle move violently and wild shadows lurched around, casting strange shapes and patterns on the wall. I asked her to tell my new family, when morning came, that I was ill and could not leave my room. Then I closed my eyes again, and slept.

Chapter 7

I awoke to semidarkness as the slats in the shutters could not prevent all the daylight from entering. I could see my wedding dress hanging on the wardrobe door: it would be packed away today. I saw the fine stitching that had brought life to the phoenixes, flowers, and characters adorning the silk. Each golden stitch created by beautiful kind hands. Yet now it looked like a skin that had been shed. I wished the seamstress was here to return us both to life. I missed watching those hands that would never harm me. I closed my eyes and opened them again but nothing had changed; apart from my dress the rest of the room was solid dark wood and lacquer. Two large *guan* of blue-and-white porcelain had been placed on a high table near the wardrobe and there was a beautiful *meiping* in copper red between them. But they were cold, and like the rest of the room made me feel nothing but alone. Yan was gone. I curled up under the sheet and cried again.

Later, Yan told me that on that morning I was traditionally required to make my new family a late breakfast, and that because I'd stayed in my room I had offended them. They had all gathered and waited for me to serve the meal, or at least tea. After Yan told them I was not coming, Father-in-law said nothing but First and Second Wives gossiped openly. They all shot accusing glances at Xiong Fa and eventually the two wives left indignantly. Father-in-law remained seated there for several hours, refusing to move. He sat with his arms folded, staring across the table at my empty seat. He could not understand how his daughter-in-law, now a Sang, could fail to keep the traditions and customs he valued so highly. Xiong Fa would be repeatedly reminded of this over the next few months and I would not be forgiven quickly.

Yan had lied to them as I had asked her to and told them that the last few days had given me a fever. I was very tired and needed time to rest and recover. She brought bowls of medicinal soup to my room every three hours, showing how ill I must be, which she lined up in a row in front of the *guan*. Eventually she poured them into the chamber pot. I had also asked her to tell them I needed a long foot massage to aid my recovery so that she had a reason to spend the day with me.

In the afternoon Yan brought me some congee, the delicious rice porridge, which I loved so much. She sat back in the chair and watched me start on it. I looked up at her and felt I should say something to bring us closer.

"Do you know if this house has any gardens? I used to walk in the gardens next to my parents' house with my grandfather. He loved flowers and trees and would tell me their names."

Yan leant forward to speak to me, resting her elbows on her knees and her chin on her fists.

"I have heard the other servants talk of gardens but they say that old Master Sang built the house over most of them. There are some on the left side of the house but they are not visited much as the family likes to be inside. The outside is for peasants and servants," she said with a smile.

"I once met a boy in the gardens next to our home. He taught me how to fish and weave crayfish baskets. He made me laugh," I said almost immediately in reply.

"Ah, my husband was a good fisherman, he used to try to teach me how to fish but I was not very good."

"The boy I knew, his name was Bi, he was very good. We used to sit on the muddy riverbank and I would watch him . . ." Suddenly I was embarrassed that our lives had been so similar. I returned to blowing on my bowl of congee to cool it. Yan leaned back in her chair again.

During the rest of the day, I slept a bit and we talked a little more about gardens and flowers and about the Sang house. Eventually it was night and she said she must brush my hair again, but first she went to light a new candle near the door. She picked up the brush and makeup from the sideboard by the door and, as she returned, beckoned me to sit in front of the mirror. She started to brush my hair slowly and gently. I looked up but suddenly I felt that I could not bear to look at myself. I just wanted to hide from the image reflected back at me, so I looked down again. As Yan brushed, I watched stray hairs drift to the floor.

Already my days and nights here felt strangely dislocated, as if they had been ripped apart. Each night the same, and each day spent scared of the night to come. I crossed from one to the other like reading across a torn page: the story continued but somehow, for that brief moment, the telling would be interrupted and the tale left hanging awkwardly. I felt I was only fully myself when daylight came again.

One night I lay naked on the bed once more, completely still, my legs pressed tightly together and my hands folded across my breasts. Before placing the sheet over me, Yan took my wrists and tried to pull my hands to my sides. At first she was just trying to guide them, then when I resisted she grew more forceful.

Still I resisted, twisting my body away in one direction while straining my neck the other way to keep looking up at her: just seeing her comforted me. She stopped trying to move me and sat on the edge of the bed, her hands folded in her lap. I returned to lying on my back with my arms tightly wrapped over my breasts. Yan looked at me as Grandfather used to do. Then, for a second, she pursed her lips in such a forlorn and plaintive expression that it made me want to cry. She knew that it was to happen night after night.

Slowly she replaced her hands on mine and I let her guide them to my sides. All the time her eyes never left mine. She pulled the sheet over me and then folded it down so that it came to just above my breasts. This was the same position as the previous nights; the one to which she would return me for several more weeks to come.

This time she pulled the sheet taut so that it pressed my breasts tighter against my chest. Its closeness made me feel trapped and anxious. I began to sweat a little. Yan saw the small beads collecting on my forehead and brought over a fan, waving it for a few minutes to cool me. Again her eyes held mine, soothing and reassuring me as if I were her child, and for a moment I forgot everything. Once I was cool, she arranged my hair across the pillow as before.

"This is a woman's role. Your husband must satisfy himself. He is not a cruel man but he has not yet learned how to be gentle and kind to another person. There is still too much of this house in him." She spoke the words slowly and softly.

How would my husband satisfy himself? I did not know what that meant. My heart began to beat hard and fast. Barely moving beneath the tight-stretched sheet, I clenched the fingernails of my right hand into my palm. Pain overwhelmed me and distracted me from my fear.

Shortly after Yan left me, Xiong Fa came into the room. He was wearing a dark-colored robe and his hair was neatly combed. He sat at the top of the bed beside me and must have seen that I was scared, because he did nothing, simply looked at me and smiled. For a moment we were both still, looking at each other, just as Yan and I had done moments before. My husband's face was round and still retained the chubby youthfulness I had seen in it when he used to visit our home to collect Sister. He had told me then that he thought Sister might be too beautiful for him. In the end it had not mattered. But now, even in the few short months since I had met him, his eyes had grown old and tired; the whites had curdled to yellow and his pupils moved slowly and cautiously, as if the world was moving too quickly for him to keep up.

Slowly he brought his hand up to my chest and, with his first finger, traced a line from between my breasts over the sheet and down between my legs. I flinched at his touch and he removed his finger, replacing his hand in his lap.

Again we remained still, neither of us making a sound. He looked around the room and I followed his gaze. Then he returned to me and folded down the sheet so that my breasts were exposed. I was sweating again and could feel him looking at the tiny droplets pooling on my chest.

I did not know what he would do next. I had no experience of such a situation or knowledge of how we were to behave. I did not understand his movements and gestures; they were all strange to me. At times he was tender, responding to my movements and changes of expression, but then he would quickly become absorbed in his own desires and almost forget I was there. At those moments, I felt that my body was like a meal that had been served to him. Ma should have explained these things.

Xiong Fa leaned down and kissed one of my nipples. Then he kissed it again and licked around it with the tip of his tongue. It felt strange. No one had done this to me before and I had not thought any man would want to do it. I had known that my breasts would one day feed a baby, but not my husband. Every new movement he made scared me, because I did not know its meaning or purpose. But he was slow and cautious, which calmed me, and I tried to lift my head up so that I could watch what he was doing. I could only see the top of his head but I could feel his fat lips and tongue. He kissed the skin between my breasts down toward my waist, and then slid his head upward again to place each nipple in turn between his teeth and suck on them.

Then I felt his left hand move under the sheet at my waist. I knew what he was going to do next and felt scared. I wanted to stop myself from feeling scared, but I knew my obligations and felt guilty that I would not be allowing my husband to satisfy himself if I tried to turn away from him. Yan had said this was the woman's role and I was the First Wife. Without knowing exactly why, I wanted to remain so.

Still, even with these thoughts, I instinctively closed my legs tight, but he rested his hand in between them and worked his fingers inside me. As they entered me, I gasped. His nails scraped and cut me, and at the sharp pain tears formed in my eyes. I tried to turn over and away from him but with his fingers inside me it was impossible. I seemed to have no control over myself or my body.

He pushed three fingers into me, not stabbing but slowly and firmly. I clenched my fists from the pain of it. I felt that I would burst. To be filled this way seemed unnatural. He pushed again, only slightly higher, and this time I started to cry, partly from the pain but more from fear and helplessness because there was nothing I could do to resist. He heard me and looked up and saw that I was crying. He withdrew his fingers, leaving me sore and exposed. I desperately wanted to put my hand to myself for protection but dared not move.

He sat upright and pulled the sheet back above my breasts. He brushed my forehead with the fingers of his right hand and kissed me on the forehead as before. Then he quietly left the room.

I curled myself into a ball and continued to cry. I clenched my fists so hard that the nail of my middle finger cut into my palm, though I only noticed this when I awoke later. The pain from my nail distracted me from the other pain deep inside me. While I cried in my fear and loneliness, I could think only of my family: of Ma and Ba eating at the table and Grandfather sitting in his chair watching the rain. I did not understand why they would want me to come here when it would be like this.

I passed into sleep without sensing I had left consciousness and found myself sitting with Sister at the small kitchen table at home. We each had a bowl of dumplings before us but the vinegar I had in mine was very sour and smelled bad. When I asked Cook if there was anything slightly sweeter, Sister came behind me and grabbed me around the neck with her arm, and with her other hand gripped my chin and cheeks as she had done that day outside my bedroom. She was crying and holding me tight against her. I could not free myself but still I struggled and twisted, trying to turn away. Her face was bony and fierce and she was shouting that I must eat the food as it had been served, she would not allow me to change anything. She held me and tried to force me to eat but I clenched my mouth shut.

I woke suddenly. My chest felt very tight and I was gasping as if I had been crying hard. I understood now why Sister had told me to think of her. She had known how ignorant and vulnerable I was. Even faced with her own death, she had relished the thought that although I would receive everything from a marriage into this family, in my innocence and foolishness, I would be frightened and damaged by it. I lay watching the candle stub flicker and burn away and realized that I hated everyone I had left behind for not protecting me.

Chapter 8

On the morning of the fifth day, Yan woke me early. She washed the cut in my palm that I had made by clenching my fist tight in fear and wrapped a clean linen bandage around my hand to protect it.

"We must get you ready quickly this morning as your father-in-law demands that all family members eat breakfast together. This morning you must be there," she told me.

She hurried about, frowning.

"You are required to serve him tea."

Then she stopped bustling and held my hand.

"Remember, because you did not appear yesterday to serve the Master the traditional breakfast, if you are late or do not attend this morning, he will be extremely offended and you will be punished. Whatever he asks you to do, you should do it carefully and properly."

After seeing for myself how Father-in-law and First Wife had rigidly enforced the rules of the wedding ceremony, I understood the risks of failure. I sat in front of the mirror but could not bring myself to look at my face, just at my hand, which had started to sting. Yan finished getting me ready and then I was taken downstairs to a dining room.

I had not seen this room before. The walls were simply whitewashed and covered with portraits of the male members of the family. Stretching around the entire room, where the walls met the ceiling, was a beautiful gold-and-jade cornice. The tables were round, according to tradition. The head table where Father-in-law would sit so imperiously was much larger than the rest, and the others were arranged around it in order of importance. At the other tables sat members of the extended family, a few of whom I recognized from the wedding. On this particular morning, Father-in-law had been sitting waiting for us all to enter so he could see who was late and who was not dressed properly.

Everyone watched me enter with Yan leading the way. I was shown to a chair next to Xiong Fa, who smiled at me as I sat down. He whispered to me that a servant would now bring me a cup of tea that I would take to Father-in-law, and every time he drained his cup, I would be required to take him a freshly filled one.

The room fell silent as the servant approached me with a tray holding a lidded cup and a beautiful teapot. I stood up and took the cup and saucer over to Father-in-law.

Holding the saucer was awkward as my hand was still very painful and sore from the angry cut in my palm. I managed to place the cup in front of him and took a step back. I waited for a moment, one pace behind his chair, expecting him to signal that I could return to my seat, but instead he lifted the lid, blew on the tea, and swallowed it in one gulp. Then he looked up at me with the hardest, most demanding eyes I had ever seen. Remembering that moment, I am glad I never saw such coldness in Xiong Fa.

I took the cup from its place in front of him and returned it to the servant, who quickly took it away to a corner of the room where the teapot was stationed, and refilled it. He returned to me and again I took the cup to my Father-in-law. I placed it in front of him, assuming that he would drink again. He looked up at me and asked me where I thought he would put his bowl with a cup in front of him. I hesitated. Still staring at me, he demanded I move it. I picked up the cup and placed it to one side. Father-in-law nodded and I returned to my seat.

I already felt tired again and sat at the table wishing I could go back to my room. I could not hold chopsticks properly because of the cut in my hand, so I chose to eat congee. That did not please Father-in-law or First Wife, as I was quietly told by Xiong Fa.

As we ate, the servant would continually appear at my side with Father-in-law's empty tea cup, which would then be re-filled for me to take to him. My hand ached from holding the little saucer. Eventually, after eight or nine cups, I dropped everything. Tea cup, saucer, and lid smashed on the floor and the whole room fell silent.

Father-in-law got to his feet and looked at the broken porcelain. I saw First Wife laughing with Second Wife. Xiong Fa also stood up and ordered the servants to clear the mess up, but his father immediately countermanded this and told them not to move. After standing there glaring at the spilled tea and shattered porcelain, he frowned at his son then left the room in silence.

Later that morning I stood by the window in my room and looked out at the courtyard and the guards by the door to the street. Winter was fast approaching. Soon it would become cold and the wind would start to stir up the dust, but in this courtyard there was no dust and the wind would not be allowed to enter. I suspected the guards would stand there no matter how cold it became, because they had been ordered to do so.

Every evening would begin with dinner. The meal was always served at half past six exactly and everyone in the household was expected to gather and be in their place before Father-in-law entered. We all stood quietly behind our chairs while we waited, with the servants standing off to one side of the room, each man with his head shaved at the front Manchurian-style and a long braided queue hanging down his back. All the servants wore plain black cotton collarless jackets with knotted buttons down the front and black trousers, regardless of whether they were women or men. Father-in-law demanded that their dress was always clean and pressed. Like Yan, all the servants were small and nimble, moving softly and quickly; none of them were ugly or clumsy, as Father-in-law could not bear to look upon anything that disgusted him.

He would arrive without greeting anyone, take his seat, and that would be the signal for us to sit. Food was put before him first, then before the two wives, and after that it was served to the rest of us.

The seating for dinner, like that for breakfast, was organized very traditionally. The great banqueting hall, being rarely used, remained locked after our wedding until over the years it was almost forgotten. The children were seated on tables of their own, as far away from the head table as possible, and the different branches of the family's adults, who all lived in the house, occupied separate tables of their own. The head table, which was slightly larger than the rest, was reserved for Father-in-law, First Wife and Second Wife, Xiong Fa and me, and the oldest members of the family.

Father-in-law only liked a few dishes for dinner and these were repeated again and again. As the food was served you could hear people around the room moaning because it was chicken soaked in rice wine for the third time that week, or tofu with Jin Hua ham two nights in a row. The Sang family never ate rice. It was peasant food, and since they had built and lived in this huge house, they were determined to leave behind any trace of their own peasant ancestry. The only people who were served different food were pregnant women, who enjoyed a special menu to build up their strength and ensure healthy plump babies.

Yan told me I must always sit next to Xiong Fa and if he moved I should follow him. I ate quietly and neither too quickly nor too slowly, trying not to do anything that would attract attention to my presence. If Father-in-law singled a person out for comment or conversation, other people would stare and gossip. They would question whether that person was trying to get closer to him, perhaps seeking a favor. Often, though, the person in question was simply being criticized for some breach of Father-in-law's etiquette and being lectured on how the family would have lost face if such a thing had occurred in public.

I wanted to be like a little flower among all these trees, perhaps *Ranunculus acris*, the tiny meadow buttercup. For many years this was my favorite flower, bright but soft, happily hiding amid the grass. It was one of the first names Grandfather had taught me in that ancient language.

I would look down at my food and concentrate on eating. The dishes were always well prepared, as the cooks had had enough practice over the years. I heard that other families joked that at a Sang dinner one would only ever get five dishes—but they would be the best in the country. Father-in-law was very proud of this fact. Each of the dishes served was a marvel to see as he would accept nothing less. The colors of the ingredients caught the eye like a perfectly balanced flower arrangement, the rich deep brown of the duck meat, like warm earth, and the bright pink of the ham, like petals. As I ate I would gaze at each dish, reminding myself of the flowers I'd seen in the gardens during my walks with Grandfather.

I had to be careful, however, never to become too distracted by my daydreams and forget the rules of family etiquette. I would make sure I picked up the right piece of food only with my serving chopsticks and never my eating chopsticks; in my old home, we only used one set each. Being careful not to drop anything, I would place the food in my bowl. Then, using my smaller, eating chopsticks, I would carefully and gently put the food into my mouth. I tried not to eat anything too big or with too many bones in it so that I would not look ill-mannered, tearing the flesh with my teeth or spitting out bones. After each bite I would lay my chopsticks on their rest.

Mostly I looked down at my bowl or at the dishes on the table, avoiding the gazes of the people opposite. Glancing down, I would often see Xiong Fa's hands holding his chopsticks, taking his tea cup, or resting on the table. I would see his fingers, knuckles, nails, and muscular palms . . . but it was only later in the evening, when I could not see them, that I came to know them.

I learned to finish eating just when Father-in-law did, so I could return to my room after he'd departed, provided Xiong Fa approved of my leaving, which he generally did. If I stayed behind I felt vulnerable and overwhelmed by the strong personalities around me, all of whom possessed such self-confidence and expected so much attention. I just wanted to go back to my room and look out of the window at the fading light; perhaps watch the guards changing duty or the old man feeding the fish. Those few hours of quiet between the end of dinner and Yan's arrival were peaceful and my own.

Once it was dark the whole character of the house would change. In the daylight, it was a busy house, family members coming and going, their children leaving for and returning from school. Then, in the afternoon, it was quiet and empty until dinner. Once the sun had set and dinner was finished, the elder members of the family would retire to their own apartments, the young might go out and the servants to bed. Without sunlight, many places in the house had no lighting at all so each section would have several servants waiting with lanterns in the corridors, ready to guide you wherever you needed to go. Unlike the servants in the dining room, these were the sort of muscled Manchurians who'd carried me here in the palanquin. The lanterns hung from poles slotted into the floor, which the servants would remove and carry in front of them when called. Otherwise they would wait on the floor under their poles and lanterns, dark figures sitting cross-legged in their loose baggy black trousers and soft slippers. Late in the evening the servants would be hot and sweaty and would often go bare-chested, which would never be allowed during the day.

Use of these servants was prioritized by a family member's place in the hierarchy. I was supposed to be highly ranked but when I was confronted by another member of the family wanting a lantern-bearer, I would always give way. I did not even know the names of many of the others living nearby but the sheer force of their pride and self-confidence frightened me. They stood their ground and did not appear afraid of any possible confrontation, seeming to know exactly what was due to them. I would always stand back and smile weakly, like Ba would have done, letting whomever it was precede me.

Alone in my room after dinner, I would often stand at the window to watch the servants light the lanterns by the entrance to the courtyard. I would watch the guards change as the last of the daylight faded. They all wore complicated uniforms made from thick dark red cotton jackets with leather straps pulled across the chest and many large metal studs set into the sleeves. Each carried a sword and spear and had overelaborate *gong fu* boxer shoes. They looked impressive but I don't think their uniforms would have given them much protection in a fight. Yan would joke about them being dainty little gate dancers; all nicely posed and balanced, trained in nothing but outward appearance and clockwork movements, without any real fighting maneuvers or bravery. She would say her husband would have shown them what a real soldier must be able to do.

An hour or so after dinner finished, Yan would come to my room to brush my hair and rub fragrant creams into my skin. I had never taken much care of my skin before, letting it become bruised and scarred as I had grown older. I liked the contrast between the rich perfumed creams and the feel of Yan's rough hands massaging me. The coarseness of her fingertips reminded me of how hard life could be, and of the many luxuries I received in this house. Her rough hands were also a reminder of Grandfather, whose fingers had been similarly worn, and the creams were scented with the aromas of lotus and jasmine, flowers we had grown together.

During the first nights of our marriage, I repeated the same routine with Xiong Fa. As the weeks passed, I learned my role and let him satisfy himself. Though my fears seemed to fade as I became used to his ways and desires, when he started to touch me I would always retreat to another place. Not the gardens at home with their vivid flowers and wild grasses like Yan had advised me. They were sacred and special, I could not go there while Xiong Fa was with me. Instead I would go to a courtyard of exacting brickwork, deep red painted walls and giant closed doors, with guards barring both entry and exit. At the center stood a giant porcelain basin containing hundreds of fish, and in my mind I would watch them endlessly circle in the water.

My husband never asked me if his actions hurt me, he did not seem to think of it. He kissed me and touched me in the same way every night. I did not understand how he satisfied himself but he seemed happy when he left my room.

It was after the first week spent like this that Yan started to come into my room immediately after Xiong Fa had left. Once she appeared I would feel less anxious and lost and would be able to fall asleep. I did not feel anything after Xiong Fa's attentions; our time together was for him, not for me.

Living in the Sang house, I felt small and vulnerable. Simply walking around made me nervous, in case I met First Wife or Father-in-law. I was constantly reminded of Sister's bitter words to me, but noticed that with each day that passed I found ways to cope with and become accustomed to this new life. Sister, of course, would have had all her new relatives adoring her; would have swept into the dining room with all eyes looking on in envy while she would simply have failed to notice them.

I was happy to go unnoticed every evening, leaving the crowded dining room to sit alone in my own room. I realized that very little was expected of me other than that eventually I should give Xiong Fa a son and the family an heir. I still did not know how I would do this, though. I understood about the child growing in its mother's stomach, but no more than that.

As I write this I feel so stupid, remembering that time and how ignorant I was then. If I had known or understood, I would never have let you leave . . . never have hurt you. I should have had the courage to ask Yan what I needed to know. She would have told me how things should be. I try to imagine your face on that day, the day I did not want to see it but should have, and I imagine the most perfect little face. My own failings and weaknesses have scarred and hurt you; when I should have done everything and anything to make your life warm and secure, I made it as hard and painful as mine seemed to me. Then I made it worse. At that moment, I should have listened to Yan's silence.

Within a week, she had become the only person in whom I wanted to confide, yet we had few real conversations. In time she would talk and I would be happy to listen, to appear the mistress but be the child. She could always read my thoughts so well. From that first week, on the few nights that Xiong Fa did not come, Yan would appear with a bowl of congee and I knew we would sit together quietly. She would bring in a small lacquered tray inlaid with pretty peonies. The congee would steam in its bowl and I would see the rice grains bobbing below the surface like a hundred little fish. Each spoonful was warm and comforting, and made even more so by Yan's sitting quietly on her stool watching over me. Once I'd finished she would take my tray and ask me if I needed anything else. She already knew that I did not like to leave my room at night. I had become afraid of the darkness in the endless corridors and preferred to be in the familiar surroundings of my room, even when most nights I must endure Xiong Fa's visit.

On the nights when my husband was expected, Yan and I developed a routine, she would come and coax me over to my dressing table with a warm little half-smile that spread across her face through her wrinkles. When I saw this smile I knew she was secretly concerned for me, but we had no choice but to do what was expected. Each night Xiong Fa would tell Yan whether or not he would come to see me. This, I learned, was Sang tradition when visiting their wives or mistresses.

Again and again I sat in front of that mirror. I tried not to look at myself but to focus on the objects around me. I remembered those few days before the wedding when I had seen myself naked for the first time and been intrigued and pleased by the shape of my own body. Now I'd grown used to looking down and seeing nothing. It had become part of the routine. I was happy not to see myself for I had been a fool not to realize how ignorant I was; to know nothing of what people want to do to each other. I had not even been able to imagine such things. I had never imagined a man would want to force his fingers or tongue into me in this way. I would sit at that mirror avoiding my own reflection in it—yet I could not stop myself from wondering if Bi had ever wanted to do those things to me.

Chapter 9

My birthday was on the eighth day after our marriage and I became eighteen. Ma, Ba, and Grandfather did not come to see me. They might have been angry that we did not honor the traditional visit to the bride's parents on the third day; it would have been a huge loss of face for them. However, Father-in-law had been so incensed when I had failed to serve him tea or breakfast and then broken the tea cup at breakfast the day after that, that Xiong Fa said we should not do anything to honor my parents when we had disrespected his. There were no presents or messages for me; maybe after the wedding ceremony this was not considered so important. I had now left one family to join another and if there were to be any celebrations it should be my new family that provided them. Grandfather had always given me a small *li shi* on my birthday, it was never much money but enough to buy sweets and things, and Ma and Ba would buy me some clothes.

My new family provided me with all these things and more anyway, just as Sister had foreseen. I would never want for anything material again. I need not save anything if I wished. I need never become attached to anything, for everything except the family name was considered immediately replaceable. But all that day I wanted someone to give me something or at least to recognize the importance of the day to me. I wondered whether

it would be best for me to relinquish my attachment to all re-
minders of my old life, such as my birthday, for these things
were irrelevant, perhaps, and not worth the pain of remembering. My wedding was my birth into this new family—maybe
this was the birthday I should remember in the future.

During the day I would hide in my room and look out of the
window, seeing the stillness and order of the courtyard, hearing
the chaos and life of the street beyond.

In the mornings I could hear children running to school,
chattering about which classes they liked and the teachers they
hated. They would shout after the old street vendors to buy
sugarcane sticks and dried fruit. I listened to the birds and the
beating of servants' feet on the road as they carried their master's or mistress's palanquin. Occasionally I heard a motorcar, a
fight, or an accident: I saw none of this but imagined it all.

There was no more school for me. I had left one year before
my last year anyway. School rules and classroom gossip had
been exchanged for invented family traditions and Sang family
politics. My days were now run according to Sang routine and
tradition. I could not miss breakfast or dinner. Lunch I could
have in my room. If Father-in-law required anything of us,
we must naturally obey, then for me came the orders of First
Wife, and finally my husband. If I were not required by any of
them I could do as I pleased, though I could not leave the house
unless I had first asked permission and even then must be chap-
eroned. Yan had told me that this would change in time but
at the moment, as they did with all newcomers to the house,
they were watching me to see if I showed the proper respect or
would turn out to be a troublemaker.

First Wife had not outright demanded that I ask her permission but I had seen how it was for the wives of lesser members
of the family. She held power by tradition, and that was a force
as old as Chinese history. None of them wished to be cut off

and cast out from the family and its wealth and protection. How would they have lived then?

So on my birthday I sat alone until about four o'clock in the afternoon when Yan appeared to help me get ready for my afternoon sleep. This time, however, she came in with a large box, which she set out before me. I opened it and inside was a beautiful fox stole. It was many times better than the one Sister had worn, which had been only the pelt of the body. This had the beautiful tail and majestic head, which had been specially preserved to make it look rich and elegant.

"Who sent me this?" I demanded excitedly, as this was very unexpected.

"Your husband's servant brought it for me to give to you," Yan replied.

I was surprised that he had remembered my birthday, unless this present was for something else. I quickly draped the fur over my shoulders. I wanted to look at myself in the mirror but was reluctant. I stood in front of the full-length mirror in the walk-in wardrobe. I saw myself in the stole, looking tired and pale. The dead ebony eyes of the fox glinted back at me.

"Is he coming to see me?" I asked.

"No, I am sorry, he is at work and his servant told me that he is going out to dinner after that. Perhaps you will see him tomorrow."

For the first few weeks of our marriage Xiong Fa would leave after breakfast with Father-in-law, to work at the Sang family offices. Sometimes he would return for lunch and if he did, I might then be invited to eat with him in his apartment. It was a place I had visited only during the day. If he wanted me to see him, I would receive a note from his servant, Ah Cheuk, an old man who some said had once served the original father of the Sang family. He said nothing and would always look away from you. I had heard the children whispering that his tongue had been cut out when he was forty years old, for gossiping about Father-in-law's mother. He should have been cast out from the house by rights, but the family apparently believed he should learn his lesson another way. By losing his tongue he would be an example to all the other servants of the dangers of talking about the family without permission. I think it was only a tale the children told each other to scare themselves, but I cannot be sure.

After five weeks, the old servant arrived at my room. I was to follow him back to Xiong Fa's apartment and meet him there for lunch. This meant walking from the back of the house, where my room was, along the grand paneled corridors to the more magnificent front part of the house where Xiong Fa and his parents lived.

As we walked down one of the many corridors of the house, I saw Yan standing outside in the interior courtyard where the laundry was hung out to dry. She was holding my bedsheets outstretched in front of First Wife. My mother-in-law peered closely at them and after a few seconds started shouting that Xiong Fa had not yet done his family duty. She called for her son's old servant twice, and then repeatedly for Xiong Fa himself. The servant heard and rushed off, leaving me standing on my own watching First Wife screaming and cursing everyone, including Yan.

When Xiong Fa arrived First Wife was holding up the sheet. She immediately shrieked at him, bundled the sheet toward Yan, and pointed a fat finger at her son.

"Do you want this family to have an heir? Or have you decided to be the last Sang man? You are not allowed to make any decisions until you are head of the family."

Xiong Fa looked angry but said nothing in reply.

"It is your duty to have an heir! Once you have done this then you can do whatever you want. You can find some woman you like or see no women at all. I don't care. Your first duty is to have an heir and carry on this family's name. You are already as old as your father was when you were born. You do not have time to waste on being a fool."

She paused here and walked closer to him. She took the sheet from Yan and clenching it in her right fist, she stuck it under his nose.

"I can see from this you are not trying to make an heir. It will never happen if you do not behave properly . . . like a man. Such neglect is disrespectful to your father and to me."

"Ma, it is not right yet. It is too soon . . ."

First Wife slapped him across the face and screamed, "It is the right time! We all say it is right. It is already over a month since you were married. The fortune-teller told us it must happen now. If you do not want to be head of this family then I will ask one of your younger brothers. They will do what they are told."

Xiong Fa said nothing in reply.

She calmed down slightly and finished by saying quietly to him, "There are many traditions and customs that have made this family great. It is your responsibility to follow these and ensure the family's reputation is maintained. You must do this. I do not wish to mention your behavior to your father."

He looked hard at his mother, still saying nothing. She thrust the sheet back to Yan and left him standing there. My husband looked very angry. When he had calmed down, he started to speak quietly to Yan. They stood together for several minutes, Yan nodding slowly in response.

This was the first time I had seen First Wife exert her power. She had been unkind and occasionally cruel to me and I was very nervous around her, but I had not so far been afraid. Now I had seen how hard and malicious she could be, and how easily Xiong Fa could be controlled by her. I realized why her face was always contorted and sour-looking; why I never saw any peace or calmness in it. It was as though her only aim in life was to confront or control every situation. If something was beyond her direct influence, then she would seek to cause as much damage or harm as she was able. Grandfather would have said that her smile was too wide to be genuine and her eyes too motionless and uninterested in others to be caring; she did not want to adjust to anything she encountered, merely to control or destroy. She was like a stale flower that has sat in a vase too long, retaining its petals and straight stem long after nature would have let a wildflower wilt and die, giving way to fresher blooms.

I stood in the dim half-light of the corridor and watched Xiong Fa talking to Yan. Then he left the courtyard, his usual light gait drained of all energy. I waited. Yan knew I was watching. She gave me the rueful half-smile I knew well, the one that always told me my life would soon become more painful and difficult.

The old servant reappeared and gave me a note from Xiong Fa, which said he was sorry that he could not have lunch with me today after all as he had to return to work urgently. I did have lunch with him the next day, but he did not mention the argument with First Wife and we ate together in silence.

A week later, I went to lunch again in my husband's apartment. We always sat and ate at a small dark marble table at the end of the room opposite from the entrance door, which I believe was set up just for our lunches. We had eaten two dishes in silence but just as Xiong Fa had started the third dish, cold shredded chicken in sesame paste, he put down his chopsticks.

"I think you have spent enough time in the house since we were married," he announced with a smile. "The tea dances at the Cathay Hotel are enjoyable and I would like you to meet my friends and their wives there. It will only be for a couple of hours. Would you like that?"

I did not know what to say, because although Sister had described these dances to me a little, and had always said how
delightful and elegant they were, I did not know if I would
like them. I had heard her talk about the hotel with its famous
European-designed entrance hall and Western-style music.
She had said that the ballroom was bright and lively, and that
men and women would dance and chat together there, wearing
beautiful foreign clothes. I decided I would be more than happy
just to go and watch.

"I don't know . . . If you want me to come, I would like to,"
I told him.

I returned to my food. He watched me eat and laughed. I
smiled and put down my chopsticks, folding my hands together
in my lap. Xiong Fa was still watching me when I looked up,
and gave me a friendly smile. I had rarely had the chance to
look at him properly since the wedding. Normally, we would be
closely surrounded by members of the family or else it was in
my room, when it was dark and my mind suffocated or simply
blank, my body in pain. This time his eyes met mine and he
looked me in the face, free from the shadows cast by candlelight. He seemed rather tired and worn, his skin pale and waxy,
but his hair was neatly parted and his office clothes were clean
and tidy.

"Thank you. And thank you for my present," I said softly.

"Well, it was your birthday and I wanted to give you one. Did
you like it?"

"Yes, I was very surprised. How did you know it was my
birthday?"

"Ah, well, a man should know his own wife's birthday." He
laughed. "Actually I make sure all the documentation for all the
people in this house, from my parents to the maids, is kept in
order, so I looked at yours. It told me when your birthday was.
Perhaps you can wear the stole this afternoon," he said with a

gentle smile from lips that were different at night. He walked around the table and kissed me on the forehead.

"I will see you later this afternoon then."

I nodded and he left the room. I ate a bit more in silence. A few minutes passed, and as the old servant did not appear to lead me back to my room, I decided I would look around. I don't know whether Xiong Fa had intended that I should but I took the chance. The room in which we had eaten was a sitting room. Three closed doors led off the room, one back to the corridor and the others to the bedroom and bathroom. I didn't dare open these and just contented myself with wandering around this room.

The furniture was traditional but on the shelves were some textbooks and a small toy steam engine, which had been dented and battered many years ago and which someone had tried to repair. On the walls opposite the windows hung portraits of his parents. First Wife looked beautiful in the picture; it was difficult to understand how she could have changed so much. She looked so young in her wedding dress. It seemed strange to think of her as ever being a child, an innocent. Ah Cheuk suddenly entered and indicated he would lead me back to my room.

I usually had a short sleep in the afternoon but today Yan came in to apply my makeup and ensure I was dressed properly. I wore a very traditional cheongsam, which swept to the floor and had long sleeves that draped over my arms and hands. It was shapeless compared to the new designs that Sister had worn, with their short sleeves, closer fit, and shorter length. But the old-style dress had very pretty embroidery and was in a rich deep red, all of which was in accordance with how Father-in-law felt young women should dress.

My hair was put up and set under a traditional headdress and I felt like a concubine waiting to be rescued by a hero. I did not look like Sister used to, glamorous and sophisticated, but like an imperial doll drawn on a scroll by an artist many years ago. However, when I added my fur stole I was surprised how elegant I looked. For a moment I forgot everything that had happened and studied myself in the mirror for several minutes, feeling happier than I had since that first day.

Yan led me to a large black car parked in front of the house. It was one of those the family had used to come to our house to meet Sister. The interior was dark, as the windows and glass panel between the passengers and driver were covered by thick curtains, and the dark brown leather seating absorbed what little light crept around the edges of these. Yan had told me that even though this was a car, the family treated it like a traditional palanquin. I should never open the curtains to look out, as the family considered it improper for a Sang woman to be seen in public in this manner.

In the six weeks since I had been married I had only left the house twice. On both occasions I had been to the house of another relative and was simply led to where we were to eat. The men stayed behind to talk and drink afterward and the women departed to another room, but First Wife had required me to go straight home.

As it was daytime, it was difficult to restrain myself from looking behind the curtains. I very much wanted to see all the activity on the streets; all the places and things I would have liked to visit and do. I obeyed, but could barely restrain myself from looking, because for weeks I had heard this commotion and energy from my bedroom window but seen nothing of it. This time it was just the same but I could at least pull down the window a little and content myself with new sounds and smells.

The weather was getting colder and the street vendors had already started cooking chili hot pot, fragrant steamed buns, and lots of delicious fried snacks such as *dofu* sticks. If Bi were here we would have gone out to share a sesame bun and a bowl of hot noodles. Like Ma and Sister, Father-in-law and First Wife considered this peasant food and did not allow it in the house except for the servants in their quarters. The cooking smells filled the car very quickly and I closed my eyes and pictured all the things that I could taste on the tip of my tongue.

Underneath the aromas of the food was the pungent smoky scent of the charcoal stoves on which everything on the street was cooked. When the car stopped I could hear utensils scraping against pans and people calling out prices. And all the way I could hear the clamor of bells as people took to their bicycles rather than walk in the cold.

I breathed all these smells in, and with my chest full of them I sensed a small piece of my old self return: some of the excitement and happiness I had once shared with Grandfather.

We arrived and a doorman opened the car door and helped me out. I was guided straight into the hotel lobby through revolving doors—the first time I had seen such things. I watched another person go through the doors before me and it looked like they just magically vanished inside the building. I vanished inside, too, where it was clean and bright, just as Sister had described. The foreign-designed buildings had plenty of windows and there were mirrors everywhere, and instead of being lined with dark wood, the walls were painted white. The floor was made of white marble and the roof was as high as a temple's. Everything around me was open and exposed, which made me feel very small. The hotel employees wore smart bright uniforms and around the lobby there were comfortable Western-style chairs and tables laid with cups and saucers. One of the uniformed young boys came up to me and led me through the lobby, past the bright reception desks, and into the ballroom.

I could hear the band before I entered the room. The music was loud and frightening yet its rhythm and boldness excited and enticed me inside. As I entered the room I saw men and women moving quickly and erratically on the dance floor, poking their limbs out to their sides and in front of them. There were waiters in white coats standing around and a few tables around the dance floor were occupied by guests. Everything was clean and white; floors, walls, uniforms, and tablecloths.

Xiong Fa appeared then and led me over to a table occupied entirely by women.

As we walked he whispered to me, "You look very beautiful in my present. I will have to spend all year thinking how next year's can be even better." He looked down at me and winked.

As we approached the table I recognized two of the women from our wedding but I had not spoken to them before. They were dressed in Western clothes like Sister might have worn. I felt foolish again in front of these sophisticated ladies but I had now become used to my embarrassment and had learned to conceal these feelings and my ignorance by not speaking too much or drawing attention to myself. I had become the pretty little flower among the trees, the tiny buttercup content to go unnoticed.

But the journey here had refreshed me and as I looked around at the strange room and all the people, I was excited by the beauty and brightness. I was sitting perfectly still but I was excited inside.

Xiong Fa sat at an adjacent table, smoking with the other men. He laughed with the others, though not as much, and seemed to enjoy sitting there quietly. He looked over at me and smiled.

One stylish woman smiled at me and in a soft voice said, "I think your fur is very elegant. Where did you get it?"

"My husband gave it to me as a present," I replied proudly.

"Ah, are you pregnant then?"

I looked puzzled in reply.

"He must have tried by now . . . Well, if not it will be soon."
She smiled again.

I blushed because I did not really know what she was asking.
The woman smiled at the others, who looked uncomfortable at
her candor.

"Well, don't worry about it. The Sang family has its own rules
and you must play along with them if you want to stay there.
Does the old man still eat only five dishes?" She laughed, showing off her beautiful teeth and flashing her bright eyes at me.

"You must be the respectful, dutiful daughter-in-law," she
continued kindly. "Your mother-in-law's last job in life is to get
a grandson for her husband. And when she does, things will get
better, trust me. My name is Ming—pleased to meet you."

"My name is Feng . . . Mrs. Sang Xiong Fa." I stumbled over
this, the first time I had heard the change of family name from
my own lips.

"It's strange, isn't it? Suddenly you belong to someone else,"
she said quietly, then announced to the others, holding out her
hand to me as men do, "Well, Sang Feng Feng, hello."

The others at the table all smiled at me and nodded gently in
my direction but said nothing. She placed her hand on mine. I
looked up at her, surprised.

"Don't worry about them, they're too busy thinking of themselves, worried they will behave inappropriately and some terrible punishment will be brought upon them from above," she
whispered with a smile. "So how old are you? I don't think you
are any older than seventeen."

"I am eighteen and one month," I whispered back.

"Really? Happy birthday for last month then. We should
have some *birthday cake*," she said excitedly.

"What's *birthday cake*?" I whispered, trying and failing to
copy Ming's pronunciation of the foreign language.

She held my arm tighter and moved closer to say mysteriously, "It's some strange Western thing. I'll tell you more one day, when we know each other better. I like you, you're not afraid."

She straightened up then and lit a cigarette.

"So, you have only been married a month?"

I nodded.

"I'm sorry we could not come to your wedding but we were in Beijing." She studied me a moment and continued, in a kindly tone. "You must have found your wedding very frightening? These large family gatherings can be very intimidating, especially when it is your own wedding." She drew on her cigarette and breathed out the perfumed smoke. "Did you go to school? You look like a girl who went to school."

Her rapid conversation made me feel dizzy, but she spoke so quickly and confidently that I wanted to hear more.

"Yes, I did."

"Good. Well, let me give you some advice then: keep reading and writing, read anything you can, because it will help you. We women, and you *are* a woman," she commented, leaning back a little to take in every aspect of my appearance, "today in fact a beautiful woman . . . need to be educated. You never know, do you?" She squeezed my hand encouragingly. "One day you may have something really important to tell someone."

I found it difficult to understand what Ming was saying; she did not speak slowly and carefully like Grandfather but quickly and mysteriously, referring to so many different things at once.

"Well, Feng Feng, I need to go dance with my husband . . . he's the tall one over there." She pointed to a man with a broad face, not Shanghainese, dark wavy hair, and dark skin color. "He is trying to grow an ugly monkey-faced beard like a hairy Westerner." She sighed. "So much trouble!

"I hope I will see you again soon." She got up to go then hung back for a moment. "I knew as soon as I saw your pretty face and that old-style dress that you were not like the rest of us older women. I'm thirty years old, can you believe it?" Her voice became slow and wistful. She looked at me. "You are beautiful and not yet affected by all this. You must stay this way."

I did not think very much about her final comment; at that time all I understood was that whatever Xiong Fa did, it was my duty to let him. This woman spoke with such wisdom and calm that I listened to her carefully even while I did not understand all of what she said.

Her husband was waiting on the dance floor and I watched her walk to him, silent and graceful, like a swan gliding across the unbroken surface of a calm lake. They danced and I watched in awe.

The music changed and a few of the men came over to the table and asked the other women to dance. No servants were needed to pass messages, the men just extended their hands and the women took their lead. I ended up sitting with another woman who had not been asked to dance, either. She looked tired and nervous, hunching in on herself and clenching her arms tight to her sides as if to make herself as small as possible. I recognized this posture.

The next tune was slow and I saw couples hold each other closer and sway together, moving in faint circles. As they held each other, some of them whispered, sharing intimate jokes and secrets. One couple was very forward: the woman rested her head on the man's shoulder. Grandfather would have been out-raged to see such poor manners.

The next song sounded similar. To my surprise, Xiong Fa walked up to me then and held out his hand. I blushed and told him that I could not dance; that I was not like Sister. This was the first time I had compared myself to her in front of him and I half-expected him to tell me that he knew this already. But he said nothing, just smiled warmly and continued to look at me while holding out his hand.

I stood up and he walked me to a space just inside the dance floor. He put my right hand on his shoulder and held my left. Then he put his left hand on my waist and we gently swayed together. I felt strange, momentarily safe in his arms for the first time since entering the house, then I felt his fingers tighten around my waist and hand and for a moment I was reminded of our nights together and my helpless suffocation.

After several minutes he said I danced very well and that he hoped we would be able to dance together often.

"I would like to take you to more dances. If that is something you would like to do as well?"

I did not reply.

"They have many in the afternoon, lots of different dancing styles. We could learn together."

We moved slowly and awkwardly over the wooden floor in silence for a while. I felt embarrassed but excited and happy at the same time, daring to imagine a different life from the one I had endured during the last six weeks. Xiong Fa broke the silence.

"I remember your sister once said you were always playing in the gardens next to your parents' house. Would you take me there one day?"

"Yes . . . Yes!"

He laughed a little at my enthusiasm but I did not mind. The idea that we might go there made me so happy. We continued the slow dancing for another few songs, after which it was half past five and we had to go home for dinner.

Xiong Fa walked me to my car, which was parked at the entrance to the hotel, and then went over to his own. On the way back to the house, I pictured us sitting in the gardens together.

Perhaps he would fish like Bi had done, and I could tell him the names of the flowers as Grandfather had taught me.

At the house I sat in my room and waited for dinner. I watched the guards change; saw the old servant feed the fish in the giant Qinghua basin. He'd brought them small pieces of food left over from the kitchens and the fish hungrily snatched at the bits of waste flesh and vegetables as they hit the surface of the water. Even though the largest and most beautiful fish were able to muscle their way past the others to take the best bits, the old man still favored them. He would drop the best pieces near their mouths until they ate their fill and then would simply toss the rest of the food into the water for the others to fight over. I had watched him do this many times and he was never moved to help the smaller fish, who were destined to fight and savage each other every day.

Usually I felt drained and intimidated by the complexity of my life in this house but attending the tea dance had made me feel different. I felt light and relieved, as if perhaps everything could change. Sister's bitter warning in the courtyard at home had haunted me every day for the last six weeks but now I dared to imagine that I was finally overcoming my fears and she had been wrong.

After finishing dinner that night, I was able to spend my usual hour sitting at my window, watching the stars come out. Today had been very different from the rest of my time here. As I sat at the window my imagination drifted through scenes of life as it might be lived in this house after Father-in-law and First Wife were gone, and Xiong Fa and I had taken their place.

Yan came in and I joined her at the dressing table. She finished preparing me for Xiong Fa and led me to the bed as always, but this time when she sat beside me, she leaned closer. She held my left hand and brought her face so close to it that I thought she might kiss it. Her breath was warm on the back of my hand, and through that little patch of warmth I felt bonded to her. She did not look up at me, just stared at my hand. Then she whispered to me that Xiong Fa's mother had demanded an heir to the family and said that he and I must do what was necessary to make me pregnant.

I listened to Yan but did not know what that meant. She looked up at me. I was already doing just what I was asked, everything that he wanted. Yan's eyes, although small and deep-set in her weathered face, held a brightness that always drew my attention. I had not studied her face so closely before; we do not generally look very carefully at those who serve us. Beneath the warm smile that always greeted me, her skin was rough and torn, unlike the elder women of the Sang family, who, although fat and saggy elsewhere, had oiled and treated their facial skin to keep it smooth. The wear I could see on Yan's face assured me that she had survived her hard life, had not hidden or sought to be sheltered. She had been scarred and defeated, but she had lived. I could see now that, whatever happened, I would live, too. She would help me, if I would let her.

But this evening, there was something more. I sensed something would now be different. Yet even in my anxiety I couldn't move my lips and tongue to ask, I still couldn't bring myself to behave contrary to my pride. I thought instead about my old life with Grandfather; walking, running, playing, and eating . . . but thinking so little. Now there was so much to understand that was new, but I could not.

As Yan turned to leave I grabbed her hand and held it, preventing her from going. She looked back at me but still I could not bring myself to say anything, just looked up at her. She was the maid and I the mistress. Even though I was vulnerable and needed her advice, I would rather wait for her to say something than ask her outright. It did not seem fitting that she should know what I did not, it was against the natural order I had been shown by my parents and by our tradition. It was still too much for me to overcome and I let her hand slip from mine. She lingered, perhaps giving me a last opportunity to speak, but I said nothing and finally she left. I closed my eyes and waited.

Although Xiong Fa was not drunk, I could smell strong rice wine on his breath. He moved quickly to the bed but did not sit on the edge as usual. Instead he moved to the end of it and knelt between my ankles. He pulled back the sheet and took off his robe. He was naked before me at the other end of the bed. It was the first time I had seen a man like this. Xiong Fa's fatty curves were very close to how I saw him clothed. The skin on his pale thighs and stomach, which sagged around his waist, had none of the sheen and beauty of Bi's, glimpsed between his shirt buttons. Xiong Fa had hair growing around his nipples, which for an instant struck me as funny. It looked like the hair on an old man's chin: those lucky hairs that cannot be cut for fear of severing the lines of prosperity.

I saw that between his legs he had hair like I did, but much more, and nestled in the middle of the blackness was something ugly. He brought himself down on top of me, not yet lying on me but holding himself above me on all fours, his hands placed to either side of my shoulders and knees resting on the mattress between my legs. He looked down at my breasts then lowered himself to lie on top of me. His smell and his breathing were heavy; his large body covered me and pressed down on me. I closed my eyes and thought of Bi holding the corner of my blouse and how I had still sensed all of him even though he was not touching me.

Xiong Fa smothered me. I could not feel my own body separate from his. My chest felt crushed. I found it hard to breathe. I opened my eyes, expecting to see Xiong Fa's face looking into mine, but he was moving down to my breasts, sucking them and licking them, while his right hand was moving between my legs.

Then he stopped touching me and touched himself instead, rubbing and pulling at himself, and after a few seconds his hand returned to me. He had made little noise so far but as he touched himself he started to groan.

His weight pinned me to the bed. I tried to look past his head but could not. He brought his hands back and placed them above my shoulders and as he did so his whole weight fell between my legs. He started to grunt more and as he did his hips pushed down on top of me as if trying to press me deep into the bed. I lay there and allowed him to do what he wanted, fearing that any movement I made would prevent him from satisfying himself and First Wife's wishes.

He grabbed my left hand and forced me to touch him between his legs. I felt his coarse hair then something more, the part of men that had so far been hidden from me. I touched and held it, and he groaned, and it swelled and grew, becoming hard and warm. It felt ugly and alien. I wanted it away from me. I looked up at his face, which was level with my chin. It looked pained. His eyes were tightly shut and his lips parted. His lower jaw jutted out as if he were forcing himself to concentrate.

Suddenly he lifted himself, propping himself up with his hands placed next to my shoulders. I quickly glanced down. It looked even larger than it felt and so odd that I was scared by what it might do to me. He repositioned his hips and waist between my legs and then I realized that he was going to push it into me instead of his fingers. In my hand it had felt big and I did not want it inside me. I did not know what it would do there and what would happen to me.

Although I was on my back I tried to move up the bed away from him, but he lowered himself and placed his elbows on the mattress above my shoulders, resting his weight on them and preventing me from moving any farther. So I tried to push him away with my hands but he was too heavy. Then he moved his arms, resting his full weight on me, and grabbed my wrists, holding my arms flat against the bed above my head. I was pressed down hard, all the breath squeezed out of me. I kicked out with my legs, trying to hurt him, and fought to shift my hips away. It was tiring, and my legs kept hitting the wooden posts of the bed.

I could not escape, no matter how I kept kicking and struggling. I could not keep going. But I was desperate to keep him out of me, for I knew once he was inside me I would be completely under his control. My muscles ached from struggling under his weight and my mind began to slow until my thinking became foggy. Even while I fought him, he still tried to kiss me and moved down to suck my nipples as though his mouth needed them. He raised himself a little and as his weight shifted I fought to struggle from under it. It was hopeless. I could feel his hardness between my legs and was terrified.

Eventually I stopped struggling and he realized I could no longer fight him. He did not open his eyes or kiss me again but maneuvered his hand between his legs. Suddenly I felt my body burst with pain. I cried out. Memories rushed into my head then: of Sister's fingers poking into my cheeks in the courtyard at home, and my mother's smile as I climbed into the bridal palanquin. I cried out again and waited for him to finish. I shut my eyes. I heard nothing but his breathing. Felt nothing but his weight, and the sweat dripping from his brow onto my cheeks and eyelids.

I thought of our dance earlier that day and the things he had said to me then. He had moved and spoken so gently. I did not understand how this person on top of me, forcing himself into me, could be the same person who had held me so protectively in his arms that afternoon. He had described to me then what my future in his family would be like and how he would visit Grandfather's gardens with me, and I had believed everything he had said.

He kept thrusting into me and the pain was almost too much, but then suddenly he stopped. He held himself deep inside me and gasped. Then he pushed once more and after a few seconds withdrew himself. He quickly got up, carelessly throwing on his robe, and went straight to the door. He did not stop to look down at me as he usually did. There was no kiss on the forehead or uncertain smile as before. My husband left with his head bowed, hurrying from the room as if he could not bear to see the scene he had left.

I was in so much pain I could only lie on my side. I put my hand to myself. There was a lot of liquid there, which was sticky, and when I brought my fingers to my nose there was both the smell of blood and of a heavy salty musk. It was strong and filled my nostrils and head. It was a dirty smell.

Chapter 10

Yan entered very quickly after Xiong Fa had left. She looked at me and tears formed in her narrow deep-set eyes. She took my hand by the wrist and carefully wiped my fingers, then slowly and gently moved me onto my back and cleaned between my legs. I promised I'd remain still while she wiped my body down. As she tended me she noted all the bruises on my wrists, thighs, and legs, telling me that she had a special balm used by *gong fu* boxers, which would help the bruises fade more quickly and take the pain away. Finally she pulled the sheet over my shoulders and tucked it under my chin. She lit more candles and went away, to return with a worn old shawl made of layers of thick gray padded cotton sewn together, and a small pot of balm. She took the sheet away and then made me sit up and wrapped me in the shawl. It smelled of Yan, which I liked as it overpowered any remaining trace of Xiong Fa. She sat beside me on the bed and pushed the hair out of my face.

"I used this balm on my husband when he would come home from the army. His body was hard and taut but always so cut and sore. He taught me how to make this balm, which he learned in *gong fu* school during his training. Young students when they first learn to kick and punch have such terrible bruises and scars. First they punch sand, then hot sand, then a pot of small lead balls, and finally wood and stone." Yan meandered through her story and her soft even tone calmed me.

As I listened to her I thought of all those young *gong fu* students trained to fight and kill. They knew how to receive pain and how to give it back.

"Their hands become so strong that they can punch holes in walls and stop bullets. This balm helps them heal after training so the next day they can fight again," she continued, looking at me with a wide smile that came from her confidence in her balm. "You just see how well it works."

She took my hand then and led me over to my chair while she changed the sheets on the bed. My legs ached and I felt a sharp pain between them from where my husband had torn me slightly. In the candlelight I could see the stains on the sheet. The red had faded from mixing with another, colorless stain, and on the white of the sheet the colors looked like a pretty pink peony coming into bloom.

Yan sat on the stool next to me. She took some balm and rubbed it gently onto the back of my hand, the one she had held so tenderly only an hour or so ago while trying to warn me of what was to come. She applied the balm to the fingers and palms of both hands and then slowly massaged it into my arms and shoulders. Next she brought over another small stool and placed my feet on it before kneading the balm into my shins and ankles. Then she parted my legs and applied some balm to a silk-and-cotton wadding, which she pressed between them. It felt cool and took the sharp stinging away. I pulled the shawl tighter around me and closed my eyes.

"Do you know what you must do?" Yan inquired then.

I could only look down.

"You must give this family a son. They'll be happy once they have their heir. This evening is your first time . . . it'll get better as you become more used to it."

She came closer to me and held my face gently in her hands as Bi had done. Her skin felt rough against my cheeks and in any other situation I would never have let her touch me that way, but she cupped my face so lightly while still giving me a warm feeling of protection that I wanted to sleep there until dawn. I closed my eyes but I could feel Yan's kindly gaze on me. She stroked my hair and caressed my cheek.

"Your husband must visit you every night until you're pregnant. He has no choice. But I'll be here with you."

Now at last I understood what the lady at the dance had said to me only that afternoon . . .

Yan pulled out a broken and frayed *wuxia* novel and gave it to me. I had not read many myself but Grandfather had read some to me when I was a child. He had told me, laughing, that they were Grandmother's favorites, and when she was reading one no one could distract her, because she was so gripped by their tales of courage and romance. While Yan applied more balm I read.

Wuxia stories are about brave swordsmen and boxers who go on many dangerous adventures and carry out heroic deeds. Over the many nights that were to follow this one, I read of lone heroes, rogues, drunks, cruel merchants, and beautiful concubines. My favorites were the stories of the heroes who fell in love with the concubines they must rescue, all the time knowing that their love could never be consummated as the concubine must be returned to her rightful owner, the Emperor. These stories had a void and an emptiness that comforted me in mine.

Xiong Fa came back each night after that first time. At first I would fight until he was forced to tear into me. After a while, though, I could no longer resist, still aching from the previous night or else too tired to struggle under his weight. He would finish quickly and go. Each time he was done I would see that he simply wanted to leave the room, could barely bring himself to look at me. I thought he seemed disappointed by my behavior, and felt guilty that I was not able to do what he needed me to do.

Yan would enter shortly after Xiong Fa left. Sometimes I

could not speak to her and she went about her work, cleaning me and the bed in silence, while I sat in the chair and watched her. She made sure our eyes never met then. She knew when I wanted to talk, and when I just wanted to listen, and she knew when I was lost in fear and anger and needed only to hurt myself or others.

There were times when I was so angry I would scream at her, my words bitter and harsh. My thoughts would flash to images of Sister and Ma. I could not move my mind forward, to other things, but saw them again, in the sitting room of my old home, discussing Sister's wedding and then greeting Xiong Fa's parents. I saw the trail of watermarks left by the rain dripping off their rich clothes, each mark a deep bruise on that house, which would never heal. I thought of Ma sitting silently across the table from me at dinner and Ba chewing slowly. The question still rang in my head but it did not matter anymore what their answer had been; I hated them.

Sometimes I would ask Yan to tell me stories just so I could hear her voice, her words filling my mind so nothing else could enter, even the hatred would be smothered for a few minutes. She would tell me about her garden and the vegetables she grew there, about the planting and the weather she would hope for. I heard her tell me the same stories many times, but it was always comforting to hear them start and finish as expected.

Late in the night when I was alone, after the candles had been lit and extinguished, I would imagine Bi coming to find me like one of the heroes in the *wuxia* stories; instead of a fishing rod he would arrive wielding a sword, and after beating the guards at the courtyard gates, he would enter the house and confront Father-in-law. These were simply dreams that occurred as I lay in the dark, waiting to fall asleep.

Each night I was devoured like the food sprinkled into the huge porcelain basin of fish at the center of the courtyard.

This house took the hours of each night from me, greedily, in little pieces; it was only Yan who returned me to life with her kindness. I felt I did not have a body of my own; there was just this flesh that was a tool for my mind to use when I was allowed control of it, but everything—my skin, lips, legs, arms, and buttocks—could be used or commanded by others at any time for their own pleasure. At night the family entered me from everywhere, leaving me hurting and red. My days and nights had been broken apart.

Weeks had passed since that tea dance and the night that followed. During my many subsequent nights of being overpowered by Xiong Fa, we had established a new routine. The candle was no longer lit, as he could not seem to bring himself to look at me and I did not want to look at him. We could now do this without seeing ourselves, our pain. I still could not think clearly while he was with me in my bed. Every night he entered me and filled me full of his seed, only to hurry away again. I saw nothing when he was with me, felt only his need to satisfy himself; to satisfy his family.

In my mind I remained in the courtyard I had created and sometimes it took me a long while after he had left to come back to my room. Yan always entered after he had left, to help heal me for the next night.

Eventually, whether day or night, Xiong Fa could not speak to me; I wanted to ask him one question, just one word.

"Yan, you come here every night after he has been. Does he make you come here?" I shouted at her as I lay in bed, tired from Xiong Fa's latest visit. She knew that I would still fight Xiong Fa, I needed to fight and I needed to shout at her.

"You know that he doesn't ask me, that would be against First Wife's wishes, mistress. Please do not ask me anymore." She did not stop what she was doing.

"I will ask you what I want!" I screamed back at her. I watched her face and hands as she moved around the room, gathering a cloth and bowl of water to wash me with and her old shawl that I would wear as she applied her balm.

"Does he talk to you? Does he tell you why he keeps coming? How can he keep visiting me like this?" I wanted to scream at her because I could not yet scream at anyone else.

"He doesn't speak to me. I am your maid and so he doesn't speak to me," she answered quietly, knowing that I would stop soon, once the fight had left me.

"Don't lie. I saw him speak to you that day when his mother was looking at my bedsheets. You saw me as well. Why do you lie to me? I know what you are thinking."

"You know it is his duty and that he has no choice. Mistress, you have asked me many times before. I have no other answers for you." She was almost pleading with me but she did not look at me, just kept working.

I followed her with my eyes until she stood near the fox stole Xiong Fa had given me as a birthday present. It now hung near the mirror on a rack with another shawl he had given me. I had not worn it since that day at the Cathay Hotel, because there had never been another dance. My attention was caught by the fox's teeth and dark gums, its ebony eyes and nose, everything false and painted to bring it back to life so that whoever wore it would forget that it really signified death. I realized it was ugly and violent and was glad I had not worn it again. I looked at it and momentarily forgot about Yan. When I focused on her again my anger was gone.

Yan had made me understand that Xiong Fa could not stop himself, he must follow his mother's wishes; like Ba and Grandfather, he would hurt me because he did not have the courage to stop himself. He knew what he should do but could not do it. How could they, these men, be so weak as to let this happen to me, when they knew how much pain I would suffer?

First Wife now waited for my monthly bleeding, examining my underclothes and sheets. Then in the fourth month it did not arrive. We all waited for several weeks and after that Xiong Fa did not appear again and I was ordered to stay in my room. I was happy to stay there and be brought my meals. I was happy not to see or be with any of them.

A doctor arrived. He examined my pulse and breathing and told First Wife that I was pregnant and it would be a boy. They gave him a huge *li shi* and everybody celebrated with expensive and rare tea from some distant part of China.

I still had to stay in my room. I slept, I read *wuxia* stories, and gazed at the guards protecting the door through which I had entered this perfectly ordered world. I did not believe the doctor. Such men with their traditional ideas and mysticism had failed Sister. If they had succeeded she would have been here instead of me. I would be with Bi in the fields or by the river, perhaps resting with him under the peaceful night of bright moon and stars he mentioned. I would be with the seamstress, working through linen and silk to create fine clothes. Anywhere else but here.

Now there was no longer fear and pain, I was left with my hatred of this life and those that had put me here.

I'm sorry, so very sorry, but I vowed in that room, my gilded prison, that if I gave birth to a boy I would gladly do what they wanted, though even they had not yet been arrogant enough to ask. I would give my son over to them, to be raised in the Sang manner, as their perfect heir: I would not want him in any case. If the child were a girl then I would not give her to them, though they would not want her anyway. No, I decided, a girl I would treat as I had been treated. Perhaps even worse.

My daughter, I vowed, would become a servant to peasants, a maid to the luckless and homeless. I promised myself that I would do this. By being given away to peasants, she would inherit a share of my suffering; Ma and Sister's legacy to her, for all their hard work, would be a lifetime spent with street vendors and itinerant peasants, the people they had hated and belittled so much.

Two male servants always sat near my door. I instructed one of them to fetch Yan. She must have been surprised to be called, because she rushed to my room. I was on the first upper floor of the house and she would have been in the maids' area in the cellars or else outside. She arrived out of breath and I could see she was relieved to find me sitting by the window staring out at the sky. Gasping slightly, she asked me, "Mistress, are you well? Is the baby okay?"

There was no visible sign of you yet. Without so much as seeing or feeling you, I'd made an oath to hate and abandon you.

"Yes, I am well." I paused. "Yan, you are my maid and you take care of me," I said then.

"Yes, mistress."

"I need you to swear something to me."

"Anything. You are my mistress."

"I want you to promise that if my baby is a girl, you will take it to the backstreets and give it away to peasant people. Like the ones we see traveling through the streets, offering to sharpen scissors and knives."

She waited to see if I had finished, then asked, "I know a son is better, and in the countryside I know many families would do this. But why do *you* want to? This family has enough money to take care of many daughters. Third Auntie has two."

I had realized Yan would need convincing.

"I know there's plenty of money, but at this time I want only sons. This family needs sons. I don't want any girls, they are useless . . . weak and vulnerable. This family needs to be strong. Girls are treated badly by everyone, even their own family. If I have a daughter, I want you to give it to a peasant couple who have no children and will need the girl because there is no one else to care for them. We can have more daughters later, after sons," I replied.

With you in my stomach, I lied to achieve what I wanted, just for myself. I told Yan the traditional reasons, the customary excuses, so that she would believe in my good intentions and promise to obey me. Yan had lived in the countryside and she knew this practice. She listened and agreed with the reasons I gave her. I could see from her eyes that for these few moments she considered us friends, as she had before on so many bruised and wakeful nights. She thought me a person to whom she could tell the truth, and from whom she expected the same. Then, seeing nothing wrong with my explanation, the maid in her returned; she looked at the bed and dressing table, prepared to tidy them, and said nothing more. I was in control. I had never felt that way before. I told her that I just wanted her promise, which she gave, and then said I would like to be alone.

According to family rules, reinforced by their doctor, I was not permitted to leave the house until the end of the second month of my pregnancy. Yan told me that from the beginning of the fourth month, I would not be permitted to leave the house at all, because it was not considered dignified for a pregnant woman to be seen in public; another disgrace to the Sang family. This was not prescribed by the doctor but was an order direct from First Wife, supported by Father-in-law. Yan then explained that even though a pregnant woman could go out during the third month, out of respect to First Wife it was not customarily done.

A month or so passed and, as part of the benefits of my pregnancy, I was moved from my old room to a larger apartment near the front of the house, with a better bathroom. My new window gave me a good view of the streets and houses opposite, too, but that simply made me want to go outside more. I called for Yan.

"Yan, please can you take me outside for a walk? I need to go for a walk," I whined a little as I asked.

"Mistress, if I go out and we are caught then I will be thrown out of the house and punished. You know what happened to your husband's servant," she replied very wisely, because if we were caught they might indeed throw her out or punish her harshly.

"Those are only old rumors . . . I will take the blame if we get caught. You can say that I forced you, threatened you, told you if you did not agree then I would throw you out of the house. I desperately want to go outside! As I told you, I used to spend all my time outside in the gardens and park. Just one hour will be good for the baby."

She hesitated but I knew that as she was from the country-side she would believe that fresh air was good for the baby, and would be persuaded.

"I'll check if First Wife and your husband have gone to their lunch appointment, then we can leave by the servants' door."

"That is wonderful. Thank you, Yan." I had become wiser now, with a better idea of what I wanted and how I could get it.

We waited until First Wife and Xiong Fa had gone to lunch with Father-in-law then left quietly by the back entrance, which led into the market. We went down side streets and little alleys. I desperately wanted to eat noodles and sweet buns, and Yan led me in search of them, for I didn't know any of these lanes. I realized I just missed being free. It was now early May and the sun was heating up. I asked Yan to take me to a place we could eat dumpling noodle soup.

When I entered the little restaurant, the owners saw my wealthy appearance and moved some other customers so Yan and I could have a table to ourselves. The attention and re-spect the owner and customers showed us gave me a sense of power I had never before experienced. We ordered quickly and were served first. The noodles were delicious. Sucking them up smudged my lipstick and left small grease spots on my dress. I started to giggle as I ate, remembering all the times I had eaten such food with Grandfather. Yan smiled at me. We finished and bought some steamed buns, walking to one of the small squares where we sat on a stone bench and watched the people around us, trading and working. I looked out of place there in my full cheongsam with fur stole but I did not care.

After we'd finished I wanted to walk to Tailor Street where all the clothes were made. I suddenly wanted to watch hands and fingers busy working as I had seen once before. I walked slowly past the shops, glimpsing hands carefully stitching and embroidering. I saw huge bolts and rolls of foreign cloth in colors that could never be worn in the traditional Sang household.

At the end of the street were the expensive shops. As we reached them, First Wife suddenly stepped out from one of the shops in front of us with two of her maids in tow. A car was waiting for her on the side of the road but she saw me and shouted for me to stop. I knew she would continue to scream but I didn't care. She shuffled quickly up to me, followed by her two maids, eventually, her face almost touching mine. I could smell the bitter, putrid odor of her longlife herbal medicine on her breath.

"What are you doing here?" she spat at me. Without waiting for an answer, she told me, "Get back to the house. It is wrong for a pregnant woman to be seen outside."

I stood and looked at her. I was taller by three or four inches and the need to look up to me was enough to make her even angrier. As she screamed, she realized that people were stopping to watch. She hesitated a moment and looked about. I straightened my back and made myself a little taller still, forcing her to look up even higher. She shouted with rage and her parted lips revealed blackened foul teeth.

I looked down at her and saw that she was ugly and rotting. She was nothing.

"Don't tell me what to do," I told her. "I am carrying the male heir to the family name. I am the First Wife. Do you understand? I am the First Wife now."

Her face filled with dark color and swelled before my eyes.

"Did your maid lead you here?" she demanded, ignoring the curious stares of the onlookers. "You are too stupid to come here yourself."

"She did not."

"Then she's insolent for following you when she knows you must stay at home."

"I demanded she should come. She had no choice."

I remained quite still but inside I trembled. I felt cold and my skin itched everywhere. I felt at any second I might cry, faint, shake violently, or just unclench my teeth and scream at her. I knew if I moved I would not be able to control myself, so I continued staring down at her, and for a moment she was at a loss. She looked at my mouth and face and then back at my eyes. Then she slapped me across the face, but still I did not move. It was she who took the first step back.

"Return to the house," she barked at me.

She walked away quickly, not allowing me time to reply, and I realized she could never win. I realized I was the future and she the past, and that she knew this. She turned back to the car, her maids scuttling after her. I watched her get in and then the car moved away, heading back to the Sang house.

I turned to look at Yan behind me. She looked sad and I knew she was worried for me.

Chapter 11

When I returned to my apartment, Xiong Fa's servant, Ah Cheuk, was waiting to ask if my husband might be allowed to see me. Now that I was pregnant he behaved as though I was a delicate child who must not be upset. I granted his request. He arrived shortly afterward and told me that his mother had complained about my rudeness and disrespect. I told him that I had not been out in nearly six weeks and there were no rules that forbade visits outside during the third month of pregnancy. He looked at me and at that moment I saw in his face the mouth and eyes of his parents.

"Yes, but it is respectful to stay inside."

I did not wish to talk to this man or his family.

"Very well, I will stay in, but you and your family will leave me alone until the birth of your son. First Wife hit me and the fright may have harmed the baby."

"I understand." He gave in so meekly and easily.

And so, for the next six months they did not speak to me unless I granted them a meeting. I spent my time either with Yan or by myself. We ate congee and she told me stories of her husband's adventures in the army. He was a man of courage yet a simple person, who lived for his Emperor and sacrificed for the family he hoped to have but never did. He traveled around the country and I asked Yan if he had ever been to Daochu, a small town near Xian, the ancient capital. She said she had never heard him talk of it. It felt exciting to hear myself ask about Bi's hometown. It made me tremble a little.

While I was pregnant, I was served special food so that you would grow up healthy and strong, tall and beautiful. No more Jin Hua ham. Fish, soup, and vegetables instead, so you would be intelligent and wise. My child would be perfect, I was sure, yet in all of this I thought of you very little. I wish now I had spent that time thinking of you, not hating and scheming. I know now I should have enjoyed feeling you grow inside me. If I had let myself feel you, you would have been a part of me and not simply an appendage that I could discard. I should have done what Sister and Ma had never done and Ba was afraid to do, then I could never have let you go. But in my fury I now took up their legacy, and forced myself to ignore you, your kicks, the sickness in the morning that you brought me, and the swelling of my breasts ready for motherhood; I ignored all these signs of your presence, these hints for me to change my mind and reconsider. I had even stopped looking at myself naked so I would never see you, but I felt you then and I always have.

During these six months, I saw that Xiong Fa had also adjusted to his new life. He had started visiting the rooms of certain maids. He had to satisfy himself and so he did what many of the other Sang men had done before him. He was discreet, though, and never disrespected me by taking them out or making any of them a proper mistress. I could tolerate such behavior, because I didn't care. As I had said to his mother in Tailor Street, I was now the First Wife. That was all that mattered to me.

When you were born, I made sure that only Yan was present. She helped me with your birth as I pushed and suffered, splitting open old scars from my nights spent with Xiong

Fa. It was so painful, and I used this pain to hate you as much as I could so that immediately after your birth I had the strength to give Yan her orders. She had her ointment. Soon I would feel better again.

Yan told me the birth had been bloody but that you were healthy and beautiful. I lay on my bed and closed my eyes. I could not help but try to visualize you, but I let my head fall back on the pillow against the headboard and kept my eyes firmly closed as I spoke to Yan, slowly and clearly. I would not let myself see you. The room was cold, as it was early in the evening. The chill of the end of November had already crept inside. I had thrown all the blankets from me and was shivering, though I did not notice this for hours.

I wish I had seen you. Your face was wrapped in a blanket and Yan held you close to her chest, which helped muffle your tiny cries.

"Is it a boy or a girl?" I asked.

"It doesn't matter, you must love all your children," Yan replied, softly and slowly.

"Answer me?" I screamed.

"You're very angry. You've been through so much and are still so young. But you must make yourself care. You must force yourself to want this baby."

"Just tell me, is it a boy or a girl?" I demanded through clenched teeth.

"A girl," she whispered.

I refused to open my eyes and in the darkness I saw Ma again, smiling stupidly as I entered the palanquin. I saw Sister, dressed like a whore in those cheap clothes cut from expensive cloth. I had learned to see them more clearly during the last year of living with this mighty family who believed so strongly in themselves and their destiny that others believed in it, too. My parents and Sister had fallen under the Sangs' spell yet had never known exactly what had captivated them. To imitate them, they had opted for clothes, manners, Society, and displays of wealth. But these people could also be poor, uneducated, and stupid like anyone else, as some of the relatives in this house were. My family had never understood that it was all-consuming pride, arrogance, and self-righteousness that kept the Sang family in their exalted place rather than merit. I had sworn I would be the last girl of my family. This would be the end of Ma's and Sister's dreams, of Ba's and Grandfather's weakness, the end of our family.

I kept my eyes closed; the flickering light from the candles washed a strange redness over my closed eyelids, which danced unnaturally in my eyes. I never saw you.

As I said before, "You now need to go into the backstreets and find a peasant couple. A couple who'll need a child to take care of them in old age. Give them the baby and don't tell them whose it was. When the family asks, tell them I had a stillborn son, which was very bloody and had to be taken away immediately."

"We may never find her again," Yan interrupted me.

"Yes, I know. Tell the peasants she is unwanted and unloved."

Yan interrupted again, "But you must try—"

"Shut up!" I screamed. You cried then and I screamed louder so I could not hear you. I wanted no memories of you. "Stop saying that. It is better she is with someone who needs a daughter." I calmed myself a little but I could still hear you. "Quickly, go to the top drawer in my dresser and you'll find some jewelry in a red velvet bag. Give it to them so they can sell it. Please, go."

She hesitated to leave the room and remained at the foot of the bed. When I remember this night, I realize Yan waited, giving me a chance to change my mind and the course of my life: not to pursue those years of bitterness and anger that followed. I could not recognize in her silence the invitation for me to turn back. I remember shouting at her, snarling for her to move. I would have slapped her and pushed her away if I had not been in so much pain. She stood there for a few seconds longer. I ordered her to put a small silk cloth in your mouth to stop your crying and wrap you up in some of the soiled sheets, as if you were laundry; no Sang would touch laundry. I heard her do this then take the jewelry and leave. The door closed quietly behind you.

I was alone. I opened my eyes and saw the red-brown of blood and shit from your birth spread across the sheet between my legs. It was smeared on my inner thighs and legs, and as I looked at myself, in pain, I felt no connection to my own body, as though it was simply something to be cleaned and put away, to be used later. I sat back and breathed in the aftermath of childbirth, using the stench to block out any trace of you that might linger and fix you in my memory.

Xiong Fa had not yet come back to the house but First Wife had sent Ah Cheuk to fetch him. By the time he returned, First Wife knew what had happened and immediately told him that his son had died at birth. The loss of a son would be unbearable to them all but they were practical and would move on.

When Yan returned I had passed out. I had contained the pain for so long that when I finally let it flood back, it overwhelmed me. She brought me around and I fully expected her to resume her duties and bathe me. Yet at first she did not help me move, only looked me hard in the eye. She took in my cracked lips and ragged hair, damp with sweat. She looked down at my body and the foul state of the sheets. She was so direct in her expression that for a moment I accepted her re-proof and did not react. Then her hold on me was broken and our usual relationship was restored. I demanded that she help me move and then clean me.

I had been lying in one position so long that my muscles had cramped. I could not remember what I had done in the hours that had passed since she left on her errand. I knew I could not have moved at all, because my muscles had seized up, but I could not remember what I had been thinking or seeing. I was only angry.

Yan massaged my legs so that I could move but still she would not speak to me, and the only words that passed between us were to tell me of Xiong Fa's request to see me. In reply I told Yan to tell him he could come and see me sometime the following day, but he had to make an appointment first.

Yan bathed me and changed the sheets. Blood enough for First Wife here, but no heir. She would demand that Xiong Fa make me pregnant again, but I had learned now that I held the power. An heir was still needed. Until then the promise of the Sang future remained unfulfilled, and First Wife's duty to Father-in-law still unobserved. I had decided to blame the supposed death of this baby on her attack on me in Tailor Street: such ferocious behavior had clearly brought bad luck on the heir and caused him to suffer during the pregnancy and delivery. And now he had died.

I woke up late in the day to find Yan sitting by my bed watching me. Her skin hung loosely from her face and her eyes were raw and bloodshot. When she saw me open my eyes she got up.

"You need some soup. I'll be back soon," she whispered, so quietly it was as if raising her voice would confirm the truth of what we had done during the night. Perhaps until Xiong Fa came we could live our lie and pretend I had not asked her to betray her own unfulfilled maternal instincts. I lay still and pulled the sheet around me. I could still smell the blood and shit that Yan had wiped from me. I ached and was desperately tired yet I wanted to wait here for her return, so we could understand each other and settle how we would continue living together after this. I remained lying on my back with my eyes closed. In the blackness, the strong smells filled my nostrils and mouth, reminding me of the dark that had filled me last night as I lay back against the bed with my eyes closed, as Yan held you tight in her arms, and I tried to mask your new smell with my own stink. I had not dreamt it, everything was true.

Yan came in and brought me a bowl of strong fish soup to accelerate my recovery. She put the tray on the bedside chair and helped me sit up straight. She brought the bowl to my lips and the fish stock cleared my nose and mind. I sipped, and coughed. Then my hunger returned and I swallowed the soup quickly.

"I also brought you some *mantou*. You should try to eat more, to be strong again." Having left the steamed buns on the bed for me, she started to leave again. "Mistress, you should sleep. I think I should ask them to bring you a doctor."

"No," I shouted, "no doctors!"

She stopped and looked at me, startled mostly that I had suddenly regained my strength.

"I'm sorry, Yan. No, doctors, please. I don't want any doctors because they cannot help. Just sit near me, please, sit near me. But first tell my husband that I will come to see him on the third day. Tell him that I will come at eleven in the morning to drink tea with him."

"But he will be at work with his father."

"If he wants to see me then he will have to be late to work or return home."

"Very well. I will also draw you a bath tomorrow," Yan said heartily, encouraged by my willingness to visit my husband.

"Yes, that will be good."

She left me with the smell of the steaming bread to tempt my appetite. I closed my eyes and thought of the huge flat bamboo baskets that the cook used to stack up on the oven in the kitchen of my old home. I would sit with Grandfather and wait for them to be ready. And just as they were done, and smelling so warm, Ba would appear from his study, and the three of us would eat the buns with thick sauce. The cook would pour it into a bowl for us to dip in our torn pieces of bread. The little pieces of white bread would slowly soak up the thick brown-red liquid. When each piece had become completely saturated with sauce, and there was no white left, we would place it in the center of our tongues and our mouths would fill with the hot bread and salty chili flavors.

When I awoke, the bread was gone and Yan had lit a few candles in the room and was ready to bring me more soup, but first I needed to piss.

"Yan, please help me up. I need the chamber pot."

I had not stood up since last night and she had to pull me from the bed. With my arm hoisted over her shoulder, she dragged me up and I shifted my weight toward the mirror. In front of it I let the blanket fall from me and looked at my body for the first time since giving you life. My stomach was sagging and I had been bleeding; there were lines of dried blood down my thighs. Yan had tied padding to me where I had split and torn myself, wrapping it thickly around my waist and between my legs. The pain was deep and still very intense; as I moved I felt I was ripping myself open again. She brought in the pot and took the padding off me. I looked again at my waist, hips, and thighs, soft white skin surrounding a mound of slack flesh and blood. I looked as though I had been ripped from something, rather than something from me. Yet I felt whole; one mind and one body. I did not think of the second body that should have been cradled next to mine.

Yan came up behind me and placed her hands gently on my shoulders to lower me onto the pot. As the piss flowed, it burned me and I bit into my lip. When I'd finished, Yan put back the padding between my legs and secured it around my waist.

"Yan, when you take the pot out, please empty it immediately," I instructed.

"But, mistress, both the doctor and the fortune-teller downstairs have asked to see this."

"I know." I fell back into bed and pulled the blanket around myself. Facing the wall, I followed the rough outline of my shadow on the wall cast by the candles Yan had lit.

"They are all downstairs. All waiting, desperate to blame me, to tell Xiong Fa to get a second wife," I murmured, watching the flickering lights throw multiple versions of my silhouette onto the wall, lending my body different shapes and layers. "Don't let them see . . . empty it out of the window at the end of the landing."

I closed my eyes to sleep.

"Mistress, I'll wake you tomorrow for a bath. We'll clean you up properly then."

"No, Yan. Please come back in a minute. I want you to tell me again about your husband and your garden. I'm tired and want to sleep, but I want to hear your voice and the stories of your home. I'm sorry for everything I have asked you to do, but it was necessary."

I heard Yan leave, the patter of her footsteps down the corridor, and then she stood still. I heard liquid hit the courtyard below and her footsteps returning. She quietly opened the door and slipped inside then sat down on the chair beside my bed. I heard her talking as I drifted away.

Maybe an hour had passed since I had fallen asleep; there was a knock at the door and Yan went to answer it. She told the servant they were too late, everything had already been thrown away. How many must have waited with Xiong Fa, his father, and First Wife? Other members of the family coming up to its three most prominent elders, offering false sympathy while relishing their pain and upset. I imagined Xiong Fa, his Western trousers and shirt covered by a long traditional silk robe, and his father wearing full traditional clothes, his stomach pushing tight against the sash. Father-in-law's face would show little emotion as usual, just narrow eyes beneath bushy gray eyebrows, made narrower still by the swell of cheeks and jowls below. His silver hair was always slicked back tight against his scalp. I would never see beyond this unchanging facade and, unlike all the other women in the household, I would not try. Xiong Fa would be sitting next to his father, but he would not be still. I imagined him getting out of his seat and walking up and down the room, speaking to the doctor and the fortune-teller about what might happen next. Whether there would ever be a son? Men and more men. What Xiong Fa needed was an heir. I would have to provide one in time.

I thought of Bi then, my imagination racing through a hundred little moments we had shared on the riverbank or walking alone together in the gardens. Watching the shadows I returned to a moment we had spent, lying side by side on our backs, under the huge willow tree by the riverbank, staring up into its branches. They fell to the ground around us like a canopy bed and I tried to trace their origins back to the trunk as they crisscrossed each other. I turned my head to look at Bi and after a few seconds he must have heard my breathing, or maybe sensed my gaze, and met my eyes. We were holding hands for the first time. It had started tentatively with his fingers finding the backs of my hands and following my knuckles down to the fingertips. I had never before had someone caress me, even in this most tentative way. His fingers crept into mine as I opened them wider, and once they were entwined I immediately squeezed them tight, binding us together. I thought then we would never be broken apart. When we met each other's eyes a few moments later, we both looked down at our fingers and slowly smiled. Together we looked into the water, watching it run endlessly past.

The images faded and I opened my eyes to see the shadows on the wall flickering restlessly.

In the morning Yan woke me for a bath. She had brought enough water for two and had ordered the male servants from the lower quarters to bring up two tubs. Within a few minutes of my sitting in the first tub, the water turned red with the clotted blood and after some scrubbing Yan helped me move to the second, in which she bathed me properly and applied oils and lotions.

I felt hollow; everything around me had no substance, only colors and shapes. It was as if with your birth all my organs had been ripped from me as well, leaving a shell. I felt nothing but an emptiness that I knew I would eventually need to fill.

After three days of rest, Xiong Fa came to visit me. He knocked quietly and opened the door slowly. He moved carefully across the room though he barely managed to get a few steps away from the open door. Yan was sitting next to me and on seeing Xiong Fa enter she stood up and started to excuse herself.

"Yan, sit down again. I am very pleased that you have looked after Feng during this difficult time. Feng, I am sorry that we lost our first child, I wanted this very much."

He stood at the corner of the bed uneasily. I watched him fumble his words and look around the room avoiding me.

"I . . . I . . . I hope you can get better soon. I think it would have been fine if . . ."

Whatever he was to say he stopped himself. He looked at Yan and then his eyes rushed from her past me and to the wall behind me.

"I will see you when you are ready. Rest and become healthy again."

For nearly four weeks I slept. Sleep punctuated only by meals and reading, I remained in my room letting the hours and days rock slowly forward like an ancient riverboat propelled by a single oarsman. I listened at the window to the world outside. Only a year ago, before I was pregnant, I had longed to visit it but now it had lost all excitement and color for me.

I remembered what Ming had said to me, that First Wife needed to give her husband a grandson and she could never rest until it had happened. Ming understood everything, I wished I could see her again. I had only met her briefly and not seen her since that dance a year ago. I heard she was traveling with her husband, working to further his career in politics and business. I had learned also that she was an exception: educated and confident, a woman with her own opinions and ideas. Many of the older women, like First Wife, hated her because she threatened everything that underpinned their existence. As she had advised, I read whatever books I could find though they meant little to me then. I seemed to exist only in the narrow spaces between the strokes and characters, the columns and the rows, a life with no form, substance, or meaning. Surrounded by all three, I could grasp none for myself.

I had excused myself from family meals by claiming that I was very weak after losing the baby and needed time to recover. First Wife had sent a doctor to check me but he knew nothing and simply agreed with me, telling Father-in-law, First Wife, and Xiong Fa that if I were to try again then I would need rest. So it was, day after day, until one morning Yan rushed into my room. It was just before half past ten and I was still in bed.

"Mistress! I have just received a note from master's servant, that ugly Ah Cheuk, saying that your parents will be coming tomorrow," she announced.

I did not move, looking at the ceiling—an unending white. I no longer felt anything.

"What do they want?"

"I don't know, but it will do you good to see them again."

"When will they come?"

I did not want to see them. What did they want to see me for? What could they have to say?

"They will come at ten o'clock in the morning. Ah Cheuk gave me this letter from Master Xiong Fa."

She passed me a sheet of paper. The letter was short, saying merely that my parents had requested to see me after hearing I had lost my son. Xiong Fa finished by saying he thought it was a good idea as it might aid my recovery.

"Thank you, Yan." I gave her back the note. "I will go back to sleep, you can leave me."

She waited for a moment, surprised by my coldness, then turned and left me.

I returned to lying on my back and closed my eyes. I saw Xiong Fa, his bulk heavy above me, his hips brushing and rubbing against my thighs. In the blackness I felt his ugliness trying to penetrate me, control and hurt me. I looked up and saw his face, contorted and red, felt his sweat drip on my face. I rubbed my face hard but it remained wet. Nothing seemed to dry my cheeks, his disgusting sweat continued to stain them.

I woke up suddenly, finding my face covered in tears. I pulled the sheet up to it and dried my eyes.

I had nothing to say to my parents. I must see them out of politeness, but this would be the last time.

In the morning I woke up in time to be bathed and then dressed by Yan and two young maids. I lay in the bath in the center of my room and looked out of the window into the clouds. The sun streamed in and warmed my shoulders and face. I hadn't decided what I would wear. I thought about meeting Ba again and what he would say to me. The last time I had seen him was the final night of the wedding when I was still his little daughter. He had held my hand tight as we parted and now I knew why. He had been anxious for me. He had known what awaited me, and though he would do nothing, he understood, as all men must, what would happen to me after that night. I thought of his face and was sad that he had loved me but failed me, like Grandfather.

I didn't think of you; just of myself. I refused to think of you.

I thought of Ma and how I would feel when I saw her. She had sent me here assuming that like Sister I would be happy at our success of joining this family and all that I, and she, would gain once I was married. She would expect me to repay my debt to her for arranging this marriage by ensuring she was welcomed into these social circles. I could find nothing inside myself but hatred for her. I would never give her what she felt she was owed but I also wanted her to know that it would always be out of her reach and that all her work and sacrifice was for nothing.

I decided to wear my most expensive cheongsam, with my most beautiful shawl over it. Everything must be perfect; there would be no flaws. I wanted to see her beg for what she really wanted, what she had fought for and used us to obtain.

At ten o'clock I sat like a dutiful daughter, waiting on one of the chairs lining the main hallway. They arrived at five minutes past ten. Ba was dressed in a Western suit with a fedora and Ma in a new cheongsam she must have acquired since I had left. The silk was dull, the colors bright but with no depth, and the embroidery loose. It was poor quality. They stood in the doorway and looked over at me, then, marveling, up at the ceiling three floors above.

"Xiao Feng, you look lovely . . . so grown up," my father said as he walked toward me. "We heard that you had lost your son. Have you recovered properly?"

He came close to me as if to take my hand but hesitated, perhaps reminding himself that I was married now and he could not be so presumptuous. He looked healthy and his eyes had regained some of the brightness they had had before Sister had fallen ill. Ma looked older still, having never recovered from the death of her beloved eldest child and the anxiety and disgust that had haunted her from having to rely on me to save her reputation.

"Yes, Ba, I feel much better now. I was very tired but feel much stronger just seeing both you and Ma. Yan will show us to a room where we can have tea," I told them.

She led us to the room where I had been forced to stand prior to the wedding, where First and Second Wife had come to prod and sneer at me, and where Yan herself had first cared for me. Shortly after the ceremony, chairs and tables had been placed in here so the room could serve as a place to meet guests on a formal basis.

We sat down, my parents next to each other and I opposite, a table with a tea set on it between us.

"You have been very lucky. This house is magnificent," Ma began.

"Yes, I have."

She looked around the room but was quickly distracted by the beauty of the scrolls that had impressed me nearly two years earlier, even while I stood here and cried.

"I hope that you often pray in thanks to your sister, for what she gave up," Ma continued.

Never.

I said nothing in reply.

We sat opposite each other in silence. Ba sipped his tea and smiled at me, his legs crossed at the knees and his back held straight against the antique chair carved with its images of cranes at a lakeside.

"I think it would be proper for you to suggest we visit you both for dinner. You were supposed to visit us after the wedding, but you never did and that was very disrespectful," Ma remarked pointedly.

"I'm sorry that we did not come."

I do not need to apologize to you.

"How is your health?" Ba asked. "Xiong Fa told me he was very worried."

"I am well, Ba. It was bad for me at first and then I was so very tired but now I feel much better. Yan has helped me so much." I looked over at her standing by the door, and smiled. My father followed the direction of my gaze and smiled warmly at her, too.

"How is Grandfather?"

"He is not well. Has not been well since that day . . . but he told me to say hello to you."

Hello is never enough from one you love.

"Feng, please make sure that you tell your father-in-law and husband that we must come for dinner. Will you do this?" Ma asked, more insistently.

"I will try."

"Try is not good enough! It is through my efforts you have made this great marriage."

"Thank you, Ma. But I can only try. We are just women, aren't we?"

"If you do not do this—show proper respect for me and your father—then I will not speak to you again."

A promise that should be kept, I decided.

"I will try," I said, assuming meekness.

"You *will* do this. You are my daughter."

"Xiao Feng, please do this for your mother," Ba interrupted.

To me, she was my mother no longer.

"I will try."

"Don't keep saying that! All these things are mine . . . I mean, they were meant for your sister," she corrected herself quickly.

Ba sat quietly next to her. He sipped his tea and looked past me into the distance. He barely moved, as if I or another member of the Sang family would have to give him permission first.

"We were told that you lost your son, that he died at birth." Ma looked at me hard and directly. "I knew you did not understand what living in this type of family would mean. Your sister understood. She understood the sacrifice and that everything must be done properly and prepared correctly. She would have done all that was necessary to have a son and fulfill her duties."

She kept her eyes fixed on me, as she used to do when she was commanding my obedience. Her fierce stare did not make me afraid anymore. It was she who did not know what being a Sang meant. And never would.

"Yes, I did lose a son. Ma, Sister is dead she will not be having any sons or daughters. Perhaps one day I will try again." I sat with my back, neck, and chin held high and straight, as imperious as I could make myself. I thought of Ming then and her poise and sophistication—so far above Ma, with her meager wisdom and endless ambition. I lifted my cup to my lips and sipped lightly, my lips feeling the heat as the liquid touched them. I thought of whether I would ever want to try again and I felt nothing but revulsion at the idea.

Ba still had not moved except to cross his legs.

Ma leaned back, satisfied I would do her bidding.

We sat in silence for several minutes. Then Ba spoke up.

"You look beautiful, Feng Feng. You have become a woman."

I smiled at him.

"Thank you, Ba."

Ma looked at the floor and then around the room.

"Feng, to me you're not a woman until you fulfill your obligations to your family and show proper respect to your mother," she said sourly. "We have given everything to ensure this marriage was achieved. Now you must give us the proper face in return."

"Wasn't this for Sister?" I asked. "You never intended me to marry."

"It does not matter which of you eventually married!" Her voice raised, she looked me full in the face.

Silence again. Ma's face was heavily lined and her mouth bitter and downturned. She had put on more makeup than usual and it sat heavily on her skin, making it appear waxy and lifeless.

"It's time for you both to go. I have a lunch appointment," I said, lying.

I stood up and Ba followed me quickly. Ma stood up slowly, looking at me all the time as she did, reminding me that more still was expected of me.

There was nothing more for her here; the only thing she would now gain from my marriage was the knowledge I had taken away what she wanted most.

Yan opened the door to the room and we walked out into the great hallway. As we crossed it to the front door, Ba paused and spoke the last words he would say to me.

"Feng Feng, you must have a glorious life here . . . just like an empress." His watery smile was quickly lost against the vastness of the hall. "Let us know when you are to have another child."

Ma and Ba continued to the front door. The doorman opened it and with a last look at each other they left. I stood and watched the door close then turned and went back to my room, dismissing Yan.

I sat at my dressing table. I removed my jewelry and makeup. I looked at myself in the mirror and saw how, in my self-belief, I had transformed myself from my mother's timid daughter to a member of this family. I thought I had understood what Ming had said that first night, what it was to have married from one family into another, to be swallowed whole. I was a Sang, and now I would learn to take all that was mine.

I was fooling myself.

Chapter 12

More weeks passed. They all left me alone. Then, one afternoon, Ah Cheuk arrived with a request from Xiong Fa. My husband wanted to see me.

As I walked across the landing, I could see fifteen or so relatives below, watching me. Ah Cheuk had obviously shown the message to other servants before coming to me. They stood silently in the hall. I looked up and could see others hanging from the balustrades enclosing the landings of the floors above. Eyes were bulging and necks craned to see me.

Yan and I walked slowly to Xiong Fa's room and Yan knocked. Xiong Fa himself opened the door. He stood to one side to allow me to enter.

"Come in." His eyes followed me. "You look like you have recovered. I was very worried." He paused. "What was wrong with our son?" he asked eventually.

"It was no son, it was stillborn." I did not bother to soften my words. I wanted to hurt him, always.

"A terrible thing. We lost a little man. What did he look like?"

"Does it matter? We can try again soon." I had been looking at the selection of food he had ordered. "You do want to try again, don't you? Or do you want to find someone else?"

He looked lost for a minute.

"Yes, I want a son . . . or a daughter. I would like a child." He moved toward me then stopped. "Let's eat. I ordered you some soup, it is what you should eat to strengthen yourself. You must still be very tired."

We started to eat and after a few minutes' silence, I said, "I would like to go back to that hotel we visited when I first came here. It had all those beautiful women, dancing and having tea." I made my request without any pretense at shame while tasting the soup, which was delicious.

Xiong Fa seemed shocked. He did not respond but slowly picked up food with his chopsticks—beef, cabbage, dumplings—and put it in his bowl. He ate slowly, pausing after every few mouthfuls. Occasionally he would look up at me but we ate in silence for the next ten minutes.

"After such a terrible thing, why do you want to go back to the tea dance?" he said finally.

"Because I want to learn to dance, to look beautiful, and meet people again. Weren't those the best people in town?"

"Yes, they are from some of the most important and notable families in this city, some very influential people," he agreed, putting down his chopsticks and leaning back in his chair, "but why do you want to go? Shouldn't you be resting?"

"I want you to take me out. I have been in this house for the last eight months and I want to see people and enjoy life in this city with you." I realized that at that moment, it was the only thing that mattered to me, and it should be mine.

I would fill myself with something more than food and tea. I wanted to take what Ma and Sister had longed for so much. I would fill my emptiness as they had wanted to fill theirs. I would take what had been theirs but was now mine, and I would consume it all.

"I want to live as my sister would have done," I stated.

Xiong Fa looked at me seriously then he shook his head and smiled sadly.

"You want to become like your sister? Is that all you can think about after what just happened to you?" The smile slid from his face and his eyes narrowed to dark slits, like his father's. "Are you certain?"

"It will become me. Yes, I want to be the wife your father wanted for you."

"Wait, I never said anything about what my father wanted."

"That is who you were going to marry." I looked up from eating. "But I will be better than my sister."

"Well then, we'll buy you new clothes and go out to dance." He breathed in sharply. "But I'm surprised you want this."

I watched him through my eyelashes. He noticed and his eyes slid away from mine.

"My parents want us to try for another child as soon as we can." He got up from the table and came around to me, brushing my cheek with the side of his index finger. "Tomorrow we'll buy clothes and all the other things you want. Now I must go to work. I'll see you at dinner tonight."

I looked up at him.

"Don't worry, we'll have another child. I am sure we will give the family a strong heir," he reassured me.

Fool.

"I'm sure we will, and I'll respect all that you say . . . but never forget that it was your mother who hit me and caused me to lose your son."

He said nothing to that but took his jacket from a hanger on the back of the door and left with Ah Cheuk, who had come to escort him back to his car.

I remained sitting and glanced around me. I realized that this place no longer terrified me. It was just a room full of wooden furniture and a few ornaments, all arranged neatly and simply. I looked down at the half-finished bowl of fish soup, which was still warm. I brought the bowl to my face and the warmth fanned my cheeks. I drank the rest and returned the bowl to the table. The soup was enough for me. I stood up to look more closely at the objects in the room.

There was a small glass cabinet standing in the corner of the room adjacent to the main door. It held many little glass bottles of different colors—the prettiest things in the room. They seemed strange things for a man to have, out of place with everything except the toy train. Three or four bottles were placed on the top of the cabinet, within easy reach of anybody's hands. I bent down and looked closely at one of the bottles, a three-sided yellow one with a tiny silver cap and a beautiful dragon climbing down from the heavens fired onto each side. I could see the distorted outline of the photograph hanging behind it when I looked through it. The picture was of Xiong Fa being held by his mother as a baby. Through the glass, the image of mother and child was tinted with yellow. They looked sick and ghostly, as if captured inside it.

I picked up the bottle by its little cap and held it in front of my right eye, closing my left. I looked at the photo again. Mother and son floated at the bottle's center. They were not captured but protected, safely locked away. I let the bottle drop to the floor. It broke into many little pieces, some of which I trod on. Without knocking, Ah Cheuk came rushing into the room. He looked at me angrily and knelt down by my feet to look at the damage and started to pick up the pieces.

I stepped back and watched him hungrily collect the tiniest pieces, cutting himself as he did so. Yan arrived some minutes later and, seeing Ah Cheuk at work, looked at me and gave me that sad half-smile that told me she was worried for me.

"It was an accident," I said. "I'll go back to my room." We walked out, Yan first, and I said to her, "I will be rejoining the family for dinner tonight. Tomorrow we are going shopping."

As we passed back across the landings overlooking the main

hallway below, I saw that some of the family members were still standing there, waiting to see what had happened between Xiong Fa and me. Perhaps they thought I would soon become First Wife of two wives.

During the weeks and months that followed, I became the woman you knew. With each day that passed I further indulged myself acquiring all the things that Ma and Sister had longed to have. The prizes they had been denied. I had asked to buy dresses and the day after my lunch with my husband, Ah Cheuk appeared at the door to my apartment to inform me that Xiong Fa was waiting in the car below to take me shopping. Yan led me downstairs to where the car stood waiting at the side entrance to the main building. The compound, for that is what it really was, had a grand front entrance, which gave onto the main street, while at the back was the entrance to the court-yard. Here were the servants' quarters and working rooms. On the right-hand side of the largest building, which contained the main hallway and our sleeping apartments, was a driveway that could accommodate several cars; Xiong Fa's was parked there.

The driver opened the car door for me and I saw my husband sitting inside.

"So do you know what you are going to buy? I'll bet you have no idea," he said in an indulgent voice.

"I'll find something," I said as I climbed in.

"Well, if you're anything like your sister, I believe you will."

Once I was seated he signaled to the driver to leave.

As before, the curtains to the car were drawn across the windows but I wanted to see out so I pulled one curtain back.

"I hope you remember our conversation?" Xiong Fa lowered his voice, sounding serious. I didn't bother to turn around. "You can do nearly everything you want but please be respectful."

I said nothing but sat back at my leisure watching the city

pass by. Everything looked strange to me; it was no longer so important or interesting. I felt disconnected from the streets and the people I used to walk among with Grandfather. I turned to Xiong Fa.

"Where are we going?"

"We are going to the best tailor in Shanghai. A man who once made the Empress Dowager's clothes," he said proudly.

"My grandfather said she was a very ugly woman," I replied forthrightly.

"Yes, I believe she was. In fact, I think that was the main cause of the Revolution. But she wore wonderful clothes!" He laughed, and for the first time I laughed with him.

I returned to looking out of the window and realized we were on the road where I had last seen Grandfather. I stared out of the car window for a few minutes to see if he might be visible but there were just street people selling food. There were beggars and peasants walking slowly along the side of the road, hoping to find a job or be thrown some money. Shortly after that the car arrived outside a small shop and out came a tiny man with a long beard and mustache. This was not Tailor Street but somewhere very exclusive. Xiong Fa got out of the car and the old man greeted him by grabbing his hand in both of his own and shaking it vigorously. The driver opened my car door and I entered the shop.

The interior was beautiful. The famous painter Qi Baishi had given the tailor two great works, which hung between the shelves of cloth. Inside, belying its appearance, the shop was large enough to hold forty people. The floor was tiled with black and white marble, but apart from the shelves, the paintings, a large clean window at the front, and four mannequins, the shop contained only a huge worktable in the middle of the room.

The old man stood me before him and walked around me.

He looked at my eyes and felt my arms as First and Second Wife had once done. He checked my legs, ankles, and feet and measured my neck. Then he paced slowly around the shop, looking at various cloths and back at me. Suddenly he started pulling bolts of silk from the shelves and throwing them onto the worktable, causing them to unravel as they landed. Then, once he had finished making his selection, he instructed one of his assistants to take each fabric in turn and hold it against me, while he stood back to observe me and make some notes.

He then presented me with pictures of various cheongsams and a few Western designs, and explained that Xiong Fa had already asked and paid him to make these for me. He asked me whether I had any comments but I was so overwhelmed that I had nothing to say, only nodded my agreement. I was the center of it all for only the second time in my life.

These clothes were but a few of the many that I bought over the following months and years. Once I became known in the shops as an important customer, Yan and I would go out in the afternoons and visit many different tailors and dressmakers, to look at new silks and embroidery. I would go to the most skilled people in Shanghai and they would wait on me, and I learned that I liked to be waited on. I passed my time being served by everyone around me. I could ask for anything, confident I would receive it. Soon I became accustomed to this service and expected it. I arranged my days and nights around pleasing myself. Day would often merge into night, with long hours spent eating eighteen-course banquets accompanied by music, performances, and dancing.

Memories I had cherished so dearly dimmed in my mind, their sharpness drowned in the unending round of pointless activity and idle gossip. The beautiful quiet of my childhood had been interrupted forever, and like most people I did not even notice its absence until it was too late. I learned to talk, eat, chatter, and, most seductive of all, found that I loved to be the center of attention. At the time I could sense the trap that Ma had laid for Sister but it was only now that I could see how delicious and irresistible it was. That Sister could have been no other creature than the one Ma had created, for who could refuse the lure of so much adulation?

Xiong Fa and I were now regularly seen at tea dances and joined a group of friends who organized banquets and magnificent meals for each other. They would be hosted at ballrooms in hotels like the great Cathay Hotel, with its strange European decoration of white walls, gilded trimmings, and mirrors. Sometimes almost a week would pass without my having to attend a family dinner. Xiong Fa was very happy that I had started to use Western makeup, and with my new clothes and haircut I finally became the woman I knew his father had wanted for his son. Even though the old man openly expressed his disapproval of my new appearance, when he saw me enter the room at family meals, wearing more fitted clothes that outlined my body and highlighted my legs, breasts, and neck in a way that traditional Chinese dress did not do, his stare betrayed his feigned scowls and repugnance.

Xiong Fa found me irresistible and would insist on staying nearby whenever we were out. At a New Year's Eve party to ring in 1936, I felt him place his hands roughly on me from behind and instinctively pull me tight against his groin but this time in return I very slightly pushed my hips back against him.

"Is it you?" I asked, not turning my head.

"Why?" he stuttered. "Who else would it be?"

I wanted him to worry and feel anxious. In appearance I was now striking and immediately the center of attention, and the feeling was something I learned to love. But inside I was filled with hatred. I wanted to hurt Xiong Fa, but women have so little power. What did I have in my armory? I had started with nothing. But now, it seemed, I had something.

"I don't know," I answered Xiong Fa and looked over my shoulder to smile at him, his fat face pressed against my neck. I could feel that he was slightly erect. "Husband, I would like to do something for you," I said.

"What?" he murmured against my hair.

"I would like us to host a party. Perhaps we can have it here, at the Cathay Hotel?" I said slowly. I looked hard into his eyes and saw his pupils dilate as he studied my cheeks, mouth, and lips.

"Yes, we should do this. I've never hosted a party," he replied softly.

Just then the New Year chimed and everyone shouted, screamed, and kissed each other. I turned around but continued holding Xiong Fa's hand. We looked at each other and then I slowly pulled my hand away, letting my fingertips trail down his hand and fingers until we were no longer touching. Xiong Fa watched my fingers and then looked up into my eyes, plainly wanting me there and then. I wandered into the crowd, threatening to disappear from his sight, but he came after me. The other guests mingled and drank, people cheering each other and singing old songs. I slithered between them and could sense Xiong Fa stalking me, weaving his way between the guests as I led him on. We went out of the ballroom and into the cavernous foyer. I reached the entrance and he made a grab for me; his strong muscular fingers held my wrist and prevented me from leaving. It was very different this time, though. He was doing exactly as I wanted.

"Please call my car!" Xiong Fa shouted. The foyer seemed to be empty and his words echoed unanswered. I pulled myself free and waited beside him for the bell boy to appear.

Once inside the car, he kissed me and I let him. His hands slipped up my legs and around to my thighs and I let him. We continued like this until we arrived back at the house then Yan met me and took me back to my apartment. Xiong Fa stood alone in the entrance hall, erect beneath his trousers as he watched me go upstairs. He would visit me soon, I knew.

"Did you have a good evening, mistress?" Yan asked politely.

"Yes, it was beautiful. *Xin Nian Dao Kuai Le*, Happy New Year. Master Xiong Fa will be visiting me soon," I replied.

"He will, because you look very beautiful tonight. He won't be able to resist coming to visit you," she said softly.

"I know," I told her and walked past her into my room.

I went to my dressing table. The window stood open. A sharp evening breeze was starting to blow through the shutters and Yan went over to close them. As she did she looked out into the night sky and sighed.

"Mistress, do you really want him to visit you? We could tell him you are ill and cannot see him."

I started to brush my hair, studying my reflection.

"I don't like to see you so hurt," she whispered.

Yan looked around at me. Standing by the long window, which reached to the ceiling, perhaps fifteen feet high, she seemed small and frail. Her face had lines on it I had not noticed before. I had done this.

"Please do not shout at me, but I do not want to have to help heal you from so many bruises and cuts as I did before. It makes me frightened."

Her eyes became watery.

"I very much loved my husband but he went to war and in the end I lost him," she said, putting a finger to her eye to remove a tear, then she shook her head and turned away from me to the window again. "I must be tired, that is all. I will be outside, mistress, if you need me. I will be waiting for your call, as always."

I watched her walk toward the door.

"Yan, please come here," I said gently.

She changed direction and stood behind me. I looked at her in the mirror. She looked back at me, confident that our relationship was different from any other between mistress and maid in the household.

"I know you are looking after me and are worried about me," I said. "It is difficult to tell you how important you are to me. I have survived because of you and you have only ever tried to make me see good sense. But tonight you needn't worry."

She bit the inside of her lower lip as if trying to stop it from quivering.

"You should not hear what happens tonight," I told her. "Please do not wait outside but go and sleep."

"I will try, but be careful. He's a big man and very strong."

"I will be. Now, you should go."

She turned and left the room quietly. I heard her stand by the closed door, deciding whether she should remain outside or not. After a few seconds, I heard her footsteps recede down the corridor.

Xiong Fa would still be another ten minutes or so. He would have another drink and would get changed into his robes. Maybe he would play with himself first to get himself aroused as he had done many times before in front of me. Ah Cheuk would then arrive at the apartment and lead him here. He would not appear to notice if Xiong Fa was already aroused, his erection beginning to strain his robe, as his job was only to follow orders and rules. He had learned that to his cost years before.

This evening I would not be lying naked in my bed, waiting for Xiong Fa. I would be sitting here, in front of my dressing table. I had decided to greet my husband as a reflection in the mirror.

I heard the old servant knock and my door opened. I had only left one candle burning, next to me. From the little light cast by it my husband could see my face and neck, but my shoulders and breasts remained in darkness. I looked up at him and smiled, my lips layered with rouge. I could see his face and body in the shadows behind me. He was already hard and I could see he wanted me immediately. The first words would be mine.

"You want me?" I asked slowly, curling my words into each other.

"Yes, I found you irresistible this evening. You looked beautiful. I saw that all the men were looking at you." He paused and looked long into the mirror at my lips. "They wanted you, but I have you."

"Yes, you do," I whispered.

I stood up and walked toward to him. I did not want to look at his body or feel it close to mine, yet more than anything I wanted control over him. I wanted him to hear and feel me. To know I had a will of my own.

I would start with all that I had: his desire for me.

I made certain that as I stood up he could see in the mirror I was not wearing anything beneath my robe. The distance between my dressing table and where he stood was about twenty feet. I walked slowly and he watched me, his eyes filled with me, and I could see him think of all the things he was about to do to me. When I reached him, I brought my hands up to the lapels of his robe and pulled it apart, slipping it from his shoulders. He stood naked before me. Taking his hand, I led him to my bed. As we reached it he tried to bend me over and enter me from behind. For a few seconds, I remained bent as he had pushed me, but moved my hips a little to make it difficult for him. He grunted and slapped my buttocks hard but I ignored him and climbed forward into the bed. I turned and sat with my back against the wall, legs apart, showing him what he desired so much. He looked at me, staring at my hair and flesh. He looked up into my face.

"Move onto your back in the middle of the bed," he demanded.

"What do you want from me?" I shot back at him, but still enticingly.

He stepped back, shocked by my aggression. Resting one knee on the edge of the bed, he leaned in between my legs.

His breath smelled stronger than in the car earlier; he must have had two or three glasses of rice wine in his apartment. I stayed still and he leaned in a little farther, his head and large body becoming a black silhouette in front of me, ringed by the warm yellow glow cast by the single candle. He pushed his face out of the darkness into mine so that the milky yellow whites of his eyes and his dilated pupils filled my vision. We remained still for a moment then slowly I brought up my hand to touch his face. But he grabbed my wrist and pushed my arm back against my chest. He was now kneeling between my ankles, one hand on the mattress supporting his weight while the other was wrapped tight around my wrist. He inched himself up to kneel between my thighs and placed both hands on my shoulders, sliding me down from against the wall to lie on my back. He lunged forward and tried to enter me then but instead of fighting him I moved my hips a fraction, making it almost impossible for him to enter me.

"I want you, too," I whispered in his ear. His head was now directly above me, his arms to either side of my shoulders. "I want you inside me, husband."

He grunted and thrust forward but did not penetrate me, only slid against my thigh and the mattress beneath.

"Come on," I whispered, encouraging more of him, demanding it. He had buried his head against the mattress and I looked over at the dressing table on my left. The light was dim but I could just see my brush, pot of rouge, and a comb that Yan had given me.

He continued to try to enter me but I clenched my muscles and moved my hips into subtly awkward angles, so that in his drunkenness he found it difficult to slide himself inside me.

"Are you my husband? Why don't you want me? You should have me," I teased softly.

He could not see what I was doing, fooled by his own lust and belief in his right to have me.

He grunted in return and pulled himself onto his hands with his arms outstretched, so that he was directly above me. But it was too late. I felt his hardness fail him.

I stared up at him and let my body go limp underneath his.

"What has happened?" I asked, feigning innocence. "You wanted me when you came in but now you have stopped."

He looked at me and I followed the yellow light from the candle as it outlined the right side of his face. Drops of sweat rolled down his fat cheeks. He blinked hard and then lifted himself from on top of me, climbed off the bed, and stood naked beside it. Between his legs I could see he was soft and shriveled, his hair matted with the sweat and stickiness that he had spilled on the mattress and down his legs. He said nothing but bent down and picked up his robe.

He looked at me angrily and put on the robe. Then he grabbed my left leg at the thigh, pressing his fingers into my flesh, and then angrily jabbed them up inside me. I gasped and saw him watching as I did. I froze for a moment and fear started to take hold, but I pushed it down, buried it deep inside so it rested in the place where I had sealed my memories.

I breathed in and looked up into his face. In the yellow glow he looked like a demon sent to take me, but I continued to look at him. I moved my hand down to his wrist between my legs and, taking hold of it, slowly pulled his hand away and his fingers from inside me. He didn't resist. I held his hand above my waist and our two hands hung together in the air for a few seconds until I felt his gently start to pull away from my grip and I let it go.

I had not finished.

I knew he could not help but look at me. I arched my back briefly, pushing up my breasts and nipples. In return he breathed in deeply through his nostrils and exhaled hard, his chest rising heavily.

"We will try again tomorrow," I continued to whisper.

"Yes."

I looked at him, silently telling him, *You will never have me again unless I let you. Do you understand?*

But I do not think he could read my eyes.

Then he turned and left me. I heard the door close and turned over on my side to face the wall. Again I watched the candlelight trace my silhouette. My body had returned to its old familiar lines from before the birth, yet it was new to me. I seemed to have flesh and limbs I had not known I possessed but had suddenly discovered.

Over the next four weeks he came to me once a week and received variations of the same treatment, ending in the same humiliation.

Chapter 13

"Mistress, you seem much happier with Master Xiong Fa?" Yan asked me one day.

We were standing in the interior courtyard at the back of the house between huge sheets of white cotton that had been washed and left hanging to dry across the courtyard. Yan and I stood in the middle walled in by bright white. It was here that Xiong Fa had argued with his mother.

"Yes, it is better. If I tried for another heir in a few months, would it be too soon?"

She looked at me hard but did not say anything.

The stone flags of the interior courtyard were huge slabs of gray unpolished granite, forced tight together; over the years, the water dripping from the laundry had still managed to find its way into the narrow cracks between them. In one place, where the crack between the stones was wide enough, the shoots of a flower had burst through. It was only very small at that time but I recognized its leaves and perhaps the beginnings of a flower, *Rehmannia elata*, a sight that Grandfather would have greeted with a smile as one would an old friend returning from a long journey. With a little care it might blossom into pretty tubular pink flowers, but it was a long way from home. I remembered Grandfather telling me it was normally a mountain flower. Maybe that was why it felt secure between these harsh stones.

Yan joined me in looking down at the fragile sight. The sun was overhead and light bounced from the sheets, brightening the courtyard. The flower provided the only speck of color.

"Should I pick this for you, mistress?"

"No, no, we should leave it here. One day it may grow so mighty that it will dislodge this stone," I joked.

"Perhaps it will bring this building down?"

I looked at Yan and smiled and she gave me a wide smile back.

"Would you like some congee, mistress?"

"Can you tell me another story of your husband?" I asked like a child.

"I think I have told you all of them, many times. But I can tell them again." Her eyes searched my face for encouragement.

"I always like to hear them."

I knelt down and touched the little flower while she spoke. No one else had noticed it. It must have bloomed very recently and the busy servants, running around maintaining the Sang household, probably only ever looked down when they were being scolded or sweeping the floor. I was the only member of the family to come here unless someone had a special reason to inspect the laundry hanging out to dry, like First Wife had. I decided I would come back and see how this little flower grew, whether it would survive this house or not. As I knelt down, Ah Meng, the head of the laundry, walked past.

"Aiii, mistress, mistress, you should not be down here. It's very dirty," he said urgently, hopping from one slippered foot to the other. He was a young man still, though older than me, and eager to show everybody that he was competent at his work. He was short and bony, but with a long thin nose above his long thin neck. His eyes were small. He was unusual-looking; maybe he was from the west, where I heard there were many different kinds of Chinese people.

"I'm quite happy here, Ah Meng."

"Shhh!" He sucked his teeth. "This is no place for you. What are you doing?"

"I've just noticed this little flower." I pointed to it.

"Wah! Oh, no, I will get rid of it . . ." He reached down to pull it out.

"No," I shouted, and he froze in mid-action.

"But, mistress, it makes the courtyard unclean."

If I had been a bird above us I would have seen the house, a huge stone building with an interior courtyard at the rear, surrounded by low gray-brick buildings for the servants to work in. There would be squares of brilliant white running diagonally across the courtyard and, roughly in the center, three people bending over a pink flower. It would have looked magical in a place so cold and bitter.

"Please just leave it, let it grow for me," I asked him.

"I will, mistress."

"If anyone, even Big Father Sang, says anything . . ." that was what the servants called him and the laundryman was surprised to hear me use this term, " . . . please tell me before you are forced to remove it. I would like to keep it."

"You can take it now," he said enthusiastically.

"No, it is too small at the moment, it has barely started to grow," I told him confidently.

"You know about flowers?"

Yan watched me proudly while I explained, "Yes, I learned some things before I came to live here."

"Good, eh? Very good." He looked at Yan and nodded. "You have a smart mistress."

She nodded in reply.

"You should go and see Lao Tung, the gardener. He knows

much. Lots of ancient knowledge we can never share." He winked at us both.

"Perhaps I will, but for now I will return to my room to have some congee," I finished.

Ah Meng continued to the laundry area and Yan took me back to my apartment where I sat gazing out of the window at swifts gathering in huge flocks above the houses opposite. The flocks must have been made up of several thousand birds. They looped and dived in a single huge mass yet never bumped into each other, never caused each other harm, and none of them ever seemed to race ahead in a bid to take the lead. The wheeling and soaring of the flock suddenly reminded me of sitting with Grandfather under the big trees in the gardens one day. During the very windy weather, when the branches would be violently shaken and all the thousands of leaves would stir up and down, rustling against each other to create waves of sound, it felt like the garden was calling us, urging us to leap up into the turbulent air and forget ourselves, simply be carried away as they were.

Chapter 14

My nighttime encounters with Xiong Fa continued, sometimes twice a week and sometimes not at all. I teased and mocked him and occasionally suffered the consequences of his humiliation. He did not beat me but tried to violate me as he had done on so many other nights before. His fingers, though, were familiar to me; I knew their movements, their angry reactions, but I wanted to torment him further.

Each night we were together I played my games, better and better, growing more confident with each turn. Watching his humiliation made me feel stronger and more powerful.

Yet I began to see he had no real appetite for abuse. His limbs and mouth repeated the same actions again and again, which I realized were learned from generations of Sang men, from somewhere not of his making. After a while, I found he would stop and look at me and at himself, his groin, or else look away entirely. Then his face would burn and he would scowl at me, but always leave.

Perhaps I was not torturing my jailer but another prisoner. He could not be provoked any further and so I simply started to refuse him my bed, which, to my surprise, he accepted. And finally he ceased coming to me.

We spoke very little during this time. It was nearly five months after Yan and I had seen the flower growing through the crack in the courtyard that we had a full conversation.

Xiong Fa suddenly came into my room one evening, still wearing his office suit. He found me just wearing my *du dou* and reading in bed and sat down in the chair beside me. He was already a little drunk.

He sat down heavily, tired from a busy day at the office, and stared down at his feet and then across at my breasts and up the line of my neck to my lips and eyes.

"My family wants an heir. It is time we tried again. Properly. Will you do this?" he asked me very directly, his voice not commanding but explaining that the need for an heir was pure fact and we must now oblige.

"Yes, I would like to try again. I would like to be a mother," I replied. But I was already your mother: an unknown daughter left to sink among the mass of the poor in the vast unknown countryside.

"But you must do everything as it should be done this time. Will you do that?" Xiong Fa asked, his tone uncertain.

I had remained staring up at the ceiling but at this question I turned to look at him. I saw he had pursed his lips and was looking at my waist and hips, still faintly visible through the sheet.

"I must do it my way." Once I had his full attention, I continued. "I did everything your family requested last time and we lost the child. It died because of your family's foolishness."

I turned my head away from him sharply and looked at the ceiling again.

"I am sorry . . ." He continued speaking, apologizing for his family's crudeness, but I was not listening.

". . . just make sure that if it happens again, if you are having a baby, that Yan looks after you. She knows what to do," my husband finished.

"I don't want any Chinese medicine," I told him. "I want the doctors that the foreign people have. The doctors with the big bags." I sat up and let the sheet slide away from my breasts.

My husband looked down and swallowed.

"Why? Master Ding has been our doctor and fortune-teller for nearly two generations. He was my bonesetter when I broke my arm cycling when I was six years old." He shook his head and I watched his jowls tremble. "No, Father will never agree to this."

"But you *do* want an heir?" I asked, making it clear this was a condition.

"Yes! Yes, of course I must have children . . . I want lots of them. There are many empty rooms in this house." He smiled at me like an overgrown schoolboy. "Okay, but you must also follow what Yan tells you."

"Yes, I will."

He smiled at my acquiescence.

"We will go dancing tomorrow and then we will try!" He paused before asking me, "And you will make sure we have boys, won't you?"

"Oh, yes," I replied, bemused.

He got up and walked across the room to the window, opening one of the shutters. He stared out into the darkness. There were fires in some of the streets and lights in the rooms of the surrounding houses.

"All those people living out there," his voice was muffled as he spoke, "and soon we will add one more boy . . . maybe more. They will all be born with a fortune and into a well-known, powerful family. They will not be so unlucky and poor as all those others out there."

I listened, studying his chubby shoulders and the back of his head. He was so happy. Your father was happy that night. I had never seen or heard him like this before. He sounded like Grandfather talking to himself about the flowers and the seasons.

He pulled his head inside and saw the pink flower standing in its pot on the windowsill.

"That is pretty. Where did you find it?"

He was too excited to wait for me to tell him that it had been growing unobserved under the noses of his family all this time.

"But what about a daughter as well?" he was saying. "A pretty little girl. That would be very good. Yes, it would be something! A boy could play with my trains . . . I have many of them. But with a little girl, we could walk in those gardens you mentioned a long time ago. My parents want boys, heirs, because it is traditional, but I would like a daughter. It would be good, wouldn't it?"

He touched a petal of the pink flower and it quivered slightly under his large finger.

He stood in the center of the room, resolutely straightened his jacket as if readying himself to make a formal declaration, smiled, and said good-bye to me. Until tomorrow.

I wanted to scream after him then. Tell him he already had a daughter. Tell him that he and his family had killed you. They had sent you out into the world, to suffer, to work and barely to survive among all the poor and unlucky ones. He should know what he had done; what he had caused. They should all know.

But I had realized, over these last few months of taunting Xiong Fa, that he alone was not responsible.

One evening, at a dinner for thirty people, I sat next to Ming again. We had not seen each other since that first tea dance and she looked at me curiously, trying to decide who it was that she recognized under the makeup and hair styling.

"Is that you, Feng? The shy little girl who married into that crazy Sang family." I remembered her bluntness, which I now found refreshing rather than frightening, as I had then.

"Yes, it is. How are you and where have you been?" I asked with a wry smile as I knew how much I had changed and that she would find it fascinating.

"I've been living in Beijing and just returned, thankfully. But what about you? You look beautiful but where is that shy little girl, the one who blushed so readily?"

"Alas, she grew up," I responded ruefully.

"She truly did," Ming declared to everyone around us, none of whom knew either of us.

"So tell me what has happened? Old man Sang still eating the same food? I guess you learned how to use rouge." She leaned forward, her beautiful dark eyes teasing me. "Managed to give them an heir yet?"

Instinctively I paused for a moment and noticed her smile faded a little. Perhaps she could see my secret because she had a secret of her own.

"Did you lose one?" she asked quietly.

I did not know how to answer. She noticed.

"It's all right. It happens more often than we would ever speak about. It's terribly, terribly sad and you want to cry forever and no man understands . . . to them it is just a thing to be replaced with a new one." It was her turn to pause. "Maybe they're right, we Chinese have seen so many killed and lost so many children that we think them replaceable. Traveling in northern China, up to Beijing, I saw how many Chinese people there are in the world, and I saw how many are lost. We don't want to understand why so many die, why there are so many starving children, we just want to live for ourselves, swallowing all the bitterness and ignoring it."

We were both quiet for a while after that.

"Anyway, what have you got in store?" she asked me brightly after a while.

"We're planning to have another child. And," I said, slightly less confidently, "Xiong Fa and I are considering throwing a party. I've wanted to do this for a while."

"Aiii, you *have* grown up!"

We laughed loudly together.

"Good, but where will you host it?" she continued.

"I don't know. Where do you think? Xiong Fa would like it to be in our family dining room," I said gloomily.

Ming pulled a face and then smiled for both of us. She was so very beautiful. I couldn't stop looking at her long lashes. Under them, her guileless eyes met mine, shining with perfect confidence. Her skin was supple and soft yet remained taut, revealing the most perfect of cheekbones. But it was her natural grace that I marveled at the most; it was not simply a matter of the perfect posture like Ma had drilled into Sister, more the easy way with which she was able to win over anyone she spoke to. Hers was the grace that Sister and Ma had never even known existed: they would have realized the folly of their work if they had. Her movements were not forced and learned through repetition; she moved as naturally and easily as the air, and when she spoke her voice was a delight.

"Now you don't want to be serving your guests chicken soaked in rice wine or Jin Hua ham, do you? Although it *would* make your father-in-law extremely pleased. Will it be just a banquet or will there be dancing as well?"

"Well, since I last saw you I have learned to dance so we should have dancing," I decided. "And as Xiong Fa wants his heir, it may be the last dance I have for a while."

"So they're in a hurry. Who's pushing the hardest—First Wife or your father-in-law?" She pursed her lips slightly and her eyebrows furrowed. Without waiting for me to respond, she carried on, "It's always the women—they are more bothered about the continuation of the family name than they are about the actual family. My own sister has given away a daughter already, but only to our cousin who could not have children of his own with his wife."

I was surprised by her admission and showed it.

"You are shocked by this," she said carefully, as if trying to gauge the depth of my feelings on the subject, "but it happens often. I know it is never spoken about because it is often the mothers who make the decision. We all prefer our sons to our daughters, and I think we always will."

I thought of you at that moment. Had you become one of the starving children Ming had seen on her travels? I would not recognize you if you were in front of me, holding out your hands to beg me for food. It is said that a mother can always recognize her child, but I would have recognized nothing about you. Your face, your eyes, your smell . . . all were unknown to me. I felt my face burn and my eyes fill, but I could not cry.

"Is anything wrong?" Ming asked with some concern.

It's nothing. It's nothing. It's nothing, I told myself, and smiled sweetly at her.

"Just worrying about my party."

"We should decide where it will be held. What about a hotel? I think the Cathay Hotel." Ming traced her finger around the edge of her tea cup and looked at the leaves. "As we Chinese are not allowed to take rooms in many other hotels and the Cathay Hotel is the best anyway, you should go there. But it must be a huge banquet with wonderful dancing. You should spend the Sang family money on something useful for a change. A glorious meal with beautiful clothes and people! No hairy, clumsy foreigners with their large bodies."

"Do you know many foreigners?" I whispered to her. I narrowed my eyes and smiled up at her provocatively. "Do you like them?"

"Me?" She laughed back. "They are too hairy . . . like those monkeys on the streets, playing for coins, with their beards, hairy lips, and big red noses. But I have heard they are also like monkeys in other ways." She winked at me and smiled.

"No, we won't invite any foreigners. I don't think Xiong Fa

knows any, apart from those he meets through business. I'll speak to him about the guest list but it'll be all the usual families. We've agreed that we'll use the excuse of my father-in-law's birthday to have it. What do you think? Does it sound exciting enough?" I was quite anxious as I really had little idea about such events.

"Yes, yes," she laughed, throwing her head back to reveal her long elegant neck and broad pale shoulders, "it's best to have a perfectly worthy reason to throw a party—and then do your best to ignore it completely! What could be better than celebrating the old man's birthday by taking him to a wonderful hotel, serving him three plates of Jin Hua ham brought from home . . . and then getting him to pay for it and completely forgetting about him?" She leaned back in her chair and put her hand to her breast, her chest heaving with mirth. She smiled at me, eyes bold but warm, and I blushed in return. I was envious of and in love with everything she was. The other women around us stared and frowned. I'm certain they were envious, too. This was the woman Ma had wanted Sister to be, but it had been impossible for her to become such a luscious creature for they are born from Nature, not created solely by a mother's relentless guiding hand.

For the rest of the evening, Ming and the new me she had returned to find became old friends. I had found someone in her who would never know my secret but who understood my life down to the last rule and obligation—and still believed in the possibility of rising above them and finding fun and enjoyment in the least likely places. She brought me some much-needed warmth and light when I was most in need of it.

After Ming's reaction to my new appearance I became possessed with the idea that my life had only now begun and that everything that went before should be disregarded. I would have another child, one I could raise to enjoy its exalted life and position. To be rightfully placed in it from the start, not beaten like tin into the necessary shape and polished to look shiny and bright.

I sat in front of my mirror thinking of the woman I had become. I was only just twenty-two, but sensed that I had already gone far beyond Ma and Sister, to a place they had never even known existed. I wanted another child to continue this life.

Xiong Fa was coming to me regularly now. He did not spend much time with me, just enough to complete what was necessary. He did not dress to see me and we were polite to each other. His servant would announce that he was coming to my room and I would have fifteen minutes to undress and lie naked on my bed. I did not feel exposed or vulnerable anymore, I simply felt I was doing what I wanted. He would arrive in a plain red robe, no longer feeling any need to observe tradition and superstition with images and lucky figures. After placing his robe on the chair by the bed, in which I had sat bleeding after his first visit to me, he would slide between my legs. Sucking my breasts and playing with himself, he would enter me. Sometimes he would take ten or fifteen minutes and would try to make me enjoy it, too, but I did not like him inside me at all, I felt nothing. It could never be what Ming called *making love*, which sounded tender and for each other's pleasure.

After a while Yan decided that it was not necessary to remain outside my door and would retire to her bed in the servants' dormitory. Once Xiong Fa had finished he would leave and I would remain still for half an hour, as Yan believed this was the best way to conceive a child.

The continuance of this family was and would remain the most important thing.

Chapter 15

Family dinner remained exactly the same as it had always been except that First Wife had now accepted she could not bully me. She still sat next to Father-in-law, always on his left, but would not look at me or talk to me. Ignoring me was the only way she had left to save face. Second Wife also still sat at the head table but she had no voice now and had simply faded into unimportance along with the rest of the older family members. Xiong Fa sat on Father-in-law's right and although no one had managed to expand the menu, Father-in-law would at least talk animatedly to his eldest son nowadays. He would tell old stories, discuss business, and joke with him about old girlfriends and mistresses. There had not been any explanation given to me as to why Father-in-law suddenly enjoyed his eldest son's company; apparently everyone except me already knew.

It was Ming who explained it to me during the first of her visits to the house for lunch with me.

Xiong Fa had allowed me to use his room to entertain her and when Yan opened the door to her and she swept in, I was so happy. Ming sat and looked around the room. She saw the battered toy train and smiled.

"Is this Xiong Fa's room?" she asked cheerfully.

"Yes, he lets me use it but this is the first time I've entertained someone here."

"Well, I feel very honored." She continued looking around

for a while then fixed her eyes on me again, smiling. "Yes, the two of you are all we talk about. Your husband has changed so much." She could engage in gossip like anyone else, only she knew when to stop.

"How is that?" I asked, extremely curious.

"It goes back to when Xiong Fa was engaged to your sister. Everyone has always known that he works very hard for the family business—he is meticulous and thoughtful and now has been running more and more of the family concerns. We have always admired him for that, but in Society he was always very shy and sometimes your father-in-law would be so embarrassed by it that he would scold him in public. His parents would tell him everything he had to do, and I'm afraid he seemed a weak man then."

I remembered how he would come into our reception room at Ma and Ba's home, shifting from one foot to the other as he stood waiting for Sister, and how nervously he would squeeze and pump Ba's hand when he shook it. I smiled to myself as I remembered these things. He was quite funny sometimes.

"It gave the family no face at all. Then suddenly the match-maker found your sister, who would march into any dinner or dance as if it were for her, and while she was not well-liked she led Xiong Fa with her . . . mostly blindly, I'll admit it, my dear, but he had more confidence. In her shadow he learned to dance a little and have a drink with us." She stopped and, looking around, asked, "Oh, can we have some tea?"

"Yes, yes." I called to Yan, "Please can you bring some tea?" I hurried her out a little so Ming would continue.

"Your sister bullied him really but she made something of him and that was what your father-in-law wanted. He believed that she would change Xiong Fa into someone who would bring this family respect. Someone who might be commanding one day." Ming laughed at the thought, then sat up straight and smoothed her gloves. "Sorry, that was not very kind of me." She cleared her throat and added, "I think your father-in-law hoped that as Xiong Fa had begun then even though your sister died, just having a wife would allow him to continue growing. But with you, with you, my dear, things have been entirely different."

"Why . . . what have I done?" I was quick to inquire.

"Well, I don't know." She sat back and smiled, her hands resting in her lap. "But I think he has become more confident *without* being constantly bullied, and we all notice how he likes you to be with him. Suddenly there is an air of strength about the two of you. Xiong Fa was too sensitive, to be honest. He's the kind of person who has kept his toy train, for instance. Very different from most men, who would have thrown it away by now.

"You and I have got to understand each other so you know I'm not being rude, but we all thought he was too weak to survive in Society, too quiet, just doing whatever anyone else suggested. But suddenly he is telling us all what he thinks . . . deciding for himself. I wonder why that is."

She laughed, cocked her head to one side, and continued.

"Anyway, the older generations have noticed and good reports have got back to your father-in-law. Whatever you have done to him in the last few years, you have forced your husband out of his shell and your father-in-law is now firmly on your side. Imagine how he will react when you give them a child."

I wanted to cry out then. Why had I given you away? What had been the point? It had been revenge against a woman whom I would never see again, and another who was long dead. Xiong Fa had not chosen to treat me that way; he had been forced and pressured into it, as I had. I continued to smile at Ming as she sipped her tea. My lungs wanted to burst and scream. Where were you now? I smiled at my graceful friend and, replacing her cup, she smiled back. My eyes dropped to the tabletop. I looked at the stains on its surface, made from my many meals here with Xiong Fa—a reminder of our history, like the water stains left by the Sang family visit that rainy afternoon.

For a moment I could not bring myself to raise my head and look at Ming again for I felt I could not stand to see another person, another human being. I knew the horror that her face would reflect if she ever learned what I had done, and deep within me I knew that such a reaction was all I deserved. I felt sick and wanted to vomit but continued to look down, swallowing hard. I looked up at her and smiled, but my eyes watered and I felt Ming looking at me with concern.

"You don't look well. Maybe I should go?"

"No, no, it was just so surprising to hear all that."

"I'm sorry. These things mostly happened before you came so you wouldn't have known."

"Yes." I looked into my past again, thinking of my last sight of Grandfather talking to himself on the side of the road as he watched my wedding palanquin bump its way to this house. I changed the subject.

"We will hold the dinner at the Cathay Hotel as you suggested. Father-in-law is very excited. It has made everything very much easier to organize . . . well, apart from the food," I joked. "But I wanted to share something else with you." I hesitated before I told her: "I'm having another baby."

"That's wonderful," she said, looking happy for me. "Now your position in this family is assured." The smile disappeared from her face then and she seemed a little guilty. "I'm sorry for returning to the subject of family politics, it seems we can never get away from them, but that's very good news!"

"Yes. Yan knows, though I haven't told Xiong Fa yet. I intend to tonight. But first I wanted to tell you."

She squeezed my hand. Our conversation turned to other matters and after another hour or so Ming left me alone with Yan, but I had not stopped thinking of everything she had told me.

My maid started clearing the cups away.

"Yan, please sit down with me."

"Mistress, I think we should clean this before master returns from work."

"Just for a few minutes, please?" I looked up at her with tears in my eyes.

Yan sat down.

"Can we find her?" I burst out.

Yan stood up and came around the table to me. She stood next to me and took my hand as it rested on the table. She let me cry.

"Xiao Feng." I looked up at her for it was like my grandfather talking to me again. She wore that half-smile that was sad and concerned for me, but more than anything loving and caring. "You know it is not possible. If I could have done this I would have brought her back to you before now." She squeezed my hand. "If she is still alive, she will be more than two years old now and in that time could have gone anywhere."

I turned from the table and leant my forehead against Yan's waist while I continued crying. Yan stroked my hair as she had done before. Her black cotton clothes smelled of washing soap but under this scent was her own particular odor: the herbal mixture of her ointment; oil from the kitchen where she and many of the elder servants went to keep warm and eat bowls of hot noodles and dumplings. Filling my nostrils with this smell I knew so well made me feel safe and less sad. Perhaps if she could, then other people, too, would one day understand what I had asked her to do. If that were possible then perhaps I myself could one day understand why I had done it and be forgiven.

I sat up and looked into Yan's face. Over the past years, our relationship had become strong and unfailing. We did not argue; we knew each other's habits and behavior too well for that. She anticipated when I was going to do or say something that she thought was unwise, and I knew when she did not approve. We had learned that we did not need to explain this to each other. She gave me a reassuring smile and I saw her cracked yellow teeth, the lines in her face, which seemed to circle and circle but all end at the corners of her eyes, now shining brightly for she was crying, too.

"Feng Feng, we can do nothing now. Just pray to the gods that she is healthy and being looked after well," Yan whispered. She let go of my hand. "Master Sang will be returning soon, I must clean up."

I moved from sitting by the table to the more comfortable armchair where I intended to wait for him, but once alone I noticed that the onset of evening with the wintry air outside had made the room cold. I got up and went to the door to ask one of the servants on the landing to fetch from my room the blanket Yan had given me years ago. However, on opening the door I found Xiong Fa standing in front of me.

"Hello, you look very pale. What is it?" he asked.

"I'm cold, I was just about to ask for my blanket."

"I'll get it." He turned and went down the corridor and across to the other side of the floor, to my room. I watched him go, looking very purposeful. I sat waiting in the armchair again.

He returned within a few minutes and placed the blanket around me.

"Warmer?"

"Yes, thank you," I replied. I saw him go over to his toy train that Ming had moved and place it in its original position.

"I am pregnant again," I said abruptly.

"Really?" He spun around, his eyes ablaze. "I'm so happy. I did not think it was going to happen."

"And then what would you have done?" I said sharply.

He looked surprised but understood my suspicion.

"Well, I hadn't thought that far ahead," he replied vaguely. "How long have you known?"

"The Western-trained doctor I found wanted me to wait a little because of what happened last time," I lied, but he was in my service this time so I was safe. "And so it has been a few weeks." In fact I had no explanation for why I had waited; I think I had wanted to experience this time without anyone else's knowledge except Yan's. These were the first days of motherhood and they were mine. But I had told Ming and now it was only right that I tell my husband.

"Maybe we should cancel the dinner then. It could be safer."

"No, the dinner is important, to you and to your father. If it was canceled your family would lose face. Everything is booked and we should continue."

"Yes, you're right." His eyes moved from side to side, as if looking at imaginary objects, then he looked back at me and frowned. "But I'll be worried."

"The doctor will be attending me that night in case there is a problem." I could tell he wasn't convinced. "Please don't worry, I'll be careful. I want this child, too."

He smiled.

"I think I will have a nap before dinner." He had looked weary when he was standing in the doorway minutes ago. With this news and our discussion, his shoulders sagged and he looked limp with relief.

"You go to bed. I will go rest myself and see you at dinner," I said, suddenly feeling a trace of concern for my hardworking husband.

"Isn't it marvelous that we might have a child? I would so like to be a father." He was rambling a little in his need for sleep. "I will try to be the best of fathers. I see some foreign men and they put their children on their knees and bounce them around, singing to them. Do you think that is acceptable?"

"Yes, I think it would be fun. But what will you do if it is twins?" I joked with him.

"Well, I have two knees." He walked toward his bedroom door and stopped by my side, resting his hand on my shoulder.

"I will help you every step of the way . . . not like last time." He looked down at me. "I will never forgive myself for not being at your side then, but I knew no better." He shook his head in self-reproach.

He withdrew his hand, entered his bedroom, and closed the door behind him. I sat there for a few minutes and then went over to his toy train and touched the roof of the tiny driver's cabin. The toy was battered and chipped, yet Xiong Fa had told me that it could still be wound and, when track was laid for it, would cheerfully run along. It was a model of those engines that pulled trucks around, a big cylinder upfront and a cabin behind with four wheels below. The tank was painted red with thin black stripes around it and the cabin was red with a circular logo on both sides. The front had been particularly dented as if thrown against something and had been repainted with some much heavier and thicker paint than the original. I replaced it exactly as I had found it, though I felt certain Xiong Fa would notice something was amiss.

I went back to my room wrapped in my blanket and sat in the chair by my bed. Yan still brought me *wuxia* novels and comics and I sat for two hours reading. These stories had provided me with many fantasies that had helped me escape into my imagination, late at night or during those days that I chose to stay in my room. They had taken me to magical places like the maze of rocky columns in Kweilin where heroes would hide out in caves high in the air and fight battles against evil robber barons, the vast deserts and steppes near Mongolia where horsemen would rush each other to capture women and treasure, or the lush mountains of Kunlun where monks would contemplate the heavens and teach young princes how to rule fairly and justly. These stories now seemed so unreal and childish, they were bloodless and feeble compared to what my life had become. I had hidden in them once but it was impossible to hide from one's life forever. I suddenly felt that the consequences of all that I had done, all that I had been a part of, knowingly or otherwise, as an adult or as a child, would always follow me; I could not avoid them.

I put down the books forever.

Yan came in to find me sitting, wrapped up warmly in her blanket, looking at nothing in particular. I smiled as she came and sat on the stool in front of me.

"Mistress, are you going for the family dinner this evening?" she asked.

"Yes. Yes, I am going," I said assertively, with a smile. "I will wear the dark blue cheongsam, like the one Ming was wearing this afternoon, with a shawl."

"They will see you have a baby coming."

"Yes, and it's time." I got up and went to the dressing table and started to brush my hair. "Yan, please can you go to Xiong Fa and tell him that I would like him to come to my room and take me to dinner?"

My husband came to my room about five minutes before dinner was due to start. We entered the room about a minute late but exactly on time as everyone was waiting for Father-in-law, who was directly behind us. I had made myself look as beautiful as I could. Heads turned as we took our places, and as we did I noticed Father-in-law looking at my swollen stomach. After taking his own seat, he leant into Xiong Fa's shoulder, whispering, and Xiong Fa nodded in reply. Father-in-law stood up and told everyone to be quiet.

"As you know, I do not believe in interrupting meals and I don't like to speak so openly." Everything was silent but for the sound of people shuffling around to see him speak. "This year has been a great year for Xiong Fa . . ." I looked at my husband.

Did I love him the way Yan had described loving her husband, or as Grandfather and Grandmother had done? His father continued speaking and Xiong Fa looked up at him and smiled, then surprised me by turning and looking at me and openly taking my hand. " . . . He has started taking the lead in much of the business which keeps you all wealthy," Father-in-law needled them, "but he has also established himself in Society with his First Wife, Feng. He has just told me that Feng is pregnant again and I want everyone to toast them! Next month there is a family dinner with many invited guests and we will have more toasts to them when we are there." With that he finished and raised his cup of tea and everybody followed.

As Father-in-law sat down, he patted Xiong Fa on the back. Father-in-law muttered something to himself, smiled, and then launched into his food. I looked at First Wife, who was beaming wide smiles at her son and her husband. She even smiled at me. It was as Ming had said. After all the things we had done to each other . . . and I wondered how many more there would be. I asked myself again whether I loved my husband. What is love to us Chinese? Yet I felt all these bonds, forged by confrontation, kindness, and sympathy, had some meaning, and that I now wanted them in my life.

I would like to see if Xiong Fa would be a good father; if I could be a good mother; what choices we would make, together and separately. As I watched Father-in-law talk so volubly and repeatedly pat Xiong Fa proudly, I wondered how he and I would treat each other in the future, what it would be like when my husband was head of this family. I wondered, too, whether he would take other wives. But with each new question about the future, I always returned to thoughts of you.

Chapter 16

Shanghai *Society* had never experienced an event like the Sang dinner. Foreign lives and local lives were mostly separate, segregation existed in many areas of life no matter how wealthy and educated Chinese families had become. It was our country and our city but access was restricted. The Sang dinner required Western dress for the men but Chinese dress for the women. Father-in-law wanted to show the foreigners what we all knew, namely that we could be as sophisticated as they were, perhaps more so.

The guests arrived in their chauffeur-driven cars and were ushered into the main entrance of the Cathay Hotel. We had taken every room in the hotel so that no foreigners could be there; even foreign envoys had to be turned away and would cause no trouble by demanding that Chinese were prevented from using certain areas of the building—of course, this also impressed the guests. The menu included all sorts of foods, some that were rare animals, other ingredients that had been transported from Southeast Asia and Japan.

The ballroom had a traditional Chinese orchestra that would play when people entered and during the meal, and then afterward there was a Western-style band that would play music to which the younger guests could dance. The family, and particularly Xiong Fa, First Wife, and I had to be there at six o'clock as the first guests would arrive at half past. Three weeks before, I had gone to the tailor Xiong Fa had introduced me to, to have a dress made. It was a copy of one I had seen in a photo-magazine and I had taken the picture so he could copy it. It was black chiffon and had a train to it that trailed on the floor behind. I also had black soft leather gloves made to match and bought some heeled shoes, which were acquired especially for me. Xiong Fa had bought me a beautiful diamond necklace that he said was made in France, and for himself he had made a new evening suit and although your father would never be a handsome man, he was very smartly dressed and had come to look quite dignified. For the first time, Father-in-law wore a completely Western-styled evening suit. Normally he would wear a *ma qua* with trousers but this evening he wanted to show the foreigners that we Chinese could be as comfortable with their customs as we were with our own, which is why he required the dress code of all guests. First Wife wore a traditional cheongsam and as she had looked at my wedding, she wore too much makeup and was quite a terrible sight. The four of us waited in the hotel lobby area, which extended into the ballroom. We had arranged for drinks outside first for people to gather and then once a good number had arrived we would enter the ballroom and take our seats. My dress was a little tight and my stomach was conspicuous. Xiong Fa made me sit down until my standing was absolutely necessary.

The event could not have run more perfectly. I had purposely sat Ming next to First Wife; she would confuse First Wife completely and as we walked from the drinks reception through the huge foyer to the dining room, Ming took my arm to accompany me. As usual she was all things elegant, graceful, and beautiful and I couldn't take my eyes off her.

"You've done it. It's you that has pulled this family from the recesses of good social behavior and put them in their rightful place. There has never been such a gathering of old cronies and the younger generation with such style. Well done, you," she squeezed my arm and faked a growl, which was followed by a hearty laugh, "the room looks very classy, I'm so impressed."

"Oh, thank you, you're my best friend," I said this jokingly but it was true. "I didn't do very much. I just chose this place and arranged for both traditional and Western ideas, a Chinese orchestra for now and a dance band for later. You look gorgeous as always."

"You always say that," she squeezed my arm again, "but tell me about this necklace you're wearing. Who, what, and where?" she winked at me.

"It was from Xiong Fa." I blushed.

"Is this the first jewelry he has given you?"

"Well, yes, it is, he specially chose it for me." I blushed again.

"It's beautiful. Now let's see some old people and give them our respect, it keeps them alive."

The meal was a success with eighteen courses including some old favorites such as chicken soaked in rice wine, red-cooked pork belly, and, of course, tofu in Jin Hua ham. At the end of the dinner, many of the elder generation went straight home as usual but the younger guests stayed for more drinking and dancing. They knew nearly all the European dance styles and as I had decided it would be safer for the baby if I did not dance I sat on the side and watched with Ming.

"So when is the *birthday cake* for your father-in-law?" she asked, very straight-faced.

"What is a *birthday cake*?" I pronounced the foreign words awkwardly and not nearly as confidently as Ming but it was very amusing to hear.

"It's a foreign tradition," she explained, "a very dry dessert with lots of sugar. It is horrible and tasteless, just very sweet."

"Well, in the end he didn't want anything, just the party and the ham." We laughed and continued watching the dancing.

"It's marvelous how a well-pressed suit can make a man. I think Westerners have got at least a few things right." She laughed.

"Well, suits and dancing, that's two beautiful things," I said, "more than you would expect."

We watched the dancers on the floor and I wished I could join them. I knew I shouldn't but I couldn't help wanting just one dance and when Xiong Fa came up to me to ask how I was, I suggested we dance one song.

He reached out and I took his hand. The band was striking up a quickstep, which was popular, and the dance floor filled within seconds. Xiong Fa and I had danced this a few times but he had been drinking and the tail to my dress was making it awkward. We moved a few steps then I tripped and fell. I landed hard on my side and felt the floor against my ribs. I know I did not land on my front and the baby was safe but I felt concerned immediately. The people near me stopped dancing just as I hit the floor and by the time Xiong Fa and a few other men nearby had stooped to pick me up the band had already stopped.

Xiong Fa noticed I was clutching my left side as I stood up.

"Are you all right? You are holding yourself," he asked gently guiding me to a chair.

"I think so. It wasn't very clever of us was it? It was my fault." It was all I could say as my side felt sore. I sat down and Xiong Fa knelt in front of me.

"No, it wasn't, we should know better. I will fetch the doctor." He stood up and then turned to face the crowd and the band, then called out, "Everyone, it's fine, band, please continue, more music, everyone dance, drink more." Then he turned and walked out of the room to find the doctor. On their return the doctor did a check of the baby, feeling around my stomach.

"Is the baby fine, doctor? I'm very worried," I asked urgently.

"Yes, it seems good," he started pressing gently against my ribs, "but how does this feel?"

I flinched a little as he pushed.

"That is a very sharp pain indeed," I shot back.

"Well, it looks like you heavily bruised this area around your ribs. Let's go to your hotel room and you can rest, I can examine you properly," he calmly suggested while beckoning Xiong Fa to lift me to the standing position.

"Yes, yes but is the baby okay?"

"I see no bleeding and there are no other signs of any complications. You seem fine."

Yan and the doctor helped me to my suite on the first floor. The corridors of the hotel are long and winding and when I got to the room I was glad to remove my shoes and simply lie down. The doctor sat on the edge of the bed and felt each rib in turn. I squealed as he touched the lower two ribs on the left side.

"Yes, it is these two," the doctor confirmed. "Now I have a pain relief and I think you should rest here for the remainder of the evening."

"But I'll miss the rest of the party. It's important I'm there with Xiong Fa."

The doctor looked perplexed but he had got to know me well since Ming first introduced us.

"All right rest here first and if you still feel fine after twenty minutes or so then return but you sit down and no dancing or running around," he said with finality, "you hired me and so listen to me."

The doctor and Yan waited with me, then as I still felt fine, they led me downstairs and back to the ballroom. Xiong Fa was standing in the entrance, half-watching the party and half-waiting for me.

"Is she all right, doctor?"

"Yes, she's fine. You should find her a seat where you can both sit to watch but which doesn't require any kind of movement." The doctor was a little impatient with our insistence on continuing with the party. "I'll be waiting outside as before."

The party finished after another two hours and once I had said good-bye to the last of the guests, Yan helped me upstairs to my suite again. She undressed me, temporarily laying the dress over the bedside chair, and then put me to bed. In the dim light of the room, I watched her return to the dress and, picking it up, she hung it up on the outside of the huge wardrobe at the other end of the room, which was almost fifty feet long, near the entrance door, opposite the main bay window. Yan was careful with the dress but I wanted to be rid of it. I had wanted to be the most beautiful and elegant woman there but it had been a hideous thing that had tripped me and nearly injured the baby. Yan disappeared around the corner toward the door and I peered into the darkness and started to become very anxious that I had hurt the child. When she reappeared, she found me murmuring to myself as I was falling asleep, worrying about the baby. I felt her sit next to me and gently stroke my stomach and my hair.

Chapter 17

The winters in Shanghai are very cold and I remained huddled in my room next to the heater Lao Tung brought me. The days passed uneventfully and I made no effort to pursue any adventures in the city. I avoided First Wife, and occasionally Father-in-law would come to my room to ask me how I was or, more conveniently, send one of his servants to inquire. With the arrival of spring, Xiong Fa worked more and was given more responsibility; his work would keep him away all day and night so I rarely saw him. He had long ceased visiting me to use my body but would simply sit with me and drink tea. I had heard from Yan that some of the younger maids were trying to tempt him to come to their beds but he would not do that, or at least not yet but I suspected he would eventually give in as he had before. I had thought about whom he might choose as a second wife, suspecting it would be a young girl from a large and well-connected family. He was much more confident than before and would have much less trouble finding a new woman.

When April finally came I was very large and had become quite fat from eating so much. Yan would not stop bringing traditional food to make the baby stronger and healthier, which of course I had to eat before my own meals.

"A fat baby is a healthy baby," she would say to me.

The morning I gave birth I woke up feeling quite well but the pain came on me suddenly and my water broke. We were in my apartment and, seeing this, Yan held me up and took me to lie on the bed. She then sent for Xiong Fa and Ah Cheuk, who would fetch the Western-trained doctor. Xiong Fa came in first and stood over me.

"It will be all right this time. He will live and be a glorious head of this family. Strong and powerful," he burbled excitedly. "He will be clever and strong, won't he?"

"I hope so," I replied with much less confidence. "Please . . . can you make sure the doctor comes quickly? I need him." I had grown very attached to my new doctor, who had trained in Europe.

"Ah Cheuk has gone for him. He will be here soon." My husband took my hand.

"I feel like my stomach will burst!" I shouted.

This time I was not driven by a greater force, which would push me through the pain. I had no other desire than to see my child, no plan for hurt and revenge, and consequently felt every tear and stretch. It was as if this were my first child. I looked at Xiong Fa and did not know how we had suddenly fitted together; the last year we'd spent planning for this baby had seemed so easy and simple, yet looking at him now I wondered whether it had all been a lie. The past does not die like plants do, fertilizing the soil for new and possibly splendid successors to grow and thrive upon. It does not fade away, but can leave behind either wondrous towering monuments of beauty and love upon which over time we build our happiness, or else it scars and disfigures us, causing endless pain. But it is never nothing; it does not simply vanish, it is only hidden from us.

Yan rushed through the door with the doctor, who immediately suggested Xiong Fa leave. I was relieved, because every time I looked at him it reminded me of the lie I still let him believe. I watched him go reluctantly, concerned for my pain at the coming of his second child. He was anxious and called out encouragement to me as he left. He could be a good man, but I realized I could not think of him as my man, as Ming's husband had always seemed to her.

The doctor asked Yan to bring hot towels and water, and told me to push. I felt myself ripping, saw bloody towels, and smelled iron and shit again. But this time I was looking and there was a head, and then I felt such an intense pain I wanted to cry, and then there were feet . . . and then everything went quiet.

"What is it?" I shouted. I heard my baby cry.

"Is he all right?" I said urgently.

"Yes, yes, but I must look at him properly," the doctor responded flatly. I could hear Yan speaking softly and the doctor saying yes.

Yan appeared at my side with a wet towel and started drying and washing me. She applied pads to stop my bleeding and I looked up at her as she busied herself.

"Yan, what is it?" I said calmly, but still she did not look at me. "Yan, look at me and tell me what is going on?"

I felt a tear drop from her cheek onto my mouth and its saltiness between my lips.

"Yan!" I screamed.

"Mistress, it is good news . . . it is a boy."

"That is good." I breathed out and felt another tear hit me. "But why are you crying?"

"Mistress, something terrible has happened. The baby has a bad foot," she whispered to me in a low hoarse voice.

I struggled to sit up. The pain was intense and I was still bleeding. The doctor was holding up the baby, a little boy, and I could see that his right foot was shrunken and deformed. I did not care; it seemed such a little thing in comparison to the joy of seeing my second child.

"Dr. Pang, is he healthy? I can see there is something wrong with his foot. I know that. Apart from that, tell me, is he healthy?" I asked. Pang cradled him in his arms and stood looking down at his tiny head, shoulders, arms, and legs.

"He is healthy and strong, but his right foot has not grown properly," the doctor said almost apologetically. "Now you must rest because you've lost much blood. I'll bring the baby to you once the bleeding has stopped and you have the strength to hold him."

The doctor took him to the cradle we had brought into my apartment. Just as he put him down Xiong Fa came back into the room. He went straight to the baby, looked him over for a few seconds, then jumped back with a start. I knew, as did Yan and the doctor, that the senior members of the Sang family would not accept this child as their heir. He would not be considered capable of fulfilling that role, no matter what he may become and no matter how useless the rest of them may be; he might as well have been born a girl, in their eyes. But to me he was perfect. I watched Xiong Fa, who, after recoiling, looked around at me and saw the blood and shit on the mattress and that I was still bleeding, and turned back to our son.

"Doctor, wh-what happened?" he stammered.

"Master Sang, nothing happened."

"Then why . . . why is it like that?" my husband continued to stammer.

"Master Sang, we don't know why these things happen but they have done so since time began. There is nothing that can be done. He is otherwise healthy."

"I must go tell my parents." Xiong Fa walked quickly out of the room.

I was so tired Yan had to help me back into a lying position. I closed my eyes and saw that twisted and stunted little foot, like a large walnut with its creases and knots. But I did not care. This boy was mine. I lay still for a few minutes, then the door was pushed open so hard it slammed against the wall behind and Father-in-law marched straight up to the cradle with Second Wife. They peered inside. I could not hear what they said though I strained my neck trying to follow them.

"Yan, what did they say?" I asked her.

"Mistress, it is best that you wait until you are well before you talk to them."

"Yan," I shouted, "what are they saying? Please tell me?"

"They are saying that this child is no good. This child is not properly human. This child cannot be an heir." Yan started to cry very hard then, tears flooding from her eyes. "I cannot say anymore . . . please do not ask me."

I tried to take her arm but could not reach her. She could not hear my entreaties through her tears. "Yan, it doesn't mean anything. He's mine," I said to her urgently. Finally she bent closer to hear me. "He's *my* child." I was choking on my own tears and the after pain from the birth was intense. "I want this child!" I was nearly crying as well. "He is just fine as he is. It doesn't matter about the Sangs . . . I don't care."

I let her arm go and she stood up again and wiped away her tears with the side of her hand.

"Let them go and when I am better, please bring him to me." I could only speak very weakly now and once I had finished I closed my eyes and passed out.

When I awoke it was late morning and I found Yan sleeping in the chair beside my bed. I pulled myself into a sitting position against the head of the bed. I was very sore, tired, and ached terribly. I shook my maid awake.

"Yan, what happened? Please, can you get the baby for me to hold?" I asked her impatiently. She looked at me with bloodshot eyes. Her skin was pale and blotchy. Strands of hair had come loose from her bun and fallen across her face. She coughed, almost choking, sounding old and close to breaking down, then she straightened her hair before standing up and doing as I said. She jumped back when she saw the cradle and let out a shriek.

"Mistress, the baby's gone. He's gone!" she called out.

"What?"

"He's not in his cradle. Master must have taken him."

"What happened last night?" I shouted across the room. "Yan, tell me what happened last night after I passed out."

Yan told me that Father-in-law and Second Wife looked angry and disappointed when Xiong Fa had come to join them. Before any of them spoke Xiong Fa stood over the cradle and stared at his son. Father-in-law spoke up first and told his son that he had discussed the baby with First Wife and Second Wife, and they all agreed that this was not an acceptable heir.

"Ah Xiong, this baby should be given away, there is no point keeping it," Father-in-Law said bluntly.

Second Wife injected quickly, "If you were my son, I would tell you to take a second wife. A proper wife, one who will produce a proper heir. Not one that gives birth to dead babies and broken creatures like this thing!"

Yan said Xiong Fa was silent. He would not say anything, just looked into the cradle at the little boy. He remained silent for several minutes then he looked from the baby to his father and to Second Wife's ugly face.

"Father, I want to speak to you alone. Please tell Second Wife to leave," he asked flatly.

"I don't see why I should go," she snapped back.

Father-in-law looked at her and nodded for her to leave them. She snorted and left reluctantly.

"Father, I've not thought of giving this baby away. Whom would I give it to? Who would take it and look after it? We have enough in our family for this child. But more than that . . . he is my son." Xiong Fa paused but his father quickly took the lead.

"Xiong Fa, you have done well this year and last. You have become a strong man, well able to run the family business. But this is not right, not for an heir to the family, a son to whom you cannot pass on the business responsibility for the family. Get another wife who can give you and this family what it needs. This wife helped you. Still, she is not right for giving you a family. You must be sensible."

Yan told me that after they left, Xiong Fa remained watching over the baby until the tiny boy had fallen asleep, after which Xiong Fa gave him a kiss on the forehead and then left himself.

As Yan finished speaking the door opened and my husband came in with a nursemaid who was holding the baby. The child was wrapped in a white blanket with a dragon on it. I could only see his face, which was light pink with wisps of black hair projecting from the corner of the blanket above his head. His eyes were closed and he looked so fragile that I almost did not believe such a being could survive a night filled with such anger and hatred.

"Good morning," Xiong Fa said, looking directly at me. His fat face was smiling and his eyes were bright as water in sunlight. "I'm sorry I woke you but I wanted to take him out."

My heart beat hard.

"Why? Where did you take him to?" I asked impatiently.

"Oh, nowhere, just around the landing."

"Please can you bring him here? I have not seen him." I desperately wanted to hold him, just to feel his weight against mine and smell his sweetness.

Xiong Fa looked at the nursemaid and nodded. The nursemaid brought him over to me and put him in my arms. His eyes looked up at me and I saw they were not narrow slits like Xiong

Fa's but wide like mine. His stumpy little arms and tiny fingers flexed aimlessly, like a sea anemone, and I let him clutch the tip of my little finger in his hand.

"Will you be able to feed him?" I had not noticed that Xiong Fa had moved closer toward me and that he and Yan were standing watching me. Xiong Fa had not said anything about his conversation with his father but still I felt suspicious. Perhaps he was only fooling me, letting me have a few minutes with my son before taking him away. I could not bear to lose two children.

"Yes, I think I can feed him. Will you leave him here with me?" I asked.

"His cradle is here." Xiong Fa pouted his lips and raised his eyebrows as if to say, where else would he be going? "I'll leave you now but I'll come back with the doctor this afternoon and we can ask then about his foot. We should find out how this happened and what can be done."

"Have you chosen a name for him?" my husband then asked me.

The generation name had been chosen many years ago, so he would be Sang Lu, and then I would choose his first name.

"Not yet, I'll think about it."

"Well, think hard because we need it for the registration," Xiong Fa responded, finishing the conversation. He had moved forward and was now standing directly over us. He reached down, sticking out his index finger, and stroked the baby's cheek. He smiled again and then left the room with the nurse-maid following close behind.

I peeled back the blanket to look closely at my son's deformity; it was his right foot. The toes had not developed properly and the foot was small, mostly bone and skin. Again I felt nothing but sympathy and love. I stared hard at the foot, which looked more like a fist. Yet, when I looked around my room— at the dark lacquered woods; the bright clothes, made against

First Wife's wishes, hanging over the doors; the old chair next to my bed; the dresser; my brushes; my flower in its pot, close to blooming; the rug from Persia that Xiong Fa had bought me, stained now with my blood—this was a place where I could raise a child, because it was mine, and whether Xiong Fa's parents accepted him or not, in this room he would be safe and I realized how desperately I wanted him. I looked back at his lumped foot and cried. The tears hurt and after some minutes I suddenly felt so tired that I could barely continue to hold him.

He would grow into the brother you have now, strong and intelligent, exceeding all our expectations, especially Father-in-law's. I believe he inherited all that was best in me, for he was lucky, born when I thought most clearly and most selflessly. I've never stopped thinking about you. I'm guilty of stealing life from you and I feel this every day. I know these characters written on these rough empty cloths are not seeds embedded in fertile soil to grow and live, becoming something more than their insignificant beginning. They're sterile and unchanging, offering nothing more than tombstones to weep over. For no matter how often they are read, they can no more bring us together than leap from the page and reorder themselves to tell a different, happier story. I know you cannot ask me why and will want to know this more than anything, as I wanted to ask Ba and Ma. I know how pained and angry this will make you, but writing these words to you is all I am brave enough to do.

Chapter 18

The eleven years that passed while Sang Lu Meng grew up seemed to disappear so quickly. Xiong Fa became head of the family. Father-in-law's health began to fail five years after Lu Meng was born, but he lived long enough to be impressed by the little boy's bravery and tenacity. Second Wife died of a bad heart only a year after Lu Meng was born but her opinion had never carried any weight; in the end, she had been nothing but a phantom.

It did not matter to me anyway. Lu Meng would always be lame and always left behind as the People marched forward, but he would outlive his elders and see a new era dawn. The war and the Communist Revolution would try to destroy everything China had grown to be; the thick roots of tradition had become tough and impenetrable limbs, entwining and constraining everyone's lives, trapping them in time and binding them in place. The People, suffocating, suddenly exacted revenge on their history, ripping and slicing through these ancient and once-powerful bindings.

In this new world it would never again matter who the Sang heir was.

I proudly watched Lu Meng attend school and ready himself to enter university, to follow in his father's footsteps. He wanted to be a botanist though. First we lived together in my apartment, then when he got older he was put in a dormitory with other children of the family. I had tried to protect him from the outside world, requesting tutors come to the house to teach him, and during these classes, when he was no more than four or five years old, I would sit and watch him work. Sometimes I would pretend to read but listen to him instead practicing his Chinese, learning arithmetic, history, and geography. I knew it could not last and I dreaded the day I must let him experience the rest of life and let him go but the terror of the Japanese occupation was enough reason to continue keeping him close to me. The other children in the family teased and bullied him, for he was the first grandchild and yet most vulnerable. They would wait until their servants had left after putting them all to bed and then they would surround his bed and call him names: "cripple" and "animal." I could not do anything to protect Lu Meng; these were the offspring of other members of the family.

I was now officially First Wife, for Xiong Fa's mother was already bedridden when Lu Meng was born, and had died a slow death four years later. I was happy she was gone, though she had not interfered with my life since I had confronted her in Tailor Street. I knew she had whispered into Father-in-law's ear, telling him lies, any lies, until the day she died, her last erratic breaths of poison filling the air and evaporating into nothing. She knew no other way to live. But her husband had been proud and pleased of the position his son had attained in Society and his success with the family business. All this was worth more to him than anything his wives were able to give him—something she was not able to understand. I had been troublesome and chosen to live as one outside of the many, the other family members could not match my status and influence with Xiong Fa, but I could not match their numbers and conformity, so in the end I could not control Lu Meng's tormentors.

At night I would lie in bed and think of him looking up into the darkness of the high ceiling of the children's dormitory, faces crowding in on him, shouting and leering, while little fists punched. Heads constantly turned to look at his halting progress, eyes focused on his foot, and ugly smiles smeared across young lips and cheeks. I wanted to punch and kick them or their parents, but realized he must learn to fight them for himself. To help him, a *gong fu* master started to visit the house, to teach him fighting skills in the laundry courtyard. They all watched him learning, and as the months passed and he became competent and strong in basic skills, the elder members of the family were impressed, which made some of the younger ones sneer even more.

One day after dinner—I think he was about eleven years old—Lu Meng, Yan, and I were walking back to our apartment when he showed me the man he would become and of whom I would be very proud.

"Ma, will you come and watch me practice today?"

"Why today in particular?"

"Because today I will learn more *gong fu* fighting techniques. This is boxing with kicking. I've been telling you about it, remember?"

I had forgotten and was surprised. He noticed that.

"You needn't worry, Ma. My legs have grown stronger now and I can stand on my left leg and kick with my right. You should come and see."

Aside from his foot, he had grown into a healthy young boy. The *gong fu* had made him quite sinewy and wiry; he looked a bit like I imagined Grandfather must have done when young. His hair was thick like Ba's, but his lips were like his father's; they were full and very red and would easily bleed when he got into fights. In fact, each part of his body and face could easily be attributed to my or Xiong Fa's family, but his eyes were unique to Lu Meng. They were very light brown, and moved confidently yet slowly over the things around him. They were warm and welcoming, offering friendship and trust, and I hoped this was how they would remain.

He had been in fights but as he learned more *gong fu*, he won far more than he lost, sometimes taking on two or three others at a time. While his foot remained undeveloped and would ache acutely sometimes, I was always more concerned about his hands; he had such long and delicate fingers—like Ba's, thankfully, rather than Xiong Fa's sausage fingers. They looked so fragile that I worried they would break or snap off. Often when he was training and would be held in a grapple or lock, I would wince and want to cover my eyes.

"I will come and watch, but what is so special about today? You know I am always worried you will hurt yourself badly," I told him.

We walked on and he pushed himself forward to come and stand in front of me. He stood there and blocked Yan's and my progress so that we both stopped and looked down, surprised by the tenacity of our little boy.

"I know you worry, but please come."

"We will."

He moved out of the way and back to my side. We walked on. At that time I was nearly thirty-four years old and felt so tired sometimes that I simply wanted to sit quietly and just watch Lu Meng grow, peacefully watching a flower bloom. I wondered what he would do and where he would go.

Yan followed him to the dormitory, though he didn't need her help.

"I will see you in the courtyard," I called after him.

I went to my apartment and stood by the window, looking outside. The grayness and cold of the Shanghai winter made everything heavy and static; people were silent as they went about their lives, scuttling across streets and into shops and restaurants to find warmth. The landscape had changed as the city had grown, suffering the hardships of war and now suffering again as revolutionary groups started to foment trouble in distant parts of the country. The houses opposite had been knocked down and new buildings in hard and cold gray monolithic architectural designs constructed instead. The war had nearly cost this family everything. My pink flower from the laundry courtyard had died many years ago, but I had replaced it and then slowly added other plants to my room. In winter there were so few flowers, particularly after the Japanese had destroyed so much.

We had been lucky during the war. Our gardener Lao Tung had created a hothouse in the basement and knocked out one wall to let in the light; if the Japanese came we would cover up the opening so it was well-hidden. In this space he grew a few vegetables, but after the war I had asked him to grow flowers as well. I had decided that I would always keep a *Gardenia jasminoides* in my window. It is a little plant but with a big beautiful white flower that in full bloom seemed to fill my window and my room. Its strong scent would carry me back to the gardens and to Bi and, wrapped in its power, I would lose myself in fantasies of all I had missed. I would call whichever flower I kept with me "Grandfather," as it seemed to help me remember Bi as my grandfather had remembered Grandmother when we had walked together among the flowers and grass by the river. I had not seen my real grandfather or Ma and Ba again. I'd heard that Grandfather died just before hostilities broke out with the Japanese, and that Ma and Ba were both killed when their house was bombed. I looked at the hardy plant and pruned a couple of dead leaves; its petals were a faded pink, as if it were disappearing before my eyes.

I looked again at the buildings across the road, built after the Japanese had burned the previous ones with the occupants inside. These new buildings changed the landscape; they were Western without Westerners. The end of the war had seen the end of the restrictions commanding Chinese one way, Westerners the other. A few days ago I had walked the Bund with Lu Meng; it was the first time we had been there together, though it had been open for some time. I closed the window and went down to the laundry courtyard as my son had asked me.

When I arrived I found Lu Meng in the middle of the courtyard with his *gong fu* master standing silently behind him. He was talking to seven or eight of his cousins. Some of these boys had fought with him and teased him before now. He looked up and saw me leaning against one of the columns, smiled at me then moved awkwardly but quickly around and took each cousin by the shoulder to move them into regimental formation. Then he took the front and center position and started to show them stances and basic techniques. He called to them by name, encouraging them to learn the maneuver as Grandfather had once called out the names of flowers to me. Across the yard I saw Xiong Fa arrive quietly and watch his son lead by example.

I walked around to join my husband.

"Are you well?" I asked him.

He had suffered during the war; he'd had to use the family's reserves of wealth to pay off the Japanese, and had been badly beaten by the occupying forces on several occasions. He was only in his late forties but moved like an old man when he was very tired and it was cold. We had not been intimate together for many years but he never took a second wife despite his father's wishes. Once I was strong enough, I nursed Lu Meng myself and did not want Xiong Fa in my bed. It did not seem right that Xiong Fa be in my bed when I had been nursing Lu Meng moments before. After some months Xiong Fa stopped requesting that he visit me and eventually he started visiting some of the young maids instead. He would go to their rooms, and occasionally he would take one of them out after we had our dinner, going to small unknown places deep in the city. I had seen him entering the servants' quarters late at night or silently leaving the house in his car from the back door. He would dress them in Western-style clothes and pretend for a few hours, but he respected my status and never flaunted what he did before the other members of the family or his friends. Our time was spent eating together at dinner, short conversations when we met in the house, or attending parties with friends.

"I am well, thank you. This is good to see, our son is turning into a fine young boy." He paused, looking from me to Lu Meng and back. "I hope I live to see him grow up," he said in a joking tone.

"You survived the Japanese . . . can it be worse in the future?" I joked back, and laughed a little.

"I hope you're right," he said slowly.

"How is the family business?"

"It's much better than before. The country is in chaos still but there are new opportunities from this. We've good contacts . . . those who survived anyway." He fell silent and I knew he had finished talking and had withdrawn from me again, as I had withdrawn from him after Lu Meng had been born.

We stood together, watching our son swaying on his damaged foot, but still with the spirit and intelligence to show the way.

Xiong Fa and I rarely stood this close together and, looking at his thick neck, jowls, and hands, my mind drifted back to the things we had done and witnessed during the last fifteen years. Our traditional way of life had been wiped away by war, and still there was no real promise of its being restored—just looming uncertainty as to where the huge population of this country would direct itself. I noticed that the collars of my husband's shirt and suit were worn. It was obvious he had quietly made sacrifices for us.

"You should take care of yourself so that you live to see your grandchildren," I whispered to him.

He turned to me then. He looked tired, his eyes gray and watery, like the sea in winter.

"Yes, I hope I will," he whispered back, "but our son is already something to see."

"I thought you were going to give him away and take a second wife," I said suddenly.

My husband looked surprised, examining my face, then turned back to look at Lu Meng busily teaching the others.

"No, that thought never occurred to me, only to Father." He turned back to me quickly and our faces were brought close together. "I never liked any of it. I remember standing here, looking at your bedsheets with my mother, just after we had been married, arguing about when to start trying for a child. You were so young . . . but it was tradition. What did I know? In the end I did what I was told." His face twisted and he stopped himself from continuing for a moment. "What's the point? I should go back to work. Make sure our son gets a good supper before he goes to bed, so he becomes big and strong."

"Like you," I shouted after him.

"You forget, I was beaten by a young girl," he said, without looking back at me, and continued walking into the house.

I watched the martial arts until they finished then clapped and asked Yan to take Lu Meng and all the other children to the kitchen for supper.

Chapter 19

Lu Meng did grow as Xiong Fa had hoped and became more like his father, but while he was confident enough with the other children, he still preferred his own company. He spent much of his time with Lao Tung in the gardens and so began his love of plants and animals. By the age of fifteen Lu Meng had become tall and muscular, not as broad as his father and with a face that was more sculpted, like my own Ba's. His fingers remained delicate as fine scientific instruments, and perhaps sometimes I thought it was a shame they spent most of their time digging around in soil. On his thirteenth birthday, Xiong Fa had moved our son into an apartment of his own next to mine.

Every night, before he went to bed, I would hear my son reciting names in that ancient language I had not heard from anyone else since I was seventeen. I would open my window and standing next to my flower I would whisper to it under my breath, as if it were Grandfather, telling him to listen to Lu Meng. I looked out into the night and listened to Lu Meng sounding out the awkward words over and over again. His pronunciation was very bad as he'd had no one to teach him like I had.

I went into his room one night and found him sitting by the open window with two candles, looking at a book I didn't recognize.

"Are you really going to learn all those names?" I asked him.

"Yes, I have to if I want to study in Europe."

"You want to study in Europe? Do you know Europe . . . have you been to Europe?" I was teasing him.

He smiled. "You know I haven't, Ma. Don't make fun." Then he cocked his head to his right shoulder as he did when he was thinking. "But I must learn these names to stand a chance. Right?"

"Would you like my help?" I asked him.

"Now, Ma, you're acting foolish," he said with a wide smile.

"That is rather rude. How do you know that I can't help you?" I kept on.

I went over to him then and took the book. I could not read the language but I recognized many of the pictures.

"This one is a photograph of *Gardenia augusta*. And this one is *Anemone coronaria* . . . and here is *Rosa bracteata*," I said to him. Lu Meng was very surprised. "Where did you get this book from?" I asked.

"Ba bought me it, and my other books." He stood up and went to his desk, opening a drawer to show me several books on plants and botany. Some were written in Chinese and others were in Western languages. "He told me you knew the names of plants, though I didn't believe it. He said you used to go to some gardens with your grandfather?"

"Yes, I did," I said, remembering.

I sat down and looked around my son's room. He had collected lots of books on various subjects and had cut out many pictures of plants and landscapes from old Western books, which were left for street vendors when the foreigners departed, and pinned them to his wall. Then I noticed he also had the battered toy train. I got up and went to pick it up, surprised to see this old friend. It was the same one, with the dent at the front and the hand-painted repairs.

"When did you get this?" I asked him, picking it up and clutching it to me as if it were my own long-lost toy.

"Ba would let me play with it when I visited him. He would tell me not to let anyone else know, even you. He said that Grandfather Sang didn't like toys and that children should grow up quickly. Did he really say that?" My son finished with a question that could lead him to a thousand unhappy discoveries.

"I don't know if he said that, but he wasn't the sort of person who liked toys," I replied truthfully.

I put the train down and then went across the room and moved a chair so I could sit down opposite him. We started from the beginning but it took half an hour for me to teach him five names and by then we were both exhausted.

"Will you promise to teach me five names every night? And more than that when I start to learn better?" my son demanded.

"Yes." I was only too glad to help him. It seemed the perfect end to any day.

Yan came into the room then, followed by the new servant girl who had been assigned to Lu Meng. She looked pretty, quite tall with lustrous black hair and broad shoulders and hips. I was worried for Lu Meng, though. He had yet to meet many girls as he was more self-conscious than most and would be rather shy with them.

"Mistress and Master Lu Meng, this is Yu. Master, she'll be your servant for the moment. She is new and is learning to serve." Yan smiled at me, which meant that the young girl was quite hopeless. "She'll attend to your laundry, make your bed, and bring you food."

"Thank you, Yan, I am grateful," Lu Meng replied politely. "Hello, Yu. Where are you from?"

Her speech was rough and the words twisted clumsily in her mouth before they came out.

"I'm from a village called Meishi, near Zhengzhou in Henan. It is very far from here."

"You are from the old capital. What is it like there?" he continued.

She looked confused.

"Master, I'm going to show Yu where she will sleep and her other duties so perhaps you can finish the conversation in the morning?" Yan suggested.

"Yes, yes. I'll speak to you in the morning." Lu Meng stood up and smiled at her. She noticed his foot and stared openly, then blushed and turned her face away.

"It is fine to stare. I have had this since I was born." He walked over to her and pulled up his trouser leg. "You see? My foot is not whole, something is missing."

"Does it hurt?" the maid asked.

"Only a little, when it is cold or when I train in *gong fu* a lot."

"My father knew *gong fu* fighters, they were very brave," she said shyly.

This girl seemed simple and innocent.

"Time to go," Yan interrupted and put her hand on Yu's shoulder, turning her toward the door. Lu Meng watched her leave.

"Ma, my servant girl seems nice. What do you think?"

I now laughed at his innocence. "My dear son, I think she is very sweet-looking, but you need to be careful with servant girls as they often come from the countryside with little experience of our city ways. Also . . ." I smiled at him, " . . . some of these girls are out to snare a young boy from a big family, though I'm sure Yu will be a good girl."

"I never thought of those things. She didn't seem very troublesome to me," he replied, sounding rather uncertain.

"That is how they are supposed to seem." I laughed then and

wanted to change the subject. "So tomorrow we'll continue learning the names?"

"Yes."

"I will leave you to sleep now." I got up and left him reading his book.

You know how pretty this girl was. She was like fresh water from a spring and her voice was soft as petals falling. Deep in my memory I knew that face; it was the face my grandfather had also seen. He would have recognized it immediately. At that time you could not see her; those who are so innocent cannot see such things, they only know what they can feel and touch. As you read these words, do you remember her? I sit here and hope that you can think of her and imagine her. If we should ever see each other again, you will find me weeping for the girl I stole from you.

Yan woke me early at around ten o'clock in the morning.

"Mistress, Madam Ming has come to have tea with you."

"Really?" I sat up in bed and Yan passed me my robe. I stood up, put on my slippers, and went over to the mirror. Yan followed me and started to brush my hair. "I think I'll do this, you go and tell Madam Ming that she should go to Xiong Fa's living room. And please can you bring us some tea?" I instructed.

Yan scuttled out of the room and I quickly brushed my hair and put on some rouge. Yu was sitting outside Lu Meng's door and smiled at me as I walked past her to Xiong Fa's apartment. I entered the room to find Ming sitting in one of the armchairs, still wearing her coat and white gloves. Her hair had been put up and she wore a Western-style hat with a small veil.

"I don't want to stay too long," she began hurriedly, "I need to get on . . ."

"Why did you come then?" I replied, and sat down opposite her.

She laughed.

"That is just like you! I'm glad we became friends, I . . ." she started to say something further but then faltered into silence for a moment. "It has been fun," she resumed, "over the years you have made my life a joy. You've made a difference . . ."

"Me? Have I? What did I do? I barely know anything," I replied quizzically, and pulled the robe around me a little tighter.

"You weren't afraid," she replied instantly. "You were always your own person. And now look at you." She faltered again. "I need to tell you something . . ."

She suddenly looked very sad.

"What is it?" I asked urgently for today she seemed very different and I was now growing worried.

"We are leaving. We have decided to move to America," she said reluctantly, giving me a tremulous smile as the last words came out of her mouth.

"When are you coming back?" I asked. I could feel my neck and shoulders becoming tense, and my cheeks turning pale.

Her smile vanished and she clasped her hands together in her lap.

"We're not coming back."

I felt angry with her then. Blood rushed to my head, making me giddy; my hands clenched into fists.

"How can you abandon me? This is so unfair! How long have you known?"

"Please, Feng. Don't make this more painful for me," she pleaded quietly. "I feel very sad already. We started thinking of moving a year ago but it is so difficult for Chinese to go to America now. There are things happening here that don't look good and the Americans know it . . . the rest of the world knows it. We're the last to know."

She had barely finished speaking when I replied. I was so angry with her; I felt I deserved more than this rushed good-bye.

"What things? There is nothing happening here."

Ming stood up and went toward the window.

"Feng Feng, please don't shout. There are many changes . . . big political changes that could ruin everything for people like us. So we've decided to take what we have and move. Our life there will be much poorer than the one we enjoy here, but we think we should take the gamble."

I stood up but did not step away from the edge of the chair. I realized I was so angry I was shaking.

"How could you not tell me? How could you?" I demanded.

"What was the point? It could not be changed," she responded quickly but with resignation. Ming raised her face to mine. She looked older today, her lovely face drained white, brows furrowed. "I must go."

"I thought we would be friends forever." I looked up as I spoke, saw that dead flies had collected in the glass light fixtures in the center of the ceiling. It would be difficult to clean them out, I found myself thinking—while the best friend I had in the world was telling me we wouldn't see each other again. I breathed out and looked at her through my tears. She folded her arms and frowned; her lips were lovely even when she was sad. She stood up and held both my hands, shaking them a little.

"Feng, I need to go."

She brought my hands to her lips and gave them each a little kiss.

"You are abandoning me," I reproached her. Then: "Do you really think it will become that bad? Will it be worse than the war?"

She let our hands drop to waist level, still clasped together.

"Many people think so. The Nationalists lost and many think people like us will be persecuted eventually," she said. "We have all lived well while others . . . I'm sorry, I must go."

She thrust an envelope into my hand.

"This is my address in America. I'll keep you updated if I move. Write to me, too. I want to know how Lu Meng grows up."

She took a last look at me, from head to toe, and smiled. Then she let go of my hands, which swung empty at my sides. She reached up and tried to touch my face but I flinched away from her. Ming bit her lower lip and smiled again, then turned to the door.

"Good-bye. Take care of yourself." She took two steps away then turned back to me. "Don't let yourself get trapped in all this. Forget everything we were once taught . . . it is too easy to become lost in five thousand years of history."

"What does that mean?" I shot back.

But she was already gone. I sat down and clenched my fists. I banged them on my knees and then on the arms of the chair. Her footsteps along the wooden floor of the hall below were loud, echoing through the house. I heard her reach the front door and then she was outside, walking to her car. I quickly went to the window to watch her leave, my hands flat against the windowpane and my breath steaming up the glass. The engine was already running. I saw her head bob down, and her long legs fold as she stepped into the back—my best friend, more to me than any sister. And then the door slammed shut and she was driven away forever.

Chapter 20

Perhaps I had lived in this house too long, like all the older members of the family, slowly drifting toward death, fed by others, unseen and forgotten. I had become blind and deaf, a lumpen creature of mud living in a cave, which had lost its senses because they were never used. When I suddenly needed them they failed me and I was only able to sense fragments of the world beyond, which I foolishly believed made up the whole.

At the end of each day, after dinner, Lu Meng sat in his room with me and learned his Latin names. He remembered them easily and quickly, at first studying five a day then seven or eight, exactly as he'd said he would. Yu would come in after a while, and she would ready his bed for him and I would leave once it was his bedtime. She would wake him early for his *gong fu* practice then serve him breakfast. Then she would walk with him to school and be waiting for him when he finished. After they arrived back home, he would study and she would sit outside his apartment waiting, sometimes talking to Yan, who would be sitting outside mine.

After a while the arrangement between Lu Meng and Yu began to make me angry; it was disrespectful. It seemed too intimate; they paid too much attention to each other. He would often gaze at her from a distance and ask anxiously if she was well. I studied them both more closely and noticed what seemed to be a strong affection forming between them. I saw that sometimes Lu Meng would wait for Yu to come from the servants' quarters to accompany him to school. One day as I was waiting in the car at the back entrance, I watched them leaving and they were laughing together. I saw him help her make his bed, help her lift some books he had bought, help her clean his room of soil he had used to plant some seedlings. This was not what I wanted for my son, I wanted him to be with someone whom he would adore and would be adored by everyone else. Not a servant. This was not what I had planned. He was crippled and disadvantaged already. This would only cause him to suffer more.

In the four years that had now passed since Xiong Fa and I had spoken to each other in the laundry courtyard, I had seen less and less of him. We spoke on friendly terms when we did see each other, perhaps at dinner or when I was needed for ceremonial duties as the First Wife of the family. I always performed these well and willingly, but I had long ago lost any interest in men and had not wanted him or anyone else since my son was born. Lu Meng had become all the world to me. Xiong Fa continued to visit the young maids of the house, which many men liked to do, but he also continued to be discreet, which saved my face and was acceptable to me. Before, I would have fought him; now, at nearly thirty-eight, I was too comfortable living in this house. As I had to do nothing to maintain my lifestyle, I took stubborn pride in mere phantoms and emptiness. I taught my son names I could not read; went into the city to buy expensive items and paraded them in front of people as if they were trophies won by my own hard work. I could hear myself talk too much, giving advice, making sure I got the final word even if I knew it was nonsense. I was making myself sick with my life of repetition, like a ghost haunting a house of mirrors, forced to watch itself repeat the same noise and gestures, every minute, hour, day, month.

Ming had made my mind beautiful; with her I had become attentive and graceful, but now I was slipping back into ugliness. I could not help myself, because I was not able to see where change was needed until it was too late; I prized everything, not knowing what was of value and what was worthless.

When I watched Yu with Lu Meng and felt such anger, I began to sense the depth of my own bitterness. Yu brought a happiness to my son's life that I had forgotten. I sat in my room, in the chair that had witnessed everything, and became furious. I did not want change; I wanted my way, everything to be returned to the way it was before Yu came. I wanted Lu Meng to laugh only with me as he had done for so many years in his childhood. I wanted Ming to return. I sat alone and shouted for Yan but there was no reply, only silence. Rather than wait for her to return from her work, I walked alone to Xiong Fa's apartment but as I drew nearer I saw him standing at the open door with Yu. He was smiling and guiding her inside his apartment, gently leading her by her left elbow. I saw his skin touch hers. She returned his smile anxiously but he nodded reassurance and she stepped inside. He closed the door. I wanted to scream. As I walked back to my apartment I grabbed a vase and hurled it over the balustrade, hearing it shatter on the hall floor below.

Yan was already sitting outside my door. She was now nearly seventy years old and knew that, unlike before, if I were enraged now she could do nothing. She had also come to learn that she could not talk to me as freely as she once had. Our old conversations, which had once been so warm and soothing to me, had become an embarrassment.

I walked past her and into my room.

Inside, I screamed loudly, the noise rising from somewhere

deep within me. I marched up to my dressing table and, grabbing my hairbrush, hurled it against the wall.

"What is it, mistress?" Yan timidly asked. I knew she was only pretending. She recognized the problem as well as I did.

"That girl is a whore! Sleeping with the father while trying to seduce the son . . . well, I will not stand for it. I am First Wife and this is *my* house!" I shouted. I was the fool and did not see it, even though I was sitting in front of the mirror with my own reflection staring back at me.

"Don't you agree, Yan, that something must be done?" I raged. I looked around and caught sight of my belt, a Western belt with a large metal buckle. I snatched it by one end and ran out of my apartment. The girl was back, sitting outside Lu Meng's room.

"Whore!" I screamed.

I ran up and grabbed her by the hair. I forced her to the floor and thrashed whatever part of her I could reach with the flailing belt. Twice . . . five times . . . perhaps once more, I did not count. Lu Meng came out of his room then. Seizing the belt from me, he threw it behind him on the landing. He picked Yu up and helped her to stand. I saw deep red run through her long black hair.

"Lu Meng, let her go! She is a whore, trying to catch you and your father. Throw her out of this house!" I howled and screamed like a devil. "Lu Meng, do as I say, I'm your mother," I shouted at him.

He did not move but stood and looked at me, his light brown eyes darkening and his lips parting slightly as he breathed defiance. He stood in front of Yu to create a barrier between us.

"Lu Meng. Lu Meng. Do as I say! I'm your mother, you must respect my wishes." I breathed harder. "You make me lose face in front of this servant whore. Move out of the way!"

Only silence.

"Move!" I screamed.

He didn't lower his arms, which remained in front of Yu, protecting her.

Xiong Fa arrived then. He stepped between his son and his wife, but his attention went first to Yu. He brushed the girl's hair aside and we saw that she had a long gash across her right cheek, starting below her ear and ending halfway along her jaw. Blood flowed freely. It was already dripping onto the floor, leaving a stain. I watched it settle and was reminded again of the water marks left by this family, my family, visiting Ma's and Ba's house for the first time on that stormy day when Grandfather and I had been told to stay away.

For a moment I was lost.

"Yan, get a cloth to stop the bleeding. Lu Meng, take Yu to the People's Hospital," Xiong Fa instructed them, and they left. "This is crazy. Why do you do this to a harmless servant?" he rebuked me.

"She is not. She is sleeping with you! Maybe even your son."

"What? That is madness." He shook his head.

He looked at me and I stared back as hard as I could, my nostrils flaring and my eyes bulging. I could not believe he was denying what he had done. He cleared his throat to talk while mine was tight, almost suffocating me; I watched him look down at the blood and then he said, very softly, "I am sorry for everything but it can't be undone." He paused and looked at me with such sorrow on his face then. His skin was sagging and he had put on much more weight. He ran his hand through his thinning hair and I saw scars on it from where he had been tortured and beaten by the Japanese soldiers. "Feng, there is so much anger in you. I can't do this anymore. Please, will you stop?" he asked.

We stood in the corridor alone but knowing the whole house was watching and listening.

"Feng, please. Please think clearly." He looked at the floor and then up and across the balcony to the unseen faces listening. "We have been through so much. There has been war, hunger, and now people all over the country are demanding huge changes. We have hurt each other and many years ago we lost a child."

I looked hard at him and suddenly thought he may know. He may have learned what I had done. That night felt so close to me again. My nostrils again filled with the smell of blood and shit of that evening. I stood still and firm on the wooden floor but my legs felt as they did that night, dead and paralyzed.

"Lu Meng would not be alone. And you and I would have another child. Another baby. Lu Meng is happy with Yu and in all that is happening around us it is something to be joyful about."

He looked directly into my eyes. It had been so long since I had seen them, they were now softer and more watery, there was now a longing that had washed out his parents' pride and arrogance, which I had not noticed before.

"Please think about this."

He stepped forward, now closer to me than in years. I could see the lines of his face, years of hardship endured for us, I thought back to the day we stood outside the door of the banquet hall during our wedding, his face shiny and plump like that of a glazed pig. I thought of what had happened since that day and in my anger I could not understand what he was trying to explain, this old man standing in front of me.

I remember taking a half-step back.

I brought my right hand up and slapped him. His head moved slightly but barely flinched.

"Shut up. It was you and your family. Always your family. Now it is your family again."

"Feng."

He pleaded with me but I couldn't understand.

"Go back to that little whore."

He looked down, shook his head, and left me standing alone in the deserted corridor. The belt still lay on the floor where Lu Meng had thrown it, its buckle covered in blood.

It was I who had lost face.

I had been wronged and my son stolen from me. Xiong Fa and Lu Meng told me that this was not true, Yu just wanted to be a good servant, they said. But I was certain I knew how good she was being, and ordered that if he could not be a dutiful son he should move from the apartment next to mine. To my shock, he did. Xiong Fa arranged for an apartment to be made ready near to his and I requested that I did not see Yu again.

I had been betrayed by my own son in exchange for the favors of a young stupid whore. Yan told me that she'd been put to work in the laundry room but I had seen her, with my own eyes, walking to school with Lu Meng and slipping into Xiong Fa's apartment again in the middle of the day.

I cut them all off as they deserved. They would never be allowed into my life again. My days were spent with Yan. I slept late, went alone to the Cathay Hotel for tea in the afternoon, and shopped in the few remaining places that still stocked foreign goods. Shanghai was changing; it had once been the most cosmopolitan of Chinese cities but now the foreigners were largely gone and with them the opulence and luxury that the Sang family had enjoyed for the last hundred years.

I lived alone again, in hatred and anger.

The city I knew was very small. I had only experienced the gardens, my school, the backstreets full of peasants and the poor, places to eat and buy beautiful things, this house, my apartment, my window, my dressing table, and my bed. After losing Lu Meng, I withdrew even further. Yan accompanied me

at a distance, wary of my narrowing focus. She knew that my
world had now become so small, so finely balanced around me,
that any alteration to it could be upsetting. My days became
locked into a pattern, like a beautiful spiderweb, trembling at
the slightest breeze—the smallest truth. Too close and I would
not hesitate. I was too frightened *not* to attack.

Every morning in my apartment I would wear the same
clothes, a cheongsam and a shawl; I would hold the same conversations, eat the same lunch in the same restaurants, repeat
the same walks and visits, greetings and genuflections, again
and again, the same feelings, gestures, vocabulary, breaths,
colors, the same light, the same darkness . . . all repeated until
I felt my muscles and senses could continue without my voli-
tion or even the beating of my heart. Each strand of my life was
carefully held in place by the others.

Then . . . change.

Suddenly, a flood of new thinking and new demands, millions of minds and bodies commanded by one man, would dis-
assemble my world, piece by piece, without my even noticing at
first. They, too, chose to wear the same clothes: not traditional
like mine, but of red, black, white, green, and dark blue . . . but
all gray nonetheless, because there was no longer any trace of
individuality allowed. They repeated the same vocabulary and
gestures; they were as unerring in their devotion to their life
as I was to mine. Closing their businesses, they gave up their
livelihoods, setting aside their own interests for the good of
everyone else. They stopped being respectful to their betters,
like the Sang family. Red was now the national color; the red of
rage. People talked of politics I did not understand; even waiters in the few remaining tearooms and the servants employed
by the Sang family held strong views. Our household workers left and could not be replaced. It was all ending. But I was
still First Wife of the Sang family, what did I care? Politics was

for people who had to work every day to earn their living; for people whose hearts still beat and minds imagined something better.

Increasingly as Yan and I went into the city, even just for a walk on the Bund, people would openly stare at me and my clothes: traditional cheongsams and elegant Western styles made by the best tailors. They would call out names I did not understand. Shanghai was busy but newly hostile, the things I remembered long gone. I returned to the backstreets where I had once strayed with Grandfather, but they seemed dirty and vulgar to me and I could not understand what I had seen in them that had made me enjoy them so much and want to keep returning. Posters were plastered on walls, calling for change; students were going from door to door, rousing the people to think and believe in something new.

Gestures, vocabulary, and manners—all had suddenly changed. People openly showed that they did not respect me.

"Capitalist roaders, greedy pigs!" a young woman shouted at me as I passed. "You should be ashamed, wearing those fine clothes when others are struggling. Who was exploited so you could live like this?"

I stopped. The streets were so narrow here that when I turned around she was almost upon me. Her face was pretty and delicate, her hair neatly arranged in pigtails. Her lips were thin and her skin almost translucent; a beauty that would have attracted Father-in-law, Xiong Fa, and their friends. But her eyes were full of hatred, and she brought her left hand up and brandished her fist in front of my face.

"Your days are running out," she shouted at me. "Get out of here! You don't belong here . . . get out of our country."

She was not part of the world I controlled. I was frightened. Yan took hold of my hand as I looked at the young girl. My maid had not held my hand for years. Our fingers instinctively entwined. She pulled me through the crowds of onlookers. As we left the backstreets, my mind was blank. Faces faded in and out of my vision. We reached the main road and the car was waiting. Yan quickly opened the door for me to get in. Behind the curtains of the car I was able to breathe and felt safe. Yan pushed the cloth aside and looked outside to check no one had followed us and then asked the driver to take us home.

I was still upset when we arrived at the back entrance to the house.

I had hidden you away in the back of my mind since Xiong Fa had confronted me in the corridor, again pushing the possibility of your existence to a place where you would be lost to me.

I got out of the car to see Xiong Fa with Yu and an old couple standing on the steps to the back door.

The old couple looked so happy to see Yu. She smiled, the scar framing one side of her smile, making her face slightly misshapen. It had been beautiful before. I knew every detail of it. I had been extremely jealous of her high cheekbones, curved lips, deep brown eyes, and her youth.

As I stood by the open car door still barely out of the backseat, Yan took my hand urgently. It had been years since she had held me like this and I looked at her sharply but her look silenced me.

"Mistress, that couple. I gave the baby to them. I need to tell you mistress."

I was not listening.

"But when I gave the baby away I gave them a drawing of the family seal so they would know and it would be recognized."

I looked at Xiong Fa and, seeing me, he smiled sadly, showing me he understood and he waved me to come to them. I could not move. He had known for so long. I had hit you, scarred my own daughter. I thought he had been with you. I wanted to close my eyes but I needed to watch those two loving people throw their arms around you. The old woman put her hand to your right cheek. She touched the scar, her finger gauged its depth. I looked behind me. The gate was still open.

Xiong Fa started to walk toward me. He shouted at me.

"Feng, come here."

I could not face any of you, even Yan, my maid, who had disobeyed me to do what was right.

I turned to look at the gate again and the open road behind it, full of traffic and crowds of people. I looked at your face. My face as a young girl. You said something to the old couple, these strangers who were your parents. They turned and looked at me. They must have been angry but they knew they could not do anything to me. I was a Sang. My mother had married me so well that nothing was sacred; I could treat my own daughter as a creature, to beat and scar.

I stepped backward. My heart raced but everything else slowed. These poor people who had raised you in the country-side, who had done everything to help you survive, embraced you with such love.

Xiong Fa continued to walk toward me, beckoning me to join them.

Everything crashed together in my mind and I stumbled backward. My left hand caught the side of the car to steady me. I looked again at the deep scar on your face, the pained expression of the woman, your mother, hurt as she touched your cheek . . . and I turned around and ran through the gate and out into the road.

As I ran I shouted, telling myself that none of this could be possible; screaming that I could not be held responsible. I stopped and thought of turning back then but I could not face that house again, with its endless corridors, balconies, and impenetrable darkness. I couldn't let any of you see me. I thought of Lu Meng, and what my beloved son would think I could not imagine. I walked on, ran, tripped and fell, and was picked up by passersby. I had torn my clothes and scraped myself.

The streets began to grow dark and lights appeared here and there. I kept going until I recognized a street corner and realized I had come to the gardens. A wind had started blowing and rained dust into my face and eyes. I stopped to rub it out and catch my breath as well. My shocked mind was starting to settle. There was nothing left for me to hide anymore.

Chapter 21

I t was cold. I stood up straight and listened. Everything was quiet, but for dogs barking and someone farther down the road packing up a food stall. I thought of Grandfather leaving on the day it was agreed I should marry. I stood across the road from the old house and its bombed-out remains. I had not wanted to see any of my family again after what they had done, and now I did not want to see you or Lu Meng after what *I* had done.

I saw the entrance to the gardens, a place of only happy memories for me, though I did not think of what I would do once I was inside. Maybe just walk. You marry from the family you are born into to the man's family: one life into another, everything that is familiar and intimate is left behind, sacrificed for the comfortable confines of another's world. I looked down the path to the front door of my old home; even in the darkness I could see that the house had been damaged. The window through which I had watched Grandfather leave that last day was smashed and a part of the wall broken. He had always known what would happen to me. He left me as I leave you now. All of us so weak, knowing what should be done but unable to do it.

The entrance to the neighboring gardens had been locked

and boarded up, but someone had broken in and made a hole to enter by. I walked inside. They had run completely wild. Whereas before the beginning of the war the entrance to the gardens had been properly kept and the rest only lightly pruned by Grandfather and the gardeners, now nature had been allowed to thrive unfettered. The grass was tall and the willows huge and dense. In the distance I saw that the boundary trees had grown much fuller, and underneath them there were scattered small fires surrounded by people huddled together. I took off my shoes and, holding them in my hand, walked barefoot in the direction of the flames. I had not felt grass between my feet since I was last there. Much of it was now waist-high. I felt it brushing my hands as I passed.

The moon lit up the bushes and the shrubs, which cast huge black shadows on the ground that swayed like strange animals from a child's storybook. I reached one of the fires and the people looked up at me and smiled, then returned to hugging themselves for warmth. One old man's eyes remained fixed on me as he rested his chopsticks on an old bowl half-filled with rice.

"Mistress, what are you doing here in that nice cheongsam?" he asked politely.

I looked at him and smiled.

"Don't go north, there are many problems brewing in Beijing. Some say new revolutions will be launched against the rich." He went back to chewing his rice.

I sat down in front of the fire, closed my eyes, and saw the hot orange and yellow light through my eyelids. I heard the wind whip through the flames, making the fire spit and crackle. I opened my eyes again and looked up to watch the trees swaying heavily, the darkness wrapping itself around them. Their branches waved me on, beckoning me again, as they had many years ago, to join them and be swept up into the air forever. I wanted to be carried away, to forget I had ever left here, and live again in those happy days with Grandfather and Bi.

I wept. While I did so an old lady stood up on bent legs. She came to me and put a shawl around me. I thanked her and crouched there for several hours, tossed between deep sleep and nightmares. When I woke it was still night and I left the huddled group to visit Ma's and Ba's house. What was left of it was boarded up as the entrance to the gardens had been but again someone had forced an entry. I did not stop to consider that the invaders might be sheltering there, and luckily it was empty. I went straight into the living area. A bomb had hit the house at the back and killed Ma, Ba, and the cook; the rest of the servants had left and presumably taken whatever they could carry. The courtyard was full of rubble and I saw that there were several piles of ashes there. For a moment I wondered where I wanted to go and then realized that I only wanted to see the room at the top of the house, the one where the seamstress had worked on the wedding dress. The room had frightened me before and I felt afraid now, but I remembered the seamstress whose hands had created such beauty and who had sat so peacefully, and I needed to see that room to remind myself that I, too, had once been a simple little girl.

The stairs creaked as I felt my way up slowly, tripping on things I could not see. I inched my way to the doorway. I looked in and saw the mannequin still standing in the back of the room. It was lit by the moonlight and a faint glow from the streetlights entering through the broken window behind it. As before, I dared not enter the room but stood at the entrance, leaning against the doorway as I had as a child, the mannequin standing facing me. It was covered in white dust, perhaps ash or whitewash from the ceiling that had fallen in the center of the room. It had a number of pins embedded in its sides and front;

it looked as if, having been abandoned, it had entered hibernation, barely alive, simply holding itself up until someone came to breathe life into it again with new colors and textures. That was how my heart felt. I needed to find someone who would bring it new life.

I remembered sitting in this doorway watching the seamstress at work, surrounded by red silk, her head bowed over the material, scissors and chalk by her left side, her long white neck shadowed by her heavy black hair tucked up in a bun. Next to the scissors and chalk, the thread pulled from the bobbin, first taut then relaxing, alternating seemingly forever as her hand swayed and stitched the cloth together or created embroidered images. Her work had breathed life into the mannequin, lending it bone, blood, and flesh almost. If someone could have taken such care over me I would have become someone new, the most dignified and graceful woman, someone who would never have done harm.

She was not to know what her dress would mean to me; she had been asked to create something magnificent and fine, that would last, and it was so. It was only in our hands that it became soiled and malignant. We had created nothing beautiful, just wretchedness and ugliness. I could not return to you, Lu Meng, Xiong Fa, or Yan. What would I say to you? Would it help? Would it make everything better? How would I ask forgiveness for something I knew was unforgivable?

You would ask me why, Xiong Fa would ask me why, and I would not be able to explain to you for there was nothing to say except: I did what I could not stop myself from doing. Now, unlike Ba, Ma, Father-in-law, Sister, and even Grandfather, I had seen and understood what pain I had caused.

"Should I kill myself?" I screamed at the mannequin.

I sat and wept then. Choosing death would be cowardice, I knew that. Like Grandfather leaving me; like Ba not preventing

Ma from agreeing to my marriage; like Ma not stopping herself from wanting what she believed she deserved, no matter what it cost others. But out of all this unrelenting selfishness came two good things, you and Lu Meng, and without me you could both escape the shadows, to live better lives. The past had poisoned the future for long enough.

I got up and walked over to the mannequin. In the center of the room I stood on the rubble of the fallen ceiling, looking at the stars through the hole in the roof. The night was chilly; I should go back to the fires in the gardens. I reached the mannequin and touched its surface. It was ripped and torn. I placed my hand against its padded breast. This rough, worn simulacrum of a human being had once been the most beautiful thing. I had kept the dress carefully preserved in one of my trunks; it was the only thing that remained from the time before. Suddenly I wanted to see once more the woman who had made it, and who had known the young girl she had altered it to fit.

I returned to the gardens where I huddled around the fire with the homeless people. The old man kindly lent me a blanket and I slept again.

I awoke with the fixed idea that I would never return home. Whatever happened from now on, both my children were better off without me if all I had to offer them was anger and hatred. I had to escape. I would go to the seamstress, I decided, perhaps Bi might still live with her. There was nowhere else I could think of going.

I remembered clearly that Bi had come from Daochu town. Maybe I could take the train there. For many years there was a street of pawnbrokers near the railway station that had catered to new arrivals to the city. The Communists had shut down many of them but I had heard gossip of some of the wealthier families nowadays selling their possessions to the remaining black-market brokers. I had the jewelry I was wearing so I walked to the street to see if I could sell it.

I had not been outside so early in the morning since I was married. The city was alive at this hour. Ming was right, though, a huge change was coming. As I crossed the pawnbrokers' street, a balding hollow-faced man beckoned me from a window on an upper floor. I nodded up to him and he stuck his arm out and pointed to an entrance below. The door was unmarked and the building itself looked deserted. I went in to find narrow unpolished stairs in front of me, the wooden treads worn by the passing of many feet. As I reached the first-floor landing, a door opened on the left.

"Please come in." I saw that the hollow-faced man was short and thin, with dark, blemished skin.

I entered a dim unfurnished room from which a narrow passageway led to an unseen back room emitting the faint promise of daylight. The room we stood in was dark, the window boarded up. Light was provided by a few candles; the whole place looked empty and disused. There was nothing in it except for an empty counter made of mahogany. The man who had beckoned to me went around to the other side of this.

"What can I do for you, madam? You aren't from this district." The pawnbroker sounded polite and businesslike, but I felt very anxious.

"No . . . no, I'm not," I replied.

He was a bony person but had a little potbelly, which strained the buttons of his white cotton shirt. He had a friendly smile that brightened his eyes under his bushy brows. His face reminded me of an ancient god's, one of the fun-loving sort who liked to drink and eat. I started to take off my necklace, earrings, and rings.

"Please put them on the counter," he requested, following this with a wide smile that brightened the room. I put the things on the counter in front of him.

These were expensive pieces and should fetch a lot of money, allowing me to travel, buy new clothes, and live for months—perhaps longer.

"I know these are valuable because I bought them myself. What will you give me for them?"

I could see the man knew what they were worth and wanted to let him know I was no fool, though my hands were shaking and my legs felt weak. I felt ashamed to find myself in a transaction of this sort, eager for his money where once the shopkeepers had been eager for mine.

"Very nice pieces, madam," the pawnbroker commented. Looking up at me, he noticed my unease. "Are you all right? You look as if you're about to faint."

"I'm well, thank you," I answered, too quickly, and he screwed up his face in a show of concern. "Please, let's just finish this?"

"Okay, as you wish, it's up to you . . ." He looked at each piece in turn more closely, taking his time. "There are fewer and fewer pieces like this around. People are leaving the country and taking their best jewelry with them. What would you like for them?" He put the final piece down again.

"I would just like to sell them to you."

"Leaving the country as well?"

"No, the city."

"You're going inland?" He laughed to himself and then sucked on his teeth to show that he doubted the wisdom of this. "Very brave of you. The countryside is wild and chaotic . . . I hear all sorts of strange things. Massive building projects . . . people working in huge farms . . . production lines making clothes, tools, and generators. I hear the women drive the tractors and the men pick rice. It's all upside-down today. Not that a lady like you would be driving tractors, of course," he joked, laughing a little nervously. "Well, let's hope not yet."

He looked down again at each piece and then played with the earrings between his finger and thumb, turning them around again and again.

"I will give you five hundred new renminbi and nine hundred American dollars. What about that?" he said, knowing that even with the foreign currency, he was getting the better deal. But I was in no position to bargain. "It's a good deal, eh?" He gave his teeth a suck for emphasis.

"Yes, I agree. I will take it."

I was desperate to leave, to get on the train to Daochu or just anywhere. I could not wander this city that was once my home, with everyone looking at me, staring and pointing. He brought out some paper and was about to wrap the money for safety, but I stopped him and took out a few notes. He wrapped the rest in a tight bundle and handed it to me.

"You should hide this, particularly on the trains. The Communists all say they are for the people, but many of them are hooligans and will steal from the same people they say they're protecting, first chance they get." He said this softly, as if he feared being overheard even in this empty room. "I wish you good luck, madam."

He opened the door for me and I went out onto the narrow landing and looked down the empty stairs to the street door below. He watched me hesitate, reluctant to set foot there again. I seemed to have walked here in a daze, because, now that I listened to it, the noise coming from the street outside frightened me. It was loud and aggressive, heralding a new order in which I, and the Sangs, would have no place.

"Perhaps you shouldn't go," the pawnbroker said behind me. "It is dangerous out there for someone like you."

Someone like me . . . what did he know about me and what I

had done? I did not react to his comment but continued to stare at the door to the street.

In the face of my silence, his attitude suddenly changed.

"That's the problem with your class . . . you're all so arrogant. That's why *they*," he pointed down the stairs " . . . want to teach you all a lesson. They have forced many of you to share your wealth—all your factories, businesses, and the other things you have—but next time they will take everything that's left! They will take your sons, your . . ." As he talked he made himself quite agitated, but stopped himself; taking a breath, he bowed his head. "I'm sorry, madam."

"No, I'm sorry." I smiled at him. "Thank you very much for your help." I looked down at the bundle of notes he'd given me.

He seemed to guess what I wanted to do next. "There's a shop just next door . . . it sells cheap clothes for young Party cadres and zealous youngsters fresh in from the countryside, keen to join the Party. Buy yourself some clothes there and get rid of that expensive dress and foreigners' shoes and hairstyle."

"I will. And thank you again."

"No need to say it. Good luck to you . . . I believe we'll all need it. Remember, the Revolution is over, long live the Revolution." He gave a bleak smile, stepped back inside, and closed the door firmly.

In the silence after his departure, I focused on the street outside. Among the masses of people walking to and from the station, I could hear young voices, calling for Shanghai workers to join them in constructing the new nation; to leave the cities and go to the countryside, working for the movement to build a new world order. I could hear chanting and singing about Chairman Mao and the new People's Republic. The Revolution had come to an end, long live the Revolution!

The whole country had changed, and we families like the Sangs no longer had any idea what was happening around us.

We had had everything we needed for so long, we had all but forgotten those who were the source of our wealth. We had turned our backs on them in order to maintain our narrow privileged existence, and now we would be made to pay for our neglect.

I descended the stairs, meaning to turn quickly into the shop next door, but was overwhelmed by the crush of people filling the street. I opened my eyes and saw the scene properly. Crowds of young people fresh from the countryside were pouring out of the train station. From their badges, posters, banners, and chants, they had been ordered by the Party to organize this movement to the cities and join the students there. The Party had sent many students to lead teams of "newly educated" peasants back to different parts of the new nation, to operate and run the State machinery that would build, feed, and clothe new China. Everyone must work to one end only. This was a huge unending mobilization, dedicated to nothing but movement itself. I saw young men and women painting slogans on the walls of buildings, ordering obedience, and posters covered the giant pillars of the station entrance on the opposite side of the road, calling for change and revolution. There were students addressing the people of Shanghai, requesting that they come out and join them at the station; others demanded the fall of Shanghai, saying that the Party must take control of the city. The sheer scale of the changes taking place around me was shocking. The people I had simply ignored were powerful now. Ming had warned me that this was coming, and I had not listened.

I hoped that Xiong Fa had made arrangements to save himself and the family, sacrificed the Sangs' glorious past for a safe if less glorious future. Father-in-law would not have done it; it was not in the Chinese tradition to gamble with the past in order to secure the future. The old man would rather have burdened the future to maintain the past. I prayed that my husband would be more farsighted in providing for our children and the rest of the family. Then my mind strayed to thoughts of you and I began to panic, standing there, that these huge crowds around me all knew what I had done. In their own striving for purity of deed and thought, they would recognize me as a liar and a demon. I must leave this city and my shame, submerge myself in the new nation. Slide into nothingness and start again: learn to pay for my own survival.

I listened to more of the madness: the shouting and screaming, the hands and arms beckoning frenziedly, demanding people should join, work and fight, give over their minds and bodies to his cause and course: the Great Helmsman.

With my head bowed, I quickly entered the building the man had pointed out to me. As soon as I was inside it the people there jeered at me. It had once been a shop with shelves and a sales counter, but was now more of a general store—selling clothes to new supporters but supplying existing Party members for free. There were piles of plain white shirts, and trousers in dark blue and khaki green stacked on a table in the center of the room or piled in heaps on the floor. On shelves racked from floor to ceiling there were hundreds of pairs of rubber-soled shoes, slippers, and sandals, knapsacks and caps.

A young man standing behind the counter noticed me.

"Look here, a wealthy woman in tatters!"

Everybody cheered and laughed at the sight.

"This is what they deserve," said another. "Let them wear nothing and suffer like we had to."

The atmosphere was hostile, I did not feel safe, and yet these were just children—the same age as Lu Meng. There were some older people looking through the stacks of goods, but they went about their business quietly and unobtrusively. I sensed that, like me, they were interested purely in survival. They did nothing to attract attention, for even in that shop, as in the street outside, there seemed to be the constant threat that a spirit of frenzy would seize control of all these young bodies, taking possession of their mouths, arms, hands, legs, and feet, directing them against anyone at a moment's notice.

I moved to the back of the shop and found a space to change between the piles of clothes and shoes. The black trousers I'd chosen were of thick loose cotton with a drawstring, and once I had them on I realized they were the same kind as those I had worn as a child, running through the gardens with Grandfather. I slipped out of my cheongsam, wrapping the bundle of notes into the material and tying it around my waist. I quickly put on a white shirt and a thick padded coat over that. I also took out the money I had retained from the bundle, ready to pay for these things.

At the counter the boy in charge looked at me and barked with laughter.

"A convert! Our first in Shanghai today," he shouted.

He leant over the counter and touched my lapels. Instinctively I took a step backward.

"Don't worry, comrade, these are free for you," he shouted.

"Thank you very much." I kept my head down and looked at the floor. Following the lead of the other older people in the shop, I turned and left quietly.

As I did I passed a mirror and saw myself in the ill-fitting clothes. I looked like a child again, and for a moment I wondered whether my life in between had all been a dream.

I looked across the road to the entrance to the railway station. The mayhem there continued, endless crowds pouring out and down the street into the city. I made my way through them and on to the concourse. I had never been outside Shanghai before and my heart was racing at the prospect, but with each step I took farther away from home I felt more relieved. I bought a ticket and, once through the barrier, breathed in more freely. There was no returning now. The journey would take nearly eighteen hours but this train went direct to Daochu itself. The carriage was old. The seats, bare wooden benches fixed back to back, were placed down either side of it. The wooden floor was stained a dark moldy brown and the smell of piss rose from freshly wet patches. A young boy slept in the rack above the seats. I sat in a corner and waited; there was still another thirty minutes before we would depart.

Chapter 22

I had not slept well in the gardens the night before and after a few minutes tiredness took hold. My eyes began to close. I remembered seeing you step down from the back entrance, and the couple rushing to greet you. Then I saw your face suddenly close to mine, our foreheads touching, and your eyes looking into mine. Your breath smelled of flowers and I felt it waft over my cheeks and lips. You pulled away a little so that I could see your whole face. I had never seen you so closely—would never have let a maid do this. I wanted very much to cry then. You smiled slightly, plaintive and anxious, your lips pale and broken. The right corner of your mouth pulled your cheek slightly crooked, where the scar ended. You turned your face away from me, sensing where I was looking. I needed to look at it closely; I had not cared before. I felt your hand against my cheek, fingertips sliding around to the back of my neck, your hand pulling me in, my cheek resting against yours. I felt the scar against my skin, hard and unnatural. I felt my whole body tense and my eyes start to sting. I was shaking and crying, the wooden seat hard beneath me. The carriage was empty except for the sleeping boy. I dropped my chin to my chest and cupped my hands around my eyes. The tears rolled between my fingers and down my cheeks, over my lips and to the floor. I sniffed hard and smelt the stale piss. Then there was a noise to my left as thirty or so Communist youth members scrambled inside the carriage and took up the seats around me.

"Hey, kid, no sleeping," one of the youths shouted at the boy, and poked him with a finger. "There is work to be done. The country is calling us."

Others laughed.

I kept my hands around my face. I heard a whistle and the train started to move. For a moment, like a child, I wanted to look out of the window and see what was happening, how this huge machine would carry us, but I just closed my eyes and thought of the lonely mannequin, waiting for someone to clothe it and give it life. The train gathered speed and its gentle rocking made me sleepy. I leaned back and rested my arms and hands on top of the money wrapped in the cheongsam tied around my waist. I watched the city speed past the window. This was my first trip out of Shanghai and I left an emptiness that told me I would never return. As I watched, the buildings grew smaller, more broken and worn, until eventually they disappeared leaving scarred ground, piles of stones and bricks, sand, dirt, grass, empty space, wooden houses tied together, fields, people with no shoes, farmers, animals, mud, river, water, grass, trees, green: endless green. Yet again I had misunderstood Ming: she had told me China was huge but I had never realized it was so vast. I forgot everything and just watched. I did not feel myself blink, my eyes drinking in everything that flickered before me. The plains of grass, hills, farms, then a small village would flash past, children waving and cows with their heads down chewing grass, or hundreds of sheep, like little white spots sprayed across a canvas of green. Our country is truly beautiful, I thought. Perhaps, as these students keep shouting, it is worth dying for.

I awoke hours later. It was night and the students were sleeping now. They huddled against each other, like cats keeping warm. The air was thick and moist. An old woman came through the door and, seeing me awake, asked for my ticket. She took it and looked at it, commenting, "You don't look like you're from Daochu."

She sat down next to me, ready for a chat.

"I know the people of that town—they're farmers." She looked me up and down, frowning. "You haven't got worker's hands." She grabbed my left hand and squeezed the fleshy part below my thumb. "Yes, very soft. I like them."

She smiled at me. She had wiry hair that sprouted and coiled from her head like fine tree roots, a fat rosy face with tiny slits for eyes, and when she smiled her mouth and eyes seemed to converge at the center of her face. She held my ticket between chubby fingers.

"I'm going to see an old friend," I said, politely but trying to shorten our conversation.

"Oh, why?" I was surprised at her forthright attitude. "Dear me, I didn't mean to offend you. It is nice to talk to someone, though. I have friends there . . . perhaps I know them?"

"Well, it is a seamstress and her son. She is a great seamstress, knows all the old traditional meth—"

"You must stop!" she cut me off, whispering close to my face, her breath bitter and rotten. "These students do not approve of people who know such things." She paused and smacked her lips a few times while she checked that they were still sleeping. "They hate all the people with traditional skills . . . I hear them shouting about it all the time, riding up and down the country." She examined me closely. "I know the woman you mean—Madam Zhang. She's very good. How do you know her?" she whispered.

I pulled my head back but answered in a low voice, "A long time ago, she made my wedding dress . . ."

"You must have been from a rich family!" she cut me off again.

"Well, no, she was a family friend," I lied.

"Yes, Madam Zhang . . . she is old now."

"Where does she live?" I quickly interrupted.

"Alas, I don't know. Her son left her and did not return because of the war, and then after that there was the Revolution." She continued speaking but I did not hear her, my mind fixed on Bi, the boy I had known. The only one I had kissed out of love. When I had woken in the gardens this morning I had drifted down to the place on the riverside where we had lain together in the grass. He had fished and I had picked flowers. I remembered the feel of the petals of a wild rose between my fingers, the slight red stain they had left on my skin, and then giving one to him, his fingers touching mine as he took it. I had visited the willow tree, which had grown thick and now hung heavily to the ground, and sitting against its trunk, I had thought of our kiss there and of our fingers entwining under that tree, years before. I wished we had been old enough to make love.

". . . here is your ticket." Her short fat arm was outstretched in front of me. "Have a good trip."

I took the ticket and she stood up.

"I'll see you later." She smiled at me and walked down the carriage, pushing past a young girl who had fallen asleep and whose head and arm were hanging into the aisle. I heard her close the carriage door and I returned to staring out of the window into the darkness outside, and in that dense black I imagined I saw Bi with his mother. I saw us meeting again; we were young and we fished and ate together and smiled. Then in the window I caught sight of my reflection. My face was dirty and my hair wild. The clothes were too large for me. Though I was dressed like I had been while I was with Grandfather, my face was older and its innocent luster lost. I looked hard and cruel, because I was.

I sat and watched the students sleep. One of them had a

puppy cradled in his pocket. It had pissed, and the piss had soaked into his coat. I slept, too.

The train came to an abrupt halt. There had been no announcements of the name of the station but at each stop a team, which had obviously been charged with working in that area, would start to chant and shout. There was tremendous excitement among them all; they believed they were changing the world. I climbed down from the train. Daochu station was small. Following everyone else, I was outside in a few minutes. As in Shanghai, there were young people surrounding the place, encouraging people to work for the Party, for the country, and for the Great Leader. There were posters hanging from every wall demanding allegiance to the Party and Chairman Mao. There were also lists of meetings to attend and orders from various work groups, instructing people to farm, fish, build, and manufacture. The station stood on a main road, though it would only be a small one in Shanghai. To my left was the town, nothing but a straggle of dusty roads and low brick houses; to my right I could see down the road to a People's Square created for gatherings, where a team of students were busily erecting a statue of Chairman Mao.

Chapter 23

I walked away from the square to what seemed to be the quieter side of the town. The streets were empty but eventually I saw an old man sitting outside a house. Like all the other buildings, it was made from gray bricks, with basic shuttered windows in front of thin glass panes. I could see inside but there was little other than a bed, a desk, and a cooking *kang*. On the wall was a picture of Chairman Mao in a green jacket with a red-trimmed collar.

"Hello, who are you?" he asked me.

"I'm looking for Madam Zhang," I replied.

"The seamstress?" he said and frowned. "Well, she is in the clothing depot just down this road. Keep going, then turn left at the fruit stall. There is a wide road with large production halls on either side. She is in charge of the clothing unit."

"Thank you," I said and turned to go.

"What's your name?" he asked me abruptly.

"Feng . . . Xiao Feng," I replied.

"Well, Xiao Feng," he said, in an abrupt tone, "you take care with Madam Zhang. Remember, she likes people who work hard."

I nodded to him and walked in the direction he had pointed me. The streets continued to be empty but the doors to most of the houses stood open and I could see into each one of them.

They all looked very similar, containing a bed, a desk, a poster of Chairman Mao or a little statue of him. Many of the walls and doors were covered with handwritten posters and printed images of strong and proud men and women, holding aloft tools and farming implements. After fifteen minutes' walking, I found the fruit stall. I turned into the next road, which was much wider than the previous streets, wide enough for trucks to come and go. I walked past four or five production halls, set on either side of me, all identical, simply constructed with double doors and large metal-framed windows to either side. Each had a plaque nailed next to the doors. The first one was producing radios, the second torches, the third was mixing fertilizer. I came then to one marked CLOTHING PRODUCTION and peered through the window. There were twenty old women sitting inside making clothes: white shirts, black trousers, green and blue jackets.

The room was a large rectangular space, the lower half of the walls painted blue and the upper half whitewashed. Seated in two lines running the length of the room, each seamstress had a long wooden worktable set in front of her. At the back of the room, standing with her back to me, was a woman I recognized immediately. Her long gray hair was drawn up in a bun; although she stood bent over a little, her neck was still long, slender, and beautiful. I watched her as before, again frightened to enter but this time frightened also to stay outside in the empty street. I left the window and went to the double doors, gently pushing one open. My heart suddenly beat wildly. I entered and stood silently just inside the hall. The women looked up and Madam Zhang turned around. She walked toward me, taking each step calmly and carefully.

"Hello, can I help you?" she asked.

"I have come to see you," I said. I didn't know how to continue. My face felt hot and flushed and my eyes became watery.

Instinctively I brought my hands together in front of me; they were very dry and I clenched them tightly.

She looked hard at me.

"You have grown much older, my dear. Did you marry that rich man?" she asked in her soft voice.

"Yes . . . yes, I did." My throat had seized up until I could barely talk. "Yes, I did." I started to cry. "I did! I did!" I could only repeat myself and sob. I inhaled deeply and gasped for air. Tears rolled into my mouth and their saltiness made me think of sitting with Yan after Xiong Fa had held me down and forced himself into me.

I cried until my whole body shook. I felt my shoulders sag forward and my head loll. Then a hand reached under the disheveled hair that now covered my face. It touched my cheek and brushed my hair back.

"Just sit down. Ah Ting, get her some tea."

Madam Zhang led me to a seat and I continued to cry into my hands. She stood next to me and lightly stroked my hair.

"What has happened to you?"

I could not talk for the tears would not stop and my throat felt strained and somehow locked. I wanted to speak but when I opened my mouth all that emerged was a whooping sound. My voice could not compete against the tears.

"Take your time," she patted my shoulder, "it will come, whatever it is, and we all have plenty of time."

"Aiiiya, time to make a million suits of green and blue?" moaned a lady behind me.

The other women laughed.

Madam Zhang gathered up my hair, now dirty and unkempt, into a ponytail. Reaching over, she took a strip of red ribbon—in that room every ribbon was red—and tied my hair back.

"We can't offer you much, things here are not good," she said flatly, then she groaned. "This is crazy. You cannot stay here. I will take you back to the station."

She walked from behind me to the other side of the work-table immediately in front of me. "We should go now so you can catch the next train."

She held out her hand. "We should go."

"No," I whispered; my breath was weak but my tears were drying at last. "I don't think I can ever go back."

"But there is nothing here for you."

"Then it will be like this cloth around us, it is not much at present but in your hands has the promise of something much more."

I continued to look down into the working surface of the table and the deep scars from all the cutting, but I felt her bend down close to my face.

"Ai, I always liked you, like my son once did. Well," she whispered in my ear, "if you stay here you will have to work and life will be difficult."

Madam Zhang walked around and stood behind me again, then and rested her hands gently on my shoulders. "We have lost twenty minutes since you arrived and we have a very strict quota to fulfill. If we miss it there are penalties, but if we do more then we receive benefits—sometimes food, sometimes a stupid badge—so for now we must all return to work." She stroked my cheek as if to wipe away the last of my tears. "If you stay, you must work." Then her hands suddenly left my cheeks and she tugged my ponytail sharply, which didn't hurt but surprised me. I turned and saw her face close to mine. She was beautiful still, more padded in her old age, but her face had a sheen and her eyes were a hard nut-brown and shone with a light I had not seen since I last saw Grandfather's. I smiled at her faintly. "Good. Now . . . what can you do?" she asked me bluntly.

"I don't think I can do anything."

"So that is how you have lived?" She sighed faintly, thinking. "But you must be able to sew a little . . . use a needle? I remember you as a bright girl, who would probably have been able to stitch on a button. Can you remember doing that?" I nodded. "Well, I'll remind you how to sew on buttons, and you can do that."

She grabbed a piece of cloth, a button, a needle and thread, and slowly looped a long piece of cotton through the needle and placed the button on the cloth. Then she started to loop the thread through the eyes of the button and back into the cloth.

"Occasionally, you must loop the thread through the knot at the back," she turned the cloth over to show me the stitched knot on the cloth, "to give it strength. And to give it more strength, you can wind the thread around underneath the button, then tie that off, and finally tie off the thread at the back of the cloth. Here . . . now you try."

She gave me the cloth and button to look at and I pulled it a little between my fingers and thumbs; it looked tidy and strong.

"Practice a few times, then Ah Sui here," she walked over to a tubby little lady three tables behind me on the opposite side of the room, "will start to give you trousers," she held a pair up, "and you will sew on the buttons.

"Now, I must get back to my planning and some sewing. The group leader will return at six o'clock and, as you will see, we must be ready for his inspection."

She came over to me once more, bringing more cloth and some buttons.

"Do some practicing," she ordered me, though in a kind voice, then turned and went to the back of the room to continue whatever it was she had been doing when I slipped through the door.

I struggled with the buttons, lancing my fingers and thumbs

several times, but by the fourth attempt my work started to follow Madam Zhang's example, which lay teasingly in front of me. Hers was so exact and tidy . . . but by the time I ran out of buttons mine did at least have the same strength. I straightened up and within a few seconds she was standing behind me again. I felt like I was back at school and let myself slip willingly into being the child again. I felt happy just having someone concern themselves about me.

She picked up my practice attempts and looked at them closely.

"Well, it's pretty ugly, isn't it, my dear?" I felt my head droop in shame, as if I had failed her. "But it is functional and that is what is important. It was good that you never made your own wedding dress." She looked at me and smiled. "I remember it well . . . you sat and watched me for hours." She left me briefly and I looked around to see her gathering together twenty or more pairs of trousers. She stacked them on the table in front of me.

"Get some buttons and thread from the storeroom through the door behind us. Do as many of these as you can, but you must do more than thirty by the end of the day . . . that means you have just four hours." She gave me a wide smile and a wink. "Then, if you want to carry on tomorrow, you will have to do ninety every day. Today you can take it slowly."

The other women all chuckled to themselves.

The room was airy and smelt slightly of flowers or grass; it had a high ceiling and long windows to either side, which stretched down to half the height of the room. The white metal window frames pivoted at the center so they could be pushed open, leaving a space at both ends. I stood up and walked to the end of the room. There was a gap of about ten feet between the edges of the desks to either side, and at the last desk on the left I could see Madam Zhang studying schedules and patterns.

Like her, each seamstress wore black trousers and a white shirt, but some had colored scarves, too, and Ah Sui wore a hat with embroidery on it. Each sat in front of a sewing machine, which, when all were working together, made tremendous whirring and clattering.

The door at the end of the room led to a darkish corridor barely big enough for a man to enter. After twenty feet or so there was another door. I pushed this open to find a large area with twelve rows of shelves, all stacked with cotton trousers, bolts of material, and hundreds of boxes of buttons. The storeroom was poorly lit, with bare bulbs hanging from the ceiling, so it was quite dark. I walked up the aisle immediately in front of me and through the shelves, between the clothes and boxes, I could see the racks stretching away to either side, all filled with finished clothes. It seemed endless. At the end of the aisle, I found the wall had two large doors that must open outward to allow work to be dispatched and materials to be delivered. I looked at the huge hinges to either side of the doors, and the bolts locking them in place; they were clean and well-oiled. Although everything here seemed basic, it was at least neat and in good order. I turned to find the buttons and return to the sewing room, realizing that I had just lost another twenty minutes.

As I passed Madam Zhang on my way back, she called out to me: "Feng, you don't have time to watch the flowers grow here." She was talking very seriously. "If you are going to stay, you must work quickly. If not you should leave." She beckoned me to come closer and I walked over to where she was sitting behind her table and sewing machine. In a whisper she told me, "This is not Shanghai—and China is no longer the same these days. You must work hard in order to live. I don't know what happened to you but this is a new China and a new time . . . for better or for worse, there is no turning back for any of us. Now . . . go to work."

I nodded and went back to the worktable. I sewed on as many buttons as I could for more than three hours. My fingers bled and my muscles ached and cramped hard and tight, so that I had to stop occasionally and flex my hands to relax them.

Madam Zhang and Ah Sui came to my table. It was twenty minutes to six.

"Well, how many have you done?" Madam Zhang asked.

We counted the pile and it was twenty-six.

"That is good," she commented, then grabbed my hands and examined the needle marks and the redness of them. "Can you do the remaining five?"

"Five?" I said, alarmed.

"Yes, you will need to do at least one more than the minimum, as the leaders like to see enthusiasm and devotion to the cause."

"What is the cause?" I asked, a bit too abruptly.

She looked back at me, hard-eyed.

"The cause," she emphasized these two words, "for you is getting something to eat, which you will only do by sewing buttons onto trousers. The cause for them is building a new China. They are sweeping into the cities and want to change everything there . . . and they don't want to do it naked. They are proud of their shiny enamel badges, basic clothing, and red scarves, so we are proud of them, too. Isn't that right, Ah Sui?"

"Oh, yes," Ah Sui answered, giggling as she did so, "we're old but we believe, too." Then she smiled at me. "I'll do two, you do two," she pushed two more in front of me, "and Lao Ding, behind, you will do two."

At six o'clock the machines stopped and through the windows we heard footsteps approaching, then the doors opened and five students entered. Immediately everyone stood up and remained very still.

They were all dressed like the youths crowding the station in

Shanghai and those on the train, all wearing clothes made in this room. Two of the five were young girls, with their hair in braids and a few spots on their cheeks and chin; they could not have been older than seventeen. Of the three young men, one was clearly older, in his early twenties, short, with closely cropped hair and a round face under his glasses. He was thick-set with large forearms and a wide waist. His expression was friendly but his manner was official.

"Comrade Zhang, please can you give me the productivity figures for today's work?" he asked flatly.

"We made one hundred and twenty-four trousers. Four more than the quota. Fifty-two shirts. Seven more than the quota. And we cut and finished three hundred scarves," Madam Zhang replied, just as flatly.

"Excellent work on the production of trousers and shirts but there must be more enthusiasm for scarves," he said, very forcefully, and the skin of his scalp undulated as he continued to instruct us: "Scarves are essential, they are a unifying symbol of the movement."

Ah Sui smiled and clapped, and Madam Zhang stared hard at her.

"Exactly! That is the spirit." Then the spokesman looked up at the roof and shouted, "Clap and sing to the glory of the nation and Chairman Mao. Let productivity rise!"

The four others repeated this feverishly, and then the leader said, "However, Comrade Sui, please remove your hat and scarf. We should maintain our diligence at all times: red scarves only are permitted, and a hat with a star at its center is better. Comrade Zhang, can you introduce the new comrade in your team?"

"Yes, this is Comrade Sang."

I looked up, trying to avoid eye contact.

"Do you have any documents, Comrade Sang?"

"No, they're lost." I looked more directly at him, though he was some twenty feet away.

He and his team had remained standing in the empty space between the door and the rows of tables, but now he came to the other side of my worktable to inspect me more closely. He smelled strongly and his breath was very acidic. I noticed that his hands, too, were soft, so, like me, he had not worked hard before.

"Well, if you intend to remain here, then we will get you some new ones. Everything must be documented and accounted for in the People's Republic. Chairman Mao will not accept anything less," he finished and studied me closely. "How old are you?"

"I am thirty-nine," I answered quickly. I was not afraid of him but this situation was very strange to me and I was glad that I had found shelter with Madam Zhang and her team. He wrote something on his clipboard.

"What is your full name?" he asked.

"Qin Feng," I answered, making up the first name I could. "I am from Wuhan."

He wrote this down then looked up and nodded at me and at Madam Zhang; I felt relieved when he left the room with the other cadres.

The seamstresses all sat down. After a few minutes of silence Madam Zhang scolded Ah Sui.

"Sui, you know you should not play up to him like that. You'll get us all into trouble."

"I know, but it's so silly! I'm glad I will be dead before these foolish children lead us to ruin," Ah Sui whispered, and then winked at me. Her face was fat and round, and when she smiled she looked like a handmade doll.

"Time to close," Madam Zhang ordered.

The women spent an hour tidying up and taking inventory

and I helped where I could. Everything was carried back into the storeroom so that the main workroom was left empty except for the worktables on which the covered sewing machines still rested. As we finished clearing the room, Madam Zhang sat down at her own table and continued checking through various schedules and lists. The other women gathered around her and Ah Sui locked the door leading to the passageway and storeroom.

Madam Zhang stood up; she held some small tickets in her hands.

"Here are your coupons for rice, meat, and other things." She started handing them out.

Ah Sui interrupted, looking at me.

"I'll give you one of mine . . . I had a few from before so you can have one, otherwise you cannot buy anything." She gave me a coupon.

The other women looked at each other. They were old, mostly in their sixties, and their faces were chapped and marked with little scars and blotches. Each of them gave me a coupon, which I was told would be enough to tide me over for a few days. If they had known my life, I doubt they would have been as generous. I feared what would happen when I eventually told Madam Zhang. I had no influence here and must rely on coupons and kindness.

"Thank you very much, I never expected such generosity. Actually, I'm not sure what I expected. Can't we use money here?" I asked, rather hesitantly.

"There is no money in this production commune anymore, at least not for this. If you meet your production targets everything is good and you have what you need," Ah Sui replied. "Soon the whole country will be like this. That is what they want anyway. I expect Madam Zhang can explain to you." She looked at the forewoman. "See you tomorrow."

They all turned and left, and Madam Zhang and I stood watching them go.

"They're very nice," I remarked in a small voice.

"Yes, they are, and many of them very skilled in traditional arts but these talents will soon be lost." She turned back to her chair, leaving me standing alone looking at the open doorway leading out into the dimly lit street. I could hear dogs barking and people shouting. Once seated, Madam Zhang resumed her work and I went to her table and sat down on the end of it to watch her.

My feet hung down. I swung them like a child; like I had with Bi, from the riverbank. I breathed a little deeper.

"You can live with me for now, but if you're going to remain here then you'll need to get the correct papers as without them you aren't entitled to any food coupons. More important, though, you need to practice your sewing techniques," she said, without looking up from her work.

"Thank you, I'd like to stay. I came here to see you," I admitted shyly, still watching my feet as I swung them.

"Well, I don't know why you did. This life's lonely, and after my husband I lost my son so I'm glad of the company, whether you stay a year or a day."

So he was gone.

"Did Bi marry?" I asked, almost embarrassed, staring hard at my feet.

She looked up at me and raised one eyebrow.

"I remember how close you two were," she said, without answering me.

She was an old woman now, but she remained as calm and self-assured as she had been many years ago, and I as upset and anxious as before, though I was now at the end of my journey and not the beginning.

"I'm sorry, but I have not seen Bi in many years and long ago became used to the idea that he was gone." She looked at me more sympathetically as she continued to speak. I felt very sad to hear this and it must have been obvious. "My child," she stated candidly, "this country has always been a violent and angry land. Sooner or later, we will suffer."

She smiled at me but it was plain that it cost her some effort.

"I loved Bi very much. He was a good boy." She seemed to look inside herself then as if remembering the brightness in him she had loved so much, that same quality that she believed must have drawn me here. "Did you hope to meet him again?"

"I thought of it, but I . . ." I could not say any more and returned to studying my feet.

"Well, he went to war against the Japanese, then against those greedy Nationalists. Someone once brought news that he was fighting them in Fujian after the war and the Japanese had been defeated . . . then nothing. It has been nearly six years and I'm afraid he's gone." Her face was hard and set; she was well practiced at preventing herself from crying. "But isn't it the same for all of us?" She laughed and shook her head in self-reproach. "Such misery we Chinese can put ourselves through. How many families have lost someone, or caused someone to be lost? How many do you think?" Her voice drifted into silence.

The mask had slipped for a second. She was all things angry, sorrowful, broken then . . . and, like all the rest of the poor, hardworking and exhausted.

"I don't know," I answered her, thinking only of my own guilt.

"Everyone. All of us. All of us collectively. You can ask anyone and they will tell you a terrible story." She paused and her expression softened a little; she blinked and rubbed her eyebrows as if to wipe away the tiredness and bad memories. "We are going to stay behind an hour or so tonight, as you are going to practice those buttons again, and I will teach you some basic straight-line stitching on the sewing machine. Go sit by Ah Sui's machine."

I went over to the machine and sat down.

"Uncover it," she instructed rather impatiently.

As I did this and folded the cover away to a small shelf under the table, which was where the spare needles were kept, Madam Zhang continued her writing for another few minutes during which I had time to think of Bi. I had shared my first and only loving kiss with him, and there would be no continuation of it in my lifetime. It was one small beautiful moment that I would never allow to be swallowed into China's bloody future; it would remain as a glimpse of brightness in my life, a wonderful chance moment, forever unspoiled. We had touched and held each other once, and although I had known it was impossible all along, a small part of me had hoped to find him here, alone and waiting for me. He would have remained young and lovely, I knew. And as I watched his mother, writing calmly and carefully in her book, I looked around me and wished I had run away with him to live here and become a fisherman's wife, the daughter-in-law of a seamstress.

Madam Zhang finished her work and came over to sit next to me.

"Now look at me—" I turned toward her—"and show me your hands?"

I held them out and turned them so she could see their palms and backs. She grabbed them and felt the muscles and bones.

"You have very weak hands but nice long fingers."

"They are like my grandfather's fingers. My son has them, too," I said proudly, which surprised me.

"We'll talk about your son some other day."

She put my hands down and for the next half an hour showed me how to use the pedal to maintain the speed of the needle, and how to change and thread the needle. Then, as before, she made me practice by repeating the procedures. After fifteen or so attempts I got it correct and felt so proud. I sat looking at the machine, smiling to myself.

"Well done, but what are you smiling for? You haven't actually made anything yet," Madam Zhang said, rather amused.

"I know, but at least I learned something. I can *do* something. I thought I wouldn't survive." I felt my heart beat wildly, my breath shorten. It felt as though I would cry again.

Madam Zhang took hold of my shoulders and gave them a shake. She came around the other side of the table and, leaning on her elbows, spoke gently but firmly to me.

"Now stop. If you are going to survive here, you must be stronger. I don't know what you did . . . you can tell me when you're ready and not until then. I've often traveled the country, working for families like yours, and like all those who move around, I have seen death, killings, disease. Have watched others lose their children and lost my own. We must swallow down such bitterness and keep living, hoping that fortune will help us." She paused then said assertively, "Everything is for the Party now. We're too old to follow the youth who will lead us to the world of devils, so we must remain practical if we want to survive."

I looked down. I thought of all that had happened to bring me here. I had run away to this place, with no idea of how I was going to live. I had been lucky already, finding her and these old women. I could have been lost like so many others . . . like Bi. I bit my lip. I knew I did not deserve this luck. I closed my eyes, but could still feel the stirring of Madam Zhang's breath as she continued to watch me closely. A few tears rolled slowly down my cheeks and dropped on the table below. Madam Zhang remained still. I saw Lu Meng limping when he was a small boy, practicing his martial arts so bravely and, later, rescuing his sister from the violence of my belt. I imagined Xiong Fa sitting alone, slumped against the back of a chair in his apartment, trying to understand what had happened, his eyes bloodshot from tiredness. I thought of you and the scar I gave you.

Chapter 24

I opened my eyes and Madam Zhang was still there.

"Are we doing something good?" I asked her. "I need to do something good."

"Feng Feng, I don't know if what we're doing is good. Like when I made your wedding dress, there is no choice but to do it with every good intention and then hope. I think we Chinese don't think so far ahead. We leave that to the Emperor . . . that is why we have such a long history." She laughed.

I laughed a little, too.

"Go get some buttons and cloth and practice for a while. I have some things to do myself," she said finally.

I sewed for forty minutes and became competent enough to be trusted with the task while Madam Zhang finished her books. When she eventually locked up, we went out into the street. We walked for half a mile and turned into a narrow road. The whole town was very quiet. There were houses to either side, built of the same gray brick, and through the windows we could see the same weak candlelight. From each roof protruded a metal pipe from which soot drifted into the air and filled our nostrils with the smell of coal dust. There were no streetlights so we walked carefully and slowly. After fifteen minutes we turned right into a small lane, just wide enough for two people to walk together. Looking up, I could see thousands of stars and a great moon. This was the peaceful beauty that Bi had described. Although I had not found him, he was still not lost to me.

We reached a house, like all the others.

"Here we are," Madam Zhang whispered, opening the door and disappearing inside.

I followed her and for a moment we stood in complete darkness before candlelight revealed the interior. The house had only three rooms. The bedroom lay immediately to the left of the front door, with two single wooden beds covered in thin cotton summer sheets. Madam Zhang must have slept here with her husband once. The living room was rectangular with a low ceiling, its longest side facing the street. It had a small bed in the far corner, where Bi had slept. Seeing the lonely little thing, I understood he had never married, never had a family of his own. I wondered if I had been his only chance?

Above the bed was a drawing of him, perhaps done by someone in the town. It was drawn when he was older than I remembered him. His hairline was more adult and his features more pronounced; he had a sharper jawline and the artist had made his eyes more intense than the expression of wild innocence to which I had been drawn. He looked kind but strong. It seemed like a long time ago since I had known him; unreal and blurred, like a half-remembered dream, yet intense in the images that still remained in my mind. As my years in Daochu passed, further memories and sensations from our time together in the gardens would be awoken for a while and then return to the deep sleep of oblivion, fading in and out of my mind, untainted. I would quietly enjoy them, like a child carefully picking its first flowers. I began to understand that everything we had been together, in that short summer, was more than Ma could ever have felt or imagined. Bi's bed only took up a small part of the room; the clay *kang* oven, which was nearly eight feet long

by four feet wide and stood immediately outside the bedroom
door, took up a quarter of it. I would later find it more than ad-
equate for keeping the room warm in the harsh winters. There
was a thick red, yellow, black, and dark blue mosaic carpet
across much of the floor, in the center of which stood a wooden
table to seat four and two heavy armchairs. On the wall above
the *kang* was a picture of Chairman Mao, which had become
gray from soot and smoke. The door in the back wall adjacent
to the *kang* led to a large bare room used for keeping foodstuffs
and occasionally chickens. It had a hard-baked mud floor with
a tub in one corner, where I was told we could wash after we
had fetched the water.

Madam Zhang boiled some water for tea and we sat together
at the table.

"We didn't always live here," she explained. "We used to live
on a farm but then my husband suffered a terrible injury to his
chest and died a few months afterward. Bi and I tried to keep it
going but we were not experienced farmers. I was a seamstress
and he was on his own. Then the local leaders suggested we give
it up for the People and allow others to farm it."

She sat looking down at the table, running her right hand
over it as if reassuring an old friend. She stared into the dark
grain of the wood and sighed.

It was quiet here. There were no Sangs demanding my attention. There was no need to speak. I was at peace. My pain
would be dulled for a while.

The pot of water started to boil and I filled our cups. I
watched the leaves rise to the surface and the steam drift from
the water. I placed the lids on top and handed one to Madam
Zhang. We sat saying nothing.

The bedroom had no windows, which was how Madam
Zhang liked it but it was also very warm with the *kang* on the
other side of the wall. A mannequin stood proudly at the end

of the little room, filling up the space between the beds. It was draped with the most brilliant colors, some large pieces of cloth and some merely scraps; she was in the process of creating a wonderful dress pieced together from each of these scraps and slivers. It reminded me of standing with Grandfather looking across the gardens in the summer and being struck by the myriad of colors we could see from the flowers in bloom against the lush greens of the grass and trees. And how, after a shower, the sun would emerge and the petals and grass, fresh with raindrops, would reflect rainbows of light.

Madam Zhang pointed to a bed, removing some swatches of cloth and a few bobbins of thread. "You can sleep here until you decide whether you are going to stay."

I lay down and was immediately asleep.

Finally, nothing.

I learned slowly and carefully. I started with buttons on trousers and taking the inventory. Then, when the others agreed I was competent with the sewing machine, I stitched straight lines on trouser seams and hems. After a time, weeks or months, it did not matter, I learned to cut, and so eventually I was skilled enough to produce things on my own.

Our days were filled with work. In the morning at home we cleaned, cooked, and washed; there were no servants to cook for me here or to help me bathe and I did not miss them, though I often thought of Yan's plaintive expression, her half-smile and maternal concern. Perhaps she would even have approved of the way I lived now. In the evening, after locking up, we would go to the People's Store or canteen and join the rest of the town for dinner or else take food home to prepare ourselves. The townspeople had become used to the Party and its demands, and all change becomes acceptable whatever the consequences once you are accustomed to change itself.

The Party would hold many celebrations commemorating its own success and longevity and the way the country had been rebuilt. People would gather in the town square, the People's Square, and accordion players and drummers would strike up marching music and Communist anthems that the local dance troupe would follow. There would be songs about the great examples of Maoist spirit sung by choirs of workers, as our ancestors had sung to welcome the coming of spring, and there would be readings about acts of great courage and Chairman Mao's principles, and we would sit entranced, listening like villagers a thousand years before to tales about ancient heroes. But unlike them we had to unlearn everything we had ever known before: traditions, superstitions, and old philosophies were now forbidden and ridiculed, we were consumed by productivity.

As the night grew later fires would be lit and still the celebrations would go on. People were banned from meeting together for purposes other than this by many policies and directives unless it was agreed in advance but, far from the eyes of Chairman Mao, in the alleys and the fields, you could see couples secretly meeting all around; groping, touching, and greedily devouring each other in clandestine but unfettered release. In the dark, with their identical clothes, you could not tell which was the boy and which the girl. Perhaps it did not matter and they only saw themselves as two members of the Party. At this time, only the words of the Little Red Book had the power to interfere in our lives.

Madam Zhang and I became thought of as mother and daughter, and for a few years, before the madness, even though I was isolated from the city, I felt at home here. Provided our work was completed, we would have enough to eat and I would enjoy walks into the fields and woods outside the town. Sometimes I would go alone, at other times we would be together. We would talk about the other women, what work needed to be done, and then fall silent. The town stood at the edge of a mountainous wooded region; between the trees I found grass and wildflowers. With each flower an ancient name and a memory of Lu Meng. My mind has rarely strayed from either of you and on these walks, such short interludes of peace, I would forget nearly everything except your faces, young and soft, as they were that night in Lu Meng's bedroom when you first came back to me.

Only on a few occasions was I tempted to tell Madam Zhang all that had happened. During our walks, our silence would sometimes become so comfortable that I wanted to tell her everything about my life. It felt important that she should know and tell me what she thought. We would walk perfectly in step, and my mind would race, searching for an opening sentence to my story. I feared that she would hate me by the story's end and so the beginning was extremely important. But I always stumbled over those first few words, and a small inner voice would always tell me that an acceptable opening sentence to this tale of cruelty was impossible. In the end, I could not force myself to say even one word about what I had done.

You would appear in my dreams, sometimes just your face, smiling and looking up at me: kneeling in front of me as I sat on my old bed or appearing between the sheets hanging to dry in the courtyard. Or I would follow you at a distance as you skipped into the house and disappeared into its darkness. Other times I could feel my own body become filled with fear as I beat you. I would see the belt dig into your skin, blood covering both of us, then the old woman would appear and wash you clean. Lu Meng, Xiong Fa, and Yan would be next to me laughing, everything would be bathed in the red glow of the candle flames, the color I had seen throughout the night you were born.

Our team became a full production unit under new Party rules. To us it didn't matter whether we were a team, a unit, or a production regiment, we had become a family. The Party didn't want such bonds of affection or love, it wanted only itself to be the beginning and the end. The Party cadres were possessed by their belief in man's ability to attain perfection, like the gods themselves. Yet in our small town, as in villages, towns, and cities everywhere, we could see the many shortcomings and failures in this relentless pursuit of the unattainable. We were able to insulate ourselves a little in our workroom from the dehumanizing process. They were only small transgressions, amid all the endless repetition, but sometimes we embroidered special patterns for people, their initials, or even small flowers, concealed inside cuffs and hems.

Chapter 25

The months and years of routine wore on; we carried our cards, badges, won production awards, set new targets, assisted other teams . . . yet in the tiniest stitches we found creation and companionship. Our lives were uncomplicated as long as we met the Party's requirements; seasons were irrelevant, production schedules defined our calendar. Then, early in the new year of 1958, the leader of the local cadres came into the workroom in the middle of the afternoon. He stood at the door. Fortunately we were all working then, not talking among ourselves. He glanced down the room at Madam Zhang and walked quickly over to her. She remained seated while he stood over her, his left hand leaning on the desk and the other waving in a very animated manner. They looked as though they were deliberately keeping their voices low but the noise of the sewing machines helped. He seemed very concerned; she merely nodded calmly in reply. When he stopped speaking, she said only two or three words to him and nodded. He looked at her and we could see there was regret upon his face. Although he wielded authority over us, we had all grown to like him very much. He made life easy for us; so long as we slightly exceeded our targets, he would be happy. He had obtained my papers very quickly, and then when he had got married, about seven months after I arrived, we had made his fiancée a plain but traditional wedding dress and a smarter suit for him. We had even used some red scarf fabric for a traditional veil. Now he finished talking to Madam Zhang and offered her his hand. They shook and he turned immediately for the door. It seemed to me that as he was closing it, he glanced back for another look at us all.

Madam Zhang got to her feet.

"Come here, quickly!" This was the only time I ever saw her panic. "The team leader has just told me that he is to be replaced . . . a new leader is coming. He says there are new instructions and we'll find out more tonight. He was very concerned about this, though he doesn't know anything more. He says he has heard that huge changes have taken place across the country . . . there's been violence in many places." She paused to catch her breath. "It's not just the greedy and the selfish, like the capitalists, who are the targets now. Many other people, guilty in different ways, have become enemies of the Party as well. Please, everyone, be very careful. He said we should work hard, make sure that whatever happens we exceed our targets, and most important of all . . . keep quiet."

As I listened I wondered whether you, Lu Meng, and Xiong Fa would already have left the country, like Ming had. Against everything I had seen and still believed, I now just hoped blindly that Xiong Fa had always known you were his daughter and that somehow he had saved you and Lu Meng from the terror that was descending on the country. I watched the other women look at each other then return silently to their desks. They had already seen and lost enough to understand that our only course now was to keep working.

After an hour there was a lot of shouting and screaming in the street outside. Madam Zhang went to the door and stepped out for a moment. She reappeared with a young angry-looking boy who was carrying a large stick.

"All of you, get outside! The new team leader wants to see you."

The boy was not much older than sixteen. He came forward and thumped the stick against the nearest worktable, which was mine. The end of it caught my box of pins, sending it into the air and raining pins across the table and over the floor.

"Pick them up, pick them up!" He was screaming at me, his face strained and red with anger, but he explained nothing of the reason for his anger, just continued screaming, "None of this work is good enough . . . pick them up!"

As he shouted he brandished one end of the stick, swiping the other through the air. We watched it and recoiled for fear of being hit.

"Why are you afraid? Why are you afraid? You would only be fearful if you had something to fear. The Party is for the people, you should not fear the people . . ." He kept screaming until his words became one endless howl.

Ah Sui and I bent down to start collecting the pins. He came forward and grabbed Ah Sui by the hair, dragging her across the floor. Initially she kicked out her legs behind her. He smacked her kneecaps hard with the stick and she screamed and kicked again. He hit her harder and she stopped kicking. As he dragged her across the floor to the door, she shrieked like a tortured animal. I froze, crouching down with my hands full of pins, and watched. It was like a hunter dragging an animal he had caught; he had not yet decided when and how to make his kill. I looked up at the other women, but they remained frozen behind their tables.

The boy took Ah Sui out of the door and Madam Zhang walked behind. I got up and followed her. Outside there was a circle of about a hundred youths, all dressed in our clothes but wearing different scarves and badges. They had the previous team leader and his wife down on their knees at the center of the crowd and had hung wooden signs around their necks. The signs said they were traitors to the Revolution and enemies of the people. Young people leapt out of the crowd to beat them, smashing their heads and backs with sticks and pummeling them with fists. They bled freely. The boy who seemed to be the new leader was shouting and holding up one arm. People in the crowd looked around as the young man who had burst into our workroom dragged Ah Sui through the howling mob. They did not have a sign ready for her but hit her anyway.

"Here is the woman who helped them engage in old practices! These are forbidden." The new team leader threw the wedding clothes we had created for them in their bleeding faces. The clothes slid to the ground, stained with blood. "Do you understand?" the new leader screamed. "To be forgiven, you must admit that you were wrong . . . will you do that? No false pride before the people," he shouted.

He was barely an adult, the others only just out of childhood. They looked blind and shouted as if they were deaf. Where had they suddenly come from? What mother had bred such animals? The new leader was thin and bony, with sharp features and large weak watery eyes behind thick glasses. His chin was covered in spots. This was not the handsome muscular worker, holding aloft a hammer, that all the posters celebrated.

I screamed, "No, it was not her—it was me! I helped them."

"You . . . who are you?" the new leader demanded. His lips curled so that his teeth and gums were left bare like a dog's.

Suddenly hands came out and grabbed my hair, forcing me to the ground. Lying on my back, I felt more hands sliding under my arms, propelling me through the crowd to its center. I could see Madam Zhang standing with her hand over her mouth, the whites of her eyes visible around wide terrified pupils.

"Do you admit that you observed these old traditions?" They picked up the bloodstained clothes and pushed them in my face. "Explain yourself!"

"Yes, it was me. I thought it was harmless. Why should we care about such a thing? It is nothing, isn't it?" I screamed then as a hand yanked a fistful of my hair and my back scraped against the ground, tearing my shirt.

"It is *everything*. Chairman Mao said that we must eradicate all outdated practices. There can be no leniency for their supporters!" the cadre leader shouted, and raised his fist in the air. People shouted all around and one stick and then another crashed down on my legs. I curled up into a ball. A woman with a short stick poked me hard in the side, to force me to open up. When she realized she couldn't uncurl me, she beat me on the head and then I felt another stick jab my hip. Over and over again.

All I could hear was the leader, shouting: "This won't be tolerated! The people must be pure in spirit."

My last thought was not for myself but it was the image of beating you and watching the blood flow from your cheek. In that deep red I lost consciousness.

When I awoke, I was in my bed with Ah Sui and Madam Zhang sitting beside me. My head hurt and I felt bandages around my forehead and on my left hand.

"How are you?" Ah Sui asked me. "Aiiiya, thank you, but you're very crazy!"

"What happened?" I whispered.

"They beat you quite badly, but not as severely as the old team leader and his wife. Aiii, she didn't live! And he was battered almost to death and lost an eye. An older party official arrived and stopped them, but they were like wild dogs. It has been chaos since then. He has told us that there will be a massive production increase. Those of us without skills will make iron—everything must be done to beat the production of the Western capitalists. We are being told to make a great leap toward modernity, challenging the West and all their capitalist prowess."

"I don't understand," I replied.

"We will give everything we have to show the Chinese are the best in the world—even if we kill ourselves."

And so we did.

* * *

slowly healed but my right leg still would not move well and I would get terrible pains in the right side of my head. In their turn, cadres in the newly appointed team were replaced, beaten, imprisoned, and occasionally just vanished. And so it went on, feeding off itself. Insatiable. Our targets became increasingly unattainable, and so, in order to ensure we made them and retained the coupons we needed to live, we made poor-quality clothes, using less stitching, and the cutting was done very crudely. We would be stopped arbitrarily, asked to produce something different; but only ever useless and point-less items, created not by design but on a whim. Eventually it became easier to lie to our superiors and get away with cutting corners as the administration imploded and our town fell into chaos. People had used up every pot, pan, tool, and utensil they had to make useless pig iron; we had killed flies, sparrows, and mosquitoes by the truckload, and beaten and kicked each other until there were no friends or enemies left, just rabid dogs run-ning, barking, and scavenging to survive.

Madam Zhang and I, like many others, learned to follow orders when necessary and occasionally to anticipate them, always being careful to use the vocabulary expected of us. Ev-erything was playacting, it seemed to me. It had been nearly eight years since I had come to find Madam Zhang, and I real-ized now that I would die here. What had happened to you, my children, to both of you? I heard that Shanghai was safer, that there was more order there than in the countryside. I hoped that Xiong Fa had used all his wealth to find a way to protect you and Lu Meng.

The worst of the winter had passed but it had been harsh. The ground had been frozen solid so that the dead could not be buried. They were piled up to await spring in the western part of the town, where it was coldest. There was also a short-age of firewood, and there had been no coal for two months.

Two women in our workroom had died just before the end of the year and we had been forced to break up their tables almost immediately so that each of us could take pieces home to burn. When I stared in the mirror I was frightened to see how much I had aged; my skin had passed from smooth and supple to tough and lined. The beating had left me with a scar on the right side of my head, cutting across my temple. When I touched it, I imagined touching you.

During the winter cold it was my chest, though, that became the worst affected. During the intervening years, I had watched my breasts shrivel and droop, the skin around my nipples becoming dry and flaky. I was happy to wrap cloth around my chest to keep me warm; beauty was no longer a concern. But it was internally that I felt the most sore; when I breathed in I ached, and my chest felt heavy as my lungs expanded and contracted.

Even though I now limped slightly, when we returned from the workroom it was so cold inside the house that Madam Zhang would have to hurry me in as quickly as possible so that we could both set about laying and lighting a fire in the *kang* from whatever scraps of wood we had scavenged. The main room always seemed cold; even after the fire had started to emit a hearty glow, I felt the cold deep in my bones. It felt as if there would never be another warm day, that the sun had changed its orbit and, even if it burned forever elsewhere, the heat would never reach us. We were to be punished by this cold until we could no longer move and it froze the life from us. At least it would save us from continuing this existence.

Once the fire provided some heat, we would cook whatever food we had and then huddle close together under a single blanket to eat. Meat had become so scarce I often laughed to myself, thinking how I would have loved some of Father-in-law's chicken soaked in rice wine or Jin Hua ham.

Madam Zhang, too, suffered terribly from the cold; her fingers in particular would become stiff and locked into claws until I massaged them. We would place the chairs in front of the fire inside the *kang* and, after eating, would sit and watch the flames, falling asleep holding each other, still wearing our thick jackets and trousers filled with cotton wadding, which we would often supplement with newspaper. We had also made ourselves large hats to cover our ears, from material taken from the storeroom, pretending that they were a new item to equip the People's Army. Like every other soul in the town, possibly in the entire country, we were hungry and tired, half-waiting to die and half-expecting to be killed.

During the spring, summer, and early warm autumn, after each day's production and then our supper, we worked on the dress wrapped around the mannequin in the bedroom. Over the years we had collected more scraps of different fabric to add to it. Madam Zhang had folded each scrap into a tiny diamond shape, which she then hand-stitched together to form a beautiful structured bodice. It was elegant and enticing, and reminded me somehow of my old friend Ming; she would have been able to wear it, her beautiful pale shoulders and arms unfurling above it like wings. She must be living far away by now, free from this insanity. I tried to help Madam Zhang with the folding and stitching but my work was a poor imitation and often she would undo my efforts and repair them. So I would just sit behind her at the end of my bed, drinking tea and watching her work, following those gentle and nimble hands as they created what was likely to be their last work of beauty. Now it was too cold to work and without firewood or coal those beautiful hands were being slowly broken and her skills lost forever.

One morning it was particularly cold and I had been up early to fetch water from a tap nearly three miles away. The walk there had been difficult because of the ice, and my slippers—we did not have boots—had become wetter than usual, causing me to slip and fall. When I stood up, I felt a sharp pain in my knee. I should have rested myself then but it was too cold and I continued. There was a queue for the water and I waited in it. The other people were also cold and hungry. The children's faces were thin and wretched; although my own life had been painful, at least I had lived. Without better food these children would die soon. There were no crops to feed them, the overworked soil having been drained of its resources. A young girl stood in front of me.

"Xiaojie, what's your name?" I asked.

"It's Comrade Li to you, old lady," she replied aggressively. "I'm collecting water for my team. We will farm the land today."

"But the land is frozen. How will you do it?"

"The warmth of Chairman Mao will break the soil and let us work it." She beamed at me proudly.

I smiled a reply.

The queue diminished and it was my turn but I was cold and could not get the tap to work. My fingers were numb and I cut myself without feeling anything. I put the bucket down and looked at the blood dripping onto the ice, the deep red instantly thinning and diluting as it hit the frozen surface, leaving nothing but a faint rose-colored shape. I sucked at my finger and my blood felt warm in my mouth. A man behind me came forward to help and filled my bucket for me. It was the old team leader who had been beaten with me. His left cheek had been crushed, his eye socket had collapsed into his face and many of his teeth were missing.

"Hello," he said, and stooped down to help me with my bucket.

"Thank you," I replied.

I looked at him briefly, smiled quickly, and nodded to him as I turned to walk away.

We could not speak any longer. If that little girl or some of her friends saw us we would be punished. Who knew how many team leaders there had been in his place since he was beaten and his wife killed? Yet his disgrace was not forgotten. I took a few steps and looked into the People's Square a hundred meters away. I could see into it from one corner. It was white and flat with the huge statue of Chairman Mao standing in the middle, presiding over his triumph for all the world to behold. I looked at all the banners and placards, demanding loyalty, self-criticism, and equality, fastened to the sides of the long low administrative buildings that formed the perimeter of the square. They had been erected six or seven years ago in the tide of hope that followed the Revolution, but now they were smashed and broken by children who should have had toys to play with instead. A huge sign heralded the Triumph of the People. I looked behind me at the ragged, wasted town dwellers in the queue, wondering which people had triumphed. It was certainly none of us.

I walked home and when I arrived found Madam Zhang waiting for me, pale with agitation.

"What have you been doing?" she shouted at me. "We have to go to work and you're frozen! What has happened to your finger? Sit down and tell me."

She sat me down and I realized that my toes were badly affected by the cold today and cried out.

"What is it?" she asked anxiously.

"My feet and toes are frostbitten, the pain is very deep this time." I moaned and started to cry. I leaned back hard in the chair and tried to arch my foot, but it was too painful. I clenched my teeth and felt myself grow faint.

Madam Zhang quickly crouched in front of me and rubbed my feet then turned around to stoke the fire in the *kang* to generate more heat. She wrapped my feet up in a towel and then started boiling some water, which was nearly frozen in the pot and would take a long time. She wrapped the rest of me in our large quilted blanket, now greasy and stinking from so many evenings spent covering our two huddled bodies.

Sitting next to me, she took hold of my finger and examined it. Then, with a needle quickly sterilized in the flames, she stitched my wound with some black medical thread. As she did I coughed hard and nearly pulled the first stitch out again, but we ignored this and looked instead at the dark red phlegm lying on the blanket in front of my chin. Madam Zhang took a clean piece of cloth and wiped it away. I closed my eyes. I felt the thread pulling on my finger as the numbness began to recede.

After she had finished I spoke, but did not have the courage to open my eyes and look at her.

"I don't think I will live through this winter. It's so cold and I'm too tired."

"Ha-ha! None of us may live through this next year," she quipped back, "bad weather is no excuse for leaving me. You must live because there is someone who wants you to live. Here, you received this letter today. It seems to have taken over a month to get here."

She handed me a dirty envelope with the words THE SEAMSTRESS, DAOCHU, SHAANXI PROVINCE, and inside there was a single folded sheet. I took it out. The message was so short but I read it ten or twenty times.

Dear Madame Zhang,

I have been given your name by our old comrade Yan, who recently died. She told us that you knew my mother, Sang Feng. If you have seen her please tell her that our father died two years ago. Lu Meng is well and I am to get married soon. On the other side is our address.

Sang Yu

My eyes filled with tears and I simply looked up at Madam Zhang standing over me. I clutched the little square of paper between my thumbs and index fingers. You had found me.

"What can I do? Is it possible to go back to Shanghai?"

I knew that a journey wasn't possible.

"You know the answer. Who is Sang Yu?"

She sat next to me and held my hand, which I suddenly remembered was cut and painful. She nursed it until my cut finger had stopped throbbing. She let my hand rest on the arm of my chair then and turned herself to look at me. My face felt cracked and blistered by the freezing air and snow, yet I was safe here and still alive. She reached across with her left hand to stroke my hair, touching my scar. I looked into her mild eyes.

"Little daughter, you don't have to say anything," she told me. "We've all witnessed and lived through terrible things. We live with almost nothing, and there's nothing for us in the future. How long can we keep going? It doesn't matter to me what you've done."

She smiled at me, her eyes as pained as mine. I smiled back and leant my left cheek into her hand, which felt warm and comforting.

"I know. I would like to tell you anyway, because the ground is so hard I cannot dig a hole to whisper my story into." I laughed a little and she along with me. Her eyes followed my movements closely: my lips as I spoke, my eyes as they looked into hers, and my brow as I frowned and sighed. In the quiet we could hear the flames crackling in the *kang* next to us.

"Very well, what is it?" she asked, continuing to cup my cheek.

"It is about my daughter, my son, and my husband. This letter was from my daughter." I was bursting; Xiong Fa had kept you both safe.

I told her how I was married: how Grandfather had lacked the courage to stand up against tradition and left me that day; how

Ma and Ba had given me away to replace Sister; what Xiong Fa had done to me; and what I had done to you. She listened and I cried, which I had not done since the first day here except while waking from dreams. But this time the tears quickly ceased. I felt too empty, too tired.

"I have missed my son deeply and regretted what I did to my daughter every single day I have been here. I have cried in my dreams, and followed lame boys down streets in the town, hoping they might have come here to find me. Each day I have watched them grow up in my imagination. What must they be like now? What must they think of me? And I am so grateful that you have loved me all these years without ever once inquiring into my sadness and silence. Xiong Fa had been a good father."

Madam Zhang remained silent when I had finished.

"We do terrible things to each other," she said finally. "Every time a dynasty ends, we hope the new one will not repeat the same cycle of tragedy and waste. But such is the nature of history . . . the cycle must continue."

"Can't we just stop it?" I asked meekly.

"Look around us. Is this not the end of one? Soon there will be a new beginning. Five thousand years since this country began, and we have stumbled and fallen, again and again. Perhaps one day soon your children may come looking for you and then you can explain things to them."

"I don't think I will last that long," I replied with a short laugh. "Who can live in this craziness?"

"But you can write . . . why not write something to tell them?" she suddenly suggested. "I'll bring some scraps of white cloth and you can write on them. We can sew them together into a book." She seemed more excited than I was by this scheme and squeezed my cheek to encourage me. "First you need to recover . . . we can tell the team leader that you are very ill and if he comes here he will see for himself. You can stay here and write." She calmed down a little and smiled at me. "The rest of us will do your work at the factory, there are so few useful materials left anyway that we are barely busy."

I nodded against her hand.

"Yes, I would like to tell them everything."

Then I was lost in that night again, sitting with my back pressed hard against the headboard, drowning in the smell of blood and shit, a glowing red light filtering through my closed eyelids, trying to escape the thin sound of your muffled crying. Yan's fearful voice pleaded with me to stop what I was doing. The pain between my legs reminded me to continue. "Why did I do this?" I said aloud.

Madam Zhang had no reply.

I closed my eyes again and dropped my head against the back of the chair. I felt the back of her hand press against my cheek again and then she stood up.

Knowing you were alive I forgot I was hungry and my pain eased but then there was a sudden burning sensation in my feet as the feeling and the frostbite returned to them. Madam Zhang stooped down, swiftly undid the wraps, and slowly submerged them in a bowl of warm water. The pain increased, then became less intense until I could move them freely. Madam Zhang put a cup of hot tea next to me.

"Your feet look bad, I will go and fetch the doctor," she grunted, "for all the good she will do."

"Yes," I smiled, "I think she is trained only in ideological health and welfare."

"Well, let's see if in this cold she is as barefoot as they say!"

She left me alone to think of you, Lu Meng, and Xiong Fa who had made himself a good father.

Madam Zhang and I sat by the opening of the *kang* with its meager flames, the light had almost dropped from the sky, and we huddled together under the thick blankets. Every minute was now spent thinking of food, sometimes I would dream of Jin Hua ham but instead we had to pick at the ground for roots and grubs and stripped the bark from the trees. I had spent several weeks writing on white cloth as Madam Zhang suggested telling this story to you. I had imagined your wedding, what sort of ceremony could you have, we had wasted such riches and you now have nothing but dark green, blue, and a little red. I looked at Madam Zhang sleeping next to me and I woke her.

"I would like to send my daughter a wedding present."

"We will have to be careful. What do you want to send? We don't have much."

"Can we create a shawl for her, with flowers on it? Each flower would be one of those my grandfather showed me. Can we do this?"

For a few minutes I was excited.

Madame Zhang looked at me sympathetically as we both knew we had few materials to use.

"Yes, we can. We can use the materials in the dress in the bedroom."

"But you have been working on that for so many years."

"Who knows how many years of madness we can endure and what will be left. Besides our fingers are rough and stiff," she stretched her fingers a little, "and this may be the last beautiful thing I create."

She laughed heartily.

"Anyway these materials I have saved should be worn. What better way than as a beautiful garden?"

We smiled at each other.

"Thank you."

Chapter 26

Dear Yu,

I will not live to see you but I am here now thinking of you. We hear that the country is falling apart again and that it's not even possible to think of a future because there is only the present. There is no education, no respect for the aged, no love, no wisdom, no truth, and no lies. But I wish you every happiness in your marriage and hope that you and your husband love each other.

I hope you have found this letter and shawl. The shawl contains all the flowers that I loved when I would visit the gardens with your great-grandfather. Madame Zhang and I have colored it with yellows, pinks, greens, reds, and gold. Lu Meng can tell you the names of each flower as I learned them from Great-grandfather. Please tell Lu Meng I love him and have missed him terribly. The garden was my happiest time and enjoyment of such things has been long forgotten.

Please live for me and someday come here. I leave two books, explaining my life. I have no right to ask anything of you, but find these lines and words when it is possible and know that I have always loved you. Don't suffer and hate the way I have. I wish with all that I have lost and all that is left of me, my useless legs, torn muscles, and blistered face, that I had only opened my eyes that night and let myself love, as all of us should. Finally I can smile, happy that you have found me.

Ma

A+

AUTHOR
INSIGHTS,
EXTRAS &
MORE...

FROM
**DUNCAN
JEPSON**
AND

WM

WILLIAM MORROW

Discussion Questions

1. What is Feng's relationship like with her parents compared to her grandfather? What important lessons does her grandfather teach her?

2. Why is Feng attracted to Bi? What kind of background does he come from, and why is it considered unacceptable for Feng to associate with him?

3. Describe the hierarchy in the Sang family. Where does Feng fit in? How does she learn to manipulate these relationships to her own advantage?

4. What is Feng's sister and mother's view of an ideal life? How is this different from what Feng wants? Does Feng finally achieve this life, and if so, how does it make her feel?

5. Do you think Xiong Fa is a good or bad husband? Is he also a victim of society's expectations of him?

6. Why does Feng decide to give away her daughter? Even if you may not agree with her decision, can you sympathize with her reasons for doing it?

7. Do you think the suffering that Feng endures during the Great Leap Forward is enough to atone for the mistakes she has made? Why or why not?

8. How does Feng change throughout the novel? Has she learned anything about herself?

9. Based on this novel, what do you feel is the prevailing attitude toward daughters in China? Is it very different from how daughters are perceived in the West?

10. Are you surprised that the author is a man, given the book's first-person perspective and subject matter? Do you think that men can write about these things?

On My Mother
By Duncan Jepson

My mother was the central figure in our family, always insisting that a core Chinese principle was that families were inclusive no matter how distant the bonds and relationships. To her, family was more than the immediate four of us but must always include the extended Chinese side of her sister's and brother's families, the latter being based in her native Singapore.

She had immigrated to the U.K. in the mid-1950s along with her siblings, on the slimmest of opportunities afforded by the British colonial government: if my grandfather passed his degree, taken in his late thirties, then his children would be allowed to continue their studies in the U.K. Working hard, she became a doctor, engaging and enjoying English culture while retaining what she could of her Chinese heritage as she remembered it.

Her profession quickly provided her with the option of independence, even the possibility of breaking from her family and building her own life as one might in a Western family, but it also provided the means to help and support her family, and this she chose, something that was and would always be her priority. It did mean that, unlike millions of other Chinese immigrants before and after her, she did not have to rely on the Chinese immigrant diaspora that existed in Chinatowns all over the world. The Chinese clans who would support lonely immigrant laborers and new arrivals were the ultimate extended family, which at its simplest level was based around one's family name, such as Tan, Chen, Yeung, and so on.

It was just after my mother was diagnosed with breast cancer in 2006 that I began to reflect more deeply on her—and therefore a mother's—role in what Asian families in particular refer to as *keeping the family together*. My wife had been diagnosed with breast cancer three years previously, and so I was not shocked or confused by the situation but was almost immediately aware of the grim reality and possibilities for the future. I was sad at the possible devastating conclusion that, in my mother's case, would come so quickly, some nine months later.

My mother was a person who loved fiercely. Even in her flashes of extreme anger, common in those who draw on deep passion, her love would eventually get the better of her darker moments. The extended family she had held together was made of disparate characters, and over the months that passed between her diagnosis and her final days, the two of us occasionally discussed what might happen if she did not win the battle. The week before she finally slipped into deep unconsciousness, I told her that without her, these relationships would surely wither and this extended family would diminish. Several days before her death, as I sat at her side, she urged me to continue her efforts to keep the family together. I had to admit to her that I could not do what she had done, and reminded her of a number of events that despite her efforts and energy had only been costly and disappointing to her personally. She waved these off and lying, thin and tired in her hospital bed, adopted a tone and demeanor that reminded me that while I may be a grown man, I would always be her child. She told me I must do this. I replied that I had thought hard about it but for various reasons I could not find the same depth of devotion as she had. Ultimately, I had needed reasons to make the effort, whereas, fortunately for us, she had not.

My mother's commitment, like many, was endless. She was never ill-intentioned though sometimes her attention and energy and their consequence were unwelcome, but there was no denying her devotion and the depth of her feeling. To be a Chinese mother is to have considerable power in determining the direction of the family. It is rooted, first, in their intense unquestioning passion for their family and, second, in the duties and responsibilities placed on them by tradition and history. Unfortunately, when this power is applied in the most unthinking manner, it can cause terrible harm.

In writing this book, I wanted to explore Chinese attitudes toward motherhood, children, and family. Similar to mothers in many Asian cultures, a Chinese mother plays a central role, with the father being the provider, often a silent provider. The dynamic in a Chinese family between father, mother, sons, and daughters is complicated. It was, and largely still is, a patriarchal structure with the mother required to focus on raising the children. Historically, there was always a preference for sons over daughters, traditionally explained by the practical need for strong arms and hands in the fields. It is difficult to accept the relevance of this reasoning today, but those urges of preference and discrimination are still present, whether among the poor or rich. It is an ugly and inexcusable way to think and act, and it is this relationship between a Chinese mother and daughter I wanted to focus on in my story.

As a Eurasian, but brought up in the U.K., over years of studying, dating, traveling, and working in Singapore, Hong Kong, and China, I have noticed that often this favoritism of sons over daughters, and often eldest over youngest, is regularly promoted by the mothers themselves. It is as though providing and raising a son, guarding the family name, must be done regardless of the cost to those around them, even though in modern Asia the cost is unnecessary. Like some atavistic calling, the prejudices must be maintained no matter that they contradict logic and fairness and, most important to me, are accumulated by many mothers in the face of their own experiences of this same attitude.

But the preference does not always stop at favoritism and its wretched cousin, discrimination; it can become an actual victimization of daughters. At worst, as is well documented, a daughter can be rejected and abandoned on the street to die or, more simply, drowned. I wanted to use this story to explore how a mother could intentionally treat a daughter in this manner, having often been treated this way herself; to understand what forces would push a woman to act this way. I wondered what must then happen for a mother to reconsider how she treats her daughter and what event must occur to awaken her to become fully aware and cognizant of the senselessness of this prejudice, particularly in a culture that declares its belief in family so fervently. Finally, I wanted to explore what prevents others from intervening and disrupting this "tradition." In the end, let's be clear, everyone is culpable for the harm caused.

My mother told me that she had made up her mind not to return to Singapore only a few years after arriving in the U.K. She might have missed home, and I think she always did, but the enjoyment and prospect of freedom from tradition and from conservative expectations was not to be sacrificed for anything. She felt that Chinese women needed to question the lives they were asked to lead and should be able to choose how and with whom they would spend their futures. I believe she would have liked the intentions behind my story and I wish she could have read it.

Further Reading

<u>FICTION</u>

Rice by Su Tong

My Life as Emperor by Su Tong
I think Su Tong is one of the world's great living storytellers, and of his many talents, his greatest is the ease and simplicity with which he builds complex and intense relationships between his characters.

Daughter of the River by Hong Ying
An autobiographical tale of growing up in poverty in rural China that is well crafted, dramatic, and heartfelt.

A Thousand Years of Good Prayers by Yiyun Li
She is one of the strongest voices among the young Chinese writers, and she speaks to all of us. Her work is modern, haunting, and powerful.

Beijing Doll by Chun Sue
A book that, in its style and story, tells the reader much of young Chinese women in the 1990s struggling with the differences between Mao's generation and their own as China modernizes.

NONFICTION

I believe the three books below will best help people unfamiliar with Chinese culture understand some of the significant challenges currently facing Chinese society. While the contents of the books are important, how they and the authors were received and treated is also worth further investigation.

The Ugly Chinaman and the Crisis of Chinese Culture by Bo Yang

Will the Boat Sink the Water: The Life of China's Peasants by Chen Guidi and Wu Chuntao

The Good Women of China: Hidden Voices by Xin Ran

Chris Lusher

DUNCAN JEPSON is the award-winning director and producer of five feature films. He has also produced documentaries for Discovery Channel Asia and National Geographic Channel. He was the editor of the Asia-based fashion magazine *West East* and is a founder and managing editor of the *Asia Literary Review*. A lawyer by profession, he lives in Hong Kong.

Duncan Jepson